The Miller of Carnac

BY THE SAME AUTHOR

The Song of the Skylark
Argentine

Antoine-Louis Duclaux,
Comte de L'Estoille
writing as "Louis de Lyvron"

The Miller of Carnac
and Other Works

translated, annotated and introduced by
Brian Stableford

A Black Coat Press Book

Acknowledgments: Thanks to Marie Duclaux de L'Estoille, Thierry Fraysse, Christine Luce and Jean-Marc Lofficier.

English adaptation and introduction Copyright © 2020 by Brian Stableford.
Cover illustration Copyright © 2020 Michel Borderie.

Visit our website at www.blackcoatpress.com

TABLE OF CONTENTS

Introduction 7
HAICKS AND BURNOOSES: ARAB SONGS 27
  The Forests of the Sahel.....................................27
  Fatma 29
  The Sylph and the Rose 32
  Thirst...34
  Sensuality...36
  The Woman and the Poet....................................37
  The Palm Tree in the Desert 38
  Aïchouna..39
  Princess Mitidja 43
  Sidi Mohamed-Ben-Abd-El-Rhaman 46
  Sidi-Embareck 48
  The Legend of Adam 50
  Great Is He Who Shrinks 56
  The Angel of Pain 57
  The Yellow Plague..59
  The Drop of Water..61
  The Land of the Sun..62
  The Daughter of the Ouled-Aïad 64
  Love Song...66
  The Death of Ben-Mansour 68
  Yamina...71
  Bullets Don't Kill 73
  The Warm Spring 74
  The Camel-Driver's Song....................................76
  The Janissary's Song 78
  The Palm Trees With the Heads of Angels...........80
  Desire...83
  The Dark-Eyed Virgin 84
ATTILA..87
THE MILLER OF CARNAC 109
FOLLE-AVOINE 124

FUSAINS..143
    The Evening...220
    The Morning 223
    The Evening...230
    The Morning 233
POEMS IN PROSE 234
    Jephthah's Daughter 234
    The Song of Arthur..238
    Rachel and Lia 255
    Symphony 276
        ROSE-DES-EAUX 276
        ALONA..298
VERCINGETORIX 326
    PART ONE...326
    PART TWO...352
    PART THREE 370

Introduction

This is the first of three volumes of translations of the literary work of Antoine-Louis Duclaux, Comte de L'Estoille (1835-1894)—work that was published in two distinct phases. In the first sequence of his publications, which extended from 1864-1869, he employed the pseudonym Louis de Lyvron, the surname being borrowed from his maternal grandmother, and it is work from that phase that is sampled in the present volume. In the second phase, which extended from 1880 to his death, he employed the signature "A. de L'Estoille." He had signed the dedications and one of the introductions to his earlier works "A. de L'", Antoine de L'Estoille being the name he employed in common usage, so the pseudonym was partly transparent, and the publications of the second phase include numerous revised versions of works initially published in the first phase; his works are still recorded in the catalogue of the Bibliothèque Nationale de France under the name Louis de Lyvron, with a note in small print recording that attribution as "erroneous."

The second volume of the present trio is a translation of *La Chanson de l'alouette* (Lemerre, 1880), as *The Song of the Skylark*; it is his longest individual work, and although it contains a certain amount of material recycled from the first phase, particularly from "Symphonie" (in *Poèmes en prose*, 1867; tr. in the present volume as "Symphony") and *Vercingétorix* (1869), it is so drastically elaborated and reformulated as to constitute an entirely new work. The third volume, *Argentine and Other Works*, is a collection of subsequent works from the second phase.

Little information is recorded about the life of Antoine de L'Estoille in addition to fragments of a journal covering the years 1856-8, which were published in 1862-3, and passages of apparent autobiography contained in his other works, most notably those in the fourth published volume signed Louis de Lyvron, *Fusains* (1868)[1] and *La Chanson de l'alouette*. As the bulk of both the latter texts consists of surreally phantasmagorical hallucinatory fantasy their suggestions cannot be taken literally, and the trivial details of the notional author's early life given therein are not always accurate. Thierry Fraysse, a French publisher desirous of reprinting some of his work, managed to locate Marie Duclaux de L'Estoille, a descendant, who kindly supplied some accurate details.

Antoine de L'Estoille was born in the Château de Taron in the small town of Renaison, in the Monts de la Madeleine, in the foothills of the Massif Central, between the Allier and the Loire—a region featured extensively in his work, to which he returned to live after his marriage in 1870. His father, Maximilien-Louis Duclaux de L'Estoille, was a soldier who was wounded during the capture of Algiers and subsequently resigned from the army, refusing to serve under Louis-Philippe. Antoine also became a career soldier in the 1850s and early 1860s; his experiences in that employment, and in particular his tours of duty as a spahi in North Africa, were the cardinal determinants of the highly unusual nature of his literary work, produced in an era when poets who had been career soldiers, and who employed their experiences as raw material in their literary endeavors, were rare. Although his fictitious

---

[1] In this context, a *fusain* is a slender stick of charcoal used by artists to make rapid sketches, and the plural was thus employed as a term for charcoal sketches made with the implement in question. It would therefore have been possible to translate this title as "Sketches," but as it represents a second metaphorical removal, drawing an analogy between such sketches and the prose vignettes often described as "poems in prose," it seemed appropriate simply to employ the French word.

alter egos are all orphans, Antoine maintained a close relationship with his father, whose death only preceded his by three years, and his mother, *née* Xaviérine de Bathelais. Maximilien settled in Renaison after his retirement from the army, establishing a steamboat service on the Allier and taking an active part in various scholarly societies.

If the suggestions in *Fusains* can be trusted—which is admittedly dubious—it appears that at some point L'Estoille returned to France, and was stationed at the Camp de Châlons before returning to Renaison to convalesce after a bout of "cerebral fever," but there is no precise indication as to when that might have occurred or in what circumstances. In *Fusains* the notional author convalesces in the home of his sister, but in a sequence in *La Chanson de l'alouette*, when the protagonist's delirious fever is prompted by a fall from a cliff in Algiers in peculiar circumstances, he is cared for by two fictitious and symbolic characters. If L'Estoille did, in fact, suffer from a bout of "cerebral fever," which was as significant as both *Fusains* and *La Chanson de l'alouette* imply, it must have been some considerable time before 1867, when the first episodes of *Fusains* were published in a short-lived literary periodical edited by Auguste Villiers de l'Isle-Adam, *Revue des lettres et des arts*, but how long before is difficult to determine. In the last of the published excerpts from his journal, dated December 1858, the author announces the abrupt departure of his regiment for Italy, presumably to join the forces of the French Empire in the campaign against the Austrian army that culminated in the battle of Solferino in 1859, but L'Estoille's work never makes any reference to being involved in that battle, or any other, and only passing reference is made in *La Chanson de l'alouette* to the protagonist having had military adventures in Lombardy.

There is a long gap in the chronology of the *Fragments*, during which a bout of "cerebral fever" might have occurred, or his regiment might well have returned to Africa after the French victory in Italy. Either way, the delirium that L'Estoille apparently suffered as a result of his "fever" is not reported in any detail in *Fusains*, where it is said to have left no conscious memory and where the diagnosis of "cerebral fever" made by an army doctor is casually dismissed, but it is possible that the experience was not unconnected with the substance and tone of his highly colorful fantastic fictions. The text in question also notes in passing that he had used both absinthe and *kif* (i.e. cannabis), which might also have made some contribution to the visionary tendencies of his literary work, but he was obviously inclined to controlled flights of fancy long before he went to Africa. He resigned from the army in January 1870 in order to marry, but was soon recalled to duty when the Franco-Prussian War broke out. When he retired for a second time, he was stationed in Besançon, where he held the rank of lieutenant-colonel.

The protagonist of *Fusain*s is packed off to the military college of Saint-Cyr, then located in the Yvelines, in order to avoid a petty scandal, but that probably does not reflect the reality of L'Estoille's life. It is, however, plausible that he shared with his fictitious *alter egos* a reputation for eccentricity based on his literary interests and ambitions and his strong interest in historical legends and mythology. It is known that, while he was on leave from the army in Paris, he patronized the bookshop owned by Noël Thibault, nicknamed "Père France"; in an article first published in *Le Temps* in 1888 the latter's son—who borrowed his father's nickname for his pseudonym, Anatole France—recalled encountering him there, the dashing spahi evidently having made an impression on a boy nearly ten years his junior.[2]

---

[2] It is unclear exactly when these encounters took place, but it is interesting to note that, although Anatole France knew that the spahi was "Louis de Lyvron," he either was not told or did not remember his real name, as he clearly did not know in 1888 that "Louis de Lyvron" and "A. de L'Estoille" were the same person, although he would definitely have realized it had he read *La Chanson de l'alouette*.

L'Estoille's early work, much of which was assembled in his first collection, *Haïcks et burnooses, chants arabes*, (Dentu, 1865) was presumably based on work initially written while he was in Algeria; although several of his early volumes are dated, those dates must refer to the completion of the submission texts, not to the original composition of the fragments making them up. L'Estoille was a compulsive reviser of his own work, and those items he published more than once—often under different titles—were always modified for republication. Although *Fusains* was the fourth volume of his work to be published, in 1868, the prior serialization of its early sections in the *Revue des lettres et des arts* and its strong links with the material in *Haïcks et burnooses* imply strongly that it is partly based on fragments that might have been initially composed some years earlier, probably in the late 1850s.

It may seem odd that the first evidential traces of L'Estoille's literary activities appeared in *Le Journal des Demoiselles*, a periodical aimed explicitly at girls aged between fourteen and eighteen, which serialized his "Fragments d'un journal d'un officier" in five parts (May and August 1862 and October, November and December 1863), but it is worth noting that alongside those fragments, numerous contributions to the magazine were signed "Sam": a pseudonym employed by S. Henry Berthoud, who did a good deal of freelance editorial work in the period and might well have been the magazine's managing editor at the time. That supposition is supported by the pattern of L'Estoille's other contributions to the magazine, which reflect very closely the policies that Berthoud had followed while editing the *Musée des Familles* twenty years earlier and which had been copied by many other periodicals. The classified contents page of the *Journal des Demoiselles* had no section of *Romans et nouvelles*, all of its fiction being classified as "*Instruction*" or "*Education*," and all of it justifying its presence, at least supposedly, by virtue of its educational value.

In addition to two travel articles and a music review. "Louis de Lyvron" contributed four short stories to the periodical: "L'Edredon de Mademoiselle Marie " [Mademoiselle Marie's Eiderdown] (1865); "Le Meunier de Carnac" (1866; tr. herein as "The Miller of Carnac), "Le Sabotier de Nuremberg" [The Clog-Maker of Nuremberg] (1867) and "Folle-Avoine" (1867; tr. herein as "Folle-Avoine"). The first is a didactic visionary fantasy clearly slanted toward the magazine's strategy, in which a girl dreams of traveling to North Cape with am eiderdown, experiencing several educational encounters on the way; it breaks the conventional pattern at the end, however, when a Lapp woman abruptly reveals herself to be the angelic "soul" of the Lapp race—a narrative move that L'Estoille was to repeat, with variations, in two of the key works of the latter part of his career.

"Le Meunier de Carnac" is far less typical of the magazine but very similar to much of S. Henry Berthoud's early work, when he attempted to become a serious folklorist of his native Flanders and became a prolific producer of "fakelore" imitating Medieval legends. L'Estoille adapted an abbreviated version of the story into *Fusains*, where its opening paragraphs are employed as a frame narrative for for two accounts of the enchanter Merlin, but the fuller version is more interesting, and it laid important groundwork for much of his subsequent work, not only in terms of its content but its rather eccentric manner of presentation. L'Estoille laid out many of his later texts in a highly idiosyncratic fashion, the seeds of which can be seen in the convolutions of "Le Meunier de Carnac."

"The Sabotier de Nuremberg" and "Folle-Avoine" are both variations of a standard plot in which a rich father stages a competition to decide between his daughter's suitors, in which the man who loves her dearly and is loved in return seems to have no chance of success, until he receives extraordinary aid. The former novelette is unfortunately interrupted in the scanned volume of the magazine available on the internet by a lacuna of four pages, but the beginning and the end survive and allow the outline of the plot to be determined. The shorter "Folle-Avoine" is far more tongue-in-cheek, straying into farce, and suggests strongly that the author had begun to find the editorial requirements of the *Journal des Demoiselles* uncomfortable; "Louis de Lyvron" never appeared in the periodical again, but elements of the fiction L'Estoille wrote for it were echoed in much of his later work, and he undoubtedly found it a useful market in the initial phase of his literary career, How he made contact with Berthoud, if Berthoud was in fact the managing editor of the periodical in 1862, is impossible to determine, but Berthoud had certainly been one of Noel Thibault's assiduous customers for many years.

The material collected in *Haïcks et burnooses* is far less orthodox than the prose published in the *Journal des Demoiselles* and poses difficulties of description. Some reviewers took the subtitle *chants arabes* to mean that it consisted, at least in part, of translations from Arabic, and that implication was seemingly endorsed by the titles of such individual pieces as "Chanson de Chamelier" (tr. herein as "The Camel-Driver's Song"). The latter was one of several works signed Louis de Lyvron set to music by the composer Augusta Holmès (1847-1903), who was then at the beginning of her career but had already adopted the affectation of adding a grave accent to her Anglo-Irish surname. When Lyvron's works began to appear in Villiers de l'Isle-Adam's *Revue des lettres et des arts* in 1867; however, they were labeled *poèmes en prose*, a term which that periodical did a great deal to popularize; he adopted that description himself when he titled his third publication in volume form *Poèmes en prose* (Lemerre, 1867).

The term "poèmes en prose" had already been used abundantly by Charles Baudelaire, who had just died when the periodical began publication, leaving unfinished the classic compilation *Le Spleen de Paris* (1869), also known as *Petits poèmes en prose*. Villiers evidently liked it; his periodical published four early poems in prose by Stéphane Mallarmé and applied the label to an item by Augusta Holmès, among others; he also reprinted the entirety of Louis Bertrand's *Gas-*

pard de la nuit (posthumously published in 1842;[3] the author preferred to style himself Aloysius Bertrand, but Villiers used his real name), which was subsequently hailed as a landmark work in the history of French "poetry in prose" and the first major exemplar of the genre.

It was not unusual for translations of poetry written in foreign languages to be rendered in prose; one of the dedicatees of *Gaspard de la nuit*, Charles Nodier, had provided models of that kind for its author, and Alphonse Lemerre also published Charles Leconte de Lisle's prose versions of the *Iliad* and the *Odyssey*. Many of the books of the *Old Testament*, especially the *Song of Solomon*, also provided key examples for would-be dabblers in the putative genre. Many Medieval romances exist in prose as well as verse versions, and there was a considerable overlap between the forms, further confused by the fact that the performances of Medieval troubadours and published versions of their works classified as *chansons* [usually translated as "songs"] included narratives in prose and verse—and, as in "Le Meunier de Carnac," L'Estoille's strong interest in such work had a enormous influence on his own work.

The label "poèmes en prose" was problematic long before Baudelaire and Villiers began to promote it, and remained so; it is significant that L'Estoille employed another descriptive label in *Fusains*, which mostly consists of material that must have been originally composed before the contents of *Poèmes en prose* but was only arranged for publication thereafter. Although many of the items in *Haïcks et burnooses* bear a close enough resemblance to prose poems by Baudelaire and Mallarmé to be considered as exemplars of the same vague genre, the great majority of L'Estoille's subsequent works, especially those in *Poèmes en prose*, are markedly and variously different, having more in common with ancient exem-

---

[3] Available from Black Coat Press in a translation by Donald Sidney-Fryer, ISBN 978-0-9740711-2-1.

plars but also developing new and idiosyncratic styles of presentation.

It is no more possible to determine how L'Estoille made contact with Villiers de l'Isle-Adam than with the editor of the *Journal de Demoiselles*, but Villiers undoubtedly knew Noel Thibault too. "Sam" Berthoud had known Théophile Gautier for thirty years; in the early 1860s, he was undoubtedly a regular visitor to Gautier's salon, as were Villiers and Catulle Mendès (who deserted his first wife, Judith Gautier, during the *Revue*'s brief lifetime, and subsequently lived with Augusta Holmès), and probably Alphonse Lemerre. Thibault or Berthoud could easily have made the introduction there.

The work with which "Louis de Lyvron" followed *Haïcks and Burnooses* was *Les Runes d'Attila* (Marpon, 1866), which certainly warrants description as a "poem in prose," but of a variety very different from the material in the previous collection. The term "runes," in this instance, is ambiguous, not only referring to the letters employed in various Germanic and Scandinavian alphabets but relating more specifically to the Finnish *runot*, a term used for the sections of Elias Lönnrot's *Kalevala* (several versions issued between 1835 and 1849), which is generally regarded as an epic poem, although it can just as easily be regarded as a collage of folk tales, of which Lönnrot had long been a collector; the closest English equivalent of the word *runot* is "folk tale," and *Les Runes d'Attila* is an imitation *runot* in the sense of the word employed by Lönnrot. The French prose translation of the *Kalevala*, by Louis-Antoine Léouzon Le Duc (1815-1889), had first been published in *La Finlande: son histoire primitive, sa mythologie, sa poésie épique* [Finland: Its Early History, Mythology and Epic Poetry] in 1845, where L'Estoille must have read it, as his own poem predates the separate publication of 1867.

The Lyvron "poem" is divided into "verses" but does not reproduce the severe metrication of Lönnrot's unrhymed verse (a schema famously pastiched in Henry Wadsworth Longfellow's *The Song of Hiawatha*, published in 1855); in fact, it resembles more closely the format of the books of the Old Testament, and although the second version of the poem, used as the lead item of the 1867 *Poèmes en prose*, retains the original title and format, the versions printed during the second phase drop the term "runes," and the version in *Les Amoureuses* (1883, by-lined A. de L'Estoille), entitled "Hildewige," numbers the "chapters" and "verses" in imitation of the books of the Bible. The Marpon edition of the poem is not available on *gallica*, so the translation included in the present volume is taken from the final, presumably definitive, version included in *Contes du Nord* (1892) under the title "Attila: conte danois" (tr. herein as "Attila, a Danish Tale").

Even the items in *Haïcks et burnooses* and *Les Runes d'Attila*, therefore, pose problems of classification, which illustrate the looseness of the term "poèmes en prose" and its dubious propriety with reference to some of the works gathered under that heading by Villiers de l'Isle-Adam. Those problems of categorization, however, become very acute indeed with reference to the material in *Fusains* and the Lyvron *Poèmes en prose*. It is difficult to describe *Fusains*, which, although it contains four page-breaks and several series of numbered sections, is not really organized into "chapters" or "stories." None of its subsections is given an individual title in the Lemerre version—although the last one has four subheadings—even though the revised versions of some passages included in *Les Amoureuses* and those sections that had previously appeared in other publications all had individual titles there. *Fusains* could, therefore, be regarded as a bizarre novella rather than a collection, albeit a signally incoherent one, but it is perhaps most appropriate to regard it as a literary collage, that label extrapolating the analogy contained in its title.

At any rate, however it is categorized, *Fusains* deliberately mingles sections of ostensible autobiography with visionary passages sometimes mimicking effects of delirium, many derived from folklore of a peculiar and distinctive kind, presented in a calculatedly disjointed fashion. It has few literary precedents, although one of the "stories" that it contains is deliberately interrupted in a fashion reminiscent of a similar tactic employed by Charles Nodier in *Histoire du roi de Bohême et de ses sept châteaux* (1830; tr. as *The Story of the King of Bohemia and his Seven Castles*), a surreal hallucinatory fantasy that Duclaux might well have employed as a model in planning *Fusains*. L'Estoille subsequently recombined some of the fragments of the interrupted story and supplied the narrative with an ending in a revised version included in *Les Amoureuses* as "Hélène," but the ending of that version would not have been at all appropriate to the deliberate surreality of the version included in *Fusains*.

Although *Poèmes en prose* is divided into separate sections, the longest of those sections, "Symphonie," itself divided into two subsections, is also a deliberately-disordered mingling of pseudo-autobiographical and folkloristic motifs. L'Estoille was evidently dissatisfied with it, because he launched the second phase of his career in 1880, writing as A. de L'Estoille, with a very extensive revision and drastic elaboration of "Symphonie," in the first volume of *La Chanson de l'alouette*, issued by Lemerre in three volumes separately titled *La Statue, Celui qui doit venir* [He Who is to Come] and *Le Moissonneur* [The Harvester].[4] The problems of classification posed by *Fusains* and *Poèmes en prose* were further increased by *La Chanson de l'alouette*, which bears less resemblance to a collage but does not really invite description as a novel—but that is a matter best taken up in the introduction to *The Song of the Skylark*.

---

[4] A later volume entitled *La Chanson de l'alouette* (1895), published in Lyon, appears, to judge by its page count, to contain the whole work, but it is not on *gallica* so I have not been able to confirm that, or to determine whether it was revised; it might well have been, as the dedication of the 1880 version describes it as an *ébauche* (sketch) and expresses an intention to keep working on it. The three-volume version was reissued on a print-on-demand basis in 2016.

The second item in *Poèmes en prose*, following the second version of "Les Runes d'Attila," is "La Fille de Jephté" (tr. herein as "Jephthah's Daughter"), a prose poem based on an episode in chapter 11 of the Biblical book of *Judges*, in which Jephthah, having won a battle, vows that he will offer the first thing that emerges from his tent as a burnt offering to the Lord, only to see his only daughter come out to greet him. It was one of Lyvron's works set to music by Augusta Holmès, and might well have been a collaboration between the two (Holmès subsequently wrote almost all the librettos for her musical works herself.) The collection also contains a dramatic piece very loosely based on a Bible story, "Rachel et Lia," about the two sisters who become wives of the patriarch Jacob in *Genesis 29*; a revised version was included in *Les Amoureuses* as "Lia."

In between the two pieces based on the Old Testament, *Poèmes en prose* features "La Chanson d'Arthur" (tr. as "The Song of Arthur"), which is based on a pseudo-folkloristic interpretation of the Medieval romances featuring King Arthur and the wizard Merlin—many of which exist in both poetic and prose versions. Lyvron's version of the romance appears to be loosely based on the interpretation of the relevant legendary material elaborated by Théodore Hersart de La Villemarqué (1815-1895) in *Les Romans de la Table-ronde et les contes des anciens Bretons* [The Romance of the Round Table and the Tales of the Ancient Bretons] (1860) and *Myrdhinn, ou l'enchanteur Merlin, son histoire, ses oeuvres, son influence* [Myrdhinn; or, the Enchanter Merlin; his history, his works and his influence] (1862), which followed up Hersart's highly successful popularization of supposed works by Breton bards, which were mostly his own invention. Like most of the "folklorists" of his era, Hersart put an enormous dose of imagination into his research, and much of what he touted as folklore is really fakelore, but such fakelore was highly influential on the work of writers associated with the French Romantic Movement of the nineteenth century, to which L'Estoille became an enthusiastic is slightly belated contributor. It was mainly from Hersart that L'Estoille initially derived the supposed legendry of Breton *fées* (fays), which he adapted very freely to his own purposes in the major works of both phases of his career.

"La Chanson d'Arthur" certainly warrants consideration as a poem in prose by comparison with the Medieval romances on which it is based, albeit in a revisionist frame of mind, and its imagery is echoed in "Symphonie" as well as the long drama *Vercingétorix* (1869), but "Symphonie" is markedly different in its style and format, much more closely linked in method and concern with *Fusains*, the visionary passages of which similarly borrow from Hersart. Like *Fusains*, "Symphonie" attempts to combine aspects of the author's personal history with the legendry of his homeland—with the *caveat* that L'Estoille was not a Breton, and thus had difficulty fitting his own presumed cultural heritage into the imaginary history concocted by Hersart. It was, however, not an insuperable difficulty, and L'Estoille had one spectacular literary example available to him of how such a transformative fusion could be wrought: *Merlin l'enchanteur* (1860; tr. as *The Enchanter Merlin*)[5] by Hersart's great rival, Edgar Quinet, then in voluntary exile from the Second Empire. Quinet ingeniously fused elements of his own autobiography with a heavily-revised version of the legend of Merlin to produce a mock-epic work that remains *sui generis*, part episodic novel and part epic poem in prose.

It is improbable that Louis de Lyvron's contemporaries did not notice the affinities between "Symphonie" and *Merlin l'enchanteur*, just as they might have noticed affinities between *Fusains* and *Histoire du roi de Bohême et de ses sept châteaux*, but none of the sparse reviews of *Fusains* or *Poèmes en prose* made any such comparison, and that silence is illustrative of the fact that Louis de Lyvron had the misfortune to be working under the Second Empire, when political censorship of literary works, although it relaxed somewhat after

---

[5] Available from Black Coat Press, ISBN 978-1-61227-303-7.

1860, was still powerful. Lyvron, who spent many years fighting for the Empire in its colonial adventures, does not appear to have been an avid supporter of the regime,[6] and although his work avoids political arguments as scrupulously as almost everything published in Paris during the 1860s, it is certainly not jingoistic and tends somewhat in the opposite direction, consistently sympathetic to the Arabs who resented and resisted colonization. Had any critic bothered to draw a parallel between "Symphonie" and the work of Edgar Quinet, whose voluntary exile made him a symbol of defiant opposition to the current regime, or between *Fusains* and the work of the ex-Jacobin Charles Nodier, who had been imprisoned and exiled from Paris after publishing a satirical poem criticizing Napoléon when the latter was the First Consul, he would not have been doing the author any favors, diplomatically speaking.

In fact, the apparent popularity during the Second Empire of works of historical and quasi-historical fiction probably had much to do with the fact that such works were far more likely to escape the stern attention of the censors than edgy endeavors in contemporary fiction, and interest in the remote history of "Gaul" was probably reckoned to be a safe subject, especially when larded with legendry and myth, because Napoléon III had a declared interest in such ideas.[7] As a native of

---

[6] In the reconfiguration of the history of France sketched in *La Chanson de l'alouette*, Napoléon I is a significant character (depicted as a supposed reincarnation of Julius Caesar, working for his own vanity rather than for France), and the Franco-Prussian war is elaborately featured there, but there is no mention of any character equivalent to Napoléon III, who is a nonentity within L'Estoille's mythicized history.

[7] Louis de Lyvron was not the only writer published by Alphonse Lemerre in the 1860s who took a good deal of inspiration from Hersart; another was the poet "Louise d'Isole" (Adine Rion, 1818-1899), although it was only in the twilight

central France, however, L'Estoille preferred to trace his own imaginary ancestry back to the tribe he calls the Arvernes, extensively featured in Julius Caesar's self-serving account of the *Gallic Wars* (where they are called the Arverni) and it is from the details given in that text that L'Estoille took the substance of his own epic drama *Vercingétorix*—which naturally takes the opposite side to Caesar, and makes its eponymous hero a reincarnation of an earlier, entirely hypothetical, legendary figure tenuously associated with the myth of the founding of "Gaul" by "Gaels" who had allegedly colonized much of Northern Europe during the first millennium B.C.— including the British Isles, where their name and language still survived.[8]

Although L'Estoille and Edgar Quinet were in very different existential situations in the 1860s, and developed markedly contrasting legendary histories in spite of numerous points of commonality, they were both outsiders relative to the tightly-knit literary community of Paris. Although L'Estoille—an ardent traveler—might have been based there for a while in the late 1860s, he certainly spent most of his life elsewhere, and although the literary associations he had in Paris, with the likes of Villiers de l'Isle-Adam and Augusta Holmès, now seem retrospectively prestigious, they would not have seemed so at the time. The association, however tenuous it was, might have done him more harm than good socially in the late 1860s.

---

of her career that she produced her *Légendes bretonnes* and her own epic *Merlin* (both 1887).

[8] Modern ethnography draws a different distinction between "Celtic" Gauls, who allegedly spread throughout Northern Europe in the fifth century B.C. and Gaels, whose later culture was narrowly restricted to the British Isles, but in L'Estoille's hypothetical prehistory is it the Gauls who are represented as a subsection of the Gaels, the former being specifically associated with the territory that eventually became France.

At any rate, "Louis de Lyvron" disappeared from the Parisian literary scene in 1869 and never returned. The dedications of *Poèmes en prose* and *Vercingétorix* to "the woman I love" and the last autobiographical details given in *Fusains* dovetail neatly with the fact that L'Estoille married Marie Roy de l'Ecluse on 5 January 1870, and settled with her in the vicinity of Renaison. That was by no means the only significant interruption to his life in that year, however; France mobilized its army for war with Prussia on 15 July, and L'Estoille was inevitably involved in and deeply affected by the subsequent catastrophe. An *Armée de la Loire* was formed in order to mount resistance to the invasion, and although it won the Battle of Coulmiers in November, that was the only significant success obtained by the belatedly-gathered French forces, which were comprehensively smashed before the signing of the armistice in January 1871. Although L'Estoille's subsequent literary work makes no direct reference to his involvement in the *Armée de la Loire*, it does include two dramas and a substantial prose poem bitterly regretting the loss of Alsace to the Prussians, which are included in the final volume to the present set, and the second and third parts of *La Chanson de l'alouette* are obviously an angry reaction to the tragedy, probably written in fits and starts between 1871 and their publication a decade later.

Although the bulk of the second and third volumes of *La Chanson de l'alouette* consists of "The Story of Ar-Braz" as narrated by a character simply called "the poet" that story is embedded in a frame narrative set thirty years after the Franco-Prussian War (i.e., in 1900), when "the poet" is dead. If "the poet" is assumed to be "Louis de Lyvron" the narrative voice that takes up the story after his death is presumably "A. de L'Estoille," and it might well be the case that by 1871, let alone 1880, L'Estoille regarded his first literary incarnation as deceased, quite separate from his second, even though "A. de L'Estoille" revised a considerable number of the sketches signed "Louis de Lyvron" for republication. The narrative voice of *La Chanson de l'alouette* is insistent, both in the text and the dedication, that what he is saying, with specific reference to reincarnation, is true, and whether that can be taken literally or not, "A. de L'Estoille" certainly seems to have thought of himself as someone "reborn." Several other *alter egos* featured in L'Estoille's fiction have manifest dual personalities who indulge in elaborate "dialogues."

Whatever the precise reasons were for Louis de Lyvron's temporary silence after 1869 and his subsequent resurrection under a different signature, that period of silence and change of signature certainly affected the reputation he had and the memory he left behind, and his work was almost completely forgotten; by the time that literary historians began to take an interest in what they dubbed the "Parnassians," borrowing that label from Alphonse Lemerre's showcase anthology of contemporary poetry *Le Parnasse contemporain* (1866, supplemented by two "sequels" in 1871 and 1876)—in which Lyvron, as a writer in prose, was not included—he had become a mere footnote in orthodox literary history. Gustave Kahn's chronicle of *Symbolistes et Décadents* (1902) mentions him in passing, but only in order to dismiss summarily him as "atypical" of the Parnassians—a drastic understatement which does no justice at all to the extreme originality of his work. The garrulous Anatole France similarly only mentioned him in passing, in an article on another subject, albeit sympathetically and in complimentary terms; France did wonder, however why Lyvron was not considered alongside himself as a significant "precursor" of the nascent Symbolist Movement—which he certainly was.

In 1880 the term "Symbolism" had not yet acquired the meaning that it subsequently took on in literary circles, so *La Chanson de l'alouette* could not be recognized then as the first full-length Symbolist work of fiction, but when the term began to be bandied about freely in 1885 none of the commentators who employed it seemed to remember Louis de Lyvron or even to have noticed the existence and relevance of A. de L'Estoille. In fact, however, Louis de Lyvron was a diehard Symbolist, greatly encouraged by the fact that he was an unusually coy writer when it came to erotic matters. As a soldier in Africa he undoubtedly had some communication with and emotional response to women, including prostitutes, but all mention of that association is unsurprisingly excised from the excerpts from his diaries published in the *Journal des Demoiselles*, and although the material in *Haïcks et burnooses* and *Fusains* is greatly preoccupied with it, it is heavily disguised, erotic impulses being described and discussed almost entirely in terms of flowers, butterflies, birds and gazelles.[9]

A few modern commentators have belatedly allotted "Louis de Lyvron" a significant transitional role in the historical development of the prose poem, his publications arriving some time after *Gaspard de la Nuit* and shortly before the posthumously-issued *Spleen de Paris*. The observation is just—indeed, no other writer was anywhere near as prolific in the production of *poèmes en prose*—but his work is markedly different in its flavor from that of Bertrand and Baudelaire, and is better regarded as a different tributary of the stream whose waters Villiers de l'Isle-Adam attempted to define and direct. It is certainly very interesting, in terms of comparison and contrast, and its peaks—including much of the material sampled in the present collection, especially the defiantly experimental *Fusains*—are definitely worthy of attention in terms of their style, method, subject matter and ambition.

Less attention has been paid to L'Estoille's contribution to the development of the French tradition of *contes de fées*, which had long been in the doldrums in the mid-nineteenth century, but he was the most significant contributor of his era

---

[9] Even in *Les Amoureuses*, which is more erotically explicit, it still requires a certain amount of decoding and reading between the lines to realize that, for instance, the reason why the relationship between "Captain Jacques" and the title character of "Hélène" is so perversely problematic is because she is the illegitimate daughter of a high-class whore who has taken elaborate steps to prevent her or anyone else discovering that fact.

to that tradition. His work is particularly significant in exemplifying and mapping the gradual elaboration and transfiguration of the idea of *fées* that took place following the suppression by the Church of the inventions of the Parisian salon writers, which became briefly fashionable at Louis XIV's court under the tutelage of the king's eldest daughter, the "dowager Princesse de Conti." L'Estoille's fays undergo a marked transition from being apparently-human enchantresses to immaterial beings of peculiar symbolic significance, in a pattern that is as enterprising and as highly idiosyncratic as every other aspect of his work.

"Louis de Lyvron" was a genuinely innovative writer, in a period when experimentation was not encouraged by circumstance, and he was a definite precursor of much of the experimentation subsequently carried out by writers affiliated to the Symbolist Movement of the late 1880s and 1890s. It is easy to suspect him of some influence, albeit uncredited, of some of those supposed pioneers, given that his formal experiments are extensively echoed in the work of various eccentric poets and short story writers, most obviously Catulle Mendès and Jean Lorrain. Although he revised the work he republished as A. de L'Estoille, sometimes drastically, it is not always obvious that the revised versions of the short vignettes are a considerable improvement on the initial versions, and the earlier ones have much to recommend them in any case, in terms of their enterprise and their relentless quest for originality. L'Estoille's overall contribution to the literature of his homeland has been drastically underestimated, and it is unjust that he was almost completely forgotten until *gallica* began to make his work readily accessible again.

The translation of "Le Meunier de Carnac" was made from a bound volume of the *Journal des Demoiselles* reproduced on Google Books, and the translation of "Folle-Avoine" from a similar volume, accessed via the Hathi Trust because the version on Google Books had mysteriously disappeared after previous consultation. The various works published in volume form included in the present collection were all made from the copies of the original volumes reproduced on the Bibliothèque Nationale's *gallica* website, with the exception of "Attila," with was made from a pdf file of *Contes du Nord* (Sauvaitre, 1892) kindly supplied by Christine Luce via Thierry Fraysse and Jean-Marc Lofficier. (The latter volume, which is exceedingly rare, is not in the Bibliothèque Nationale.)

Brian Stableford

HAICKS AND BURNOOSES: ARAB SONGS

"Where are you going, horseman?"
"To the desert; my heart is empty, I want to fill it."
It's necessary to rattle one's spurs!

The Forests of the Sahel

Praise to the unique God!

What I say is true; repeated and your words will not be diminished by anyone.

The forests of the Sahel are beautiful and sad.

They resemble a young widow who is still thinking of the dead man while combing her hair and weeping, with one tress braided and the other scattered.

They ornament themselves for the Sun, the forests of Mitidja, they weep in thinking about the Hadjoutes, dead under Christian bullets.[10]

---

[10] Mitidja is a plain in what is now northern Algeria, outside Algiers. The Hadjoutes were the tribal inhabitants of the region, the town that the French called Marengo having subsequently reclaimed the name of Hadjout. Here, as elsewhere in his work, L'Estoille manifests far more sympathy for the indigenous victims of French colonization than the forces for which he had fought, but the poetic form of his work and its

"Weep no more, forests of oaks, today is Man's but tomorrow is God's; weep no more, you are beautiful and the Hadjoutes had sons.

"O you who wear spurs, you for whom beauty is as sweet to the eyes as milk to the lips, come and visit the forests of the Sahel."

In the plain, all around, the roots have darts, the flowers have thorns. But under the trees, bindweed run through the grass, clematis hangs from the branches, and butterflies with golden wings flutter over the oleanders in the forests of the Sahel.

The heart of a forest palpitates, like the heart of a virgin at the first rendezvous.

In the depths of ravines, the pomegranates shed the petals of their coral flowers over dormant springs; the tamarinds dip their silky crowns here; the fir-trees plunge their shiny roots between the rocks like sleeping snakes; the reeds sway their feathery heads, the spotted ferns incline softly; and the acanthi support their satin leaves on the trunks of oaks, in the forests of the Sahel.

The eyes of a forest are like those of women; they have the depth of the sea and the calm of the sky.

But the North wind has dispersed the Hadjoutes and the eyes of the forests of the Sahel are filled with sadness and ennui.

"O you who wear spurs, you whose hands can hold a bridle, come and tell the forests of the Sahel that the sons of the Hadjoutes have grown up, and that the Christians are going to die."

---

description as "Arab songs" presumably served to deflect the attention of Napoléon III's censors.

Fatma

In Algiers the victorious, at the back of a house with an arched doorway, in a blue chamber paneled with faience, on cushions of striped silk, Fatma the virgin is braiding her golden hair with coral.

Then she crosses her haïck over her brocade jacket, hides her feet, reddened by henna, in her yellow leather babouches and says to Zora the African, in front of her father: "Take me to the bath before midday."

When Fatma the virgin and Zora the African pass through the streets of Algiers, the Moors with peach-colored cheeks withdraw the amber bowls of their chibouks from their lips, and sigh in whispers: "Fortunate is the man who will see without a veil that figure more supple than the palm-tree of Bab Azoun."[11]

But Fatma does not turn her head as she passes before the Moors who are smoking under the cool arcades of the cafés where there is singing; she does not turn her head when the janissaries make their lustrous stallions rear up before her; she does not even turn her head when the pacha smiles at her.

Fatma, the swallow of Algiers, loves Ismael, the falcon of the plain, whose horse is thin and whose rifle is rusty. She loves Ismael with the forehead burned by the sun, whom she saw for the first time at the festival of the fava beans, on the sandy beach near Mustapha.

---

[11] Bab Azoun is one of the city gates of Algiers. The other places mentioned in the poem are outlying districts of the city, nowadays incorporated into its suburbs.

Walls stop thieves, veils cause debauchees to despair, African women drive away gallants, but amour soars over walls, plunges beneath veils and tames women.

At the festival of the fava beans, Ismael said to Fatma: "For you my heart burns like a star in the blue sky with amour," and the virgin responded to the horseman's words with a tender gaze.

On the day when Fatma says to Zora the African in front of her father: "Take me to the bath before midday," she knows that Ismael is waiting for her, and instead of going to the bath she goes to the lentisks of Hussein Dey.

As soon as Ismael perceives her he seizes her in his arms, and without saying a word, without giving her a kiss, he lays her over the mane of his horse and departs at a gallop.

Zora the African slaps her cheeks, rolls in the grass and cries; "Allah!" But the Arab disappears in the direction of El Harrach in a cloud of dust. His horse flies like a bird, and Fatma's haïck remains hooked on an olive branch.

The child of the tents shivers under the flashes that spring from the dark eyes; he drinks the breath of the torso over which the breasts beat like the wings of a dove; he bites the gilded tresses that writhe under his lip like snakes; but his horse is traveling so rapidly that he does not say anything.

The road becomes stony, the horse slows down and the rider sighs to the virgin: "Fatma, the sultana is less beautiful than you! I must give you a nuptial bed finer than the sultana of the harem of Stamboul."

The virgin smiles. "I have your broad chest for a nuptial bed; it is whiter than ivory; I have your heart for a wedding-gift; it is purer than gold. Ismael, the sultana would envy Fatma's nuptial bed.

The road become stony, the horse moves less rapidly and they hear the sea. "I want," the horseman continues, "to see you always as beautiful as today. I do not want your hair to pale, your eyes to be extinguished or your throat to wrinkle. I would like to give you a nuptial bed in which you will always be virginal and I will always be strong."

The virgin smiles and touches the flyssa[12] whose copper hilt is shining under the burnoose. "It cuts, your flyssa, Ismael, it is long enough to reach the heart... Draw your flyssa and give me your lips, Ismael, my beloved."

The horse flies over the crest of the cliff that the sea licks with its blue waves. "If your blood flowed, Fatma, the dust would drink it and I would be jealous; I want you for myself alone, your body and your soul in our nuptial bed."

The virgin smiles and takes the bridle of the obedient horse. "Ismael, here is our nuptial bed... Master, clasp your slave hard and make your spurs ring."

The spurs ring, the horse bounds, Ismael's lips stick to Fatma's lips and then…a circle spreads over the blue waves.

---

[12] The flyssa—a long single-edged knife, or short sword—was the traditional weapon of a Berber tribe known during the era of French colonization as the Kabyles.

The Sylph and the Rose

Roses have the souls of woman in their velvety calices.

One morning, a rose bloomed beside a river.

The sylph that gives flowers their perfume found the rose so beautiful that he fell in love with her, and in order to caress her all day long he curled up in a cluster of white lilac that the zephyr swayed nearby. But the coquettish rose was smiling at the butterflies and, in allowing itself to be teased by them, she stung the heart of the amorous sylph.

He flew away, swearing to avenge himself.

He said to the red-haired demon who drives the storm-clouds: "Go into the garden beside the profound river; you'll find a cheerful rose there; take her, I give her to you."

The demon plucked the rose from her stem and, after having respired her perfume, he threw her, paled, into the middle of a marsh.

The rose wept for her sweet perfume, and then she wept for the beautiful butterflies, but she did not weep for the amorous sylph.

He flew away, swearing to avenge himself.

In the garden, he heaped up the flowers fallen from the cluster of lilac and he sowed them on the black braches of a thorny bush that steeped its leafless head in the marsh.

On seeing the flowers on the black branches, the rose remembered the cluster of white lilac around which the butterflies fluttered in the garden, and she loved the bush because of the remembered flowers.

At the first kiss, the flowers fell and the long thorns of the soiled bush dug into the petals of the amorous rose. She realized that it was the sylph and not the cluster that had loved her before, and she wept for the departed sylph.

The sylph forgot his anger, but, in spite of his amour, he could not render to the rose either her lost perfume or her paled splendor; the future belongs to sylphs, but not the past.

He cut out large leaves from his emerald mantle and he extended them over the marsh like a satin carpet; then he laid his dying beloved on the freshest.

Of the withered rose he had made a nenuphar, the white rose of the waters

Roses have the souls of women in their velvety calices.

The one I love is pale, butterflies have buzzed in her ear, thorns have lacerated her, and destiny has cast her on to a marsh of dull water, but in my heart she will find the where-withal to tailor a stainless robe and weave an immortal crown of youth and beauty.

Amour effaces the wrinkles that pleasure has hollowed out.

Thirst

A warbler was singing, the pomegranates were turning crimson in the sunlight, and a coral cup shone beneath the young woman's veil.

"I'm thirsty," said the child.

The bees were buzzing, periwinkles brushed the stream, a sweet liquor was quivering in the cup.

"I'm thirsty," said the adolescent.

The shadow of the orange-trees extended in the direction of the orient and the cup filled up.

"I'm thirsty," said the cavalier.

The cup broke, the young woman paled, and her heart was visible in the depths of a wound.

The child became a man.

The city was scintillating with flowers and weapons, the crowd pressing around the victor. A blonde feather trembled on his turban, a red burnoose floated over his shoulder.

"I'm thirsty," said the warrior.

The city presented him with a cup full of a vermilion beverage, and words fell, as sonorous as waves, from the warrior' lips.

"I'm thirsty," said the visionary.

The men who read him gave him a rose from which to drink. His lips found nothing there but ashes and the crowd began to laugh.

The man became an old man.

The sun was setting, the tent was deserted and a virgin sustained the ancestor's head.

"I'm thirsty," said the old man

The virgin handed him an ivory cup; he emptied it and his eyes closed.

"I'm thirsty," sighed the cadaver.

The virgin bore away the soul

Sensuality

My babouches weigh like a bronze cannon, my burnoose is heavier than a tombstone, my temples are throbbing and my eyes are troubled.

Wave the fan with the silky plumes, make sprays of icy water spring from the nacreous basin.

Bring me flowers: jasmine and roses. The perfume of jasmine is as sweet as a woman's smile and the perfume of roses warms like a houri's kiss.

Enlace your naked arms, flex your ivory hips, turn more rapidly, daughters of the Beni Mzab.[13]

My tent is as wide as the plain, taller than the palm trees. Let your veils fall; I am the voice that commands, I am the hand that gives.

My horses are stronger than the desert wind, my spahis more rapid than a flying bullet. Curb your heads, slaves! I am the Emir.

Stirrups ring, heads fall, virgins scream. Strike, strike…I am the arm of Allah, the saber that touches and kills.

The sand fumes where I have passed. I am the devouring flame, the fiery vapor that glides westwards.

The course of the Earth is less rapid than mine; the crimson clouds cradle me and lift me up.

The moon opens to embrace me with her snowy crescent…

---

[13] The Mzab is a region of the northern Sahara south of Algiers; the Beni Mzab were the tribe inhabiting the region in the era of French colonization.

The Woman and the Poet

In a garden there was a sylph and a rose: a sylph with dark wings, a rose with a golden heart.

When the stars lit up, the sylph approached the flower. "I'm in love," he said, "and dying of it..." and the flower smiled.

"I'm also in love," she replied, "I love a beautiful butterfly as brilliant as a flame."

"I'm in love," said the sylph, "and dying of it..." and the flower smiled again, and the sylph flew away.

The next day, he came back, but he no longer spoke, and the rose said to him: "What flower do you love—doubtless a *belle-de-nuit*?"[14]

"I love a rose with a golden heart.

"Roses are lovers of the sun, and your wings are dark, poor fool."

"My wings are dark but my soul is aflame. I divine what the butterfly does not see, I dream what he does not know, and in my dreams you say to me what you do not say to him. He opens your lips but I alone have your kisses.

"Your disdain has killed me, tomorrow I shall be dead; but tomorrow, you will no longer be in love, because I have spoken to you."

The sylph shook his dark wings over the rose, something akin to sparks fell therefrom, and then he died.

The next day, the rose was inclined on her stem. "Yesterday, however," she sighed, "I believed that I was in love."

The butterfly was only a man, the sylph was a poet.

---

[14] The name *belle-de-nuit* was applies to various flowering plants, most commonly to *Mirabilis jalapa*, which originated in South America but was naturalized in various subtropical regions of Africa and Asia.

The Palm Tree in the Desert

In the desert, where the sand flows, the great palm tree stands alone.

Its trunk crackles in the sun, and laments fall from its calcined palms.

From its palms, beside which amber-colored clusters have never swung.

But the wind blew from the sea, where peaks were hidden in the coral, drops of dew in crimson crops.

Under the warm caress, the palm tree quivered.

Like a stallion when the acrid odor of mares dilates its silky nostrils.

"Your kiss intoxicates me, said the palm tree to the breeze; who are you, then?"

"I am the language that is spoken everywhere," replied the breeze, "Which is understood everywhere, the language that sings the ardent hymn of the heavens to the earth.

"Listen, solitary palm tree..."

Then the breeze spoke...

Amorous strophes streamed over the palms, and unknown words, like blonde oil, slid all the way to the roots of the great thirsty tree.

One evening, the angel who brings to the date palms the kisses of their sisters, flew as far as the solitary palm.

He departed weeping.

He had not found any golden dust in the pale flowers of the great palm tree.

Aïchouna

When the Arab did not wait to fold up his tent until the pickets rotted, when he had the plain as the eagle has the Djurdjura mountains, Dellys of the white houses was the city beloved by scholars and flowers.

"The hand of Allah is open, it has let servitude and death fall upon the believers; you have taken Dellys, the twice holy city.

"Those whom the lead has touched no longer come to ask its thalebs for talismans; those who have shared their hearts no longer come to pick geraniums in the tomb of Aïchouna.

"Nothing any longer remains to the children of the prophet but hope and memory; the hope is for our sons, the memory alone inhabits our bald foreheads. It was written.

"You are not, like your brothers, incredulous and impious; listen to the story of Aïchouna. It is true, because the first man who repeated it had learned it from those who knew the virgin of Beni Ammal; it is sweet on my lips, for my mother nourished me under the olive-trees of Benchoud...

"Listen:

When Hassan Barberousse commanded in Algiers,[15] the Turks built Bordj Sebaou and made Beni Ammal pay taxes; but Achemed, whose heart alone opened his hand, withdrew

---

[15] The Pacha known as Hassan Barberousse [i.e, Redbeard] (1517-1570) ruled Algiers for many years while it was part of the Ottoman Empire, having inherited that sovereignty from his similarly-nicknamed father

into the forests of the hill of Beni Aïcha with those who knew how to light gunpowder.

Every day, there were eye-to-eye encounters at the end of rifle-barrels.

After three years of battles the janissaries were preparing to abandon the Bordj when a young man named Kaddour came to find their bey and said to him:

"I love Aïchouna, the fiancée of Achemed; if you promise her to me I will deliver the rebel to you."

The bey promised, and the same evening, Kaddour hid janissaries in the wood of Benchoud.

As soon as the stars paled, a shadow passed under the trees not far from the ambush; it was Aïchouna. Every night she came to the olive grove, and every night Achemed descended from the mountain and only returned at dawn.

In order to find one another in the midst of darkness, Aïchouna imitated the song of the warbler, and Achemed uttered the cry of the white heron three times.

Aïchouna sang, but she stopped, trembling; she had heard an unknown footstep...

"Don't speak," said Kaddour. "I could carry you away, but my love is less powerful than my hatred; I want him to die."

The heron cried three times on the mountain.

"Mercy, mercy for him; perhaps I can love you. Let's depart, Kaddour, let's depart..."

"It's necessary that my bride be ornamented under my tent. The blood of Achemed will be brighter than henna; you shall have pink fingernails and a crimson haïck; you shall be beautiful, Aïchouna."

The heron cried three times under the first olive trees.

"Depart, my beloved...," said Aïchouna.

Kaddour's dagger fumed all the way to the hilt.

A flame shone in the darkness and Kaddour writhed on the grass. The Turks launched forth, but Achemed's flyssa traced a circle that death could not break. They fell, to the last man.

Achemed took the bloody veil of the virgin with the golden hair and departed at a gallop.

More rapid than an eagle returning to its nest, his horse crosses the rocks and cleaves through the undergrowth of the hill of Beni Aïcha.

"On your feet, companions, on your feet! The sister of my heart is dead; the Turks will not see tomorrow's sun."

The bold horsemen leap into the saddle and traverse the plain of Issers like a hurricane. Far away, far ahead of them, rides Achemed, upright in his stirrups, holding the bloody scarf in his hand.

"It's today that men are recognized," he cries, in a terrible voice. "Mount up, companions, mount up! The powder is about to talk,"

At every village, at every tent, his troop swells.

Before the Turks have extended their long bronze cannons from the crenellations, the ditch is filled in, the gate broken, and the bloody scarf takes the place of the standard of Algiers.

Achemed returned to the olive grove and he saw red flowers emerging from the arid soil everywhere that a drop of Aïchouna's blood had fallen.

He had a granite tomb constructed for the daughter of the Beni Ammal and he planted flowers the color of blood on the heaped-up earth. The flowers were as red as Aïchouna's lips and the leaves had the odor of her breath.[16]

One evening, the sepulcher was opened, and enclosed Achemed with his beloved.

While traversing the olive grove, pick geranium flowers from the tomb of Aïchouna and take them to your mistress; if

---

[16] Aïchouna is the name given to the spirit inhabiting one of two symbolic sphinxes in *La Chanson de l'alouette*, where she identifies herself as Mort [Death].

you are betrayed, they will lose their perfume as soon as she touches them.

Princess Mitidja

"Never drink from the spring in the ruins. Your body will tremble like a corn-stem when the wind blows from the south; your cheeks will become as yellow as a ripe orange."

Meyrin was the most beautiful of the virgins of the Sahara, but her heart was mute.[17]

Meyrin only loved her black greyhound, and when the stars gazed at the sand, she went far from the douar in order to listen to the esparto-grass singing in the south wind.

One day, she did not come back until dawn; she had found the king of the djinn in her path and she had listened to him.

The next day she waited for him, but he did not come back.

On their return from Tell her brothers went pale on seeing her. "You're going to die," they said to her.

The next day, the tribesmen rode southwards, and the pearl of the Sahara remained alone under a torn tent.

In the evening, she was dead, beside a wailing infant.

The deceiver heard its cries and felt pity. He dug a grave for the shredded rose, and took her daughter in his arms.

His servants built an immense palace for her and changed in order to serve her into saves and cavaliers.

---

[17] Meyrin is the name given to the spirit inhabiting the second symbolic sphinx in *La Chanson de l'alouette*, who identifies herself as Volupté [Sensuality].

For fifteen years, somber vapors hid the domes of the place and blue flames watched before its bronze doors.

The place was in the middle of a grassless plain.

In the morning of her sixteenth year, the cloud tore, the flames were extinguished and a shady garden covered the arid plain.

The slaves poured gilded barley in the ebony mangers, the spahis leaned on their flexible lances, shook their chabirs rusted by the fog, and the two great lions crouching under the porch passed their tawny paws over their wrinkled muzzles.

The blinds rose, and a young woman as brown as an autumn morning leaned on the balcony.

She was beautiful, the sultana; her hair was as brown as an autumn morning...

Every day the sultans departed for the hunt with a brilliant retinue of almahs and musicians, and while her companions followed the sloughis,[18] she watched the cavaliers.

Her smile stopped them.

She was beautiful, the sultana; her hair was as brown as an autumn morning...

The next day, a cavalier found beside his horse two camels laden with flowers.

In the evening, he was dead.

Every night, a cavalier went to sleep on the crimson bed...

---

[18] A sloughi was, and is, a Berber hunting dog of the "sighthound" family.

One day, Mitidja met as handsome traveler near the spring. "Come," she said to him, "you for whom my heart was waiting."

The traveler did not reply.

The sultana leaned over the spring and she saw in her limpid mirror the head of an old woman next to that of the young man. She uttered a scream and hurled herself into the deep water.

The palace crumbled, the trees disappeared, and the pools were filled in; only the spring remained, transparent and fresh.

But woe betide anyone who wants to drink from it; the sultana is hidden under the moss and her lips kill as they did on the crimson bed.

"Never drink from the spring in the ruins. Your body will tremble like a corn-leaf when the wind blows from the south."

Sidi Mohamed-Ben-Abd-El-Rhaman

Sidi-Mohamed-ben-Abd-el-Rhaman, sensing his hour approaching, wanted to finish his days in solitude and departed for Algiers with a servant.

Solitude renders wisdom. The human heart resembles a spring, which remains transparent and fresh in the hollow of a rock but is corrupted and evaporates as soon as it divides into a thousand streams.

He retired to a gorge in the Djurdjura, and six months later he died there.

The kabyles laid the body of Sidi Mohamed in a tomb covered with slab of slate and built a marabout next to it for his servant.

Every grain of dust that covers a just man is surrounded by benedictions, and the Algerians wanted the saint to sleep in their midst.

As the kabyles were brave, the Turks employed cunning, and a few artful men climbed the Djurdjura under the pretext of going to pray at the tomb of their friend.

The kabyles received the sons of Algiers as envoys of God, but the next day, Sidi Mohamed's tomb was violated.

The guilty parties fled after the crime and two old men were sent to Algiers in order to reclaim the body.

The Dey, wanting to gain time, said to them: "The pilgrims left before dawn in order not to inconvenience their hosts, but their hands are pure. Return to the Djurdjura, then, and dig in the tomb; you will find the man we have loved there. The jackals alone have shifted the slabs. May Allah go with you."

The old men departed without having unsaddled their horses. They had the sepulcher opened and saw the saint lying in his white burnoose.

The Almighty had not wanted war to break out between the friends and the hosts of his servant, and he had permitted the venerated body to repose both in Algiers and on the Djurdjura.

The kabyles and the Arabs were reconciled, and Sidi-Mohamed-ben-Abd-el-Rhaman was no longer called anything but Bou-Koubarrin, the father of the two tombs.

Sidi-Embareck

God always sustains the hands that are held out toward him.

Listen to the story of a servant of God, and may his prayers keep plague and thirst away from you.[19]

One day, Sidi Embareck of the tribe of the Hachems was forced to flee from the douar where calumny had blackened him in the heart of the Sheikh. He had numerous friends in Milianah; he went to ask them for hospitality.

"It's necessary to dread the wrath of God and the arm of the powerful," they said to him, "put the earth between your enemy and you."

Sidi Embareck remounted his horse and departed for Cherchell. *There*, he thought, *I will find people for whom my hand was always open.* When he knocked on their door his burnoose was torn and his horse was thin; he no longer wanted to be recognized. The rich have no friends; those who surround them are like locusts; they fly away as soon as there is no longer anything to eat.

Sidi Embareck gave away his horse and hired himself out as a laborer to the Kadi of Koleah.

Instead of blaspheming, he prayed while laboring.

One day, when he fell asleep fatigued, he saw when he awoke the entire field sown. The oxen had traced the furrows of their own accord. The following day he went to sleep again and his work was done, as it had been the day before. While he traversed luminous palaces full of amour and perfumes in

---

[19] An earlier version of this story appeared in one of the "Fragments du journal d'un officer" in the August 1862 issue of the *Journal des Demoiselles*.

dreams, the angels guided his oxen, swallows sowed his wheat, and partridges hunted the flies that landed on his face.

The kadi, informed that Sidi Embareck was sleeping instead of working, went out in order to catch him at fault. He found him lying down, his eyes staring at the sun, but the plow was tracing regular furrows without a conductor.

He fell at his servant's knees, and gave him all his wealth.

Sid Embareck distributed the kadi's wealth to the poor and retired with him into the ravines of Ank Djemmel, where the birds of the sky nourished them both for half a century.

The saint and his companion died on the same day, and a marble mosque was erected over their tomb. The lightning never touches it, and when the earth trembles it remains unmoved, alone in the midst of houses that collapse.

Fortunate are those who visit the Kouba of Sidi Embareck!

Fortunate are those who pray on the tomb of a just man! In their hearts they take away shade for all their middays.

The Legend of Adam

In the name of the Clement and the Strong, salutations to those who believe...

When the earth, still warm, was fuming upon its axis, the djinn, sons of flame, blasphemed the name of Allah.

And the Almighty said:

"Hareth, bind them with chains."[20]

Hareth, who watched to the right of the throne, took his golden shield and his heavy lance; he opened his wings, and the stars thought they saw a crimson star flamboyant in the heavens.

Lightning sprang from the crest of his helmet, and the worlds crushed by his bronze heel flew up behind him like grains of sand.

The djinn hid in the depths of caverns, and the archangel, crushing the mountains, imprisoned the rebels forever beneath their uprooted peaks.

Then these words fell into the silence from above:

"Hareth, your name will mean Sovereign and the earth shall be your domain."

"In the heavens I am the second, but on earth I am the first; why should I not be equal to the Master?" said Hareth.

The Almighty elevates those who lower themselves, and lowers those who raise themselves up; he made a sign to Gabriel, whose feet have the color of the dawn, and said to him:

---

[20] Al-Harith or Hareth [the sower, or the laborer] is one of the titles attributed in the Koran to Iblis or Eblis, the Islamic equivalent of the Christian Satan.

"Go in search, in each of the seven stages of the earth, of a handful of dust; I want to create a man, who will take the scepter of Hareth the proud.

He departed. But the earth did not want a master to be extracted from its bosom, and Gabriel returned with empty hands.
"Lord, he said, the earth is afraid."

The Almighty knows what others do not now. He made a sign to Azrael, who carries the balance and the sword, and said to him:
"Take from the earth what it has refused."
Azrael cut the earth with his sword and weighed the seven handfuls of dust in the balance.

The rain changed that dust into mud, which the angels kneaded, and the great Architect made a statue of it, to which he gave respiration and life with a breath.
Adam was created.
The Sage made him sit down to his right and said to the angels:
"Bend a knee before the man, my lieutenant, and my beloved."
Hareth murmured:
"Why should a son of fire bow down before the son of mud?"
"Proud One," replied Allah, "You want to contend with me. Go away."
Lightning inscribed the sentence of exile on the forehead of the accursed, and Hareth the sovereign became Eblis the despairing.

Allah took Adam into the garden of Eden, where a river of milk and honey flows.
"This garden is yours," he said, "but I forbid you to touch the tree of knowledge and that of life."

"You are the Almighty," replied the man, "but why am I alone? The animals all have companions that resemble them.

The Sage put the man to sleep, and with one of his ribs he made Eve.

When Adam awoke he saw her, smiling; swallows brushed her lips and tigers licked her hands.

"Here is my companion," said the son of the breath.

Eblis pondered; and one day, at the hour when the nightingale slips into its nest, he spoke to them.

"If you taste the fruits that Allah forbids you to pick, you will be immortal, like him."

They believed him.

Then the Lord said to them: "You have disobeyed, and because of you the earth will be nothing but a sepulcher, where, in order to live, it will be necessary to kill."

Then the angels drew their flamboyant swords and expelled the condemned couple from Eden.

Adam ran all the way to Ceylon, Eve all the way to Giddah.[21]

Adam had been wandering alone for a hundred and twenty years when, one day, he woke up on a sheer peak. No cloud stained the crimson of the Orient.

He raised his arms toward the sky and cried: "Allah, you are the Almighty!"

The arm that breaks pride sustains those who repent; the Sage sent Gabriel to take the man his pardon.

Gabriel transported the reconciled to Mecca, where Eve was waiting for him under a tent built by the angels.

---

[21] The name Giddah, employed idiosyncratically here, was applied to several places at the time when the story was written, including the port of the Arabian city of Macoraba, then thought by many people to be identical with Mecca— evidently the intended reference.

Adam took Eve to Ceylon.

One evening, after a warm day, the mother of life leaned on Adam. "It seems to me that I am carrying a heavy burden, sustain me, as a vigorous olive tree sustains a vine.

Eblis asked Eve what she was carrying in her womb.

"I don't know," she replied. "Adam doesn't know either."

"It might be a monster that will devour you," continued the deceiver.

Eve began to weep.

"Don't weep; if I wish it, you will give birth to a son who will resemble Adam, but it's necessary swear to me to call him the servant of Hareth."

"She swore it, not knowing that the lapidated had been called Hareth before his fall."

Eve brought into the world, at the same time, a son and a daughter. She named the son Abd-el-Hareth, as she had promised, and the daughter Acclimia.

But the Lord said to them:

You have called your son Servant of Hareth and not Servant of God; I shall turn my face away from him."

Then Eve, hugging the little child to her heart, sighed the word *kabil*, which means; *he is mine*, and Kabil became the name of the first son of man.

Abel and his twin sister Lebuda were born the following spring.[22]

---

[22] In the apocryphal document known as *The Cave of Treasures*, probably originated in the fifth or sixth century A.D. it is Cain rather than Abel who has a twin sister named Lebuda, while Abel's sister is named Kellmath, so that Cain's desire to marry Lebuda rather than the wife allotted to him by Adam is

Sixteen years later, Adam said to his sons:

Kabil, you know how to bind sheaves, you will take Lebuda for your wife; her hair is as golden as ripe crops; Abel, who guard the flocks, will take Acclimia; her eyes are as soft as those of a black mare."

Kabil replied: "Why separate me from Acclimia? Wood-pigeons born in the same nest always love one another. Abel is your favorite, you are giving him the more beautiful."

"Children," replied Adam, "the Lord has commanded, but consult him yourselves. The one whose sacrifice is better received will choose."

Abel offered to the Eternal the plumpest of his lambs, Kabil the lightest of his sheaves.

The fire of Heaven consumed Abel's lamb and the wind dispersed his brother's ears of corn.

Kabil married Lebuda, but hatred grew in his heart, and one day he cried: "If only I could kill Abel!"

Eblis heard him.

"Watch," he said, crushing the head of a bird between two stones.

Kabil searched for his brother and killed him as Eblis had killed the bird.

When the first drop of blood touched the ground, the earth cried: "Kabil, Kabil what have you done to your brother?"

Kabil wrapped his brother in a sheepskin and having loaded him on his shoulders, fled toward the woods.

---

incestuous, but the legend has numerous variants in the so-called Arabic Apocrypha, including a document known as *The First Book of Adam and Eve*, from which L'Estoille was able to derive his idiosyncratic variant.

But to hide the cadaver no thicket seemed thick enough to him, no torrent deep enough, no precipice dark enough.

He searched day and night; and as soon as he stopped, streaming with sweat, vultures and wolves came to sniff the cadaver.

On the fortieth day he put Abel in a deep ditch, and then he returned to Adam.

"Kabil," Adam said to him, "what have you done with your brother?"

Instead of replying, he ran away, and Lebuda went with him.

For eight centuries he walked; as soon as he stopped, the earth turned red.

Fruits changed under his teeth to ashes. He was obliged to nourish himself on flesh.

He became similar to a wild beast, and one day his grandson, mistaking him for a bear, pierced him with an arrow.

Like palm trees that stand up again after a storm, Adam and Eve resisted the breath of dolor.

One evening, at sunset, they inclined toward one another like two stems of corn whose ears have ripened, and Azrael carried away their souls to Eden, where no one weeps any longer.

Adam and Even are buried on the peak of Ceylon, and when the trumpet of the resurrection makes the world tremble, they will be the first to rise.

To prevent demons from troubling the repose of their tomb, angels watch over it, and every night, when the angels are guiding the stars, great lions replace them next to the Father of Life.

Great Is He Who Shrinks

Great is he who shrinks; the Infinite leans toward him, and one no longer sees even where his head rises, where the hand of Allah descends.

Strong is he who does not know his strength; the Invincible fights for him. The breath of Allah breaks the palm tree and raises up the reed that bends.

Sage is he who sleeps; the Clear-sighted sees for him, and there is not as much sensuality on the entire earth as in a dream of Allah.

Fortunate is he whose spirit has no wings...

The poet resembles an eagle; he only soars in the region of storms; and on the day when he surpasses it, he breaks his head on the level of Allah.

The Angel of Pain

When Allah punished the man, he did not want to leave him alone between memory and dolor.

Alone, he would have succumbed.

He said to the angels: "Descend to the earth and be the man's companions. Love him like an unfortunate brother, sustain him like an enfeebled brother, and on the day of justice bring him to me repentant and consoled.

The angels departed.

The earth shivered on seeing again the guests it believed to be lost forever.

It saw again the angel of hope who bears a star on his forehead, the angel of amity with the pensive mouth and interlaced fingers, the angel of adieux who engraves oaths, the angel of return who hides wrinkles, the angel of amours who tints eyelids blue, the angel of slumber who lulls the heart, and the angel of death who pays all debts.

The seraphim sang again around the throne; the Sage enveloped the most brilliant with a radiance of amour and said to him:

"Depart also, my beloved son, you shall be the angel of my clemency."

The seraph departed.

The earth did not shiver on seeing him.

"Your hair is unbound, your wings have black plumes," it said to him, "you are not an angel."

"I am," replied the seraph, "the angel of pain, the one who comes when the others go away."

The earth shivered and said to the man: "Tremble; God has sent you the angel of his wrath."

The man ran away, but the seraph followed him at a distance.

He caught up with him when his heart bled, when fever ran in his swollen veins.

Then the man obtained patience and courage, and the pain went away, for a day if he had still to live, forever if he died.

The Yellow Plague

"Where are you going, yellow plague,[23] where are you going so quickly?"

"To Cairo, Azrael, to Cairo, where men are buzzing like avid flies over the wounds of camels."

"Stop; I can't follow you. Souls are forcing me to wait in their bodies already cold. I'm weary."

"I'm going to Cairo, where men are crowded together like seeds on an ear of corn."

"Turn back, turn back, yellow plague. Return to dip your bloody mantle in the Ganges and sleep all winter on the fuming waves."

"I'm going to Cairo, Azrael, to Cairo, where men are laughing in their house of mud.

"Listen to the orders of Allah, whose hand is heavy: Only strike a thousand heads. We shall count them this evening; woe betide you if you deceive me; death is my slave."

"You can count, Azrael; I shall give a thousand kisses."

---

[23] The reference is unlikely to be the disease nowadays known as yellow fever, which plagued French colonists in the Americas but did not make much impact in Africa. It is perhaps more likely to be cholera, which affected Algeria severely during several nineteenth-century epidemics, but it is not impossible that it refers to malaria, which often causes jaundice as a secondary symptom and was commonly associated in the nineteenth century with the term "cerebral fever," of which the protagonist of *Fusains* suffers a bad bout. Malaria also tends to recur, and if L'Estoille did contract it in Algeria it might have produced further bouts of fever long thereafter, but it is not the only parasitic disease that has that unfortunate property.

Woe betide you, yellow plague, there are two thousand cadavers."

"Look closer, Azrael, they do not all have the mark of my lips of the forehead, Some are black, others are pale. I have only given a thousand kisses, but my daughter, Fear, has given a thousand more. We always travel together; you had forgotten that."

The Drop of Water

The storm threw a drop of water into the heart of a periwinkle.

The periwinkle was thirsty.

But the wind of the earth blew over the flower and bore away in a muddy torrent the drop of water fallen from the sky. A great river carried it all the way to the sea,

"Where have you come from?" said the angel with salty wings to the drop of water.

"I've come from the forest where a periwinkle was thirsty."

"Where do you want to go?"

"I'd like to return to the heart of the periwinkle."

"On the waves you'll shine like star in the blue sky."

"The heart of the periwinkle is larger than the blue sky."

"You'll warm up in the sun in the fine sand of the gulf."

"The heart of the periwinkle is softer than the fine sand,"

"You'll sleep by night between the ivory breasts of the undine with glaucous eyes,"

"The heart of the periwinkle is more beautiful than the breasts of the undine with glaucous eyes."

The angel changed the drop of water into a pearl, and the sultan put it on the hilt of his dagger.

The pearl encrusted in the hilt of dagger still repeats:

"I'd rather be a drop of water in the heart of a periwinkle..."

The Land of the Sun

It is close to Allah and far from sultans, the land where we are erecting our tents.

By night it sparkles like the sea that rolls silvery waves; by day it shivers like a crimson veil fringed with diamond and bouquets of emeralds.

Its hills undulate like the veins of thoroughbred horses, and its immobile lakes are deeper and more limpid than the azure-tinted eyes of houris.

"O you who live and die in cities of mud, who respire air that others have already soiled, who, like a tortoise, never quit your house, envy the lot of the Arab, the swallow of the Sahara.

"Our tents emerge from the sand like firm breasts from an open haïck—our great tents grouped in a circle on the musk-scented sand. They are cool by day and warm by night, and the demon does not approach them.

"O you who life and mores curb over a métier, who bear sacks on your back like a donkey, who pull the plow in order to sow the wheat we eat, envy the lot of the Arab, the cavalier with the soft hands.

We only know how to sing and fight, but our verses are so sweet that they make your women pale and our spurs are so long that they hook your carpets and your barley as we pass by.

"And you of the West, beware of the Sahara; our sabers are sharp, our bullets never fall to earth and our young men pick up at the gallop, without quitting the saddle, the necklaces that the lovers of their heart throw to them.

"Our young men mount horses covered by dazzling blankets, horses as white as the shooting stars that the angel of the night launches against the demon, horses as red as the calyx of a rose, and horses spotted like a panther's flank.

"On days of fantasia our horses disperse over the plain like the pearls of a necklace, and the hearts of virgins palpitate. But when the hour of confrontation comes, eye to eye, our horses are eagles mounted by lions and human hearts freeze.

"We are the kings of the plain where the ostriches graze.

"We are the kings of the mountain where the white antelope bounds over the rocks.

"We are the kings of the land of thirst where caravans pass without leaving a trace, like a cloud over the ocean, and we want no masters or neighbors.

"Don't touch the smoking rifle; our bullets never fall to earth and cause the open mouth to die."

"But if you have peace in your heart, if you want to admire and not to take, we will receive you like the envoys of Allah. Our liberality has no measure, our speech has no circuits, and our hand always goes further than our tongue.

"If you have peace in your heart, erect your tents beside the blonde oasis where the jasmine enlaces the palm, where the ash-gray pigeons caress in the shade, where the women dance in the orange grove and you will know amour.

"Come to the land of the sun and your days will flow like a limpid steam.

"Come to the land of the sun and your years will accumulate like the grains of sand on a moving dune."

The Daughter of the Ouled-Aïad

See that cloud gliding over the plain, more rapid than a partridge flying toward a spring, darker than the smoke of esparto-grass. It is not the wing of the simoom, it is our horsemen returning from a raid.

"Put crimson aatatiches on the camels,[24] put tufts of white feathers on the aatatiches, arrange your camels in a line, daughters of the Ouled Aïad.[25]

"Throw your necklaces to the chosen of your heart, but smile at everyone.

"Daughters of the Ouled Aïad, pour balm where the bullet has passed,

"Hasten, hasten; the burnooses of our brothers are red, their hands are black. It is pleasant to lean one's head on a red burnoose; it is pleasant to kiss hands black with powder.

"Their horses are buckling under the weight of the booty.

"We shall have, my sisters, Sudanese babouches, perfumed kohl, and resounding krolkrals encrusted with gold and coral.[26]

---

[24] An aatatiche was a silk-curtained palanquin in which women rode on the camels of caravans.

[25] The tribe Duclaux calls the Ouled Aïad is more commonly known in English sources as the Ouled Nail. Its members played a leading role in resistance to French colonization, and its traditional dances, popularly known as "belly dances," especially when performed by women forced to leave home and seek an independent living as entertainers during the colonial era, became legendary.

[26] In Algeria, krolkrals were silver ankle-rings

"Let us hasten; my beloved is always the first of the goum.

"Cowards, what have you done with Mohamed, the right arm of the Ouled Aïad?

"He cried to you when you mounted the rumps of your horses: 'Fatma, daughters of Fatma, hold on to your souls, everyone's hours are counted,' and you have not followed him.

"They have fled, those who stood up in their white stirrups on feast days and sang as the powder burned.

"Cowards, take your rifles, give us your rifles; you have the skin of a lion and the bones of a cow.

"Cowards, may God curse you, may your sons tremble on touching a rifle and your daughters never say no.

"Cowards, may your fathers and your fathers' fathers be cursed because of you."

"And you, Messaoud, who cherished his stallion, who knelt down on days of fantasias, who bit the enemy on days of powder, what have you done with your master?

"After having allowed him to be struck, why have you not brought him to my tent? I would have closed his wounds with my lips.

"After having allowed him to be killed, why have you not brought him back dead? I would have put his head on my knees and I would have gazed at him until the tears had burned my eyes."

"The sultan of my heart was as handsome as a plane tree, and I have not slept beneath his shadow.

"He was as strong as a lion and he has not pressed me against his heart.

"His lips were a cup of honey and I have not drunk there.

"Like the solitary palm tree I shall not give fruits; half of my soul is too far away."

Love Song

The calices of roses need vermilion leaves; human amours need perfumed evenings and bloody mornings.

"El-Biod, shake your silvery mane, your nacreous flanks will turn blue. Fly like a wood-pigeon toward the sister of my soul, toward the sister who is waiting for me, and whom I have not yet found.

"A man with a narrow heart, a man with veins of snow, loves in closed rooms, behind bolts and sabers, but the swallow of the plain, the bearer of spurs, loves in the open air and the sunlight. El-Biod, fly southwards; the flower of my life must blossom in the sun.

"My flyssa has rusted in its sheath, the powder has turned white in the copper bassinet. El-Biod, fly on, my heart has swollen in solitude like a forgotten cadaver.

"Where are you, then, sister of the stars, half of my soul, where are you? For weeks the earth has been extending behind me and I have not yet encountered you, you whose first glance will enter into my heart like a dagger-thrust.

"Half of my soul, where are you, then?

El-Biod has buckled on his fetlocks, I have stopped him short under the tamarinds; I thought I saw a lily opening.

I have mistaken a haïck for white leaves and a round breast for a golden calyx.

It is not a lily but the sister of my soul who embalms the tamarinds.

"El-Biod is strong, my beloved, sit down on his rump.

"El-Biod, my spurs are ringing, fly, fly like a falcon.

"Fly toward the pink mountain fuming out there in the setting sun; stop near the stream where the sand is very fine, where the grass is very soft and the virgin will kiss your wild nostrils, El-Biod my good horse.

"Beloved, the stars are jealous of your moist eyes, the spring is jealous of your clear voice, the reeds are jealous of your flexible waist, the grape-cluster is jealous of your icy breasts and I am jealous of the star that gazes at you, the spring that licks your feet, the reeds that you hear and the grapes that you eat.

"Your teeth shine like a pearl necklace... Keep my head on your knees... When pearls are mounted on crimson strings, they appear even whiter.

"Do you hear your brothers coming? The powder is about to speak, may Allah be blessed!"

Human amours need perfumed evenings and bloody mornings.

"Sit down on El-Biod's neck, you shall guide him; I shall watch from his rump, and the bullets will spring from my rifle like sparks from a fire of dry wood."

Human amours need perfumed evenings and bloody mornings.

"Is it your amour or is it a bullet that is weighing on my heart? Your lips are cool...what does it matter?

Human amours need perfumed evenings and bloody mornings.

The Death of Ben-Mansour

What is that head drying on the door in Ouargla, whose lips full of worms allow the teeth to be seen?"

"It's the head of Kleddache, the chief of Djebel Hoggar, whom Ben-Mansour's horsemen killed at the spring of the Oued-Mia."

"Who is that woman weeping in front of a house of clay, whose blue eyes are launching dark flashes in the midst of tears?"

"That's Fetoum, the pearl of the Touaregs, the partridge of Djebel Hoggar, the beloved wife of Kleddache, whom the horsemen of Chamba killed at the spring of the Oued-Mia."

Kleddache, the chief of the Touaregs of Djebel Hoggar, was a brave man among the camel-riders, and all the men with veiled cheeks weep in thinking about him.

Kleddache, the chief of the Touaregs of Djebel Hoggar, had a lake of amour in his heart and the beautiful Fetoum with the thick lips weeps in thinking about him.

Fetoum, who governs while waiting until her son can take up the sword, gathers all the veiled men and says to them: "The man who brings me the head of Ben-Mansour will have me for a wife."

The next day, all the young men of the mountain, cross their legs over their white camels. Their long lances in their hand, their round shields on their arms and their broad sabers in their belts say to Fetoum: "We're setting forth in search of the head of Ben-Mansour."

They resemble a flock of crows and they have taken for their chief Ould-Biska, Kleddache's cousin.

They marched for a day. In the evening they saw a cloud running over the plain and they stopped in order to wait.

They soon saw that the cloud was a cloud of dust, and as they loved battle, they struck their elephant-hide shields with their lances.

But they were mistaken in believing that they were waiting for an enemy; the dust was raised by the camels of Fetoum, the beautiful widow with a starry forehead. She was accompanying the men in order to empty sooner the sugared gourd of vengeance.

"We shall give you the head of Ben-Mansour," cried the Touaregs, following her northwards.

The Touaregs encountered the Chambas near the Oued-Mzab on a moonless night... They had no suspicion, and were almost all killed before being able to mount their horses.

Only one fled on a horse without a bridle, but he had not had time to put on his spurs; the lance of Oued-Biska entered between his shoulders and emerged through his breast.

He fell, and a little child fell with him.

"Do you know Ben-Mansour?" the Touaregs asked the child.

"There he is," replied the child, pointing at the cadaver. "I am the son of Ben-Mansour."

"I will be yours, said the woman with the blue eyes, but before then, cleave the breast of that accursed with your dagger, rip out the heart and give it to the dogs."

Ould-Biska gave the heart of Ben-Mansour, the chief of the Chambas, to the dogs, and since that time Ouargla is like a widow whose hair has been cut.

"Bearers of rifles, I am the son of Ben-Mansour; let us mount horses and enable our dogs to eat the heart of Fetoum, the heart of Ould-Biska and the hearts of all the men, all the women and all the children of the Djebel-Hoggar."

Yamina

"O you who know what the bullets say, you who have slept on braided hair but who do not know the sister of the stars, my beloved Yamina; children of the powder, listen!"

Yamina is a ray of sunlight sparkling after a storm, a limpid spring that one finds in the evening, a golden orange that bleeds between the lips, an embalmed breath that intoxicates and engenders dreams.

Yamina shines under the tent like the moon of summer nights over a lake bordered with salt; she runs through the esparto-grass like a gazelle with curved horns; she balances on her mahari[27] like a date-palm of the Beni-Mzab whose fruits are so high they cannot be reached.

Yamina has no sisters among the daughters of the desert. Yamina is a bean-flower that the Eternal has perfumed.

"Yamina, my heart has melted under your gaze and you have drunk it in a kiss. Yamina, you have no sister among the virgins of the desert.

"Your eyebrows are two bows from the negro lands, your eyelashes the beard of an ear of corn on the eve of the harvest, your cheeks are ripe peaches, your teeth, more tightly-packed than hailstones brought by the west wind, are pearls encased in coral, and your lips have the taste of honey."

I could tell the bee where honey in sweeter than in asphodels.

---

[27] In this context a mahari is a dromedary adapted for saddling,

"Yamina, you are a bean-flower that the Eternal has perfumed. Your neck stands up like the standard that braves the enemy, your ivory neck more polished than the marble columns of the mosque of Ouargla.

"Your bosom resembles a cluster of grapes swollen by dew and sugared by the sun.

"Your shoulders are two blocks of snow and your ribs are rounded like Damascene sabers.

"Butterflies mistake your fingers for rosebuds and your feet for lily-pads.

"Yamina, you have no sisters among the daughters of the desert.

"Where are you now, flame of my heart, warmth of my blood, light of my eyes? For a year, my gazelle, where have you been?

"You are out there, out there where the ostriches run in huddled bands, where the white camels sleep in the shadow of tents, where the lustrous foals whinny next to their mothers, who are awaiting great thin stallions.

"For a year I have been wandering in this accursed Tell where the flowers have no perfume. I would be dead if I had not kept the perfume of your breath on my lips.

"O cherished pigeon, you who know the green path where my heart has passed, tell Yamina the white star that I would like to be the pin in her haïck, the porcupine quill that blackens her eyelid, the carpet that conserved the imprint of her bare feet.

"Tell her that she has struck me with two dagger-thrusts, one in the eyes and the other in the heart, and that my life is flowing away through those two wounds.

Tell her that the pain of her absence is more bitter than a green olive.

"Tell her that amour is a heavy burden to bear."

Bullets Don't Kill

Bullets don't kill; only destiny kills. Run, sons of the powder.

The moon is as thin as the blade of a saber, but are we not the sons of the night? Her veil is our armor, and her darkness cannot deflect our blows. Where we have passed the sun rises in blood. Run, sons of the powder.

We'll find our enemies asleep. Their virgins will be devoid of belts and their horses devoid of bridles. Strike until your arm goes stiff, your burnooses are as red as a coral necklace and your pistols are as hot as ardent coals.

Fortunate are those whose blood will flow; a kiss closes a wound and women love the brave. Run, suns of the powder.

Tomorrow you shall have velvet saddles and thoroughbred horses; I shall have Meyrin, the gazelle with the blue eyes.

We're entering the douar... Strike, sons of the powder, bullets don't kill.

The Warm Spring

"Open your wings, handsome pigeon, open your blue wings and carry my song to where my heart has remained."

The Sultan of the Maghreb, the one who built Tlemcen, the sultana of the desert, encountered a red-haired virgin near a spring.

"Open your wings, handsome pigeon, open your blue wings and carry my song into the striped tent."

The virgin with amber arms was washing at the spring. Her pink feet shone on the wool like a coral bead on an ebony gun-butt, and amour touched the Sultan of Tlemcen.

"Open your wings, handsome pigeon, open your blue wings and carry my song to the black swallow."

"Some and choose at Mechouar," said the Sultan, "necklaces of sequins and bracelets of pearls. You shall be the rose that will make the roses of my garden pale..."

"Open your wings, handsome pigeon, open your blue wings and bring me the perfume of her moist lips."

The young woman fled and the Sultan returned to Mechouar. "Eblis," he said to the demon, "tomorrow I want to be loved by the virgin who was washing a woolen burnoose."

"Open your wings, handsome pigeon, open your blue wings and bring me the word that she sighs as she goes to sleep."

"Vengeance is ours, but amour is God's, Sultan of Tlemcen," replied the lapidated. "If amour lulls, vengeance intoxicates. Crush the flower that you cannot pick."

"Open your wings, handsome pigeon, open your blue wings, the wind of amour is lifting up the quivering palms."

"I shall crush the flower that I cannot pick, Eblis, I shall sell the red-haired virgin to you."

"Open your wings, handsome pigeon, open your blue wings; I want to know whether my gazelle is gazing southwards."

"Master," said the young woman in the palm grove, "I prefer your kisses to the sultan's treasures..."

A soft sight was heard, and then mocking laughter, as the virgin disappeared underground with the cavalier.

"Open your wings, handsome pigeon, open your blue wings; I want to know whether my star is jealous."

The next day, wild olive-trees had replaced the palm grove. Only two date-palms swayed their pale heads. A spring was fuming at their feet.

"Open your wings, handsome pigeon, open your blue wings; I want to know whether my fiancée is a mother-of-pearl casket to which only I have the key."

The water of the spring is limpid, but instead of flowing continuously it spurts forth, and then dried up momentarily, to spurt forth again. The accursed one has dragged the virgin and the cavalier underground.

"Open your wings, handsome pigeon, open your blue wings; I want to know whether my fiancée is a stainless mirror over which my image alone has passed."

The tears that swell at the ends of her eyelashes and then fall, warm and dense, form the spring of the two palm-trees.

"Open your wings, handsome pigeon, open your blue wings and carry my song into the striped tent."

The Camel-Driver's Song

Further away than Algiers the white seagull, further than Tripoli the black pearl, further than Fez, where the camels sleep weighed down by sacks of gold, in the land where the sky is aflame, a great sphinx is asleep.

"Never sleep on the sand without rolling yourself in your burnoose."

In the land where the sky is aflame, a great sphinx is asleep, but when the pale-lipped moon caresses its long lowered eyes, its eyelids lift, and then it sings. Listen:

"When your camels lower their heads, sing while striking them with the bat."

Its eyelid is raised, and then it sings; listen: I understand the two words that the stars say to the south wind, I understand the two words that the waters of the Nile say to the red sand.

"Never drink at a spring except from the hollow of your hand."

I understand the two words that the waters of the Nile say to the red sand, I understand the two words that humans weep over graven walls, and I understand the two words that rise from granite obelisks.

"Never listen to the djinn that hide under rocks."

I understand the two words that rise from granite obelisks, and of those that words the angel bears to the azure tent of Allah I make songs for the sage who looks into the past.

"By night, look at the stars in order to find your way."

These verses were made to regulate the march, by a soldier, the son of a soldier, dreaming while going to Mecca, to the songs that he heard one evening fluttering on the pink lips of a great sphinx on the edge of the Nile.

"Beautiful verses are engraved on the sky, between the verses of the Koran."

The Janissary's Song

For the one whose voice is sweeter than the song of the nightingale on a branch of jasmine, for the one whose gaze is more profound than the sea where the coral grows, for the one whose forehead resembles the blue vault sown with stars, for the daughter of the west, the janissary has made this song.

"Allah, give to the sister of the ripe corn days without clouds, give to the janissary a horse that goes far, and give to all those who believe hope and peace."

The sun twisted the palm-trees and the white cavalier sang as he caressed his fuming stallion.

"This evening you shall eat barley from a virgin's haïck, a fine silk haïck in which amber breasts have throbbed, a haïck still warm, my beautiful horse with nacreous flanks...

"I have beneath my burnoose the heart of a lion.

"This evening you shall eat dates from a virgin's hand, a dainty had that my saber has bruised, a hand still warm, my beautiful horse with nacreous flanks...

"I have beneath my burnoose the heart of a lion.

"This evening you shall drink pink blood from a virgin's breast, an open breast that your shoe has broken, a breast still warm my beautiful horse with nacreous flanks...

"I have beneath my burnoose the heart of a lion."

The cavalier who is singing is a son of the powder, a handsome cavalier.

The sun set and stars as pale as a pearl necklace were distributed in the heavens when the cavalier saw the virgin with the somber eyes in the palm grove.

"My heart is a wild bird, in the sunlight it had made its nest. Pass by, handsome cavalier."

The Palm Trees With the Heads of Angels

"What are you looking for, with your head bowed?"

"I'm looking for what no one has found," replied the traveler.

The traveler was alone and his weary camel placed its feet heavily on the sand.

The air was mute, the sun red, the sand yellow and the sky blue.

The pink peaks of the Djebel Amour were slowly magnified, and somber crevices opened one after another in the amethyst flanks.

"Death is long in coming, but it will come," sighed the traveler.

"What are you looking for, with your head bowed?"

"I'm looking for what one loses as soon as one has found it," replied the traveler.

The traveler was alone. His camel knelt down slowly, turned its large soft eyes toward him, shivered and died.

The air was mute, the sun red, the sand yellow and the sky blue.

The pink peaks of the Djebel Amour hid their heads in a vermilion mist, and a large crevice opened up like a gulf in their polished flanks.

The traveler wiped his bloody lips and sighed.

"You are dead, you whom she caressed when, like a dove allowing a wing to hang out of its nest, she passed an arm whiter than a lily through the flap of her tent.

"You are dead because you loved me, and I have killed you as I have killed the gazelle with the velvet eyes."

"What are you looking for, with your head bowed?"

"I'm looking for what I do not want to find," replied the traveler.

The traveler was alone.

The air was mute, the sun red, the sand yellow and the sky blue.

The pink peaks of the Djebel Amour made a crown of pearls for the round valley in the depths of which palm trees swayed their light heads near the icy spring.

The traveler dipped his thin hands in the water, but he did not drink.

"I let my beloved die of thirst, I must also die of thirst," he sighed. "My heat was a desert in which there was only one spring; I have lured the gazelle with the velvet eyes into the desert, and I have not shown her the spring, She died of amour, and I want to die of thirst."

He lay down on his back, uncovered his head, extended his arms in a cross and gazed at the sun.

"What are you looking for in the sun?"

"I'm looking for love," replied the traveler.

The traveler was alone but the palm trees what were swaying next to the spring had the heads of angels.

The air was mute, the sun red, the sand yellow and the sky blue.

The pink peaks of the Djebel Amour leaned over to hear what the angels were saying. "Why did you let the gazelle die of thirst?" asked the angel with green wings.

"Because my mouth did not know how to speak the language of my heart," replied the desperate man, still gazing at the sun.

The tallest of the palm trees bent down, and the angel with the green wings closed the traveler's eyes with his lips.

"Stay with us," he said, "We will teach your mouth the language of your heart.

The traveler died, and his body became a palm tree.

When the moon shines, the palm tree sings and the gazelle who died of thirst stops her star in order to listen.

In the round valley of the Djebel Amour, the palm trees have the heads of angels; in the desert where men pass by, many gazelles die of thirst because they are not understood.

Desire

"I would like a philter that gives death, a philter that kills like lightning; I shall rub his lips with it, and this evening, I shall have his last kiss."

In the cedars nests a beautiful blue bird; fly over the snow, beautiful blue bird.

"I would like a flyssa as sharp as a gaze, a flyssa with a solid hilt, a flyssa long enough to go from my heart to his, and this evening, I shall drink his last breath."

In the cedars nests a beautiful blue bird; fly over the snow, beautiful blue bird.

"I would like to seal our tomb with a stone heavier than the Atlas and harder than a ruby, in order that the angel will not see us on the Day of Judgment.

In the cedars nests a beautiful blue bird; fly over the snow, beautiful blue bird.

The Dark-Eyed Virgin

The sun rose and the dark-eyed virgin sang under the palm trees:

"Like a stork, my heart has two wings, two ash-gray wings; it has flown toward the great river... It has flown so far, so far that it will never come back again, never...

"Braid your hair with wool.

"Like a swallow, my heart has two wings, two black wings, two silken wings; it has flown toward the Orient... It has flown so far, so far that it will never come back again, never...

"Braid your hair with wool.

"Like a vulture, my heart has two wings, two sharp wings; it has risen toward the sun... It has risen so high, so high that it will never come down again, never...

"Braid your hair with wool."

The dates were ripe and the dark-eyed virgin sung under the palm trees:

"Like the Ocean my heart has waves, great green waves, great blue waves, but the wind of solitude weeps there and its kisses make me weep...

"Why does my heart have waves on which nothing can float?

The dark-eyed virgin gazed in the direction of the Orient and saw a cloud of dust.

"That's the simoom coming! Why does my heart not have wings, like the simoom, which skim the earth?" she sighed in a whisper, very softly.

She went back into the yellow tent, and let her tears glide over her gilded tresses, like pearls.

It was not the wing of the simoom but the feet of a flock that were lifting up the desert sand.

A pastor was following the rams, and he sang as he watched the grass grow:

"In a blue lotus I had put my heart, my dormant heart; a passing stork has broken the flower and my frozen heart on the rolling river.

"My rams go where the grass grows.

"In an eglantine I had put my heart, my amorous heat; a passing swallow has broken the flower and my wounded heart on the bloody thorns.

"My rams go where the grass grows.

"On a tall fir-tree I had put my heart, my inspired heart; a vulture has broken the tree at ground level and my body, crushed on the stone, is mute.

"My rams go where the grass grows."

The pastor followed them, watching the grass grow, and he arrived outside the yellow tent where the virgin was weeping.

The pastor who was singing had bleeding feet and a furrowed brow,

"What are you doing while your rams are shearing the grass?" the virgin asked the pastor.

"I'm listening to the tears falling in my empty breast."

"What are the tears saying as they fall in your empty breast?"

"Your heart is a leaf, the wind has cast it on the river without banks where the storks with ash-gray wings fly."

The virgin leans on an ebony coffer encrusted with copper.

"Pastor, what else to the tears say as they fall in your empty breast?"

"Your heart is a leaf, the wind has cast it on the tower without windows where the swallow with silken wings nest."

The virgin raised her dark eyes toward the pastor.

"The tears falling in your empty breast also say: 'Your heart is a seed; the wind has sown it in the gold and azure sky where the vulture with sharp wings soars.'

"Pastor, the seed has germinated, and my heart has alighted on the green tree."

"Strike in cadence the bronze disks.

"You, almahs without veils, swell your satiny necks like doves as you turn. Enlace your bare arms and let your pink heels trace silvery circles in the sand."

Strike in cadence..."

"Lord, give the virgin a flower-bed of roses and a grove of palm trees!

"Lord, give the pastor a basket full of splendid flowers and embalmed fruits."

ATTILA

A Danish Tale

The wind weeps in the leather sail, the blonde young woman smiles at the hollow waves and the pilot, standing at the front of the boat, says:

"You are the white reindeer of my green prairie, Elf of the tempest; whip the dormant waves with your wings, my boat is a salmon playing in the foam; whip the dormant waves with your wings, my boat is a falcon fishing in the foam."

The waves howl, the boat groans; the stiffened pilot listens and, with her head on the shoulder of the man of the North, the blonde young woman says:

"The Elf of the tempest loves the song of the brave; sing, my blue elk, until the promised kiss, until the night of amour; I am like the teal that smoothes its feathers in the first days of April, like the snow awaiting the spring."

"I know many songs! Regarding my oxen I have searched for them in the spots of the reeds, under the tongue of the reindeer and in the mouth of the squirrel; but my ear is full of the clash of words...

"Thrush with green plumage, make your nest in my helmet; squirrel of the woods; make your nest in my shield; crow, perch on my ash-wood bow; until the snows of winter I want to sing runes to my bride.

"I know many songs! I have found them along the roads, on the heads of swallows, on the shoulders of geese, on the bark of beeches; but my ear is full of the rumble of waves...

"Snowdrop with the golden heart, blue periwinkle, pale violet, scatter your seeds, your little seeds, in my fir-wood boat, in my new sail; until the dews of spring, I want to sing runes to my bride.

"I know many songs! I have sung while arrows flew like seagulls; I have sung while cups filled up beneath open veins; today, I shall sing better, my ear is full of the sound of a kiss.

"Rocked by the swell in my floating net, go to sleep smiling, undines with blue-green eyes; I shall sing to my bride a song of love, a song of war, the runes of Attila, the king of horsemen."

I

At sunset, the old world slumbers in its ruins. At dawn, in their maple-wood chariots, the awaited awake, hungry. Over the land, Attila weighs.

In the flat valley cut by a road as broad as a sea and as straight as a spear, under ragged willows, in the confines of two worlds, the great river is silvery.

Dew spangles the plain; on the road, crows are croaking; two elks are drinking from the river... But a dark cloud appears, and the dew freezes, and the crows fly away.

Under the cloud of russet wings race twenty thousand horsemen; wolves gallop behind. In front, the chief with the shaved hair mounts a white stallion. The two elks flee...

The stallion cleaves the waves; the horsemen stop; the chief releases the reins, raises his arms and cries:

"Old river, Attila salutes you!"

A gust of wind passes through the willows, the dew falls as frost, in the steppe the echo rumbles:

"Attila! Attila…!"

"Greetings, Brother!" cries the king. "I am the river with crimson waves."

"Greetings, Brother!" the Volga responds.

Attila crosses the river. He has blackened the marble, he wants to redden the snow; but before then, he wants to dream where he played as a child, while his mother milked the mares with curly manes in the reeds.

Before attacking the Purs,[28] the unvanquished sons of the Aesir, the man driven by the Unknown comes to ask the voice of the desert, engendered by the wind in a clump of aspens, for his route...

He dreamed alone until sunset, until moonrise...[29] When night fell, he laid his wolf-skin lined with crimson on the russet grass, and went to sleep bare-headed.

The horsemen waited on the soil of Europe, but the vultures and the wolves had accompanied the king on to the soil of Asia, for the vultures and the wolves followed Attila, not the horsemen.

---

[28] *Purs* is L'Estoille' translation of a term in runic script whose first letter only resembles a P, and which probably mans "giant"

[29] L'Estoille often switches between present and past tense in his works, in a fashion that sometimes seems arbitrary; he is not the only French writer of the period to do so.

Alone, his head bare, Attila sleeps, but he is well guarded; the gray backs form a steely circle around him; the tawny
wings make a rounded tent above his head.

As he fell asleep, he sighed—the voice of the desert not
having replied to him, the future loomed up before him like a
black shield—but now he smiles; he dreams that he is playing
with the foals...

He awakes; he sees the white teeth, he hears the yellow
beaks, and he sighs: "Amour! I do not have amour, which is
necessary to all those who desire, to all those who found."

However, in his maple-wood palace he had priestesses
and courtesans, dancers with starry foreheads, singers with
rosy lips, and virgins trembling like an ear of wheat.

But in his maple-wood palace he did not have amour.
That is why he sighs while the dawn with full udders gaily
strews the grass of the plain with its necklace of pearls.

She runs, laughing, but she perceives, on the russet grass,
the reaper of forests, the bloodier of rivers, is horrified, and
flees. Then a dull murmur rises from the corrupted grass.

Attila hears the voice of the grass, and he is afraid. He is
so fearful that he crosses the river without looking back; the
blades of grass were asking one another how they would cause
the death of the man who crushed them.

They were asking one another that, but, none of them
finding a means, the heather began to weep, while the sun,
irritated by still finding darkness, bounded into the starry sky.

"Why has the dawn not waited longer for me?" said the
most handsome of the great Aesir, who watches from the city

of gold over the hills where the beech has grown. "Is she too afraid of the king of horsemen?"

And the blond young man, leaning over the ardent manes of his horses with winged hooves, says to the tearful heather: "Before your flowers fade, I shall cause the death of the king of horsemen."

The sun said that, but the sun is not the master; into the dark abyss the Aesir will fall one day; only the Old One will remain over his devastated work; the Old One alone in the master.

On his throne of ice, the Old One, the father of the world, hears everything, and his voice growls: "The hand of a man cannot kill, and the hand of a god must not kill Attila the reaper!"

He hears the voice, the Aes with the golden lips, and anger swells his heart; he hears the voice, the red sword-bearer, and his brow furrows. The weeping heather also hears the voice.

It says: "The promises of the gods shine like the frost, but melt likewise."
"Before your flowers fade, he will die," replies the blond charmer, the sweet singer of runs.

In the meantime, Attila thought: "I am the master's scythe; where his grain is about to sprout, I cut the brambles; where his grain is about to ripen, I cut the tares; the scythe will never be blunted.

"I shall do my day's work, but at the hour of noonday the reaper may repose momentarily in the shade. O Thou whom I meekly obey, make a clear spring well up beneath my feet.

"The flame has burned my lips; I am thirsty, Master! The blood is during on my hands; make a clear spring well up before me; in the hour of noonday make a woman love me."

The sun hears; his mares are already razing with their brazen hooves the green hill where the Northern dew comes every morning to dream under the birches while gazing at the sea...

The eyes of Hildwige are beautiful; they are neither blue nor dark, they are as brown as rushes; but the eyes of a virgin ought to gaze at the spindle and not at the clouds.

The great Aes said: "The hand of a man cannot kill him, the hand of a god must not kill him, but the eyes of a woman slay like a serpent's tongue, like the tip of a sword.

"You have blackened the marble, but you shall not redden the snow, man with the shaven hair; those who have loved me do not forget me, their kisses are no longer for sale, and you shall love the Northern rose."

On the white moss at the foot of the sorb-tree, her chin in her hand, the virgin who is dreaming instead of spinning, said while watching the hawk soar over the blue gulf; "Oh, if I only had wings!

"If my soul had wings, like the hawk, I would glide over the bottomless gulf." Slowly, she passes her hand over her forehead; slowly, she passes her fingers through her hair.

She bounds to her feet, her lip disdainful, her breasts swollen; her foot trampling the moss she says: "Oh, if I had wings like he hawk, I would fly to where the swords are blunted!"

Confused, she lowers her eyes; a man is smiling at her. She has not seen a swan fall from the cloudless sky; she has not seen him change into a soldier, the great Aes with the curly hair.

"If I had wings," said the blond warrior, "I would break them on the green hill; your eyes are more brilliant than the fire of swords, your gaze is sweeter than the mist of the gulf..."

And Attila went back to his horsemen, where the heavy carts, buckling under the booty, arranged in circles, awaited him. In the breath of the wolves, under the wings of the vultures, he is dreaming of the clear spring...

When the night, shaking her veil, sowed star over the crimson of the evening, the blond warrior was still smiling at the intoxicated virgin, and the man with the shaven hair went to sleep in order to dream...

"Under the birches of the hill, what does the hawk say to the dove, my beloved? You would like me to speak like a god, and the feet of the hare to efface my amorous runes in the snow..."

The stars shining, the palpitating virgin has descended the hill of birches; the blond young man resumes the form of a swan and he flies toward the tent where Attila is falling asleep.

"King of horsemen," he says to him, "on a Northern eglantine bush, a rose is blooming; if you want to pluck her, follow me to where the raspberry-bushes are growing, where the sorb-berries are reddening.

"Her arms are whiter than my wings, follow me, her cheeks are softer then my neck; if you want to love her, follow me to where the raspberry-bushes are growing, where the plum-trees are in flower..."

Attila followed the swan. For a week, two weeks, nearly three weeks, he marched every night, stopping when the swan was lost in the whiteness of the morning.

For two weeks, nearly three, he went. His horsemen fell behind him, the vultures letting their wings hang down, the breathless wolves drooling; the swan flew so rapidly!

Shining like an emerald, the green isle finally appeared; but the spotted stallion did not want to enter the unfurling waves. "I am also the king of the vultures and the wolves!" Attila cries.

"Vultures that I have sated with flesh, wolves that I have intoxicated with blood, bring me to the green isle where the raspberries are growing."
"Our feet are tremulous!"
"Our wings are limp!"

"From my sword a river flows that summer does not drink," cries the reaper with red hands. "Foamy sea, part thy pale waves; I am the divine river that washes mud in blood."

A wave casts its foam over Attila's forehead.
"Were thirsty!" howl the wolves.
"We're hungry!" cry the vultures.
The wolves approach, menacingly, the vultures fly lower...

But the great Aes has crossed the ivory threshold; he has released the golden reins, and now, a rapid salmon is gliding through the waves. Then he makes a boat out of seaweed and changes into an old man.

White teeth shine, yellow beaks click, the sea laughs. Attila nods his shaven head, the boat appears in the sunset, with its divine pilot.

The boat glided over the waves; it was neither large nor small; its sail was blue, its mast bent like a reed, and the old man said to the king of horsemen:

"King, I have set up for you in my new boat thing with a mast as thick as a mountain pine; for you I have hoisted this sail like a juniper of the hills; come to where you want to go..."

"Thrush with green plumage, make your nest in my helmet; squirrel of the woods, make your nest n my shield; crow, perch on my oaken spear; until the snows of winter, I want to sing runes to my beloved!"

II

The old man says to the king: "I have set up for you in my new boat thing with a mast as thick as a mountain pine; for you I have hoisted this sail like a juniper of the hills.

"Come into my red boat, into my oaken boat, into my new boat; mount my dragon with broad wings, and I will take you where the Northern rose blooms."

Attila sits down on the fir-wood bench and the boat steered northwards. The wolves swim in its wake and the vultures whipped the blue sail with their sharp wings.

The coastline shrinks, the waves swelled. "Fly, fly, red boat," said the old man, dance on the waves like a light bubble, glide like a lily in the midst of the waves."

The wind roars, lightning flashes, waves rise up; saliva drips from gaping mouths; feathers fall from crumpled wings; Attila sings, nodding his shaven head:

"When the harvest is complete I shall wash my red hands in the river of fresh water, and my soul will go to a palace of clouds. Attila will always be king!"

The waves rear up; their green arms grip the flanks of the wolves, their white tongues lick the wings of the vultures, and Attila sings, nodding his shaven head:

"Row, row, old man, Attila will always be king!" The old man takes the oars, and the boat lands on the green isle where the raspberry bushes grow, the green isle of the pale sea.

Attila leaps on to the sand...he can no longer see the boat. The boat, however, was moored to the shore, but it was not the hands of women that had woven its blue sail.

The swan was no longer there to indicate the route. He was not in the red boat, he was already on the hill, in the birch-wood, where the Northern virgin waited for him every evening.

He is more beautiful than the rainbow when Hildewige perceives him. She sees him in a moonbeam, and stops, trembling, like a hint that hears the baying of the dogs.

Hildewige's eyes are neither blue nor dark; they are brighter than an iridescent bubble, browner than the rushes of the marsh, shiner than the leaves of water-lentils.

"Like the serpent's tongue, like the tip of a sword, the eyes of a virgin slay, and I am lying down like a wounded hind at your feet," said the great Aes, changed into a warrior.

"Like the flowery peat, like the sparkling dune, the oaths of warriors attract; but his cold the water is beneath the sand! How black the mud is beneath the flowers!"

"Under the glacier iridescent with the fires of the setting sun, dwarves have forges a bed of copper with silver feet; Elves have woven a sift cushion of white linen for you."

"For a bed, Master, you shall have my heart, for cushions my blonde tresses. In the iridescent grotto, my beloved, you shall have my lips for a cup and my amour for a breastplate..."

Sweeter than honey, the sonorous runes glide from the lips of the great Aes, and the cheeks of the Northern rose redden like the petals of the eglantine under the kisses of the sun...

"Sing, my master, my sweet master, what the blond charmer, the handsome warrior, said to his beloved; I want to see whether you can speak better than a great Aes."

"The words of the god! On the foreheads of old men, on the door of the temple, on the hill of tombs, I have read them...but my ear is full of the noise of swords..."

On the cold sand of the pale gulf, in his wolf-skin, the king awaits sleep. His gaze follows the rising moon, a falling star; his soul follows his dream.

And his dream says: "Where the raspberry-bushes grow, the virgin is a seamew, the mother a bee, the father an elk. There, the wheat has no chaff, the temple has no nettles."

"From dawn to sunset, I have passed like a river," replied the king of horsemen; in the fertile mud, the future can germinate. To the white land of runes, I am going to repose.

"On these sonorous beaches, on these green hills, my people will camp...and the bloody river will no longer be anything but a lake, entirely limpid and blue, and the great killer of men will be happy…"

When Attila awakes, he sees on the sand a pear-wood sleigh harnessed to two black horses, the manes of which are braided with wool.

A golden cuckoo opens its wings at the tip of the helm; two golden cuckoos are flap their wings over the circles of the collars; silver bells are tinkling on the breasts of the horses.

Attila mounts the sleigh. He cracks the whip garnished with pearls, shakes the reins of gold and silver, and the sleigh glides rapidly over the nacreous snow.

The vultures had smoothed their wings, the wolves were marching like cavaliers, a hundred before and a hundred behind, a hundred to the left and a hundred to the right of the pear-wood sleigh.

The host of the green isle was on the threshold of the painted house; he heard the sound of the sleigh and he looked in the direction of the sea. On seeing the vultures and the wolves he cried:

"A god is coming to repose in my painted house, under my oaken beams, on my polished bench, before my red fire!"

Attila stopped his sleigh and said to him. "Have you a virgin for me, a bride, a swallow to sleep beside me?"

"I have a virgin, a bride, a swallow to sleep beside you," replied the host.

Hildewige appeared then on the road of the hill. Her hair was undone, her eyes were moist; she was thinking about the blond young man, the handsome warrior.

"Virgin, for two weeks, nearly three, I have been marching in order to find you. Come to sleep in my tent; I am Attila, the king of horsemen."

"There is no virgin here who wants to become your wife. No swallow here who wants to sleep beside you," the Northern virgin replies, putting up her hair.

"Host of the green isle, I am Attila; give me your daughter, and I will give you ten boats full of silver and two boats full of gold."
The host replies to the king of horsemen:

"I give you my daughter, my swallow, to sleep beside you. Hildewige, comb your hair, put on your bracelets; you are the bride of the king of the vultures and the wolves."

"We are not sold for silver, we do not give ourselves for red gold to passing heroes," replies the Northern rose, frowning.

"Attila, I give her to you," says the host...
An elk was slain for the king, an ox for the guests, a hundred sheep for the vultures, a hundred sheep for the wolves, ant the marriage was made.

At the end of the meal, the aged mother, the venerable hostess, took Hildewige behind the hedge, near to the door of the cowshed where the oxen were ruminating, and said to her in a whisper:

"Let your ear be as fine as that of a mouse, let your feet be as light as those of a hare, let your heart be as tender as the crown of a young plum tree."

"Oh, my mother, you who have nourished me, why have you sold me? I do not love the king of the wolves; I love a warrior that I saw last night on the hill of birches."

"Oh my daughter, my golden apple, my flowery staff, let the sorb-trees of your husband's orchard be sacred to you. Oh, my daughter, let their fruits be more sacred still...."

But the cups were empty, and the sleigh was harnessed! Hildewige combed her hair, weeping; she put on her bracelets weeping; she bid the painted house adieu.

She already has one foot in Attila's sleigh and she says adieu again to the trees of the orchard; but the sleigh pulls away and at sunset. It stops near the red boat.

Hildewige sits down at the bow, Attila sits down at the stern, the old man takes the oars, the wolves enter into the dark water and the vultures fly into the gray sky...

In front of the palace of maple-wood, where they are stationed every evening, the riders sitting on the heads of aurochs say sadly: "Under the threshold the grass has paled; already, ivy is attaching itself to the walls."

In the round hall of the maple-wood palace, on the crimson cushions, the women leaning sadly on their elbows say sadly: "The hall in already full; which of us will make way for the master's chosen one...?"

It was not the hands of women that had woven the blue sail; it inflates, the mast bends and the boat dances on the waves like a light bubble on an iridescent cascade.

Hildewige sings, letting her white hand dangle in the green water, she sings letting her blonde hair float fee, she sings in the old language of the runes.

Attila does not understand what she is singing, but the vultures and the wolves understand it, and the fish too, and the daughters of the sea who rear up on the waves.

She says: "When he calls to me this evening under the silver birches, only the echo will respond..."

Attila smiles; he does not understand the language of the runes.

The wolves weep as they swim. The vultures weep as they fly, the daughters of the sea weep and the fish say to one another: "The Northern rose will wither."

The old man sings, while dipping the oars: "when one sows blood, swords grow! When on sown swords, blood grows! Perhaps...often!"

The boat touches the sand. "Attila!" cry the horsemen. The king leaps into the foam, but when he turns round, the boat has disappeared, and a short sword is shining in Hildewige's hand...

"Snowdrop with the golden heart, blue periwinkle, pale violet, scatter your seeds, your little seeds, in my fir-wood boat, in my new sail; until the dews of spring, I want to sing runes to my bride."

III

The king leaps into the foam, but when he turns round, the boat has disappeared, and a short sword is shining in Hildewige's hand. "Attila!" cry the horsemen.

"She has a sword for a distaff, your bride, hurrah, hurrah! Her veil will have red pearls, hurrah, hurrah! For the morning gift well shall deck her tent with the heads of kings."

101

The horsemen launched their arrows at the clouds; their feet muffled, the wild wolves howl; the vultures circled like dry leaves; Attila smiled.

And the Northern virgin, her cheek pale, her eyes lowered, folded her two pale hands over the agate hilt. "Hurrah for the bride!" cry the horsemen.

A dappled stallion has been saddled for the king, as light as oat straw, as sleek as the stem of a sweet-pea. Hildewige sits down on the silky rump.

The Northern rose holds the naked sword in her hand.
"What is that sword?" asks Attila. "Did the old man give it to you?"
"Perhaps. Who knows?"

Attila spurs his horse and murmurs: "Fly, white stallion. Fly to the maple-wood palace, to the hall of the golden shields; I know how to speak to women as well as horsemen."

In the evening, a tent of felt was erected for the virgin. Before the lowered flap, Attila plants his spear, and he lies down next to his horse, bare-headed, his arms folded.

He dreamed of the time when the young women forgot their full pitchers in the spring, in order to watch the indefatigable horseman circling, and while dreaming, he smiled...

"Has he slipped into the tent of felt, the sweet charmer, the handsome warrior?" At the bronze table of the palace of the great Aesir, in his marked place among the Strong and the Sage, he is seated.

He speaks, and everyone falls silent. "Why, Father of Men," he says, "do you allow the son of a deformed dwarf to turn like a mill-wheel over the crushed world?"

"Is it wheat or chaff," replies the Father, "that the wheel is crushing? Who knows? Who knows? The Old Man alone is the master; tomorrow is his secret.

"For as long as the sun shines in the sky of the Aesir, the ash-tree will flourish on the green hills of the Northern isles; the raspberry-bushes will not be trampled by the feet of Attila..."

Attila marches for two weeks, nearly three, and he arrives at the maple-wood palace, the palace with the polished beams. All his warriors are waiting for him, all his women are waiting for him.

When they saw Hildewige, the warriors uttered a cry of joy; she was beautiful. When they saw Hildewige, the women uttered a cry of dolor; she was the most beautiful.

The wolves, fatigued, lay down before the door; the vultures, fatigued, perched on the top of the roof; and the women, pale with jealousy, set the table for the feast...

Attila had all his men sit down. He had a silver plate and a golden cup set before each of them; he had one of his women stationed behind each of them, in festival garments.

Then he sat down, with his bride, on the wooden bench with the twisted feet. Hildewige places her naked sword on the bench, and in the battle hall the feast commences.

It is a fine feast; the cups are overflowing, the table buckling, the women moisten their lips in the cups, the men plunge their swords into the tables, and a hundred bards sing.

Then, at the door of the hall, a stranger appears, a shield over his shoulder. He says: "The coward only comes when invited, but the brave man knocks and enters the palace of kings.

"The brave man sits down at the table; his invitation is engraved on the blade of his sword." He is handsome, the stranger; dazzling flowers shine on his shield.

Attila invites him to sit down on the bench with the twisted feet and he says: "The unknown guest must be received like a god; Queen of the World, fill the stranger's cup."
Hildewige smiles.

The cups, filled a hundred times, have been emptied a hundred times; he king says: "Take the golden cups, and also take the women, but bend the knee before the Queen of the World."

Everyone has bent the knee, but the blond young man has said, as he bent his nee: "Amour has wings like white birds..."
Hildewige smiles.

She is still smiling when the king carried her away in the hall where the golden shields are flamboyant. She is still smiling when the king places her on the bed of bearskins with ruby claws.

The men cried: "She has a sword for a distaff, hurrah, hurrah! We are the ones who will put flax in her distaff, hurrah, hurrah!" Wine was foaming in the cups like blood.

The king places Hildewige on the bearskin bed, and then he kneels down and opens his mouth to speak...

But he does not have time to speak; she plunges her sword into his heart.

Attila cries: "Men of the Orient, lacerate your cheeks, a woman has killed me."

She says: "My oaths have roots like the iris; they yield fruits like the pear-tree."

Hildewige is pale but her eyes are dry. Attila said: "Weep, gray wolves! Weep, tawny vultures! A woman has killed me!"

Blood flows from the breast of the king over Hildewige's robe.

The blood flows and the king says: "Let me sit down next to you. Will you sustain my head? Don't withdraw the sword, don't take back your kiss."

Attila smiled.

The Northern rose gazes at the man who is smiling with a sword in his heart; she gazes at the man who speaks of amour with a sword in his heart, and her eyes widen, astonished.

The king sang softly: "I have a palace of clouds for my bride; I have washed my red hands... Weep, gray wolves; weep, tawny vultures; weep, men of the Orient!"

The shields groan, the wolves howl, the vultures flap their wings, and a loud voice cries: "Weep not, heather, I have kept my oath."

The shields groan, the wolves howl, the vultures flap their wings, and in a ray of sunlight the unknown guest of the feast appears, the warrior of the green hill.

As soon as Hildewige sees him, she applies her lips to the blue lips of Attila. "I am coming to join you, king of swords" she says, "I shall pour you hydromel in the palace of the brave."

Then, pale, her hand raised, she says to the great Aes: "When your enemies pursue you, let your horse fall! Let the arrow that you launch turn back upon you and avenge Attila!"

She draws out the sword...
Attila falls; the wolves flee; the vultures fly away; the shields break...
She draws out the sword, strikes herself, and falls upon the heart she has struck.

Then, on his iceberg, the Old One says: "the hand of a man cannot kill, the hand of a god must not kill, and a woman has not killed Attila the reaper.

But when the sheaf is tied, in the hour of noon, the reaper may repose for a moment in the shade; he may moisten his lips in the cool spring...."

A lightning bolt has ripped through the maple roof; a mare with black wings and a fiery mane launches forth into the fall where the shields are flamboyant; Hildewige smiles and Attila get up.

"The Old One alone is the master!" sighs the radiant Aes, frowning.
"Tomorrow is his secret," replies the man who is still the king of horsemen.

"Why have you not taken the form of a swan? I recognize you, owner of the boat with the blue sail. You have not lied; the arms of my bride are whiter than the foam.

"You have not lied; from the eglantine-bush of the green isle I have plucked the rose of amour; now take me to the celestial spring, where I must wash my red hands.

"From dawn to sunset I have passed like a river; in the fertile mud, the future may germinate; handsome swan, carry me to the blue land of the runes... Attila! Attila!"

Beneath the muscular thigh of the king of horsemen, the mare bucks; quivering, she extends her bloody wings. Lightning flashes in the fiery sky; the mare launches forth.

The virgin leans her hand on the king's shoulder, her loose blonde hair caresses his brown cheek. The mare bounds; on her ebony rump the bare feet of the virgin shine like seamews.

"Attila! The Romans!" cry the horsemen. "Attila, get up! An iron circle is closing around us, wake up!"

Trembling, they raise the lowered curtain, the curtain of the hall of golden shields.

But in the round hall, through the torn roof, a ray of light slides... On the sandy floor, a red patch is fuming; on the empty bed, a sword shines...

"Attila!" cry the horsemen.

Like a swallow in the paling sky the mare describes great circles as she rises.

"Beloved," says the virgin, "your children are calling you; the iron circle ids closing in."

"The straw is dry, the sheaf is tied," replies the reaper, "tomorrow we shall take up our heavy scythes. The hour of rest is sounding; come with me to the pathless plains!"

Like a black whirlwind, the squadrons take flight; the heavy cartwheels turn; the great bulls shake the clouds with their horns; the surprised army rises toward the stars...

And ever since, Attila's army, like a river of milk, has been shining between the stars; in order to descend again to cut the brambles, it is waiting for the hour to chime...

In the leather sail the North wind is weeping. "Until the promised kiss, until the night of amour, sing, my master, my sweet master."

"I know many more songs, but my ear is full of the sound of swords..."

THE MILLER OF CARNAC

Equidistant from the river in the Crach and the peninsula of Quiberon, at the extremity of an immense heath strewn with little hamlets, between the growling waves and the singing pines, in the midst of dolmens and menhirs, some fifty white houses are clustered around a gray steeple. That steeple is the bell-tower of the church of Saint Corneille,[30] the patron of animals and the poor in spirit; the white houses are the houses of Carnac.

Carnac does not resemble Auray, which is a town, nor Trinité, which is a port, nor Plouharnel, which is a farm, nor Saint-Columban, which is only an anchored boat; Carnac is neither a town nor a village, neither rural nor marine.

Carnac is a place of pilgrimage for sick animals, a tranquil nest in which mariners worn away by the sea can go to run aground, a sacred field to which poets and scholars come in order to dream. It is not loved by its neighbors, jealous of its such church, its two notaries and its physician. That enmity has endured for centuries, and takes advantage of any excuse

---

[30] Breton legend associates the Saint Corneille who was pope from 251-253 A.D. with the Breton Saint Korneli or Cornely, who was allegedly pursued pagan soldiers, whom he turned into the stones of the impressive megalithic alignments of Carnac, constituting more than 4,000 individual stones, nowadays an important national monument and tourist attraction but not as well-known in 1865, although they had ben visited and publicized by several Romantic writers, including Prosper Mérimée and Gustave Flaubert

to burst forth. During the Chouannerie Carnac sided with the blues; in 1848 it was in favor of the whites.[31]

Today, peace is on the lips but not in the hearts. The people of the heath think that there are too many mariners around the church of Saint-Corneille, and the fishermen of Pô think that there are too many peasants in the mariners' inn.

I, who am neither a man of the sea nor a man of the heath, would love Carnac passionately if one were not rubbing shoulders so frequently with poets, scholars and collectors fanatical about enriching their museums with a pebble, over-turning menhirs and disemboweling old tombs.

The poets who think they can speak as loudly as the sea, whereas their empty strophes tinkle like little bells, deafen me; the scholars searching for Roman roads, the Commentaries of Caesar in hand, annoy me, and the vandals who destroy what they cannot understand irritate me. So I only like Carnac for six months of the year, and I wait before visiting it until the breeze is too brisk for the sensitive wings of those linnets, parrots and owls The heath is, however, charming when the oak leaves redden above the wash-houses, when the gray willows shine in the middle of the meadows, when the sunlight gilds the rows of menhirs and when the dormant Ocean extends its long blue arms between the sparkling salt-mills and the flowery islets of the river of the Crach.

Tourists, be accursed!

In winter the landscape becomes grim; the furious sea howls, the west wind breaks the pines, and rain drowns the heath. But the Ocean's wrath is even more beautiful than its caresses, and the rush-flowers have an even sweeter perfume than that of honeysuckle. If I could choose between winter and summer, I would still choose winter for visiting Carnac.

It is true that I have a friend out there, and one can converse better when the evenings are long.

---

[31] The Chouannerie was a general term applied to the royalist uprisings of 1794-1803. The Revolutionaries were the "blues" and the Chouans the "whites,"

My friend is the miller of the mill of Kermau.

You don't know Kermau, the diamond of Carnac? It's necessary to go to Carnac, if only to see Kermau. The menhirs of Carnac are small by comparison with that of Lochmariaker, as big as an obelisk; the funereal grottoes of Carnac are trivial by comparison with that of Gavriuis, the holy island of Morbihan, the heath of Carnac is not a large as a thousandth part of that of Elven, the cliffs of Carnac are only half as high as those of Croisic and the hats in Carnac are not as pretty as those of Guérandes, but only Carnac has Kermau!

Kermau is a former manor huddled under old oaks. It backs on to the heath and gazes at the sea. Between the sea and it, broad meadows snake long a crystalline stream.

I don't want to describe Kermau to you; even a photograph wouldn't give you an idea of it, for a photograph wouldn't tell you that its mossy walls are as pink as the cheeks of cherubim, that its sharp roof is s shiny as the throat of a wood-pigeon, that the ivy that embroiders it is as fresh as an emerald, that the pond that bathes it is as silky as a Milanese breastplate, that the spring that sings at its door is as limpid as your eyes, my charming reader. But I shall simply tell you, in order that you can recognize it at a distance, that it is composed of a main building flanked by two small towers, that its windows have lattices as light as convolvulus stems, and that the skylights in its roof resemble two spear-heads.

From the road to Auray you can perceive it between the heath and a clump of oaks. It is in the middle of a square formed by thick walls flanked by corner turrets. The wall that touches its two flanks encloses a small courtyard in front of its façade, and a large garden on the other side. The garden, surrounded by terraces, is planted with apple trees. On the terraces here is a double row of laurels twenty feet high. In the corner facing the rising sun two large pink stone slabs cover two tombs; in one of them a Templar reposes, and in the other a fay.

The limpid spring is beside the courtyard, between Pierre the Miller's farm and the château. When you go to see

Kermau, mention me to Pierre. If he isn't at the farm go to the mill and you'll find him there.

The mill of Kermau is a windmill perched on a funerary mount ten minutes from the château; it has four red sails, a slate roof and a blazoned door. Its owner is the finest player of the binlou in all of Morbihan and one of the best storytellers in all Bretagne.

While the millstones turn Pierre plays the binlou[32] when he is alone, and he tells stories when he receives visitors. He receives a great many visits, because one can't go to Carnac without following the alignments, and one can't pass the mill of Kermau, situated in the middle of those alignments, without stopping to listen to the original and charming melodies that take flight from the window of the blazoned mill. As soon as one stops, a floury hand shows itself and invites you to come up.

One climbs a steep granite staircase and enters a round room, in the middle of which he millstones are purring. Sacks of wheat on one side, sacks of flour on the other, are leaning against the walls. Pierre is lying on two or three of them; one sits down to get one's breath back and the conversation commences. To the local people Pierre talks about the most recent wedding, to mariners the most recent storm, and for strangers he names the seventeen bell-towers and the twenty-two islets that can be seen from his two windows. The tassel of his cotton bonnet serves the designate the places he is talking about. About every bell-tower, every islet and every clump of trees he knows an anecdote. Listen to him:

Between that round tower, which is the bell-tower of Sainte-Anne, and that wooded hill, which is on the edge of the Auray river, you can see the smoke of the farm of Marie-Jeanne, the sister of Georges Cadoudal. She's a countess and she hasn't been made a cardinal.

---

[32] A binlou is a Breton instrument closely related to the bagpipe, also known in the Auvergne; L'Estoille would probably have encountered it in the Monts de la Madeleine.

"There's the steeple of Auray. Beside it is the Charter-house, all marble inside; the field of martyrs is there, a little to the right.

"That village at the entrance to the peninsula of Quiberon is Plouharnel; two gold necklaces were found in a tomb there, one of which weighs eight hundred grams. That strip of sand is the camp of Hoche, the famous general![33] The émigrés disembarked in that cove. That's the burg of Quiberon, opposite Belle-Isle.

"On that point is Saint Colomban. Facing you, to the right of the Château de Kermau, is Bomer, where there are proud lads. One day they said to themselves: 'We're from Bomer, we don't want to drink in Carnac.' And they summoned an innkeeper from Plouharnel. The first evening they got him drunk and they left him between two wines for three months. At the end of the third month the innkeeper sobered up and saw that his cellar in which he'd invested two thousand francs, was empty The lads had only paid him seventeen sous; he died of chagrin. They're proud lads, the lads of Bomer!"

"That fine yellow pigeon-loft is the château of a baron who made himself a park.

"In a field of rushes near that pond, my uncle was shot by a firing squad—a worthy man if he hadn't had ideas that he didn't understand..."

The millers of Bretagne are all free spirits, to some extent. The peasants claim that they're also thieves, to a degree.

Perhaps the peasants are often right, but Pierre is an exception to the rule, so you can address yourself to him in confidence, provided that you're not an antiquarian. Oh, he doesn't like antiquarians. One day, he said to me:

"Those messieurs from Vannes are true rats, they dig everywhere. The proof is that they've hollowed out Mont Saint-Michel, that big hill over there with a chapel on top. They're rats who know the best places; they found a basket in

---

[33] Lazare Hoche (1768-1797), famous (or notorious) for his suppression of the Vendean counter-revolution.

the Butte Saint-Michel full of precious stones, which they took away, but they made a portrait of it which they gave to Carnac. They're good lads in Carnac! All the same, I wouldn't want to be in their place; they've touched the fay's stones."

"What fay?" I said to him.

"The fay of Kermau, the one whose tomb is in the garden."

What if I were to tell you the legend of the fay and the Templar? It is more interesting than anything I could tell you about the monuments of Carnac—and then, I have already written it down under Pierre's dictation. He read the beginning of it to me from a greasy piece of paper which is part of his family papers, for Pierre is the last of the Comtes de Kermau, and he has the right, as he puts it: "to put in embroidery on his bonnet" the escutcheon that is engraved on the door of his mill.

Pierre claims that the manuscript is as old as the story, but he is mistaken; his manuscript is a modern translation of a "*chanson*" of the crusades.[34] A Kermau, a rector or deacon, amused himself by translating from Breton to French an old story whose conclusion has been eaten by rats.

This is what remains of the Kermau manuscript entitled *The Song of the Templar*:

In the name of the Father, the Son and the Holy Ghost!

Noble barons, unfasten your helmets, and noble ladies, put down your spindles, in order to listen to the song of a pilgrim overseas.

---

[34] As noted in the introduction, *chanson* is usually translated it English as "song," and I have done so here and, more importantly, in translating "La Chanson d'Arthur" and *La Chanson de l'alouette*, in spite of the ambiguity of the French term, which made troubadour *chansons* significant models for modern poetry in prose.

114

I have arrived from Jerusalem, where Christ preached; I have wept on the Mount of Olives where Christ wept; I have prayed on the Holy Sepulcher, where Christ was buried.

Be silent, noble demoiselles, and your tears will flow in listening to the story of Richard the Templar.

I

In the name of the Father, the Son and the Holy Spirit!

When one descends the Loire one finds the city of Blois and then the city of Nantes, and if from Nantes one marches in the direction in which the sun sets in April one enters into the land of Bretagne.

The knights of Bretagne are noble knights; a thousand of them followed their Duc to the Holy Land.[35] But Richard de Kermau did not follow them because he was still a child when they departed for the crusade.

Richard de Kermau was an orphan, and his château was in the parish of Kermau.

Noble gentlemen, his your horses leave hay in the manger, noble ladies, if your hackneys begin to waste away, make a vow to Saint Corneille, whose church is in Carnac, and your horses will rediscover their appetite and your hackneys will raise their head again. Saint Corneille is the patron of beings who have no souls. He died at Carnac after having changed into stones the pagan soldiers who were pursuing him. The entire pagan army was out there on the heath, arranged in battle order. In the first rank were the knights, in the last the varlets. There are nine rows of stones, and fifteen hundred stones, fully counted, in each row. The king was at the head of his army.

---

[35] Alain IV, Duc de Bretagne, joined the First Crusade in 1098.

Richard de Kermau, who had been an orphan since birth,[36] went up every day on to the Butte Saint-Michel in order to watch the pack of the Comte du Lac, the seigneur of the river of Crach, running over the heath. Richard only had three basset hounds, because he was not rich, but as he was a good gentleman he liked to watch dogs running.

One evening, he went to sleep on the butte and he woke up when the watchman of Carnac struck the dozen chimes of midnight on the bell of Saint-Corneille. It was the first night of the full moon of June.

When he woke up Richard rubbed his eyes; he could no longer see the stones on the moonlit heath, and although the night was calm, the sea was seething in Saint Columban Bay.

The stones were no longer on the heath because they had gone into the sea, and the sea was seething because they were drinking. They went there once a year and they will go here until the day of judgment; then Saint Corneille will baptize them and open the gates of heaven to them.

Richard trembled when he no longer saw the stones and he took the road of Carnac at a run. When he was in the meadows he heard a loud noise coming from the direction of the sea; he looked and saw the stones running after him and bumping into one another. He fell to his knees and made a

---

[36] In one of his more literal quasi-autobiographical fictions L'Estoille says that there was a point in his writing when he realized that the protagonists of all his early stories were versions of himself, and burned them all. The present story, in which aspects of his exploits in Algeria might be transfigured as Richard's adventures as a crusader, was presumably written subsequently, and more deliberately; the circumstances of Richard's enlistment make an intriguing comparison with the prelude to L'Estoille's enlistment sketched in *Fusains*, and the present story contains, in strange embryo, the elements of many of his subsequent quasi-autobiographical transfigurations.

vow to Our Lady to take the cross if the stones were deflected away from him.

As soon as he fell to his knees a white woman who was holding a branch of furze in her hand appeared to him. That woman touched the stones with the flowery branch and they veered to the right and the left. When the last one had passed by, the white woman touched the knight's forehead with her branch and disappeared, leaving behind a perfume of violets.

The next day, the knight armed himself, mounted his best horse, and went to Vannes in order to take the cross.

II

Richard rode without stopping all the way to Constantinople. He passed over the sea in a ship, and after much fatigue, much thirst and much hunger he arrived in Jerusalem.

There we prayed for one day on the Holy Sepulcher, one day on Calvary and one day on the Mount of Olives, and then he departed for the desert in order to see the place where Saint John baptized in the Jordan.

On the way he encountered a Templar who was riding alone with his squire.[37] They agreed to travel together, but that same evening, near a spring surrounded by palm trees, they were attacked by Saracens. Soon their horses buckled on their hocks and fell. They were about to succumb when a white woman descended from a cloud with a branch of furze in her hand.

Richard recognized the woman who had deflected the stones of Carnac away from him and he cried: "Our Lady, if you save me from the pagans as you delivered me from the stones of Carnac, I swear to make myself a Templar."

The white woman struck the Saracens with her flowery branch and they feel dead.

---

[37] The military order known as the Knights Templar was founded in 1119.

The next day Richard drank the water of the Jordan, and he returned to Jerusalem and made himself a Templar.

III

One day, he learned that the Saracens hidden in the desert had cut the pilgrims' route. The Grandmaster told Richard to arm himself and to go with five hundred knights to exterminate the miscreants.

Richard departed with five hundred knights and encountered the pagans in a narrow gorge.

The combat commenced with the day and only finished at the hour of vespers. It was a sad day; all the Templars fell one after another. Richard was the last to fall.

When he was on the ground he could not see anything because he was blinded by blood, but he heard the bursts of laughter of the pagans who were cutting off the heads of the knights and suspending them from their saddle-bows. He also heard the steel grating on the bones, and he fainted.

Suddenly, he felt someone unfastening his helmet and he cried:

"Ah! Our Lady, you who deflected the stones of Carnac away from me, you who have killed he Saracens near the spring, protect me!"

He opened his eyes.

He was alone in the midst of bushes, his faced had be wiped, his wound bandaged, and on the grass he saw loaf of wheat-bread and a golden cup full of wine, in which a branch of furze was dipped.

Richard thanked Our Lady and then drank the wine and ate the bread. As soon as he had eaten he no longer felt his wound, but he was too weak to get up. Then he looked at the furze branch and he thought about the great heaths of Carnac. At that memory tears came to his eyes, but he was so tired that he fell asleep.

As soon as he fell asleep he had a dream. He saw himself in the meadow. Beside the fays' altar; next to him, the lady who had saved him three times was motionless beside him and the...

The Kermau manuscript ends there. Fortunately, Pierre knew the end of the story. He continued:

"You see, Monsieur, the knight thought he was dreaming, but he wasn't dreaming. He really was in the meadow, against the large stone around which there were brambles, which I showed you yesterday evening.

"During the night, the fay had transported him through the air from Judea to Kermau.

"The knight was very astonished when he saw the smoke of the kitchen rising through the trees and when he recognized the black colt that he had left two years before.[38]

What I am telling you was in the pages that the rats have eaten; my grandfather read them to me so often that I still know them by heart.

"Have you seen on the Butte Saint-Michel a great trench that those messieurs from Vannes had dug last year? Before being filled in, that trench traversed a layer of stones, and then a layer of mud, like that found on the bed of coves, and then another layer of stones; it led to a cave like that of Plouharnel, in which the golden necklace as found. That cave is a grotto, the sides of which are formed by huge stone slabs and the ceiling by a single stone. That chamber is only two and a half feet high, but it is broad enough for three people to be able to move therein.

"In that grotto, thirty-nine stone axes of various colors were found, beautiful green pearls, and a ring formed of little white beads like those that are sold at the fair of Auray...but no body was found.

---

[38] It may not be insignificant that the term *poulain*, which I have translated literally as "colt," and which recurs frequently in L'Estoille's work, was also applied metaphorically at the time he was active to inexperienced but promising writers.

"The messieurs from Vannes said that they had found the ashes of one, but they were mistaken. There had never been anyone in the grotto of Mont Saint-Michel except a fay that Saint Corneille had imprisoned there on the day when he changed the pagan army into stones. In order to prevent her from escaping from her prison, the angels had thrown the mud and stones over the grotto.

"You know that the fays always ended up being converted, and that is why there are almost none left today, because no new ones are made. On the day when they're baptized, they become women like other women, except that they're milder and they always love their husbands.

"My opinion is that I haven't married a fay myself, but no matter, I'll go on with the story such as it was written in the manuscript.

"When Richard saw the black colt beside him in the meadow of the château he thanked the fay, whom he mistook for the Holy Virgin, but the fay said to him:

"'I'm not the Holy Virgin, I'm the fay whom Saint Corneille had imprisoned by the angels under the butte Saint-Michel because I swelled the sea in order to drown fishermen and because I unleashed thunderbolts on the houses of Christians. I wept there for a thousand years, and then I invoked the saints of paradise. Then the angel Michel descended into my prison and said to me: *The Bretons are departing for Judea; if you watch over them for a hundred years, and if, by means of your diabolical power, you aid them to triumph over the pagans, the Bishop of Vannes will baptize you and you'll become a woman to whom Saint Pierre can open the gate of Heaven. But if you become wicked again, you'll fall into Hell, from which you won't emerge again.*

"'I left under the butte the stone axes with which I launched thunderbolts, the green pearls with which I swelled the sea, and the white ring with which I poisoned springs, and I cut a branch of furze from the heath and went to the Holy land in order to watch over the Bretons.

"'On the nights when the stones went to drink I returned to Carnac to prevent them from crushing people on the heath. They went to drink last night, and as you were still too weak to remain out there alone I brought you with me. Spend the day in your château and I'll take you back to Jerusalem tomorrow night.'

"While he fay was speaking, Richard gazed at her, and he found her very beautiful, so beautiful that he fell in love with her.

"Then he said to her: 'Beautiful fay, when can you be baptized by the Bishop of Vannes?'

"'Today, if I weren't obliged to return to Jerusalem; the hundred years end at noon.'

"'Well then, take me to Vannes, to the house of the bishop!'

"The fay carried Richard to Vannes, to the house of the bishop. They arrived just as noon chimed. The carillon of the cathedral bells was being rung, the deacons were wearing white surplices and the bishop was under the portal of the church.

"As soon as he saw the fay the bishop said: 'Fay, Saint Michel has informed me that you would come in order to be baptized, and he told me to call you Margareth. Come.'

"The bishop baptized the fay. The Duc de Bretagne was her godfather and the Duchesse was her godmother.

"As soon as she was baptized, Richard de Kermau approached her and said to her: 'Now that you're a woman, would you like me to marry you?'

"Margareth blushed, but the Duchesse cried: 'Certainly, it's necessary that they marry.'

"The bishop relieved Richard of his vows, and the marriage was made the same day. As Margareth had no armories, the Duchesse gave her her own, and that is why there is the ermine of Bretagne over the door of my mill.

"Richard and Margareth lived to be very old. They died on the same day and they were buried next to one another in the garden of their château. As soon as Margareth's grave was filled in, white violets, the like of which are found nowhere else, grew on her tomb."

When Pierre had finished his story I asked him whether he believed that it was true.

"Certainly it's true," he replied. "My grandfather has read the marriage contract between Richard de Kermau and Margareth. That contract was signed by the Duc de Bretagne, and since that time the eldest of our daughters has always been named Margareth, and their godmother gives them eyes that the other daughters of Carnac don't have. Here, I'll show you my Margareth."

He put his head out of the window and called to a girl of fifteen who was guarding five dappled cows and two black sheep on the heath. She arrived at a run.

"Look, Monsieur," said Pierre, when she came into the room of the mill. "Don't be afraid, it's necessary to see whether her eyes resemble those of her godmother, the fay."

The girl, who was twisting a corner of her apron between her fingers, lowered her head and raised an eyelid shaded by long brown lashes. She was charming, in her large white headdress, and her eyes had the glaucous color of the Ocean in the month of August.

"She's as kind as she's pretty," the father told me, as he embraced her. "She's as hard-working as a honey-bee and she sings like a skylark. Sing your godmother's song, child."

Pierre picked up his binlou and Margareth sang without being begged the most adorable Breton melody that I have ever heard.

"The tune is mine," said Pierre, when she had finished.

"And the words?"

"They're Margareth's."

When you go to Carnac. search on the heath for the little shepherdess who could embroider on her gray linen handkerchief the ermine of Bretagne, and ask her to sing her song.

Margareth speaks French, but don't speak ill of Carnac, or she'll run away, because:

> *The daughters of Margareth*
> *Like the gulls, only love*
> *The bay of Quiberon*
> *And the fishermen there.*

If you go to Carnac in order to know what the old tombs contain, listen to Pierre's stories; if you go to Carnac to learn to sing as the sea sings, listen to Margareth's couplets; and believe me, go to Carnac in winter, when the Ocean foams and the heath is flowery.

FOLLE-AVOINE

I

In the time of fine tales, a proud château overlooked a great plain. That château belonged to a baron whom, being the son of a baron himself, was named Hugues, like his father.

Hugues was a widower; he had a daughter, but he was scarcely occupied with her. From the first of January to Saint Sylvester's Day , falcon in hand, he hunted the marsh and the heath, Berthe grew up as free and wild as the wallflowers of the keep.

Messire Jean, the falconer, who was a man of good sense, said one evening to the baron: "Monseigneur, Demoiselle Berthe is approaching her sixteenth year; it would be good, I think, to teach her to distinguish a sparrowhawk from a goshawk."

"Go fetch my daughter," replied Hugues. I've been a widower for fourteen years; how time passes when one can dine at one's hour and digest in peace!"

Messire Jean went to fetch demoiselle Berthe.

II

"Oh!" cried the baron, striking the table, "Berthe is taking a long time. How does she spend her evenings, then?"

Berthe spent her evening with Margot, her nurse, who was as deaf as a pillow, and Folle-Avoine,[39] her page, who was as talkative as a tinkling bell. She came in, followed by Messire Jean, who was holding the page by the ear.

---

[39] Folle-Avoine is the French name of the wild oat, the original plant from which cultivated oats were developed.

"You've kept us waiting for a long time, Mademoiselle."

"Father..."

"It's the fault of this fellow," the falconer interjected. "He was making so much noise with his damned lute that Mademoiselle didn't hear me knocking on the door. Ah, you play the lute instead of chopping up the bird meat thinly! I'll take care of you, handsome page!"

The page was much the same age as Berthe; he had been found as a baby in a field of oats, and the baron had brought him up out of charity. He was s cheerful as a wren.

After having given a kick to the basset hound warming himself in front of the fire, Hugues said: "Sit down, daughter, and listen. You're approaching your sixteenth year, and it's high time you learned what a well-brought-up young woman ought to know. When one wants to train a falcon..."

Berthe sat down. In order to hear better Messire Jean removed his otter-fur cap, and Folle-Avoine leaned on the back of the young chatelaine's armchair, sighing.

"Are you listening, Berthe?"

"Yes, Father."

"When one wants to train a falcon, one takes it as soon as it commences to fly and one attaches a short strap to each foot, from which one suspends a little bell. That thing is called a jess. One then accustoms it to the lure..."

Folle-Avoine whispered something in Berthe's ear, and Berthe smiled. The baron saw that smile and frowned.

"Why, when you don't understand a word, are you laughing instead of waiting for me to explain it? The lure is a piece of wood to which two pigeon-wings have been attached. One accustoms the falcons to descend to the perch and to come, at a signal from the falconer, to take their nourishment on the lure. One does that so that they'll know that they'll have something to eat every time they obey their master."

"Yes, Father."

"Why are you affirming something that you don't know yet? As soon as the falcons are obedient, they're taught to let themselves be held on the wrist and to tolerate the hood. The hood is a small piece of leather ornamented with feathers and tufts of wool…"

Messire Jean, who had until then, approved of what the baron was saying with gestures, threw his otter-fur cap behind Berthe's chair, and Folle-Avoine jumped.

"Are you mad?" cried Hugues.

"The fellow was sleeping while you were speaking so well."

"He was asleep, the fellow? He's right, ten o'clock is chiming. Let's go to bed, and tomorrow, at daybreak, everyone mount up. You hear, Berthe?"

Berthe held out her forehead to her father.

III

In his great square bed with heavy serge curtains, Hugues went over through his mind the events of that memorable evening.

He said to himself: *Berthe's hair is as bright as poor Dame Odette's was. Her big blue eyes are as soft as my beautiful bride's were on the day when I carried her through the ripe wheat, smiling, to my château. That was a long time ago—a very long time! The peasants at the crossroads threw us flowers and shouted: "Long live our good lady!" Poor Odette…*

He said that, and went to sleep.

Hugues would have been the best of fathers if he had not loved hunting so much.

While Hugues was looking into the past, Berthe was looking into the future. She saw buffalo-hide garments, burnished breastplates and velvet doublets. She saw huge horses rearing up, cavaliers with serious faces leaning toward her and looking at her heron-plumed hat. She also saw…what young women see nowadays on the eve of their first ball.

Berthe was like a vigorous jasmine whose branches had not been guided by a gardener.

Old Margot was snoring; Messire Jean was dreaming that he had a falcon strong enough to stop a stag; and Folle-Avoine, his little dagger in his hand, was sleeping across Berthe's doorway.

IV

The next day, at dawn, a joyous cavalcade shook the wooden bridge of the Château de Beaucresson.

It was fine hunting weather; the sky was rather cloudy, the wind light, and scattered dew-drops glittered on grass withered by the early summer sun. Hugues was mounted on an ardent stallion the color of foam, Berthe was trembling slightly on her meek bay mare, and Messire Jean was prancing around the falconers, urging some and scolding others. Behind came the baron's officers. In front, Folle-Avoine, followed by two furry griffon dogs, made his black pony bound. Old Margot shouted from the window: "Oh, my sweet Jesus! Oh, my sweet Jesus!"

The cavalcade traversed the plain and stopped on the edge of a marsh in the middle of which was an islet covered with old oaks.

Folle-Avoine whistled to the griffons and launched his pony into the reeds.

"The fellow has the right idea!" muttered Messire Jean. He made a sign to a valet who was carrying eight falcons on a padded frame. He took the largest, and approaching Berthe, he said: "Demoiselle, the tercel that you have on your wrist is a worthy bird, but the prey we're about to hunt is too strong for him. Tercels are only good for magpies, partridges and skylarks; a heron requires more solid claws and more powerful wings. This is a Norwegian gerfalcon; with him you'll always be the queen of the hunt. She how broad his breast is, how white his belly and how the plumes of his tail fan out."

Berthe caressed the proud bird, whose golden claws scratched her deerskin gloves, and she raised herself up in her saddle impatiently, in order to see further. Folle-Avoine was making a racket in the reeds. A heron whistled and rose vertically into the sky.

Hugues launched his falcon, but Berthe was trembling so much that she could not take the hood off hers.

"Wait, demoiselle," said Messire Jean in a low voice.

The heron received Hugues' falcon on its beak, and threw it into the marsh, dead. The baron uttered an exclamation of anger, and Messire Jean, who had taken off the gerfalcon's hood, said to Bethe: "Raise your wrist, Demoiselle!"

In a second, the bird saw the heron and extended his great wings. He rose so high that he seemed no larger than a swallow. The heron fled, stretching its neck, with its feet dangling; but a gerfalcon flies rapidly, and as soon as he was above it, he closed his wings and fell on to its back. Feathers flew. Folle-Avoine cried *hurrah*, and five minutes later he attached a white heron-feather to the fur bonnet of his beautiful mistress.

V

They returned by way of the heather, and forced quail and skylarks; thus, by sunset, Messire Jean's face was radiant, the baron was content and Berthe was delighted.

"That Folle-Avoine will be a hunter," said the baron, suddenly.

"To become a hunter," replied the falconer, "it's necessary not think about anything but hunting. When I was his age, instead of playing the lute, I read good authors in the evening."

"Folle-Avoine," Berthe put in, "tells me every evening what he has seen while hunting."

"Bah!" said Hugues. "Where is he, then?"

The cavalcade was reentering the château, but Folle-Avoine was not with it.

In the depths of the heath, on the edge of the royal forest, there was a small pond bordered by willows, where tall loose-strifes inclined their red heads over the white umbels of meadow-sweet. The peasants dared not go along the path alongside that pond by night because, they said, an undine hid in the rushes there. Several had seen her!

You know that undines are fays, that they have ashen hair and that their eyes are speckled with golden dots. Some people claimed that undines were malevolent sorceresses who came to dance at village fêtes and drowned their dancing partners; others affirmed that they were good fays who rode on the backs of swans and played the harp in autumnal fogs. Everyone agreed in saying that they were recognizable by the drops of water that dripped from the green hem of their skirts. I don't know what to believe, but Folle-Avoine believed the latter, and he went alongside the blue pond hoping to see the undine.

While Berthe was riding merrily with the falcon on her wrist, the page, sitting under a willow, was searching the white evening mists for the pleats of a green robe. The pony was grazing nearby, and the two griffons were asleep, their heads on his knees. He gazed for a long time, but the moon was shining, and he stood up, sighing. The pony whinnied, the griffons growled; a beautiful young woman was coming along the causeway.

Folle-Avoine fell to his knees.

"Oh, good fay, good fay!" he stammered, all a-tremble.

"I'm not a fay," the beautiful young woman replied.

"Pardon, Madame, pardon; I know that you don't like to be called that, but I've been waiting for you for so many evenings."

"You want to become rich, then?"

"I want to learn our songs in order to repeat them to Berthe; the ones I know are ugly."

"Who is this Berthe, whom you love?"

The page blushed and replied in a whisper: "Berthe is a noble demoiselle and I'm only a poor page who doesn't know his mother's name."

The young woman smiled and drew away slightly.

"Return to your mistress," she said. "If she finds your songs ugly, it's because she isn't worthy to hear them."

A cloud passed before the moon, and Folle-Avoine no longer saw anything.

VI

The next day, all the baron's vassal lords knew about Berthe's exploit, and the day after, they all came to hunt with their suzerain.

During the first week, Hugues was proud of his cortege, but he soon perceived that those handsome hunters were not hunting seriously, and that they were more occupied with Berthe than the pursuit of the game. He remarked on that to Messire Jean.

"Monseigneur," said the falconer, "it's necessary for Mademoiselle Berthe to marry."

"Why?"

"Because she's nearly sixteen years old. She's acquired the habit of following the hunt, and if you don't marry her off, no good will come of it. The falcons of the amorous hunt the game while their masters chatter, and their dogs bay at the moon while they roll their eyes."

"You're right," sighed Hugues. "It's necessary for Berthe to marry; but as I want her to marry well, I'll invite all the sons of my friends the princes to the autumn hunts. Berthe can choose."

The baron invited a great many princes to the autumn hunts at the Château de Beaucresson.

VII

Folle-Avoine had lost his gaiety.

When Berthe returned from hunting she was tired and she went to sleep during the first verses of his songs.

"If the undine wanted to teach me what she sings on moonlit evenings," the page sighed, "perhaps my mistress wouldn't fall asleep."

He went to the blue pond, but he only saw glow-worms under the furze of the causeway.

During the day, Berthe conversed with the hunters.

VIII

A thousand princes of all lands, of all sizes and all colors, headed for the Château de Beaucresson as soon as they had received Hugues' message.

On the first of September they arrived on horseback, in carriages, on camels, on ostriches, and some even on huge dragons with blue wings and green tails. Their squires, their pages, their musicians and their buffoons formed a veritable army; and when Berthe saw them from the height of hr balcony, as brilliant as buttercups on the plain, she said to her page: "Folle-Avoine, we're going to have some fun!"

Folle-Avoine uttered a deep sigh.

Hugues received the princes as best he could, but after a week of introductions and salutations he perceived with terror that he only knew two of them by name. He had them introduced again. When the operation was concluded he did not even know the name of one. He wanted to begin again, but by dint of shouting out names, forenames, titles and qualities, his chamberlains had all lost their voices.

"Damn!" he said. "I'll never get to the end of knowing even the names of these estimable princes. After all, it's not me who's marrying; let Berthe choose!"

The thousand princes were assembled in the reception room; Hugues said to them, in his most gracious voice: "Messieurs…!"

The thousand princes bowed.

"And dear friends…!"

The thousand princes bowed again.

"My falcons are growing thin and my dogs are getting fat..."

The thousand princes said: "Oh!"

"Which proves that I, who invited you to the autumn hunt at the Château de Beaucresson, haven't been hunting for a fortnight, so I have a head as heavy as a mill-stone and I'll say this to you briefly: If you want to marry my daughter, be gallant in her regard. With that, I have the honor of saluting you, and I'm going to fly a magpie."

The noble princes uttered a simultaneous sigh of satisfaction, which agitated the panoplies on the walls, and the high chancellor, who was bald, caught a cold in the head of which he died ten years later. They uttered such a sigh because each of them, thinking himself more handsome that the other nine hundred and ninety-nine believed that he was sure to be welcomed.

Folle-Avoine and Messire Jean also uttered a sigh of satisfaction, Messire Jean because he could not sleep when there was no hunt and Folle-Avoine because he still hoped to please Berthe, whereas he was certain that the baron would not choose him for a son-in-law himself.

Old Margot did not sigh, because, being deaf, she had not heard her master's speech.

IX

Berthe decided immediately that there would be a tourney every morning, a contest of wits at three o'clock, a concert at six and a ball at nine.

The chronicles of the time are full of details of fêtes of that sort. The prince of Nigritie was seen there mounted on an ostrich, fighting for six hours running with the prince of the poles mounted on a sea-lion with a mane of holly. The prince of the Saracens and he Prince of Asturias were seen fighting at such close quarters that their breastplates became welded together and three blacksmiths were required to separate them, not counting the bellows-puller, Seventeen thousand, three hundred and twenty-four speeches, epistles and petitions, were made; rondeaux, ballads, acrostics and sonnets were composed for the occasion, in all the languages we know and many that we no longer know. There were also many things that have been lost. In brief, the fêtes were so magnificent that after a month, when the baron interrogated Berthe, she replied: "Oh, Father, they're all so charming!"

"You can't marry them all, so find one more charming than the others, and hurry."

"Yes, Father," Berthe replied.

And he fêtes resumed, more splendid than before.

X

The good princes, riding in the morning, rhyming in the afternoon, singing in the evening and dancing at night, grew so thin that by the end of the sixth week it became necessary to summon tailors from a hundred leagues around, the baron's no longer being sufficient to adjust the doublets. Berthe generously sacrificed forty-eight armchairs and a sofa to pad vacillating armor, and the fêtes continued.

Folle-Avoine had also grown thin, but Berthe did not even notice it. Whether one is brunette, or even blonde, who has time to look at a page when a thousand pages are looking at one? Old Margot took pity on him and said: "Child, you're at the age of growth; it's necessary to drink a good cup of warm milk when you wake up. You're getting as thin as an ant; tomorrow, when I bring up Berthe's milk, I'll bring one up for you."

Folle-Avoine stifled a sob and turned his head away, which brushed the old nurse and caused her to say:

"Little one, your page is beginning to be a little too big; to be a page it's necessary to be as insolent as a squire; it's necessary to ask your father for a different one."

"You find Folle-Avoine too big to be a page," replied Berthe, "but he doesn't have the shadow of a moustache. Besides which, I'm going to be married soon, and the prince I marry will give me one."

Folle-Avoine was behind the door; he put his hands over his heart and fled to the stables in order to weep at his ease. His pony licked his cheek and his two griffons licked his hand.

"Poor friends," he said to them, "You love me, and for six weeks I've left you shut away while the other horses and the other dogs are running in the sun. Help me to forget Berthe."

He saddled the pony and, followed by the two griffons, he joined Hugues on the plain.

"Ah!" said the baron, on seeing him arrive. "Those fine princes are boring you! Be patient for a few more days; when they've gone, when we're alone with Messire Jean, we'll amuse ourselves like kings, and you can be my squire."

Folle-Avoine hunted every day with the baron, but by the end of the seventh week he was so pale that Hugues said to him: "These princes are definitely annoying you too much, and me too. You feel forced to wait for the end of the ball before going to bed, and I'm forced to wait until the end of the ball in order to go to sleep. This evening I'll talk to Berthe, and tomorrow I'll have a son-in-law."

"You'd do better to talk to her right away," muttered Messire Jean.

"What are you saying?"

"I'm saying that girls are, with all due reverence, like falcons, and it's necessary only to take their hoods off within sight of the game one wants to capture."

"You're right, Messire Jean."

During the hunt, Folle-Avoine let his bridle hang loose on his pony's neck, and instead of going back with the baron he went to the blue pond.

XI

The sun was setting amid long golden clouds; water-fowl were playing among the nenuphars, frogs were hopping in the grass and Folle-Avoine, his head in his hands, was looking into his heart.

He said: "I wish I had stables full of horses, cellars full of gold, and coffers full of pearls. If I had all that, I'd load the gold on to the horses, put the pearls into necklaces, and I'd say to Berthe: 'Take them and love me!' But I'm only a poor page, and tomorrow I'll be dead!"

"Why?" said a soft voice.

Folle-Avoine raised his head; the young woman was smiling in front of him.

"Because Berthe is get married tomorrow. If I were a rich prince, perhaps she would have loved me..."

"And you'd like me to make you rich? But then, if Berthe loved you she'd only love your wealth."

"You're a good fay and you know what we don't. Help me."

"Will you promise to obey me, no matter what I command?"

"I swear it."

"Well then, return to the château, put on your new doublet, go to the ball and don't talk to Berthe."

XII

When Folle-Avoine went into the ballroom, Berthe, who had not seen him for a week, exclaimed: "Bonjour, handsome hunter."

Folle-Avoine bowed respectfully, but he did not approach her. Berthe looked at him, astonished.

"Folle-Avoine," she said, "Sing us a *chanson*."

The princes drew nearer.

"Stand aside a little, Messeigneurs, I'm stifling," she said, and, leaning toward the page: "Aren't you going to sing any more *chansons* for me, then?"

Folle-Avoine shook his head.

"Monseigneur le Baron!" cried the usher, opening the two battens of the door.

135

Hugues came in, holding the hand of a beautiful lady whose silver lamé robe was embroidered with emeralds and sapphires. A murmur of admiration ran through the hall, and Berthe, blushing deeply, advanced toward the stranger.

"Madame," said Hugues, "may I introduce my daughter Berthe and a thousand princes, the sons of old friends. Berthe, the daughter of the Duc, our sire, is doing us the honor of spending the night under our roof."

Berthe blushed even more deeply, and Folle-Avoine smiled; he had recognized the undine.

"My lovely child," the new arrival said to Berthe. "I know that you have to choose a husband among the thousand princes. I don't want to risk depriving you, this evening, of your preferred dancing-partner, so I'll take your page for a cavalier. Folle-Avoine, give me your arm."

"She knows my page's name," Berthe said to herself, in a whisper.

The thousand princes were jealous of the page, and, instead of competing for the hand of Berthe in order to dance the minuet, they watched the duchesse smiling at Folle-Avoine.

The baron gook Berthe into the embrasure of a window and said to her: "Berthe, those princes are getting so thin that I feel sorry for them, and furthermore, your dances are preventing me from sleeping and your concerts are aggravating my dogs. So, you're going to introduce me immediately to the one you've chosen, and Madame la Duchesse will sign the contract."

"Father...!" stammered Berthe.

"That's enough!" cried the baron. He advanced into the middle of the room and said: "Messieurs and noble friends, my daughter finds you all equally charming, and I'm forced to choose for her. Tomorrow we'll hunt a red deer stag, and whoever brings me the animal's foot will be my son-in-law. I have spoken."

When the baron had said "I have spoken," there could be no further argument.

Folle-Avoine tottered.

"You're a good hunter," the blonde-haired woman murmured in his ear.

"But I'm not a prince."

"What does it matter?" And, addressing Hugues: "Messire, I shall follow the hunt tomorrow."

The baron's face was resplendent. His nose was also resplendent, but his suntanned cheeks were only resplendent under the shock of a violent emotion, and he asked for permission to go and make everything ready for the next day.

"You are at home, Madame, command" he said, bowing.

"Well, then, I believe that we should go and repose."

XIII

Folle-Avoine sat outside Berthe's door and began to sing songs so sad that a yellow parrot that was more than a hundred years old went blind by dint of weeping, but Berthe did not shout through the door "Adieu, Folle-Avoine," as she had before the arrival of the princes, and Folle-Avoine began to weep with the parrot. He wept for a long time, but then suddenly stood up, saying: "The undine has promised to help me."

He went downstairs stealthily and went into the stable where his pony was asleep. He woke him up gently. He held his furry head between his hands and said to him: "My lovely Corbeau, I'm going to give you an armful of Lucerne and two measures of oats. You're going to eat well, in order to be as light as a roe deer tomorrow and as nimble as a cat. If I can force the stag, I'll marry Berthe."

The pony whinnied, and as the two griffons licked the page's hand, Folle-Avoine lay down on the litter and said to them: "Mouflet and Mouflette, you'll need to be very obedient and very reasonable tomorrow, and not amuse yourselves with the other dogs; if we force the stag, I'll marry Berthe."

The two griffons looked up at the page with their big golden eyes, wagging their tails and bounding in the stall in order to talk about all that to the pony. The pony lowered his ears because they were scattering his Lucerne, but he did not bite them because they were his best friends.

Folle-Avoine embraced all three of them and went back upstairs as he had come down.

While Folle-Avoine was weeping with the parrot and talking to his friends the thousand princes were saying to one another under their silken tents: "What if we were able to please the duc's daughter?"

"They only looked at her," sighed Berthe, sitting on her bed. "She loves Folle-Avoine, that duchesse... Good night, Folle-Avoine!"

Folle-Avoine did not reply. Berthe woke up old Margot, who was already snoring, and told her to go and see who was weeping on the landing. Old Margot got up, took the night-light, and returned to say: "It's the yellow parrot."

"Why isn't Folle-Avoine consoling it?"

"Your Folle-Avoine is too big to be your page; instead of sleeping on the straw mattress, as he ought to be, he's probably drinking with the men-at-arms.

Berthe uttered a sigh that Margot did not hear, because she was deaf.

XIV

The next day, when everyone had mounted up, Hugues said:

"I've promised to give my daughter to whoever brings me he stag's foot, but I've promised to chose among the thousand princes, so let them follow me."

"I'll go too, then," said Folle-Avoine, "Because if I force the animal..."

"Word of honor, he's superb!" exclaimed Hugues. "He has a horse the size of a dog and two dogs as big as hares, and he wants...oh, he's planning some trick. I played plenty when I was a page. Stay, my lad, stay; if you bring me the stag's foot, by the devil's horns, you'll be my son-in-law, but if you bring me the foot I'll drown all my dogs. I have spoken."

138

They set forth. The duchess spoke in a low voice to Folle-Avoine; the thousand princes looked at the duchesse, and Messire Jean, who as a man of good sense, said to the baron: "Monseigneur, I believe those princes like your château better than your daughter."

"You think so? Well, personally, I'm sure of it, and I'd like Folle-Avoine to bring me the foot... Without seeming to do anything, Messire Jean. give him my horse, which follows deer like a bloodhound."

Folle-Avoine, preceded by Mouflet and Moufiette, set off at a gallop.

I won't describe the hunt to you, but I'll tell you in a few words that the beautiful duchess was only able, so she said, to move at a walk, and the thousand princes did not want to leave her alone.

The thousand princes were not as culpable as you might believe; she had said to them, with such sweet smiles: "Messieurs, I don't want to hinder anyone; I have the habit of hunting alone. In my father's court people aren't as gallant as you are."

Folle-Avoine forced the stag, and when he took the foot to the baron, the baron said: "I'll drown all my dogs."

"Never!" cried Messire Jean.

"I shall drown all my dogs because I only have one word, and I'm giving Berthe, my only daughter, to the page Folle-Avoine. Come and embrace me, my son-in-law."

Since the halloo, the duchesse had let her horse gallop, and had soon left the stupefied princes behind.

"Monseigneur," said Folle-Avoine, don't drown your beautiful dogs; "I'm too petty to marry Mademoiselle Berthe."

He whistled to his griffons and departed at a gallop in the direction of the royal forest. Berthe fell in a faint.

The duchesse leapt to the ground; blood was flowing from Berthe's forehead, but the wound was slight.

When his daughter opened her eyes again, Hugues turned to Messire Jean and said: "Have you ever understood anything about women?"

"No, Monseigneur."

"He loves you," the duchesse murmured in Berthe's ear.

"He doesn't love me any longer, and it's my fault," sobbed Berthe.

The thousand princes arrived, out of breath.

"Handsome princes," said Hugues, "return to your families, and never marry, for fear of having daughters."

"Monsieur le Baron," the duchesse interjected, "my father the duc is expecting you his evening with all these messieurs." And, leaning toward Berthe: "He wants to give you a surprise, and I want to console you."

Berthe, the baron and the duchesse followed the duchesse into the royal forest. Messire Jean took the dogs back to the château.

During the journey, Hugues muttered into his gray beard: "When I married, one didn't search for so long. I was introduced to my cousin Odette on Sunday, the notary came on Monday, the curé on Tuesday, I got drunk with my cousin on Wednesday, I hunted foxes on Thursday and on Friday it seemed to me that I had known Lady Odette for twenty years. I'm too feeble!"

Berthe wept, and the thousand princes, who were all thin, trotted in the English fashion order not to trot otherwise.[40]

Messire Jean, who was taking the dogs back to the château, swore like a Saracen when he went past a pond; he knew that Hugues only had one word, and he could already see the fine basset hounds and the huge bloodhounds being thrown into the moat with stones around their necks.

XV

Folle-Avoine traversed the royal forest and saw a fortress, on the keep of which the ducal banner was floating.

---

[40] The so-called English trot involves the diagonal pairs of legs moving together.

Poor Folle-Avoine had a very heavy heart; he thought about a story that Old Margot had told him. In that story it was said that undines were wicked fays who drowned their lovers.

"If I were her lover she would drown me," he said, " and it would be over; but I'm not in love with her; only the baron's beautiful dogs will be drowned and I…what am I going to do in that great castle she comes? I won't find anything there but sprites and fays."

Folle-Avoine, as you have been able to see from this story, had tears a little too close to his eyes, which is a fault in a page; but he was as brave as a sparrow and he passed under the heavy portcullis without hesitation.

A quarter of an hour later, the duchesse arrived.

Then something happened that astonished everyone. The old duc was waiting for his guests in the main courtyard, and he took them into an immense hall, the walls of which disappeared under panoplies, and where long banners hung down from the vault. At the back of the hall there was a platform, and on that platform were two blazoned armchairs.

The duc pointed to the platform, had Hugues sit down beside him, and said to him: "My dear Baron, your daughter is charming; would you like her to be my daughter-in-law?"

"That's all I need!" cried the baron.

"That request astonishes you?"

"It breaks my heart, my suzerain, it breaks my heart., for I only have one word, and I've promised my daughter to my page Folle-Avoine."

"Oh, Father," sobbed Berthe, "don't forget what you've sworn."

"Wipe your eyes and shut up. I've been feeble, but I'm no longer feeble, and I don't like girls who, after having made a thousand princes thin, weep like a willow because a page they care as little about as…as *that!* doesn't find them as beautiful as the moon and as tasty as a galette!"

Berthe hid behind the duchesse. The thousand princes, who would have been very glad to sit down, struck dignified poses, and the duc said to the master of ceremonies: "Introduce my son!"

The something happened that astonished the audience even more; Folle-Avoine was the duc's son. He threw himself down at Berthe's feet, and the baron, suffocating, blessed them.

XVI

Would you like me to explain how Folle-Avoine came to be the duc's son, and how it came about that Blancherose, his sister, was walking in the moonlight on the causeway through the ponds?

That must seem very strange to you.

It's quite simple. In those days, ducs thought that spoiled children became ridiculous adults, and as a duc's son is always spoiled at his father's court, they sent their sons to grow up among their vassals.

The old duc had been even more prudent than his contemporaries, on the day when his son as weaned he had laid him down on the edge of an oat-field in the baron's passage. He knew that the baron as charitable and he had said to himself: "My son will be well brought-up at the Château de Beaucresson, and as he won't be brought up to be a duc he'll probably make a good duc." Only Blancherose, who was five years older than Folle-Avoine, knew the secret, and she only went along the causeway of the pond to see whether her brother had the instincts and sentiments of a true gentleman.

The wedding was magnificent. Blancherose married one of the princes, and the baron, who didn't want to drown his dogs, went to Rome in order to be liberated from his oath.

Folle-Avoine and Berthe accompanied him, and since that time young couples have acquired the habit of going to spend their honeymoon in Italy.

FUSAINS

One evening, I was sitting at the foot of a tree and I began to weep—perhaps it was yesterday, perhaps ten years ago. I was weeping because she had said, as she raised her soft eyes toward me: "I'm suffering, soothe me. I'm afraid, reassure me." Being ignorant, I had not been able to soothe her; not believing in anything, I had not been able to reassure her,

That is why, one autumn evening. I was weeping under a poplar.

At sunset, a bitter north wind blew and the gilded leaves swirled. They fluttered like butterflies, and then fell into the water of the pond. The leafless branches sang.

"If I were a poplar," sighed my soul, "I would sing while my summer leaves fell."

Then a voice in the branches said: "In autumn, the poplars sing because they know that the earth is only a landing on the luminous stairway."

I wiped away my tears and I ran to repeat to my beloved what I had heard. Smiling, she held out her soft eyes to my lips.

Now my beloved is no longer trembling. Every morning, she picks the pale flowers of my nights, and when she has woven a bridal crown with them, she will say to the autumn wind: "Carry our souls away to the land where the spring is eternal."

A. de. L'.
18 September 1867

I

"Beautiful angel Gabriel, you who dictated the holy book to the prophet, what is it necessary to do to be a poet?"

"It's necessary to write what one says between two kisses and what one dreams between two rendezvous."

"What I say between two kisses reddens the lips of my mistress; what I dream between two rendezvous burns my blood like thirst; but the verses that I write writhe duly like a crushed snake. Beautiful angel with green wings, beautiful peacock of paradise, my verses are like rocks of salt after sunset."

"Have you wept upon the paper that your pen blackens?"

"No; my friend is a cool spring."

"Lean over the spring, drink long draughts, and do not think any longer. Verses are only the wings of desires and the shrouds of regrets."

"Adieu, beautiful angel with feet the color of the dawn; my mistress is a lemon tree on which, next to ripe fruits, perfumed flowers open."

II

I have bathed my eyes in the cool spring and I can now see further than a falcon. I have put a pink bud in my heart, a bud of the lemon tree, and my heart now illuminates my thought like a fire of aloes.

"*Ah! ah! ou! Ah! ah! ou!*" Make your stirrups ring, son of the Prophet.

I want peoples to kneel before me from sunset to dawn, and when, standing alone, I feel the earth tremble beneath my heel, I shall go to kneel down before the woman I love place her foot on my neck. "*Ah! ah! ou! Ah! ah! ou!*" Shake your silvery mane, son of the wind.

III

She has kissed my bloody hands...

If I knew how to sculpt those phrases that sound to the ear like the gallop of a horse, which slip between the teeth like the seeds of a pomegranate, and which go to the heart like a saber, I would write, my beloved, a poem about your eyelashes, a poem about your hair. If I were a poet, I would explain why your eyes are two stars fallen from the heavens of which one dreams, why your lips are two leaves from the tree of forgetfulness, and why your breasts are two waves of the sea where coral shines.

She has kissed my bloody hands...

If I could give verses the flavor of your kisses I would knead them slowly, and while my pen glided tremulously, a bee would pose on my finger and a nightingale would build its nest in my hand.

IV

I have not been able to put a saddle on my thought; it bounds like a wild sheep from the sand to the rocks. I have not been able to put a golden rein on my tongue; it only knows how to cry "Charge!" when the rifles are lowered, and to roar like a lioness when I think of you at night. But I know how to cut off heads. Don't be jealous, my beloved, of the poet's mistress; tomorrow she will only have a sonnet for a mirror, but you will have for a cushion the head that dared to sing of a beauty other than yours.

V

"Cavalier, tell me about your last combat; I shall write your story in immortal verses."

"Poet, my beloved wants your head, and I've come to cut it off."

"I've never seen a man who knows how to love; I thought that love was dead on earth. Let me look at you, man who still knows how to love."

"My beloved is waiting."

"Don't make her wait..."

VI

His verses shaded the waterless roads, they put fevers to sleep. I sang them when I was cheerful, I sang them when I was sad, I threw them like a challenge, I sighed them in my friend's white arms.

I killed him without regret.

VII

"Friend, here's the head of the poet.

"Where did you cut it off?"

"On Meyrin's knees."[41]

"Blue lips, you shall not sing the beauty of Meyrin again; the saber has broken the flute, the world is as mute as a tomb... Blue lips, you will no longer kiss Meyrin's lips; the saber has crushed the bee, life is as bitter as a laurel leaf... Blue lips, I loved you when you were pink, and I told lies for twenty nights in order that my soul could touch you as it went away."

---

[41] Presumably not the same Meyrin who is described in *Haïcks et burnooses* as "the most beautiful daughter of the Sahara" and is seduced by Eblis, but probably the same one whose name was used as a title for the section of *Fusains* that was revised for separate publication in *Les Amoureuses*, where it substitutes for "Messaouda," and who also features in *La Chanson de l'alouette* (1880) as a sphinx symbolic of Sensuality.

VIII

I've killed him...

Now I am like a wild tulip; my cheeks have the color of fire, my heart is as black as an extinct ember...

Throw me, Gabriel a feather from your wing; verses are the shrouds of regrets.

IX

"For you I have torn out a feather from my wing, and you're not writing?

"My dolor burns the parchment. It's too vast to hold on a copper blade. It's so heavy that it would bury itself under the sand."

"Tell your companions to dig a grave, and while they're digging, engrave our verses on a stone slab."

"And when I've engraved my verses on the slab?"

"Lie down in the grave, and the slab will be your tombstone."

Here one can dream at one's ease, there is nothing but ruins; Julius Caesar is no more and Cherchell is not yet.[42]

To hide my dreams I have chosen a white house outside the walls, whose door is reinforced with iron.

It was a family dinner—the return of the prodigal son was being celebrated. Old aunts were whispering in the ears of their aged neighbors: "As a child he was wild and idle," and old uncles were whispering in their neighbors' ears: "He kept bad company, artists and actresses. He's a man without principles." The old aunts sighed: "It's unfortunate, very unfortu-

---

[42] The town of Cherchell on Algeria's coast, to which reference is made in *Haïcks et burnooses* as well as elsewhere in the present collage, was known as Caesarea in the days when it was a Roman colony.

nate!" Little female cousins, white and pink, with their noses over their plates, said: "His waistcoat isn't fashionable."

Louise, her fingers plunged in her hair, was gazing at the mountain through the open window.

The old aunts do not like Louise; the little female cousins detest her; the old uncles embrace her gladly, and all the little male cousins adore her, because her lips shone like holly berries after the frost.

The little male cousins are great hunters of skylarks; in soft boots they mount maternal carriage-horses; they tease chambermaids on the staircases and shepherdesses in the thickets; they go to mass and know how to lead a cotillion as gallantly as the deputy magistrate. They would not want to marry Louise—she has no fortune—but she is their cousin and they hope, one evening or another, to kiss her between two doors.

At dessert, an old aunt who made verses under the Directoire asks the prodigal child for a camel-driver's song. At a sign from their mothers, the little female cousins leave, and the prodigal child says:

"Near the gulf where the stars sow sparks while curling their hair, a bronze palace is flamboyant. It's the palace of Saba, the eternal city that men no longer see, the palace of the queen who speaks as a prophet and sings like a bird.

"In the palace of Saba, Solomon himself built a room without windows, the iridescent vault of which is sustained by a thousand silver palm, trees. It is the chamber of the queen with lips as soft as a dream, a brow as high as a poem and eyes as clear as a pool.

"In the room without windows a swallow with broad wings soars beneath the iridescent dome; a panther with thin flanks watched it fly, and Solomon, the poet king, who only likes flowers in sheaves and pearls in necklaces, has been

148

spelling out the same word for three thousand years without wearying.

"When the swallow opens its wings, the waves sing in the round gulf, and when the panther roars, kisses sing on lips in Saba, the eternal city that men no longer enter, Saba, the city sought by those whose lips are dry and those who kisses are fiery."[43]

The prodigal child suits down again; Louise smiles at him through the branches of the jasmine that frames the window...

If my door were not reinforced with iron, the Evil One would come to steal that memory from me.

The three bedrooms in my house open under a gallery sustained by twisted columns. A hand with six fingers, a talisman against spells, is sculpted at the points of the swollen ogives, and in my whitewashed rooms, a thin garland of pale red runs beneath the joists.

I can dream at ease; to perfume my dreams, the enameller has strewn blue roses on the walls of my gallery; in order to bear them away he has painted blue ships on the walls of my stairway

All the roses are in bloom; all the ships have their sails aloft.

If I found in my path the woman of whom I dream, I would love her all my life. I might even love her for longer, for I am beginning to believe that death is only a night's sleep.

Probably, the woman of whom I dream does not exist. She is neither blonde not brunette—brunettes do not know how to say "I love you" and blondes say it too often and do

---

[43] This "song" is recapitulated in *Les Amoureuses*, where it is incorporated into the prose-poem "Balkis," translated in the companion volume to the present one.

not prove it enough—she has copper-colored hair, pale cheeks, red lips and dark eyes. Her shoulders are broad and her feet are small, her waist is slender and her arms are strong. She has learned nothing but she knows everything; she has seen nothing but has divined everything...perhaps Louise resembles the woman I shall love....

Bear away my dreams, blue ships.

My garden extends from the stream escaping from the aqueduct to the crest of the white cliff whose vertical flanks bear a few lentisk bushes and clumps of furze. It is planted with orange trees and pomegranates

When the nightingale sings in the pomegranates, when a fine vapor floats like a veil over the broken aqueduct, when the stars speckle the sleeping haven, I see the one that I would love if she were a woman passing between heaven and earth. Her long hair is undone, her eyes are looking upwards and her fingers are drawing vague chords from a ebony harp...

Blue roses, perfume my dreams.

Pietro is a tall, thin old man with prominent cheekbones, a straight and slender nose, and thick eyebrows falling over blue-gray eyes. He is the owner of a boat with a triangular sail, and I go fishing with him when my dreams are higher than the twisted columns of my gallery.

Yesterday the night was warm, the sky the color of corn-flowers, the sea the color of amethyst. When the moon rose the waves were tinted green, the silvery foam turned blue, the haven came to resemble a meadow traversed by a sinuous stream bordered by forget-me-nots, and the one I would love if she were a woman appeared to me. She was walking alongside the stream, picking the flower of memory while gazing at me. She smiled as Louise smiled....

Blue ships, carry away by dreams; Louis will love one of the little cousins.

It is said that under the tents there are virgins with eyes like gazelles. I shall know tomorrow; we are departing for the south.

A man is traversing the plain with a flowery branch in his hand. He kneels down under a solitary palm tree and he sings: "Son of the sun, make your bark supple, do not lacerate my knees; I have come to the forest where the date-palms speak to the embalmed flowers. The most beautiful one said to me: "My sister is too far away, take her my kisses if the angel of the desert has forgotten her."

A man is at the top of the date-palm and he is singing, while waving a palm that the rising sun gilds: "Allah! Allah! In your name I am sowing; your angel is fatigued. "Allah! Allah! In your name I am sowing; ripen what I have sown."

The man has thrown away the palm. He turns to the Orient with his hand on his brow and he cries in a loud voice: "Allah is the greatest! Allah is the master! He makes the dates and the barley of the desert grow,"

This evening when the moon sets, be out here near the ruins. Amour smiles on the brave who are discreet.

"Woman, who sent you?"

"Ask this bouquet."

"A branch of myrtle?"

"Amour."

"A leaf of hemp?"

"Intoxication,"

"A sprig of cypress?"

"Death."

"Woman, is the sprig of cypress for the virgin or for me?"

"Adieu, handsome cavalier."

"When the moon sets, I shall be near the ruins."

"Why are you trembling? Your fingers are rosier than the foam on a silver-plated bit; your waist is more supple than a reed on a lake. Lift your veil; your eyes are shining like flyssas... Your haïck is lifting; don't hide the turtle-doves with satiny wings..."

"Their wings are red..."

"Why are you trembling? Sit down; the sand is fine."

"If you did not love me..."

Next to the leaf of hemp there was a sprig of cypress..."

She is as beautiful as an oasis in the midst of the sand, she is as tender as shade in the middle of the day...

Never unveil your lover in front of your brother; the breasts of a woman charm like the gaze of a snake and the flame of her eyes withers the flower that has only two roots, the red flower of amity.

Never unveil your lover in front of your brother; the heart of a woman is like a dune, a breath of wind effaces the trace of footprints there.

The branch of cypress was not for me, but let the other beware!

What would our painters say if they could see what I see? In the desert, everything is gray and there are no long shadows.

The desert wind is blowing.

I have my horse saddled and I depart, hoping to find a little air on the hills that separate the plain of Angades from the Sahara.

The night was black, but the crests of the mountains shone with a phosphorescent gleam. I went into a stony defile. My horse only advanced regretfully; as soon as I let the bridle loosen he extended his neck, sniffed the air noisily and made a half-turn.

At sunrise I stopped on a plateau formed of large slabs of rock. Below me, the great desert was full of a red vapor that billowed like the sea. My horse trembled.

I do not know how long I had been gazing at those waves of light and sand when I perceived that they were beating the ridge of the plateau. Gripped by an unspeakable terror, I tried to flee. But they passed over my head and I fell heavily, hitting my forehead on the edge of a rock.

When I opened my eyes again I saw my horse lying by a green-tinted pool in which palm trees were mirrored.

I stood up; hot dust blinded me.

I sat down again, half-suffocated, and I saw a palace of emeralds with a porch of diamonds. An impetuous river plunged beneath the porch and cascades of sapphire sprang from windows that opened blackly.

I turned round and I saw the points of our tents down below.

Thunder growled duly, a rain of sand fell, my horse whinnied and I no longer saw anything but the stony plain over which red dots were running. The spahis were searching for me.

Salut, nest of vultures! Salut, nest of doves! Salut, city where storks dream on the minarets! Salut, city where the balancelles. Like weary gulls, furl their silvery wings! Salut, queen of the waves! Salut, queen of the sand! Salut, Algiers!

While climbing the Kasbah I love to stop outside the shops that perforate the bulging walls.[44]

---

[44] This passage is modified from "Fragments du journal d'un officier," which was serialized in the *Journal des demoiselles*; the original version appeared in the November 1863 issue, from a diary entry dated December 1857. It is conceivable that some of the following passages are extracted from the same

There pumice stone shines beside a display of pome-granates and orange; here a potter traces capricious designs in white chalks on a brown clay stove. At intervals, the hammers of fabricators of babouches resonate and the turntables that launch chips of blonde horn purr.

At the top, near the old walls, one finds embroiderers, smiths, silk-weavers and carpenters making shelf-units with gaudy flowers.

All are working cheerfully. A caouedji is running, brandishing a lighted coal at the end of brass forces. A merchant of angelica is rotating a plank on the palm of his hand garnished with white and pink pastes, and a woman wrapped in her blue loincloth is offering strollers little loaves sprinkled with anise and saffron.

Pescade Point is a jagged cape about three hundred meters long, strangled in the middle and expanded in the form of a trefoil at its extremity. Two islets polished by the waves show their white heads at its feet.

The sea is deep at Pescade Point, and dull bands like great rivers run over its green waters. The Turks built three batteries on the cape, now dismantled. I often go there in the evening, in the company of my dog, to smoke on a large bronze canon with a sculpted breech....

More fortunate than many others, you are not frayed by cables and crumpled by wheels. I would like to fall and sleep like you, old cannon of Pescade Point.

The polygon is near Hussein-Dey in the dunes of Harrach. If one climbs one of them in the morning, one can see something that one does not forget.

The dark blue bay is strewn with flecks of foam; thick mists hide Algiers; the Emperor's fort is black; the peaks of the Djurdjura are azure-tinted.

---

journal, but were considered unsuitable for inclusion in the *Journal des demoiselles*.

In the east, where the sea touches the sky, a luminous band extends. It catches fire without broadening, and three orange rays spring from it. One stripes the sky with a broad crimson furrow; the other two, dancing on the waves, give a golden hue to the sails of balancelles and the rocks of Saint-Eugène.

Suddenly, the sun launches forth and inundates the white mistress of the Mediterranean with light.

She is as beautiful as a moonless night, as the water of a cistern hollowed out in granite. Her lips have the color of blood, her large dark-ringed eyes shine like nails on a velvet saddle. She is a dancer in the theater.

One morning when she had supped at Les Platanes with a sheep-trader and a councilor of the Prefecture, she was on a balcony, with a glass in her hand. I stood up in my stirrups and she held out her glass to me. The Prefecture councilor having remarked to me that he had drunk from the glass, I threw the champagne over his head.

An hour later we drew swords and I received a solid thrust under the third rib.

The councilor is a charming fellow. Léonie is adorable.

She's adorable; she isn't a woman but a thoroughbred animal, a supple lioness, very graceful and very wicked. As soon as her dainty paws touch you, you feel her claws... I can hear her coming up...how gaily her little heels ring!

"Bonjour, chérie. You're very late today; why?"

"Bonjour, Monsieur."

"Why, instead of curling up on that sofa, don't you come to kiss me?"

"I'm thinking about the eyes you rolled when the worthy Edmond said to you: 'Monsieur, I've drunk from that glass.' Oh, one can't only drink from new glasses. You'd die of thirst, friend."

I told you that she had pretty little claws.

"I love you."

"That's not true. You love a beautiful phantom, as brilliant as a flame, as perfumed as a flower. You're a poet."

"Madwoman!"

"Shut up. We understand poets. We also love handsome phantoms who traverse our dreams with flashing eyes, saber in hand. I thought I was dreaming when I saw you outside Les Platanes. Your horse was white with foam, your saber was ringing. Do you remember? The sun was bright, and yet I thought I was dreaming."

"You're more beautiful than my most beautiful dream."

"You don't know me. Twelve years ago I was an ugly child and I held out my hand, My mother beat me, my brothers beat me. They didn't know who my father was. When I was fifteen, my mother wanted to sell me and I ran away. A young man found me beautiful, he gave me jewels and masters, and I took his best friend for a lover. They fought, and I don't know which of them killed the other,

"If you love me a little, throw me out..."

She has left with the sheep-trader.

If I weren't afraid of making a fool of myself, I'd weep. Damn it, too bad, I want to weep and I'll weep.

Sémon, go to the Moorish café and bring me some *kif*.

I

"You're cold? Are you cold in the head or cold in the heart?"

"I'm cold in the head and the heart."

"Come with us this evening."

" Charles will tell me that he loves a Venus, Jacques will tell me that he loves a warbler, Léon will tell me that he loves a dead woman, Armand will tell me that he loves Cleopatra, Pierre will tell me that he loves them all, you'll tell me that you don't love anyone, and I'll say: 'I'm cold.' But I'll come this evening."

II

"When have you brought us? Those Argand lamps are smoky, those tables are greasy, these glasses are dirty, those woman are frightful, those men are ignoble and that orchestra is out of tune..."

"Patience, patience! We weren't expected so soon. In an hour they'll extinguish the Argand lamps, wipe the tables, rinse the glasses, send away these women, chase away these men and change the orchestra."

"Where are we, then?"

"At the ball the *Unknown Woman* holds for those who have a head where others have a heart. Waiter! Seven glasses of absinthe."

"I'm not thirsty."

"Louis, man is an animal who drinks without being thirsty. Waiter, leave that bottle and bring another. There are seven of us."

III

"You see, Léon, the soul is in the line...in the contour...in..."

"The soul is in everything, because..."

"Drink, all of you, and shut up; the stage isn't lit yet. Shut up; when the time comes I'll rap three times. You're putting in too much water Louis."

"This absinthe is bitter."

"Because you're putting too much water in. Waiter, change Monsieur's glass. My beautiful child, we're not drunk yet, leave us alone."

IV

The stage is lit, the curtain rises, the play commences!

Listen and watch. The *Unknown Woman*, before making you dance, likes to make you laugh. The eternal comedy is about to be played before you of those who have a head where others have a heart. Approach, charmers. Waiter, another bottle, cigars and glasses.

In all good plays there's a chorus, you know. *Vox Populi*. As there aren't any people, I'll be the chorus. Blondinette, my angel, leave Monsieur alone, he isn't playing; he'll compose our public. Pay attention, the rest of you! Open all the drawers where you keep your virtues and your vices. I'm the chorus and I'll begin with an invocation of the great goddess:

Virgin with emerald eyes, virgin with perfumed lips, cradle us in the folds of your opal mantle, clasp us in your wiry arms. We only love you and we won't believe in immortality any more if you break our glasses.

JULIE

When my glass is half empty I see all men as handsome.

THE SCULPTOR

Give me your glass and I'll take a photograph.

JULIE

When my glass is full, I see all men as ugly. When it's half-empty I see them all as handsome. When it's empty, I can no longer see them.

PIERRE

And your glass is sometimes empty and sometimes full.

THE POET

Julie, you resemble Cleopatra.

JULIE

Why?

THE POET
Because Cleopatra was a brunette,

BLONDINETTE
What about me—don't I resemble anyone?

THE POET
You resemble Helen, because you're blonde.

THE SCULPTOR
That one's nice.

THE POET
Why do you say that one's nice, you who, like Prometheus, fashions with clay that is soft to the touch...

PIERRE
Charles, make pitchers, fine pitchers with broad bottoms, fill them with old wine and you'll have created a body and a soul. Make pitchers instead of making faces.

THÉRÈSE
Ha ha!

LOUIS
The gazelle is dead under the lemon tree. I had hidden her memory in the depths of my heart, and, to prevent life from tarnishing it, I had put a necklace of jasmine flowers around it; but the flowers, one by one, changed into a desert song, and with the last one, the memory flew away.

ALL
Bah!

LOUIS
Flew away!

ALL

Flew away!

LOUIS

And I don't love her any more

THE CHORUS

I love the daylight with pink hair
And the night with jet hair.
Blooming flowers,
And rosy lips
Never love.

THE MUSICIAN

I love the laments of the breeze,
I love the song of crickets.
I love the cries of the wind that breaks
Old walnut trees over the furrows.

LOUIS

I'm cold.

THE POET

I love the archangel with pink wings,
The strophe that marches with a long stride.
Blooming flowers,
And rosy lips
Can't fly.

LOUIS

I'm cold.

THE SCULPTOR

I love the nymph who arches her back
Torso bare, thyrsus in hand,
Broken stumps, amber necklaces
And cracks in the path.

LOUIS
I'd like to love a woman. That's why I'm cold.

THE CHORUS
Drink, friends, drink, and the angel of your dreams will emerge radiant from the mud. Drink, friends, drink!

Can you see him in the center of the crescent that the cavaliers in red mantles form behind him? Can you see his horse flying toward that hill of sand, above which crowns of blue smoke are trembling? Can you hear what Ahmed, the chaouch,[45] is singing while reloading his long rifle? Listen to Ahmed's song:

"A child, I was picked up on the sand in a bloody bur-noose; then I led caravans; now I'm a cavalier. I love to feel warm heads, like open pomegranates, bleeding on my bare thigh. I love to feel lips as cool as spring rain on my lips burned by the kisses of the desert."

Can you see the rifles lowering? Can you hear the horses screaming under the spurs? The bullets are buzzing like a swarm of bees... Can you hear what Ahmed is singing while staggering?
Listen to Ahmed's song:

"When I guarded the sheep, the stars spoke to me; when I guided the caravans the moon smiled at me; today my bride-to-be has dug me a soft bed of sand....

He falls smiling. Red death is a beautiful bride-to-be!

---

[45] In colonial Algeria, a *chaouch* was a servant, the term being borrowed from Turkish.

Bougie is built in a amphitheater on the Gouraya, the sterile flanks of which fall steeply into the sea.

She's a proud amazon who is allowing her armor to rust.

In the valley of the Oued-Sahel, an hour's march from Bougie, the route of the Beni-Mançour goes past a mill.

One evening in November, a horseman knocked on the door of that mill. It was raining in torrents, the Oued-Sahel was eating away the slope of the route. A kabyle looked through a judas-hole and, seeing the braid on the traveler's sleeve, opened up.

"Put my horse in the stable," said the officer, "and take me to the master."

"Sidi, there is no master," the kabyle replied, "there's only a mistress, who is sleeping now, but tomorrow, when you leave, will say to Kadour: "You've done well to give the kébir and his horse something to eat."

They headed for a large two-story building in which the mill-wheels were purring when a young woman came out of another building and said: "Monsieur, Madame will come down to receive you."

Kadour shivered. The officer, guided by the pretty soubrette, went into the smaller building.

The miller of the Oued-Sahel was twenty years old, with the hands of an aristocrat, hair like a Rubens undine and eyes like Leonardo da Vinci's virgins.

When she bid the officer welcome, the young man, dazzled, stammered.

"It's necessary t be imprudent, as you all are," she continued, "to travel in such weather along roads which are as yet only a dream of your engineers."

"I'm going to Bougie to fetch orders, and I bless the storm that has given me the right to knock on your door."

"You're wet. Light the fire, Pepita, then serve. You'll have a poor supper."

The next day, while the officer was saddling his horse—Kadour had disappeared—a curtain was agitated at the window of the smaller building. He smiled and departed at a gallop.

He was galloping under the aspens five hundred meters from the mill when a bullet whistled past his ear. "It's time to get reinforcements," he said. "Marauders are already beating the country."

That evening, the mill was nothing but a heap of ashes and Pepita was weeping over the cadaver of her mistress, whom Kadour had strangled.

The village of Beni Mansour is an agglomeration of huts made of plants and clay, inhabited by people who have come from everywhere—no one knows why—and who devote themselves to industries unknown elsewhere.

In our frontier posts, the colonists prefer to have vegetables come from Algiers than sow them at their door. Instead of bringing a spade they bring two or three barrels of vitriol and alcohol, which they baptize absinthe and eau-de-vie; they procure a dozen glasses, a few dusty bottles, and sell the liquor. If the garrison is numerous, they almost do well—one is always thirsty in Africa—but as soon as the troops leave they invite their neighbors, who invite them in their turn; the barrels are soon empty, and the fever arrives.

Winter is imminent, the wind is whipping our tents, erected at hazard on a sandy heath strewn with juniper bushes and clumps of twisted pines. The fog doesn't lift until midday, and every evening, a storm rumbles n the valley. The water of the Oued-Sahel flows viscous and dull.

It is no longer Africa with its intoxicating perfumes and its dazzling light; it's our county with its gray mists and its odor of fir trees; it's our Bourbonnais in melancholy and wild autumn.

I think about our amber-tinted woods, our long sinuous meadows that seem, in the morning, tranquil rivers dotted with green islets. I think about our somber ponds where wild ducks alight whistling, where dry reeds crackle in the wind. My isolation weighs upon me, an immense sadness envelops me and numbs me.

My pipe is no longer good; I'm homesick.

I'm homesick, but for what country? Perhaps the one where one finds oneself again, where I'll find the woman who smiled at me in the morning, and whom I saw dead in the evening...

The tents fall, the mules are laden, the soldiers are cheerfully buckling their knapsacks. Today we're traversing the snowy mountains, and tomorrow we'll be in the land of palm trees.

On the horizon, the sky, like a steel dome, leans upon the uniform, dry, bare plain. The sun is setting. To the south, a large cloud of dust is flowing; to the north, thin columns of smoke are rising. The east is blue-tinted, the west violet; the sun is red.

Tents are erected, white behind the fires. A trumpeter hurls three shrill notes at a gallop. Black dots group together forming a battalion. The cloud running southwards is duplicated. The sky is blue-tinted. The sand is silvery.

The wind brings a vague rumor. Spahis pass by, rifles across their saddles and burnooses lifted, heads over the necks of their horses, and are lost in the shadow rising slowly from the horizon to the zenith. The rumor grows, companied by a dull rumble. The battalion stops in front of the tents. A star lights up and a spark flies from the tip of a lance from which a blue pennant is floating. It's the general. Behind him, large flags flutter.

The rumor grows; camels can be heard bellowing, sheep bleating, horses whinnying, women screeching, children wailing. Gunshots crackle here and there in the darkness. The flames of fires writhe redly.

The spahis of the escort empty sacks full of heads. A confused mass appears. The soldiers run forward and come back with sheep, which they butcher as they march.

The clarions sound the appeal, and a great silence falls.

Scarps of flesh are grilling over the embers. Butter is running from slashed gourds. Soldiers lying on carpets are playing with jewels; others are breaking sheep's heads with saber-cuts and throwing the tongues into mess-tins; others are rubbing their feet with grease.

Naked children emerge from the confused mass, slip between the sentinels, drink from a water-bottle and flee.

Groups of officers form and talk about the raid.

The fires are extinguished. The camp is asleep.

The moon shines, and the confused mass brightens. Here, camels sway their necks anxiously. There, sheep are heaped together. Here, unkempt women are huddling. There, in a circle of spahis, crouching men with hoods pushed back are gazing at severed heads whose lips are creased.

A turco on sentry duty is playing a flute.

In the oasis, at sunset, people gather under the orange trees. The old men think while telling their chaplets, the women dance, the men smoke and watch. If one moves aside slightly, one can see white forms seeking one another between the palm trees.

Fortunate are those who meet under the palm trees of Beni-Mezab!

I

West of the bay of Algiers, near Pescade Point, in a white house lived—the year is quite irrelevant—a ravishing child who was beginning to be a woman.[46]

I won't make you a portrait of that child, because if she were brunette and if, by chance, you prefer blondes, or vice versa, you wouldn't listen to me any longer. I'll simply tell you: Hélène was lying on a sofa when Dorothée announced Capitaine Jacques.

Capitaine Jacques was the intimate friend of my heroine, who, for the convenience of the story, I shall call Hélène, because that wasn't her name.

"Capitaine, I thought you were dead," said Hélène.

"Mademoiselle, I have been resuscitated in order to tell you a story."

"A story of the other world?"

"Yes."

"If the story is nice, I'll forgive you."

"For being resuscitated? Thanks."

"I'm listening."

"Do you known Auxonne, the great green frog that watches the Saône flow, amorously?"

"No."

"Well, I know Auxonne; I'd describe it to you if I didn't have to tell you about Monsieur Jean Philibert, who spent his days fishing and his evenings in the intimate company of a yellow parrot. That parrot came from India, where it had been a Brahmin in the time of Solomon, in a pink pagoda on the bank of the Ganges.

"Dear Monsieur, of what malady did you die?"

---

[46] A revised, expanded and reconnected version of this episodic story appears in *Les Amoureuses* as "Hélène," where it is supplied with an ending conspicuously absent from the present version.

"A malady of the heart."

"Ah! Continue…"

"That Brahmin was condemned to three thousand years of existence for having told a young woman on the edge of a field of rice that her eyes were larger than those of Cita, the goddess with the golden eyes. That is why he spent his evenings in the intimate company of Jean Philibert, who was in love with a moonbeam."

"And was Jean Philibert's love reciprocated?"

"Inevitably."

"Inevitably?"

"Yes, inevitably.

"Hold on, you're too charming; loving a moonbeam! Men are stupid; they hurl themselves like cockchafers into the web of the spider of amour. They give a pat of the hand here, a head-butt there, and they change into a great greasy ball of that fine fabric as velvety as flame and as shiny as an evening in July, which it's necessary only to touch with one's heart and to look at with closed eyes. Whereas moonbeams…let's get back to the town of Auxonne.

"I'm there."

"Good."

"One night, Jean Philibert, his hand on the doorknob, looked at the bell-tower where the bells were ringing and he said to himself: *It's the twenty-fourth of December, the town's celebrating New Year's Eve*. He opened the door and the parrot screeched in its hoarse voice: 'Noël, Master Jean, Noël! Let's party like Monsieur le Maire and the officers of the garrison.'

"'With pleasure, old man, with pleasure,' replied Jean Philibert. I was thinking about that, but we won't amuse ourselves much.'

"'And the lotus flower who's with you? Be welcome, lotus flower, the Brahmin salutes you.'

"The parrot was addressing a woman whom Jean Philibert had not seen entering. That woman was the moon-

167

beam about whom he had been thinking while the cork on his fishing line was bobbling about between the nenuphars of the Saône. He was desolate, because his beard wasn't trimmed.

"The woman sat down beside the fire and, in order to warm her little feet better, she lifted her muslin skirt starred with gold a little higher above the ankle.

"Those little feet were charming; they resembled yours. I'll wager that if you put on a muslin skirt starred with gold the yellow parrot would have said, on seeing you: 'Be welcome, lotus flower.'"

"You think so?"

"I'm certain of it. Jean Philibert, who had only contemplated such dainty ankles in a moonbeam, fell into an armchair, suffocated, and the yellow parrot hastened to say: 'Star of the Orient, your ankle is finer than that of Cita,[47] the goddess with the amber feet. If my master had shaved, he'd already have told you so.'

"Jean Philibert, trying to understand but not understanding how a moonbeam could be sitting down in front of his fire, fell asleep.

"Poor Jean Philibert! He woke up with a start, standing on one leg, in the body of the yellow parrot..."

"Permit me, Captain to ask how many glasses of absinthe you've had?"

"Two, but the second had gum."

"You should have put gum in the first; you are, I fear, a little..."

"No, Mademoiselle, I'm not drunk; but..."

"You're yellow and you have blue wing-tips?"

---

[47] In the later version of the story this name is rendered, as it usually is, Sita; she is a central character in the Hindu epic *Ramayana*.

"Perhaps. It's stifling in here. If you'd like to come with Dorothée to Pescade Point, I'll tell you the story of the lotus and the parrot."

II

Hélène's father was dead and the uncle who had brought her up was usually at sea…between Algiers and Rio de Janeiro. He was an eccentric. Under the pretext that he preferred eglantines to Bengal roses, he let his niece grow up without a gardener.

When Jacques made the acquaintance of Hélène she was as ignorant as a swallow. All day long she played on her sofa with her slipper, or watched butterflies fluttering over the lentisks. He brought her the great poets, and she understood them so well that perhaps he regretted having brought them.

Hélène was a ravishing child who was beginning to be a woman. She had admirable eyes, those admirable eyes that say nothing to the indifferent, those large hard eyes whose eyelids need to be blue-tinted,

Capitaine Jacques was neither young nor old, nether short nor tall, neither handsome nor ugly. When he was sad he chatted with Papillon, his black dog.

He was a little bit mad, but his madness wasn't dangerous, as you can see by this page taken at random from his memoirs:

Dormans, 1ˢᵗ August 186
At Dormans there is a little church, a church so pretty that men have daubed its nave yellow and the swallows have embroidered its hammered bay windows and its roses without stained glass with their nests.

The church is very pretty but I'm very sad. Julie no longer loves me. A portrait has told me so; a beautiful portrait of a brunette woman whose hands are smaller than her mouth and

her moth smaller than her eyes. That portrait is hanging on the wall of a bedroom above a chest of drawers in the home of my host, who is a carpenter.

When I entered I cried: "Sacré bleu, what a beautiful portrait." The portrait replied: "Julie no longer loves you." I had gone so pale that the carpenter asked me whether I was ill.

I wasn't ill, I was dead.

Yes, I remained dead for a second. In that second, my soul, in the form of two butterflies, one black and the other blue, flew into a star where the flowers were all the good I had done on this earth and elsewhere.

The two butterflies alighted on an eglantine bush whose branches were my amours. The bush was as large as an oak, but it only had a single rose. The blue butterfly hid in a rose and the black butterfly went back down alone to the room where the carpenter was looking at me, frightened. I asked him for a glass of water and while he was giving it to me the portrait said to me again: "Julie no longer loves you!"

It appears that the human soul is composed of two souls, one of which has blue wings and the other black wings, but when one is no longer loved, the blue butterfly rises up to the star where the rose of amour flowers, and the black butterfly flutters from your half-empty head to your completely empty heart.

I'm not half-dead; I'm completely dead; I was only living for her.

You can see from that page that Capitaine Jacques was one of those madmen who believe the soul to be immortal, one of those simpletons who seeks in amour something other than sensuality, one of those dangerous beings who gaze at death. But you can also see, by means of the beginning of that story, that he had forgotten Julie.

III

In the battery, Jacques told the story of the lotus and the parrot like this.

"The Ganges traverses a grassy plain sown with clumps of woodland where lianas float from the round heads of palm trees and the knotty boughs of gray fig trees.

"Since the time of Solomon, two tribes, one rich in cattle, the other rich in horses, had occupied that plain. They lived in peace, but no man from one of them ever sought out a woman from the other; the warriors were too proud of their strength, the Brahmins too proud of their science.

"The Brahmins had a pink pagoda on the left bank; on the right bank, the warriors had a porphyry palace.

"One morning, a young pastor who was searching for his cows in the reeds saw a young woman come down the porphyry stairway and go into the river. The waters of the Ganges are transparent; he forgot his cows.

"For a week, he dared not return to the bank of the river, but he composed a poem in twelve verses in which he compared the bather to a wild antelope, a magnolia the color of milk, and a drop of dew iridescent in the sunlight. When his russet cows lay down in the dark he declaimed his poem to them, and the verses were so sweet that the little cows, their eyes half-closed, followed the rhythm with their heads.

"On the eighth day, he slipped into the reeds, but instead of bathing, the young woman sat down under a tamarind.

"He went home sadly, and added a thirteenth verse to his poem, in which he asked the Ganges why the daughter of soldiers no longer came to refresh herself in its waves. In searching the verses one by one, he became jealous of the waves that pressed the torso the color of milk between their lips."

At this point, Hélène burst out laughing.

171

"Don't laugh," said the captain. "If I had been the herdsman I would have been as jealous as him...

"Do you know what there is in these waves that leaves the imprint of kisses in the sand? There's a great soul, and I'm jealous of what I sense to be stronger than me..."

"The next day, the herdsman traversed the river and hid behind the trunk of the tamarind.

"When the last star paled, the young woman came down the steps of the palace; she saw the herdsman and, instead of fleeing, came to sit down next to him...

"The tamarind was on the edge of a field of rice, and in the middle of the day the herdsman said; 'Your eyes are more beautiful than the eyes of Cita, the goddess with the golden eyes.

"'It's necessary to flee where no one will be able to overtake us.' the young woman replied, drawing him toward the river.

"In the middle of the current there was a clump of lotuses. The two young people, as beautiful as gods, swam toward it.

"When they reached it the waters of the Ganges seethed, and they disappeared."

"Did my story please you?"

"It's pretty."

"I forgot to tell you, in conclusion, that the soul of the herdsman passed into the body of a yellow parrot."

"And the soul of the young woman?"

"Into the body of a beautiful child."

"I thought it was in a blue lotus."

"Adieu, Mademoiselle."

The captain got to his feet and left, but Papillon, before following him, licked Hélène's hand. Dogs sometimes have more intelligence than their masters.

Hélène found a bouquet of bean-flowers on the window of her bedroom.

Flowers have souls, and they can speak. Each one only knows a single phrase, but in that phrase there is one of the Creator's ideas. Bean-flowers say, at sunset: "Open your hearts to love."

Hélène dared not listen to the bean-flowers, and as there was a wood opposite the white house in which a man and a dog could hide, she extinguished her lamp.

The bouquet had a strangely sweet perfume.

While braiding her hair, Hélène sighed: "Why did he tell me that story? Is it to tell me that he loves me? He could simply have told me."

Hélène was a ravishing child. She slapped her forehead and rang for Dorothée.

"Dorothée," she said to her, "have you ever loved anyone?"

"Me…? Never."

"Too bad. Well, go away."

"Asking me that…going to bed without a light, chatting for hours with a captain…"

The bouquet had a strangely sweet perfume.

Hélène nestled under her coverlet. As soon as her eyes closed, she dreamed. Sitting under a tamarind on the edge of a rice-field, she was listening to Jacques read her a poem. When the poem finished he took her in his arms and threw himself with her into the Ganges. Then she went into the bedroom in Auxonne, where Jacques was chatting with the yellow parrot, on a moonbeam. She smiled, the captain disappeared, and instead of the yellow parrot she saw a young man draped in a white robe. The young man resembled the captain; he said to her: "Hélène, you are as beautiful as you were in the porphyry palace; I am such as I was in the pink pagoda.

"When our bodies die, our soul does not; it goes…I don't know where, but it comes back from wherever it has gone.

"The divine spark that has once animated matter returns to animate it again, combined with a new spark. The new spark is brilliant, the old one is hidden in the ashes. If one blows on the ashes the ash flies away, and the two similar sparks shine with the same splendor.

"Hélène, I blew on the old spark on Christmas Eve, and I saw you. You were so beautiful that I blew on the ash of the old spark again, and the ash flew on to the new spark."

Hélène woke up and ran to the window. The bouquet, spangled by the dew, had a strangely sweet perfume. She detached a flower from it and was slipping it into her corsage when, astonished, she listened attentively. She no longer recognized the sound of the waves. As they reached the coast, the waves vibrated like the strings of a lyre; the great sea was singing a sublime symphony.

She waited for Jacques that evening, but he did not come. She waited for him all winter, and he did not come. By night, however, she often heard barking, which resembled Papillon's, and every week she found a bouquet on her window.

Jacques did not come because he knew that the flower of amour blooms n solitude.

V

Every day, Hélène became more beautiful. In spring, she resembled those fine and energetic profiles sculpted in agate by the artists of Syracuse. Her forehead had broadened, her eyes were open, the corners of her mouth were lightly elevated and her hair, full of sap, curled over the nape of her neck.

174

Oh, she was a woman, a true woman; within her there was the splendor of sunlight and the profundity of the night, the mildness of lakes and the implacable anger of the Ocean. She was not a woman such as the arrangers of words create—an ethereal being, half cloud, half light—she was a true woman with red lips and a large bosom.

True women are like true poets; they often fall, because they want to march too quickly; they often die alone because no one has been able to follow them.

In spring, Hélène's cheeks were pale.

VI

In spring, Hélène's cheeks were pale, and Jacques did not come back...

It is evident that Jacques came back, because if he had not come back, my story would only have a beginning and no end, which would be contrary to the simplest laws of esthetics. I could and I even ought to tell you what happened then, but that would bore me, and as my intention is to amuse you, I'm going to talk about something else.

What if I were to tell you a little about myself?

I was born in a château.

In that château a gray mare with stiff legs slept alone in a corner of the stable. The kennels served as a store for vine-stocks and chickens laid eggs on the cushions of carriages devoid of wheels. The cellars no longer had any doors, the cisterns had no stairways, the greenhouses no frames and the hay-lofts no floors, but I found in the attics old harness, old weapons, old garments and old robes. I dressed up as a cavalier, I dressed up as a monk; I disemboweled rickety armchairs with sword-thrusts and I delivered long sermons to blackened portraits that grimaced on the walls.

In that château foalfoot ate away the lawns, and brambles hung down from fissured terraces, but blackbirds whistled in the high hornbeam hedges and a stream sang gaily over the rots of walnut trees. I chased crickets in the grassy pathways, I wove wicker nests in the crowns of ash-trees, I fished for frogs in the green-tinted basins and, on moonlit nights, I went to look out for the princess with golden eyes on the bank of the canal.

One evening, while plucking a duck, Françoise the cook had told me the story of that princess. It's a very fine story, judge for yourselves.

The branches of the lindens say, on moonlit nights: "We've seen, in the meadow, two knights mounted on two horses. They fought one another from dusk to dawn."

"They're two damned phantoms,' say the hazel trees, 'two brothers that God had cursed because they killed one another for a princess whose black hair fell all the way to the ground, a hundred years ago."

"I've seen the princess,' say the chestnut trees, 'combing her hair on the grand canal. I've seen her weeping when the knights lowered their lances a hundred years ago. I've seen her combing her long black hair, and I've seen her weeping as ferns weep after the fog.

"A hundred years ago," says the old ash tree, "I saw an owl hide the golden eyes of the pale princess in its hole."

"Never, never," sigh the fir trees, "do the golden eyes sleep; the owl had taken them into the hollow of the walnut tree."

Fortunately, I have never seen the pale princess, because, if I had seen her, I would have fallen in love with her and she would have drowned me as she had, it's said, drowned my great-uncle, a Knight of Malta.

Being unable to love the pale princess, I loved my Aunt Thérèse, whose hair was blue-tinted in the sunlight and whose brown eyes were speckled with golden dots. My Aunt Thérèse didn't drown me; she taught me the Chanson de Roland and made me lose the habit of running around barefoot.

She's asleep now in the cemetery in the middle of the vineyards, and bindweed is growing over her tomb.

How my mistress would enrage me if I loved her as much as my aunt, but how I would like to be loved as I was then! When I came home, wet to the knees, my head full of spiders' webs and my hands dirty, I slipped into her room. She combed my hair, brushed my clothes, poured sweet-scented water over my hands, knotted my cravat, and then showed me beautiful engravings or sang me pieces by Mozart.

She was one of those people who gaze elsewhere.

Bindweed has grown over her tomb and my heart is hidden in a pink flower-head. That is why my mistress cannot damn me.

Don't repeat that to my mistress; she believes that I would die of fear if she frowned. Don't repeat that; in a spirit of contradiction she'd be capable of loving me, which would be very sad for her and very unfortunate for me.

When my aunt died, I became wild. Instead of roaming in the park, as before, I plunged into the forest of beeches, I wandered over ridges where the heather is flat, I crawled under brambles that grew over torrents. In winter, I went to the plateaux where the wind prevents the snow from accumulating.

When I was asked what I was doing up there I replied: "I'm not doing anything."

I wasn't doing anything, in fact; I walked at random, without thinking, eating myrtle-berries, picking bouquets, climbing a tree because it was tall, a rock because it was sheer.

In bed I reread the books that I had read to my aunt. I couldn't write, and I was very happy.

Friends of the family said: "He'll be a good peasant who loves hunting."

The friends of my family were sensible people, but I'm not a peasant and I don't like hunting. That's the fault of hazard.

One evening—I was seventeen years old—night surprised me under the fir trees. Gray lichens were floating like muslin curtains and the smooth trunks resembled columns of green marble. I was populating that mysterious palace—for the first time since Thérèse's death I took the trouble to think—when I saw at the foot of a rock. near a hut built of fragments of beech-wood, a man and two women, one old and the other young. The man was carving a shovel with a billhook, in order that it could be used to shift grain, the older woman was weaving a basket and the young woman was stamping on firebrands with her clog to extinguish them.

"Father," I said to the man, "I got lost trying to descend to Renaison. Is there room for me in your hut?"

"The hut is too small," replied the old man. The woman whispered something to him. "But since you're the monsieur," he added, "we'll squeeze up a little."

The young woman was as pretty as a devil who had stolen the body of an angel. At first, only her velvety eyes could be seen, through which gleams passed at intervals. The whites were blue-tinted and when her blue-tinted eyelids drew together her lashes surpassed the projection of her eyebrows. Dark tresses hid her forehead. Between her thick lips her pointed teeth resembled drops of dew. Her voice had a crystalline timbre, her cheeks the transparency and hue of a Chasselas grape. Her name was Régoulaï.[48]

---

[48] The word "regoulaï" is a version of the first person singular of the verb *regouler*, meaning "I drive away with harsh words."

"Where are you from?" I asked the old man,
"The village of Chargerauds."

My Aunt Thérèse had often mentioned that village, built in the middle of the woods of a rock that overlooked the valleys of the Allier and the Loire.

My aunt believed that the village of Chargerauds was debris of one of the Moorish tribes that had settled in the Lyonnais mountains after the battle of Poitiers.[49] She was probably right.

I lay down in a corner of the hut on a pile of heather; it was impossible for me to remain there—others had certainly slept on it—and I went to sit down beside the fire.

In those days I barely knew the name of the prophet, and by the fire I was not thinking about the battle of Poitiers; but in those days I was seventeen years old and I was thinking about Régoulaï's large eyes when she emerged from the hut with her finger over her lips. "Come," she whispered to me.

I followed her, and red clouds passed before my eyes when a moonbeam fell on her bare leg. She went up as high as the dolmen of the Pierre-de-jour. There she turned round and said: "Do you think I'm pretty"

I was only seventeen. I stammered.

She leapt on to a large stone slab and started to dance. Her heavy fustian skirt impeded her; she took it off...

I was only seventeen! Well, if I close my eyes I can still see that girl, as beautiful as a statue, whirling in her chemise on the granite table...

---

[49] Not the famous battle in the Hundred Years War but the less well-known battle, also known as the Battle of Tours, fought in 732, in which a Moorish invasion of the former Roman province of Gaul was repelled by a Frankish army led by Charles Martel, helping to pave the way for the Kingdom of the Franks to lay the foundations of modern France

At sunrise, she had put her clogs and her fustian skirt back on; but we were hidden in a hole at the summit of a rock. She said to me: "You can buy two monkeys and a little carriage, and we'll do the fairs over Lyon way." I found that project quite realizable and I left to go in search of my savings.

Régoulaï was the granddaughter of the old man who carved shovels to shift grain; her father had only passed through, her mother had departed, no one knew where, and she had been brought up by an uncle who showed monkeys in fairgrounds. One morning, gendarmes had taken the uncle away, and the imperial prosecutor had sent Régoulaï to her grandfather. She was regretting her spangled dress and the bravos of the crowd when Providence sent me to her.

When I got back to the château I saw my cousin the colonel, the old woman and the old man on the perron. My cousin the colonel smiled, the old woman tore her gray hair and the old man struck the steps with his staff.

That is why, instead of being a good peasant, I am a teller of foolish stories.

Please lend me a little attention; I'm returning to my subject.

One day, Hélène's uncle returned from Brazil and, as that uncle was the best of uncles, he brought some transients to the white house. Jacques was invited to take sorbets with them.

Among those transients, some were witty and others were not, but they all found Hélène so beautiful that they fell in love with her and Hélène was delighted by it. Hélène was a beautiful fragile diamond, a gracious bee.

Jacques smiled so graciously that Hélène was on the point of forgetting the bouquets of bean-flowers.

Fortunately a transient suggested an excursion at sea.

Pescade Point having been doubled, the boat was bobbing gently on the great waves and Jacques, who was holding the tiller, said to Hélène: "Can you hear what the sea is saying, Mademoiselle?"

"It's saying that we love one another," the young woman replied, in a whisper.

Jacques smiled, launched the boat forward on to a sandy beach, leapt ashore and vanished in the shadow of the cliff.

"That fellow is an eccentric," declared the transients.

"I'm an eccentric too," muttered the uncle.

That evening, the uncle's ship had lifted anchor and Hélène went to see Jacques in the battery. On seeing him, she tottered, and then threw her arms around his neck. "Did I trouble you yesterday, then?" She asked him.

Hélène was a brave young woman.

They sat down on an overhanging parapet and talked for a long time. What did they talk about? I don't know. One forgets charming phrases devoid of subjects and verbs, with say as much with the hand and the eyes as with the lips, as soon as one has pronounced them.

When Jacques got up to leave, he said: "See how blue the sea is!"

"What do you want?" Hélène replied, leaning over.

Hélène was a brave young woman... What would you have done in Jacques' place?

"I would have..."

"You would have done something stupid. Jacques squeezed Hélène's hand and said to Dorothée, who raised her arms to the sky: "Take Mademoiselle away; the night is cold." He said that, and he fled.

The battery is closed on the landward side by a wall over which large clumps of clematis dangle. Hélène stopped under the arched doorway while Jacques went down the rugged stairway leading to the beach. At the first landing he turned round and he saw his beloved under the somber vault, silver-tinted by the moonlight. Hélène applied her two hands to her heart, then put them to her lips, and her head fell back. Her heavy tresses tore away from their comb and covered her all the way to her feet with a mantle of sparks.

She was as beautiful as Cita, the goddess with the golden eyes, when she marches luminously over the dormant waters of the Ganges.

VII

Instead of following the road to Algiers, Jacques plunged into the bushy ravine where the streams of the Boudjareah come together. He wanted to watch Hélène's lamp shining. Suddenly, a white form blocked the path. Papillon ran forward, lips curled; but he stopped, wagged his tail and came back to lick his master's hand. Jacques shivered as he distinguished a white haïck striped with pink. "What are you doing here, Aïcha?" he said.

"He recognizes me!" sighed the white phantom.

"What are you doing here, Aïcha?" Jacques repeated.

"I was waiting for you. For many weeks I've hidden here every night in order to see you pass by—you forbade me to return to your abode—but today I saw you embrace the Frenchwoman and I didn't have the strength to hide. Adieu, *mon capitaine*, I shall always love you. Adieu! Adieu!"

She fled in the direction of the sea, and Jacques continued his route toward the white house...

Let us chat while Jacques is watching Hélène's lamp shine.

At Boghar, the Tell finishes and the Sahara commences; one often passes through it and one gladly halts there.

Those who stop in Boghar are going to the land of death or returning therefrom; they all have a terror or an amour to forget; so Boghar is a town of flute-players and almahs.

182

After the evening prayer, when the camels are ruminating, their heads on the sand, the great mares are licking their meager flanks, and the Orient is shelling out its necklace of stars, when the fires are burning brightly in front of the brown tents, a flute-player leans against a pack-saddle and an almah, hidden beneath a red haïck, crouches at his feet. He draws a few vibrant notes from the reed and the believers approach one by one. He extends a carpet on the sand; the believers sit down, and the almah gets up.

She gets up slowly, her arms folded—her haïck rises as far as her eyes and trails all the way to the ground—she enters the circle, arms folded, and stops still in the middle of the carpet. Vague sounds, trailing notes like fearful kisses and distant appeals emerge from the flute. The believers stroke their beards.

A note hisses like a snake, the red haïck falls, and the almah rounds out her arms above her head. Her hair, braided with wool, winds around her temples like a ram's horn; her eyes, elongated by kohl, have no gaze; her teeth glisten between parted lips; the nape of her neck touches her shoulders and her sharp breasts are erect.

She is naked to the hips, she has a blue star on her forehead; the palms of her hands are red, and beneath the white muslin her legs are the color of honey. The believers stroke their beards.

The flute sighs, a derbouka resonates. The almah flexes her hips and slowly, slowly, her torso rises and falls. She turns slowly, and her hips quiver slowly. Her eyes reflect the starlight; stifled sighs swell her neck.

A horseman stands up in his stirrups, a negro laughs while stoking the fire, and the believers stroke their beards...

VIII

Jacques returned to Algiers along the sea shore, his heart overflowing with joy.

"*Mon capitaine*," cried a clear voice, "*mon capitaine*, I love you!"

Jacques raised his head and saw Aïcha on the crest of the cliff. She blew him a kiss and hurled herself into the void.

Aïcha was a Beni-Mezab dancer whom Jacques had found beautiful one evening under the palm trees of Boghar.

He found her beautiful one evening and he departed in the morning, because her large velvety eyes did not allow her soul to be seen. But the daughter of the desert had a soul, and she came to Algiers in search of the man she called her *capitaine*. Jacques was already in love with Hélène...

Let us leave the captain carrying the beautiful broken body in his arms—the water of life is already dull enough, why blacken it further by throwing ink into it?—and let's talk about cheerful things.

I have a close friend, a philosopher who would be no more stupid than three-quarters of philosophers if he were not completely mad. That poor friend believes that he is a druid. "I have not," he says, "listened in the grotto of words to the sage. The pontiff has not murmured in my ear the three words that command, but I know what the druids knew and everything that humankind has learned since then." He is very droll, because he is convinced.

His favorite book is a collection of old bardic maxims from the land of Wales,[50] in which one reads things like this:

---

[50] Presumably the collection of "Bardic triads" compiled by the self-styled Iolo Morganwg (Edward Williams, 1747-1826), supposedly translations but more likely original compositions—classic examples of fakelore. It is not possible to de-

There are three circles of existence: the circle of the void, where, except for God, there is nothing living or dead, and no being except God can traverse it; the circle of migration, where every animate being proceeds to death, which humans traverse; and the circle of felicity, where every animate being proceeds after life, and humans well traverse it in the heavens.

The three calamities of the circle of migration are: necessity, the absence of memory, and death.

Three things will be rendered to humans in the circle of felicity: primitive genius, primitive amour and primitive memory, for there would otherwise be no felicity...

At first sight, these maxims are not clear, but it appears that by meditating on them one can draw strange conclusions from them. Here are a few passages from a letter that this philosopher of the future has just written to me

The one who has had no beginning was alone, containing in himself everything that has been, everything that is and everything that will be. He thought, and the universe, as handsome as a bridegroom, inclined before him.

He thought, and evil, which was not in him, was created by his wisdom in order to permit the universe to struggle, and, in consequence, to live.

Evil is not the opposite of good. Good is a goal, evil is a means; when the goal is attained, the means will be annihilated.

---

termine with confidence who this philosophical friend might have been, but one of the sources that L'Estoille used for concocting his pseudo-history of France was undoubtedly Amédée Thierry's *Histoire des Gaules* (1828) and the historian's son, Gilbert-Augustine Thierry (1840-1915) wrote several volumes of mysticism and fiction that make much of Morganwg's triads.

The closer the creature approaches the creator, the less possible struggle becomes. The crystal struggles to live, the plant struggles to move, the animal struggles to think, the human being struggles to comprehend.

When a human has understood, he quits the battlefield, where one is sometimes victorious and sometimes vanquished, and he goes to struggle where one is always victorious. But, humans only being part of a whole—humankind—he cannot be completely happy for as long as the whole is not happy, and he often descends again into the arena to die again, in order to advance the hour of the definitive victory of good over evil..

Those humans who descend again voluntarily from the circle of felicity into the circle of proof are prophets or poets: prophets who trace the route to the future and poets who illuminate it. They are not understood when they speak, because they know what other humans have forgotten and what other humans have not yet found, but...

"Sidi! The Chambas have taken four men from the *goum* and they have disemboweled them."[51]

"Damn!"

IX

I would like to finish the oft-interrupted story of the amours of Jacques and Hélène, but, not knowing any longer where I am—for a fortnight I have been following the men who have filled the bellies of my cavaliers with stones—I shall conclude briefly.

I am Capitaine Jacques, Hélène never existed, and I have been telling you a dream of amour.

---

[51] A *goum* was a company of Moroccan soldiers allied with the French colonial forces.

The ensemble of that story is a dream, but the details are real.[52]

Here and there, in the thickets and on the sand, under the fir-trees and in the reeds, at dawn and at dusk, I have picked flowers, beautiful proud flowers and poor pale flowers, buds that open astonished and clusters that dangle, quivering. Instead of putting in a herbal those flowers of the woods and those hothouse flowers, instead of sticking them on a leaf of white paper under a name and a date, I have put them where my good tears fall.

Life has thrown its ashes in my eyes, and I believe that they have dried up the source of my good tears; but over the flowers of my youth, the tears of the past have changed into liquor.

Now, I am going to sculpt in a fragment of steel a cup for my old age, a cup from which, drop by drop, I shall drink the intoxicating liquor of the flowers of summer.

When my hand drops the empty cup, I shall chose my eyes, and my soul, as it flies away, will say: "Beautiful flowery earth, I am quitting you without regrets, but I am quitting you without hatred. Land of exile, you have been mild for me, and I shall never forget you in the luminous fatherland.

---

[52] Readers must decide for themselves whether or not a jealous Moorish woman really might have committed suicide by jumping off Pescade Point during the author's sojourn in Algiers, but it is worth noting that in the first part of *Le Chanson de l'alouette*, the protagonist become delirious after a fall from Pescade Point to which one observer refers as a suicide attempt, immediately after a confusing encounter with two young Moorish women, and in the revised version of the story of Hélène in *Les Amoureuses*, Captain Jacques and Hélène contemplate committing suicide in that fashion—and the ending is sufficiently ambiguous as not to exclude the interpretation that they do. Amorously motivated suicides are a recurrent feature of L'Estoille's works.

Aguzza qui, lettor, ben gli occhi at vero
Chè'l velo è ora ben tanto sottile
Certo, chè'l trapassar dentro è leggièro.

Dante[53]

At an equal distance from the Crach river and the peninsula of Quiberon, at the extremity of an immense heath strewn
with little hamlets, between the growling waves and the singing pines, in the midst of dolmens and menhirs, some fifty
houses cluster around a gray bell-tower.

That gray bell-tower is the bell-tower of Saint-Corneille,
the patron saint of animals and the poor in spirit. Those white
houses are the houses of Carnac.

The heath is charming when the oak-leaves redden over
the washing-troughs, when the gray willows glisten in the
midst of the meadows, when the sleeping Ocean extends its
long blue arms between the salt-stacks and the gilded islets.

Under the dolmen of Plouharnel I encountered a young
woman. She told me the legend of the enchanter Merlin.

I

The son of Konan-Mériadek,[54] the great king of Armorica, reigned over the isle of Bretagne, and the cattle grazed in
peace.

---

[53] The quotation is from Canto VIII of the *Purgatorio*. The
tercet asks the reader to focus his eyes on the truth, because
the veil concealing it is now so thin that it is surely easy to
pass through it. Immediately thereafter, the dreamer sees two
angels descend from Heaven with flaming swords.
[54] This version of the name of the legendary founder of Britta-
ny, more usually rendered Conan Meriadoc, is used extensive-

The Picts no longer dared to descend from the mountains, the Saxons no longer dared to approach the coasts, and the bards, their fingers charged with golden rings, sang in long festivals.

The barrels were full of beer, the orchards full of apple trees, and the houses full of children.

One night, the vassal Guortigern killed his master, the king, and exiled his two brothers, Embreiz of the broad shield and Uter of the sharp lance.[55]

Guortigern is king, thanks to the Saxons, to whom he has given half the kingdom that he stole; but he is afraid of his allies who are always making demands, and his subjects, who are dreaming of the exiled Embreiz. He is so fearful that he wants to build a tower on an inaccessible plateau.

Thousands of workmen set to work, but by night everything that they have done during the day disappears. Then the diviners, who had learned magic among the Saxons, said to Guortigern: "Take a fatherless child, wash the foundations of the tower with his blood, and it will no longer collapse every night."

The king was brought a young boy who was born of a virgin and a spirit of the air.

"Your diviners claim that it is necessary to wash the foundations of this tower with my blood," said the child, "but do they know what there is beneath our feet?"

The diviners did not know that.

---

ly by Hersart de La Villemarqué in his collection of supposed Breton folk-songs.

[55] Guortigern (i.e. Vortigern) and Uter (Uther) are both found in Hersart's *Myrdhinn*, on which this fantasy is loosely based, although the name Embreiz is rendered there is it familiar form, Ambroise. The similarity of the name to Ar-Braz, the name subsequently attributed by L'Estoille to his fictitious archetypal Gaulish hero, might not be coincidental.

Then the child said: "Beneath our feet there is a basin full of water, and in that basin a huge shell."

The king had the earth dug, and the basin was found. He had the basin emptied, and the shell was found.

"Do you know what there is in that shell?" he child asked the diviners.

The diviners did not know that.

Then the child said: "In that shell there is a flag, and in that flag a white serpent and a red serpent."

"What does that signify?" asked Guortigern.

"It signifies," the child replied, "that the Bretons, who have a red dragon for an emblem, will fight against the Saxons you have summoned, who have a white dragon for an emblem. The Bretons will fight for a long time, but they will be victorious in the end."

"Who are you, then?"

"I am Merlin, and you are no longer king."

A horseman was galloping in the plain; he announced to Guortigern that Emerik had just been proclaimed king.

II

For twelve years Emerik fought against the Saxons, and he expelled them, with Merlin's aid.[56]

The child had become a man as handsome as a red deer stag and as strong as an ash tree; and the man as a bard.

When the last Saxon had reembarked, Merlin said to Emerik; "Adieu, my master; you no longer need my aid now and I'm going into the woods to ask the leaves for advice for the future. Adieu, my friend, I'm going into the woods on the

---

[56] Emerik is not found in Hersart, and the source of the name remains enigmatic. Guortigern's successor in Hersart's version of Merlin's fictitious history, and elsewhere, is Ambroise.

banks of springs; the gazes of young women don't make me quiver, and the heart has need of amour."

In order to console himself for the departure of his bard, Emerik wanted to erect an imperishable monument to the warriors who had died in the Holy War. He consulted the most skillful masons, but the masons did not know how to construct imperishable monuments and they went to consult Merlin.

Merlin said to them: "In Ireland, at the summit of a mountain, there are stones arranged n a circle. Time will wear away its wings on their sharp edges. Send men to fetch them, and have hem erected here as they are erected there.

Emerik sent his brother Uter and five thousand men to fetch the enchanted stones from Ireland.

Merlin manned the tiller of Uter's ship.

The Bretons disembarked in Ireland and they found the stones; but they were so heavy that, in spite of their combined efforts, they could not shake a single one.

Then Merlin played the harp, and the stones formed a line. He headed toward the sea and the stones followed him over the heath. He went back aboard Uter's ship, and the sons followed him over the waves.

They followed it all the way to the plain where the tombs of the brave warriors were. There he stopped playing, and the stones arranged themselves as they had been arranged on the mountain in Ireland.

"Emerik," he said to the king, "you're going to die soon, but your name won't die. Adieu, friend, I'm embracing you for the last time. We'll met again aboard the crystal ship."

Merlin returned to the forest, and Emerik died, as had been predicted. Uter of the sharp lance succeeded him on the throne of Bretagne.

Uter loved the Queen of Cornouailles. He had a son by her, who was named Arthur, and he died.

Then Merlin quit his solitude and, for fifteen years, he instructed the boy who was to be the Breton hero, the man with the heavy hand. Then he forged him an invincible sword and he returned to the woods.

While Arthur traveled the world victoriously, Merlin followed him with his soul, and when danger menaced him, he borrowed a crow's wings or the fins of a salmon in order to rejoin him.

One day, Merlin was leaning over a spring and he saw Arthur's court, as if in a mirror. He saw treason sitting next to the king, he saw a foreigner pressing the knee of the queen with the golden hair; but he had to obey the One who commands, and he fell asleep, his eyes full of tears.

When he woke up, the Picts had been vanquished at Camlan, Modred the felon was dead, and Arthur had been carried by the fays to the isle that floats on the Ocean.

The flock no longer had a shepherd. Merlin picked up the bloody crook.

He reigned for a long time. Men whom he had seen born died of old age around him but he remained ever young and ever strong.

He reigned for a long time, only loving the Bretons and his sister Ganieda,[57] the blonde daughter of the spirit of the oaks, who had married a king.

---

[57] Merlin is credited with a twin sister named Ganieda, or Gwendydd in the *Red Book of Hergest* and other Welsh sources; she is referenced in Hersart but not adopted into his history, where her role is attributed to Viviane—a figure of which Edgar Quinet's *Merlin l'enchanteur* and other French neo-Romantic fiction make much. L'Estoille incorporates a Ganieda of his own into the pseudohistory mapped out in *La Chanson de l'alouette*.

But the old men died, and their sons, who had not known Arthur, sharpened their axes for a fratricidal struggle. They fought on the sand at the bottom of a gulf. Their blood reddened the waves.

When Merlin saw the bloody waves beating the granite rocks he broke his harp and, his arms extended, he fled over the heather.

He was mad.

Now he wanders in the forests of oaks, only seeing the future.

That is the legend that the Armorican virgin told me under a dolmen.

Kermau is an old manor huddled under old oaks.

Between it and the sea, narrow meadows wind along a crystalline stream.

I don't want to describe Kermau for you. Even a photograph would not give you an idea of it, for a photograph would not tell you that its mossy walls are as pink as the cheeks of cherubim, that its pointed roof is as shiny as the throat of a wood-pigeon, that the ivy that embroiders it is as green as an emerald, and that the pond that bathes it is as silky as a Milanese breastplate.

It is composed of a main building flanked by small towers; its windows have lattices as light as bindweed stems, and the skylights of its roofs resemble spearheads.

From the road to Auray you will perceive it between the heath and a clump of oaks.

Its garden, surrounded by terraces, is planted with apple trees, and in the corner that faces the rising sun, two large stone slabs cover two tombs.

Go to Kermau and you will know the story of the fay and the templar who are asleep under the apple trees.

Go to Kermau to pick the white violets sown by the fay.

I encountered the Breton virgin under the pines of the Crach river; she was crowned with vervain and she spoke to me about the enchanter Merlin.

I

The man who had been king had been mad since the evening of the great battle in which the brothers murdered one another.

When he saw the red waves in the moonlight he broke his harp, tore off his crown and fled into the woods.

He wanders alone in the woods. He only eats the berries of the bushes and the roots of the grass. He sleeps naked on the bare ground, and his only companion is the wolf that had licked his hand when he was king.

He crawls like a bear, he runs like a wild boar and the crows say to their chicks: "Look at the man who was a bard!" He crawls like a bear, he runs like a wild boar and
The hinds say to their fawns: "Look at the man who was a king."

But the snow hides the grass and the frost destroys the berries on the bushes. Then Ganieda leans over the bard lying beside the wolf, she speaks to him softly, and she takes him away.

II

Ganieda had a palace built in the oak forest for her brother, a palace with granite walls pierced by sixty doors and sixty windows.

Ganieda, the blonde queen, no longer goes under the willows to talk of amour with the pages. When the nightingale sings, Ganieda, the queen with the even eyes, no longer listens to the nightingale. She has read back to her what Merlin has said while the snow whitened the knotty boughs of the old oaks.

When the snow whitens the knotty boughs of the old oaks Merlin comes with his gray wolf to warm himself before the bright fire of the palace of Ganieda, the queen who forgot her pages in order to console her brother.

Before the crackling fire, Merlin casts to the wind the words that he has read in summer on the thorns of brambles and under the leaves of apple trees, and a hundred and twenty secretaries leaning on the battens of the doors and the window sills write the prophet's words on vellum.

As soon as the buds elongate on the branches of the hazel tree, the diviner who was a king flees into the forest.

While the Armorican virgin is speaking, the Crach river carries furze flowers away to the sea.

Why does anyone want to persuade the people who live between the Alps and the Ocean and between the Pyrenees and the Manche, that it is a shoot of Latin stock. Why do all sworn mouths open to affirm that a few thousand soldiers have filled the empty veins of Gaul?

If I said that Italy, all the way to the Tiber, is Gallic, the gravest of my contemporaries would burst out laughing, and yet the Gauls occupied the north of Italy for longer than the Romans occupied the south of Gaul.

Why also say that England is Saxon? Is the land of Wales Saxon? Are Scotland, the isles and Ireland Saxon,

In Europe there are three sisters, daughters of light: France, Great Britain and Ireland; the day when they will hold hands is imminent.

The vanish is cracking on the oak.

The windmill of Kermau is perched on a funerary mound. It has four red sails, a slate roof and a blazoned door.

The miller's name is Pierre. Pierre does not like antiquaries. "Those messieurs from Vannes," he said to me, "are true rats; they dig everywhere. They've followed out the Butte Saint-Michel, the stout butte that has a chapel on top. They're rats that know the good places; in the Butte Saint-Michel a basket full of precious stones.

"All the same, I wouldn't want to be in their place; they've taken the fay's stones.

"What fay?" I said to him.

"The fay of Kermau."

What if I were to tell you the story of the fay and the Templar as Pierre told it to me in the windmill with red sails?

I

Richard de Kermau, who was orphaned since birth, went up every day on to the Butte Saint-Michel in order to watch the dog pack running of the Comte du Lac, the seigneur of the Crach river.

One evening, he went to sleep there, and was only woken up by the watchman striking the twelve chimes of midnight on the bell of Saint Corneille.

Saint Corneille is a great saint. He died at Carnac after having changed the soldiers of the pagan, who were pursuing him, into stones.

The entire pagan army was there on the heath.

It was the first night of the full moon of June

When he awoke, Richard rubbed his eyes; he could no longer see the stones, and although the night was calm, the sea was seething in the bay of Saint Colomba.

The stones were no longer on the heath because they had gone into the sea, and the sea was seething because they were drinking it. They went there once a year, and they'll go until the day of judgment. Then Saint Corneille will baptize them and open the door of Heaven to them.

Richard started running along the road to Kermau, but when he was in the middle of the meadows he saw the stones coming after him. He fell to his knees and made a vow to Our Lady to take the cross if she deflected them away from him.

As soon as he fell to his knees a white woman touched the stones with a branch of furze, and they moved apart to the right and the left. When the last one had passed by, the white woman disappeared.

The next day, Richard mounted his best horse and went to Vannes to become a Templar.

II

One day, Richard encountered the pagans near the place where Saint John baptized.

The battle commenced at daybreak and only finished at the hour of vespers. It was a sad day; all the Templars fell, one after another. Richard was the last to fall.

When he was on the ground he could no longer see anything, because the blood blinded him, but he heard the pagans' bursts of laughter as they were cutting off the heads of the knights. He also heard steel grating on bone. Suddenly he felt someone unlacing his helmet, and he cried: "Ah, Our Lady, who deflected the stones of the heath away from me, protect me!"

The visor of his helmet was raised. He was in the meadow of Kermau; the moon was shining and the white lady was smiling.

Have you seen the great trench in the Butte Saint-Michel that the messieurs from Vannes dug last year? That trench traverses a layer of stones, then a layer of mud, and then another layer of stones, and leads to a chamber whose walls are made of large slabs of stone and its ceiling from a single rock.

Thirty-nine stone axes of different colors were found there, beautiful green pearls and a ring made of little white beads like those that are sold at the fair of Auray, but no body was found.

The messieurs from Vannes claimed that they picked up ashes there, but they're mistaken. The chamber of the Butte Saint-Michel is a prison in which Saint Corneille enclosed a fay on the day when she changed the pagan army into stones.

The fays are not daughters of Hell, and they always end up converting; there are almost none left now, because there are no new ones. When fays are baptized they become woman gentler than other women.

On seeing the white lady before him, Richard cried: "Ah! Our Lady!"

"I'm not the Holy Virgin," the apparition replied, "I'm a fay. Saint Corneille imprisoned me underground because I drowned sinners. I wept for a thousand years, and then I invoked the saints of paradise, and an angel opened my prison.

"I left under the butte the axes with which I launched thunder, the green pearls with which I swelled the sea and the white ring with which I poisoned springs, and since then I've been in the Holy Land watching over the Bretons.

"On the nights when the stones go to drink I return to Carnac to prevent them crushing people on the heath. They went to drink tonight, and as you were too weak to remain alone out there, I brought you with me. Spend the day in your château and I'll take you back to Jerusalem tomorrow night."

While they fay spoke Richard gazed at her, and he found her so beautiful, so very beautiful, that he fell in love with her. "White fay," he said to her, "when can you be baptized by the bishop of Vannes?"

"When a knight loves me."

"Well then, take me to the bishop."

The fay took Richard to the cathedral of Vannes.

III

In the cathedral of Vannes the deacons were wearing white surplices, the bells were carillonning, and the bishop said: "Fay, the angel Michel has announced your coming to me; you shall be called Margareth."

The bishop baptized the fay. the Duc de Bretagne was her godfather and the Duchesse her godmother.

Immediately after the ceremony, Richard de Kermau approached the Christian and said: "Now that you're a woman, would you like to marry me?"

Margareth blushed, but the Duchesse cried: "Certainly, it's necessary for them to marry."

The bishop released the Templar from his vows and the marriage was made the same day.

As Margareth had no armories, the Duchesse donated her own.

That is why I have the ermine of Bretagne on the door of my mill.

Richard and Margareth lived for a long time; they died on the same day and I am the last of the Comtes de Kermau.

I encountered the Breton virgin on the strand. Foam was silvering her feet, seagulls were caressing her hair with their wingtips; she talked to me about the enchanter Merlin.

Merlin was weeping in the forest for his beautiful apple trees with vermilion fruits, his beautiful apple trees that were all equal, when Taliesin the bard called him by his name.

"Merlin, Merlin," he said to him, "I have come to you to talk about the past; for I have lived in the hundred isles, in the hundred isles I've resided.

"Merlin, Merlin," he said to him, "I have come to you to talk about creation; for I have been a viper on the hill and a partridge in the wheat.

"Merlin, Merlin," he said to him, "I have come to you to talk about the future; for I am sitting on the green throne in the circle where faith opens the eyes of death."

Merlin replied: "You who have seen the waters of the Deluge, tell me why winter does not strip the branches of the fir trees like the branches of the oak...

I need to go!

Adieu, virgin of the broad brow. Adieu, daughter of the heaths. Adieu, brunette guardian of the flowers of the past.

Will you come to sit down with me when I light my lamp? Will you put your arm in mine during the long marches?

Come without dread, daughter of the druids; you will find books on my table that speak of the Gauls. Put your arm in mine during the long marches; I have engraved the word of the future on my saber.

Let me sleep. Fortunately, it isn't daylight and I have time to finish a beautiful dream. Beautiful dreams are even rarer than hares. Good hunting, friend.

Let's see. I was in front of a palace of pillow marble with sculpted balconies, pointed minarets tiled with faience and white domes. Jasmines embroidered the terraces and pomegranates leaned over the alabaster basins of a shady garden, in which tall lemon trees sowed the silvery sand of the pathways with pink stars. A woman appeared on the balcony and... She was certainly about to tell me charming things, to open the door of an embalmed chamber and draw me to a soft divan. Then...we would have smoked a narghileh and eaten conserves of roses in crystal saucers... I can no longer sleep. Devil take the hunters!

The woman who appeared in the balcony resembled the nice brunette who was chatting so gaily yesterday with the beautiful blonde, and the palace of yellow marble was only an idealized portrait of the house in which she lives.

Dreams can only be memories or presentiments.
What if my dream were a presentiment?

Yesterday, on the edge of the pond, under the poplars, in the rays of the setting sun, like a Byzantine virgin on the golden backcloth of a chapel, the daughter of the druids appeared to me. She was clutching to her heart a harp with seven strings, and she talked to me about Merlin.

Old age has killed Merlin's wolf and the bard has brought his friend to the beach facing the setting sun.

All day and throughout the night he had carried in his arms the stiff cadaver of the old wolf of Cornouailles, because the soil of the forest was too hard to dig a grave therein.

The bard who had been a king, the bard who had felt the red blood of hearts palpitating under his hand, dug out the sand with his fingernails in order to bury his wolf.

Why are you dead, old wolf of the Gaels? If you weren't dead, the foreigners' dogs wouldn't be barking so loudly.

When the grave was filled in, the bard sat on the sand and started to weep. Letting the tears wet his beard, he said:

"I never put a collar on you, but you always followed me. You slept under my table and you never ate bones.

"When you died, I saw your soul in your dull eyes, and your soul was like a golden shield fresh from the forge.

"What will the Unknown engrave on that virgin shield? I can no longer lift the veil; I've broken my harp!

"Cloud passing over the sky, descend on to my knees! Soaring seagull, give me seven feathers from your wings!

"With the cloud I shall make a harp, with the seven feathers I shall make seven strings, and I shall lift the veil."

The cloud passed without stopping. The gull dived into the foam, and the bard hid his head in his hands.

Why are you dead, old wolf of the Gaels? Since you died, the dogs of those who speak Latin bark louder!

The bard had hidden his head in his hands; he did not see a wave that came from the Occident, a wave that came from the coast of Erin. On that wave a woman with long hair was lying.

The wave was as green as a meadow, the woman was as white as a drop of milk. The wave left the woman on the sand and returned, growling, toward the coast of Erin.

She was beautiful, the daughter of the waves, as beautiful as an autumn morning, as beautiful as the day after a victory, as beautiful as the last verse of a sublime poem. She kissed Merlin on the forehead.

"What do you want, daughter of the waves?" said the bard. "I've seen the oak leaves fall a thousand times. I've seen the leaves of the apple trees fall a thousand times, and three hundred times more."

The daughter of the waves folded her arms and tipped back her head; her blonde hair touched her feet. Merlin had before him an ivory harp.

Then the daughter of the druids kissed me on the forehead, and I forgot Latin, and I was able to speak the language of the Gaels.

Are you really dead, old wolf of the Gauls?

My dream was a presentiment.

If she asked me for the moon, I would unhook it for her and I would fish with a line in order to look at her pretty head in the water.

Once there was a king and a queen who were scarcely occupied with their subjects.

They paid so little heed to them that they did not even know the names of the Chevalier du Loup and the beautiful Fleur d'Iris.

If the king had known Fleur d'Iris he would certainly have said: "That's the prettiest young woman in my kingdom!" If the queen had known the Chevalier du Loup, she would certainly have said: "That's surliest of my knights!" But neither the king nor the queen would have supposed for an instant that the beauty might love the soldier.

However, one evening in December, Fleur d'Iris, sitting in a huge leather armchair, said to the soldier lying at her feet:

In the ballroom, the husband smiled as he watched his wife waltz with a stranger.

How beautiful she is, the bride—but how pale she is!

Waltz, waltz, beautiful bride; a waltz is a tender dream.

They are whirling so rapidly that their hair mingles... How beautiful she is, the bride!

They are whirling so rapidly that their hair mingles, and their two bodies are no longer more than one body, and their breath is confounded... How pale she is, the bride!

Waltz, waltz, beautiful bride; a waltz is a tender dream, and your master is smiling...

Fleur d'Iris offered her lips to the soldier.

When she raised her head again, the young man said:

The Seigneur des Lerres was the best singer in Forez. When he entered the church, the beautiful ladies blushed under their lace head-dresses; when he traversed the pain, the shepherdesses shouted to him:

"Winter is past,
Sing, sing, nightingale!"

*One Sunday, he followed the King of France to Paris.
The beautiful ladies wet for a day, but the shepherdesses of
Ambierle, who dared not weep, said throughout the winter, at
the end of their couplets:*

*"When will the almond-tree flower again,
When will you return, nightingale?"*

*On the first day of summer, a cavalier galloped along the
road to Roanne. The shepherdesses saluted him politely, but
he did not look at them; the king's daughter, sitting on her
horse, said to him:*

*"If your château is nearby,
Sing, sing, nightingale...!*

Then the soldier sighed: "Will you sit on my horse?"
Fleur d'iris blushed and said:

*The boat glides between the willows, and the stranger
says to the bride:*
*"Let the boat drift downriver, the stars are smiling at us
and your master is sleep."*

*The river foams, the boat breaks, and the handsome
dancer swims in the waves.*

*How pale she is, the bride, in the swimmer's arms! But
how many things her eyes are saying...!*

The soldier gazed into Fleur d'Iris' eyes and he said:

*The king came with a thousand soldiers to demand his
daughter, but the moats were full and the portcullis was lowered. The king had the ditch filled in and the portcullis torn
down... The seigneur said to his good friend:*

*In winter as in summer
The nightingale will sing...*

Then Fleur d'Iris, smiling, extended her lips to the soldier's lips. When she lifted her head again, her eyes were full
of tears, and she said:

*Around the spring, the young women whisper; in the
square, a woman clad in black advances with her eyes lowered.*
*The woman clad in black advances with her eyes low-
ered, and the young women whisper: "Here comes the woman
who ran away on the evening of her wedding and whose lover
quit her the next day..."*

The soldier applied his heart to the head of Fleur d'Iris
and he said:

*The king had the lovers taken to a subterranean prison;
then the door was walled up and the tower was demolished
over the door. Since that time, the shepherdesses of Ambierle
say at the end of their couplets:*

*"When winter has passed
The nightingale will sing again..."*

Then the cricket sang on the hearth.

If the king had heard what the cricket had heard, he
would have been jealous of the knight; if the queen had seen
what the cricket had seen, she would have been jealous of
Fleur d'Iris.

We were sowing white and blue bindweed...

"Lieutenant!"

"What?"

"The reveille is sounding."

"In winter we shall have a warm little nest, full of books and flowers..."

"Lieutenant!"

"Let me be!"

"The clarions are sounding."

"My tunic, quickly! They're sounding the appeal. My gloves! Where are my gloves?"

"You have them in your hand."

"*Capitaine*, someone is missing.

"Have you checked whether the rooms are in the utmost state of neatness?"

"I've just got out of bed."

"That's bad, very bad! Go see whether the camp in placed as the report indicates."

"Yes, *mon capitaine*... She's promised to come this evening, but will she be able to?"

"Lieutenant! The commandant is summoning you."

"*Mon commandant?*"

"Monsieur, look at number four in the second rank."

"It's certain that that monster, number four, has only waxed his right boot. He must have a reason for only waxing his right boot; he would not have compromised lightly the military future of our beautiful fatherland. Perhaps he too is in love."

"Lieutenant Castor, when would you like to heed the commands?"

"Peloton, right turn—to the right. File to the left, march."

If I'm not shot by a firing squad at the camp at Châlons, I'll be lucky.

Adieu, high street where the girls have eyes as black as the devil's cloak, when they aren't as blue as the eyes of cherubim.

"The cantinière has two sabots.
"The cantinière has two sabots."
She owes them to the corporals.
"She owes them to the corporals."
"The corporals are soldiers!"

Good—here comes the rain! The water is running down my neck.

"The cantinière has two white stockings.
"The cantinière has two white stockings..."

My left boot is digging gently into my little toe. My pipe is out.

"Say, Pollux, why are you drawing your head back into your shoulders like a tortoise whose feet have been trodden on?"

"I'm wet."

"Me too,"

"And I'm furious. Every time I start a route march, it pours with rain. If I'd known, I wouldn't have quit my regiment."

"It never rains in your regiment?"

"You're boring me."

"The cantinière has two mittens.
"The cantinière has two mittens.
She owes them to the capitaines..."

"Halt! And form ranks!"

"The regulations say that after having marched for an hour, one rests for five minutes. Pollux, repose on this fresh grass; don't give your subordinates an examples of indiscipline."

"If I'd known, I wouldn't have quit my regiment."

"Get away, come and drink a drop."

A drop is a good thing; I'm completely cheered up. I can no longer feel the paving stones.

"I can feel them; my little toe is in a terrible state."

Yes, we'll pluck her,
The skylark, the skylark!
Yes, we'll pluck her.
The skylark,
All day long"
We'll pluck her head, her beak,
The beak of the skylark…

Devil take the paving-stones!

"Where's Thomas?"
"He's down below."
"Where's Michaud?"
"He's up above."
"Ahoy Thomas, row, row,
Ahoy, Thomas
Pick up your mitts…!"

"Mon lieutenant, you're lodged at the end of the high street, in a winding street, next to a baker on a little square, on the first floor."

"Pardon, Monsieur, can you indicate to me a winding street that leads to a little square?"

"We have three squares: that of the Mairie, that of the Palais-de-Justice and that of the Market. There's the Rue des Grenouilles, which only winds slightly, but winds, there's the Rue des Marmousets, which...

We're camped near Mourmelon, at the extremity of an immense plain strewn with meager clumps of pines.

Between the tents the paths are white; between the barracks, the road is white.

It's midnight. The sentinels are going back and forth, arm in arm, in front of the gray sentry-boxes; the dogs are barking at the moon, the lights are extinct.

The sentinels who are going back and forth arm in arm in front of the gray sentry-boxes won't see you; the dogs barking at the moon won't see you either; come into my tent, it's alone in the middle of a big square of grass...

How pretty she is when she's asleep with her arms folded behind her head, when the silky locks of her blue-tinted hair trace shiny arabesques over the mat ivory of her breast!

And there's a heart in that ivory coffer, a heart as gay as a sparrow, a heart as tender as a morning in May, a heart as faithful as...

"The heart of a woman is like the sand; a breath of wind effaces your footprints there."

"Who said that?"

"The past."

In the direction of the firing range, on the crest of one of those undulations that descend the mountain of Reims, I encountered a young woman.

She was walking, collecting those little golden flowers that star the chalky plain.

I encountered her on quitting the one whose eyes are the color of irises, and I am following her involuntarily.

I am following her because I find her beautiful, but I would have liked not to follow her, because I still have the perfume of the kiss of adieu on my lips.

She is as beautiful as a wheat-field on the eve of the harvest. Is she a woman? Skylarks are fluttering around her.

"Who are you, then, young woman?"

"I'm the one who weeps when the wheat doesn't ripen. I'm the older sister of the Breton virgin."

"And what is it necessary to do for the wheat to ripen?"

She spoke briefly to me, in a whisper.

On a stormy night I have seen an eagle flee before a skylark. Perhaps the predicted time is near, perhaps the wheat is about to ripen...

The tempest is rumbling, but it isn't yet hollowing out the waves so that Arthur's sword can be seen. Let's dream.

Then Louis rolled up the manuscript and said: "Have you understood?"

"No," Henri replied.

"So much the better, for if you'd understood, I would have burned these pages. I'm not one of those who would like to live in a house of crystal, and I don't open up to just anyone the cupboard in which I keep the garments that have withered my passions and my dreams."

"Are you in love with a woman? Once, you only found your brainchildren beautiful."

Henri was a scholar, Louis was a dreamer. The former shrank the world in order to be able to look at it through a magnifying glass, the latter pushed back the bounds of infinity in order to be able, without falling into the void, to stroll with closed eyes.

"What tells you that my lover is not my brainchild?" Louis sighed. "Light a cigar and listen; I'll translate my poem into vulgar language.

"I lived in a city overlooked by a vast plateau.

"In the evening, that plateau is silent and philosophical hares dream there, their ears flat on their backs. I went there to dream with the hares when the sun descended behind the hills, when the moon silvered the broad pathways in the wood, when the stars were mirrored in the little pond where the water-lilies flowered. The roe deer told me strange things.

"Perhaps roe deer know what humans have forgotten."

"Perhaps."

"One evening, the sky was clear, an embalmed breeze was singing in the white ears of blades of grass, in the shiny leaves of the irises, in the eglantine bushes, in the crimson bells of the tall foxgloves; I traversed the plateau and descended into a ravine.

"Do you like mossy paths, which snake at hazard over the sides of ravines, going up and down, and end in a thicket or fade away in a clearing?"

"I don't take paths that don't go directly to where they need to go."

"I take them. When I follow them, my soul flutters, laughs, weeps, remembers and hopes.

"I went down, stopping as soon as I heard a rabbit, as soon as I saw a glow-worm, and the moon was shining when I arrived on the edge of a stream. There I rubbed my eyes.

"I sometimes fall asleep while walking."

"You're always slightly asleep with your eyes open."

"But I wasn't asleep that evening, and I really saw a woman in the meadow. Her long hair as floating and her feet weren't touching the ground.

"I hid in the shadow of an oak tree."

"We're falling back into poetry; only fays dance on the grass in the moonlight.

"She wasn't dancing, she was singing, and I've never heard such a sweet song. I applauded.

"'Greetings, Brother,' the singer said to me.

"Not knowing how to reply, I responded: 'Greetings, beautiful fay.'"

"More poetry!"

"We chatted for a long time. She taught me to understand what the trees were saying, and when she disappeared, I was madly in love with her.

"The next day I went back to the bank of the stream, but she wasn't there.

"I thought that I was going to die, and I forgot her."

"It's crazy to get tied up."

"I departed. I went to revisit Norway, Africa and Syria, stopping as soon as I was weary and writing in order to repose.

"When I returned I reread my manuscripts and I perceived, with terror, that all my heroes resembled me and all my heroines resembled her. Then I went to the bottom of the ravine, into the little round meadow; I made a fire of dry branches, and when the flame rose up brightly I tore up what I had written, leaf by leaf, and I burned it.

"The last page was about to be extinguished when my beloved appeared."

"Do you see her often?"

"I see her everywhere. Look, I can see her in the smoke of your cigar; she's rising toward that red star."

"Let's go out on the water."

The two friends detached the dinghy. There wasn't a ripple on the Seine, and the wind that swayed the high branches of the poplars didn't brush the summit of the reeds.

"Where are you taking me?" said Louis.

"There," said Henri, pointing at a chalet whose balcony extended over the willows. "I want to talk to you about my mistress."

"You have a mistress?"

"Yes, and perhaps she's as beautiful as your dream."

They went into the chalet, and Louis saw books and scientific instruments on a large table, a furnace in one corner, a skeleton in another, shelves along the walls laden with bottles and flasks, and minerals specimens and herbals on the floor.

"In your turn, listen to me," said Henri.

"One evening, when I was gazing at the stars, seeking the why of creation, I encountered a beautiful young woman who was telling the night her vague desires and vague sorrows. Her forehead was high, her breast broad, her desires were as chaste as the desires of flowers and her sorrows as healthy as the sorrows of heaths.

"I took her hand and I said to her: 'Child, you're seeking, and you're sad because you haven't found what you're seeking. Wait, the hour has come; the wind is bearing to the palm tree the kisses of its brother.

"She had gone astray under the oaks; I showed her the path and I left her.

"I haven't seen her again, but I'm waiting for her, and shell come."

"And they call me mad!"

"She'll come, because I can't love any other woman than her.

"Look carefully inside yourself, and you'll only see halves of virtues and halves of vices. The woman who ought to love you is the one who has the halves that you lack. As no two souls are identical, no hesitation is possible, and as beings must reproduce, they've been created in pairs.

"The woman who confided to the night her vague desires and her vague sorrows has the halves that I lack; that's why I'm waiting for her."

The last light was extinguished over the hills of Marly, the leaves were asleep and the moon was trembling like an opal pearl in a nacreous disk.

"She'll come, but time is passing," sighed Henri. "The flowers that only open in the autumn sun languish and die without producing seed.

"When the snow falls I'll make a soft carpet of it; my beloved's feet are whiter than snow. When the snow falls I'll make a white shroud of it, and my soul will go to a star in order to rediscover spring.

"I want a sun for a nuptial bed."

"I'd like for a nuptial bed a boat rocked by the clear wave, pushed by a warm wind; I'm a son of the land. I'd like to shiver like the trees, to build a nest like the birds, and then die without regrets and without doubts, knowing that my task is finished..."

When will I be able to tell you what I want to say?

Perhaps when I'm able to write well enough to write as one speaks.

I'd like to explain to you why I no longer love the woman whose eyes have the color of irises.

I no longer love her because one day she calls me Louis and the next day Henri. I no longer love her because I always have a desire to weep when my mistresses laugh, and to laugh when they weep. I no longer love her because I'd like to kiss her when she sings and hear her sing when she kisses me. I no longer love her because she's charming, like all those who've been foolish enough to love me for an hour.

When I encountered her, I was voyaging in the blue, and the poor swallow, who only wanted to build a nest, opened her wings in order to follow me where the roads have no limits. When she was very, very high, I thought that I was a son of the earth, and I kissed her so rudely that she fell and broke her wings. Now, I'd like...

I'm a malevolent madman, and I'm locking myself up.

Tomorrow I'll love another woman—it's stronger than I am—but I won't tell her that I love her.

It's said that a man loves until death the woman who has the other halves of his virtues and his vices; but when one has one half one day and the other half the next of the same quality or the same defect, what the devil do you expect him to do?

It's necessary t love a blonde on even days and a brunette on odd days.

I shall profit from my sojourn in camp to learn what I don't know; I want to become a profound tactician, a savant administrator

Shut up, fool, and listen to the sage lessons that...

"Castor, is your cane one meter long?"

"Why do you want my cane to be a meter long? Is yours a meter long"

"Oh, if only my cane were a meter long!"

"He's mad."

"I'm a decorator."

"Of what?"

"Of the camp, of course."

"If you have a mission to make an Eden of it, I feel sorry for you."

"Don't feel sorry for me. While you're savoring the pleasures of lining up in the sun, I'll be drawing up plans in the shade. While you respond to the appeal at four o'clock in the morning, I'll be coercing those plans in my bed. I'm exempt from all service."

"For how long?"

"For as long as there's something to do, and that'll be a long time; I won't have finished on the eve of departure. Would you be capable of sculpting a statue?"

"I've never tried."

"I'll need an artist! I'll also need masons, hod-carriers, carpenters, fitters, gardeners, canteen staff..."

"And hatters."

"To do what?"

"To coif your statue. Come on, seriously, what have you been charged with doing?"

"I'm charged with the confection of a monument on which we'll plant our flag on the thirteenth of August. The monument has to be in chalk—if there were no chalk here they'd never have thought of making the camp of Châlons a branch of the School of Fine Arts—and it's necessary that it's surmounted by a statue. A regiment is dishonored if it doesn't have a colossal statue. Make one."

"I don't even know how to draw."

"All the more reason; it'll have a certain cachet."

"I'll search for a sculptor in my company. What else do you need to do?"

"I need to design gardens in which there are heaps of stones, dig ditches in which water can follow, see to the education of vegetables, supervise the pumps and have the streets sanded. But for that I need a cane a meter long; yours is too short. Bonsoir."

Sing, sing, fool.

The woman I love doesn't exist; she is neither blonde nor brunette; she has learned nothing but knows everything; she has seen nothing but divined everything; and I...

"You're forgetting that love is a recompense, not a goal, and you're on the road that leads to the folly of idiots, the folly of cowards. You're forgetting that love isn't a drop of dew shining in a furrow, and you're weeping instead of plowing up the heath.

"Are you dying of old age, then, land of the Sunset? Yesterday you nourished oaks with knotty trunks and birches with sonorous branches; now I only see elders and willows.

"The wolf has allowed itself to be muzzled! The southern wind has burned the vervain."

That was the elder sister of the Breton virgin speaking under my tent.

Yes, we're no more than trembling elders and weeping willows.

We're trembling before a phantom, weeping before the void.

Lightning has blasted the oaks, the worms have eroded the birches, and the southern wind has burned the vervain.

She doesn't yet have wrinkles in her brow, however, the beautiful queen of the West, Her veins are blue and beneath her green robe I can hear her heart beating. Wake up, daughter of Heaven!

The willows are weeping over her eyes; the elders are trembling over her heart… She's dead!
"She isn't dead, but you wouldn't dare to pronounce the only word that could reawaken her."

I asked the muse of the bards for the mysterious word; she whispered it to me, and I smiled because I had divined it. I don't know how to tell you... Can you hear?
"We can hear the thunder rumbling in the distance."
"You can hear the ivory harp singing the song of the future. Listen to what Merlin said on the hill in Ireland.

At sunrise the bud will open, and the green leaf will sing tomorrow!
It will sing the holy triad, and the sons of Erin will say to the Bretons: "This is the day, soldiers of Arthur! In the darkness, we mistook you for enemies, but the sun is rising; embrace us, brothers!"

At sunrise the bud will open, and the green leaf will sing tomorrow!
It will sing the holy triad, and the Bretons will say to the sons of Gaul: "The south wind brings thirst, the east wind brings death, but the wind with green wings brings inebriation and life."

I

Lower your large eyes
Serious.
Lower your large eyes.

II

Veil your face
White and pure.
Veil your face.

III

Above all whisper
In my footsteps.
Above all whisper.

IV

For your beauty kills
Whoever sees it,
It inebriates and kills.

(Brizeux.)[58]

---

[58] August Brizeux (1803-1858) was a Breton poet, who wrote in the Breton language as well as French. His most celebrated work was the narrative poem *Les Bretons* (1846), and his *Histoires poétiques; suivies d'un Essai sur l'art, ou Poétique nouvelle* [Poetic narratives, followed by an Essay on Art, or New Poetics] (1855) was surely a significant influence on L'Estoille's work.

The Evening

Yes, Monsieur, I was commencing the first page of the general history of the Gauls when I fell asleep; I slept for a month, and when I woke up, entirely well, I asked what time it was.

"He's saved!" cried our aide-major.

"Saved from what, my friend?" I said to him. "I've slept very well, and I invite you to dinner."

"You've had a cerebral fever."

"Get away!"

He didn't want to let it go, and declared that I had need of a change of air. That's why I'm in my sister's house instead of at the camp of Châlons.[59]

---

[59] The Camp de Châlons, later known as the Camp de Mourmelon, was created at Napoléon III's behest and inaugurated in 1857. The chronology of this and the preceding section suggest that L'Estoille spent some time in France after his sojourn in Africa, presumably after the posting to Italy that he anticipated in the last of the published fragment of his journal (dated December 1858). The protagonist of *La Chanson de l'alouette*, by contrast, experiences his bout of "cerebral fever" after a fall suffered in Algeria. If, as is certainly possible, that "fall" was symbolic, the reader might be able to form hypotheses as to why the protagonist of the present collage was confined to the hospital at Châlons before being sent to the Auvergne to convalesce. "Cerebral fever" was a term frequently applied in the late nineteenth century to complications caused by infection by the malarial parasite, but imaginary cases cited in literature are often brought on by severe emotional distress, and the term as also sometimes applied in a medical context to neurosyphilis.

I'm bored in my sister's house; I detest Gothic architecture. Those little turrets hanging on to other turrets, those winding stairways and those weather-vanes that grate on and on, are particularly disagreeable to me.

In the evenings, we chat, since you're kind enough to keep me company.

You please me greatly; you don't speak but you listen.

Men who are able to listen are so rare. Everyone nowadays has a hobby-horse on which he gallops through life, without shouting a warning to passers-by and without reading the signs that a few simpletons like me put over the potholes. Even my aide-major, a grave man, has a hobby-horse like all the rest; he has an obsession with cerebral fever; everyone whose pulse he takes has a cerebral fever.

He's completely mad, and it's not astonishing. When one turns over the same idea for years, the lobe of the brain that is working alone grows at the expense of the others; the entire mass exchanged spherical form for conical form, it tapers, and the brain becomes so pointed that there's only room at its extremity for the pampered idea that holds it in equilibrium. All the others fall away...fall away...

I've never been able to love, but it isn't my fault, my dear monsieur, for I've often loved. Don't laugh; amour is a science, a difficult science known only to those who haven't learned it.

Imbeciles don't love, and they're loved; people of intelligence love, but they don't know how to make themselves loved.

I've sworn not to have any more mistresses; I'm tired of breaking my heart into little pieces in order that the blonde and the brunette can chew it more easily, with a seasoning of angelica or Cayenne pepper. I've sworn only to love beauty from now on, the eternal beauty that people are always talking about, because it probably doesn't exist. I'm searching in history... You haven't forgotten that I've been studying Gaulish history since the night when I heard Merlin's harp.

Are you sleepy, my dear monsieur? I can see it in your eyes. Me too, I'm sleepy; let's go to bed.

I like you very much because...you're mute, which is probably disagreeable for you, but very agreeable for me, because I detest argument.

A handshake, dear monsieur. Stretch out your arm a little, the table is broad. You don't want to touch me with your fingertips? A matter of habit; there are people who, instead of shaking hands, run noses... Who's knocking? Is that you, Marie?

"Yes, uncle."

"Come in. You're not in bed yet? Do you know this monsieur, to whom I'm talking?"

"What monsieur?"

"He's gone! That's astonishing."

"Perhaps it's the little gray man who sees everything I do and tells Maman?"

"Perhaps. You've never seen the little gray man?"

"No, uncle, nor the little blue bird. Adieu. uncle."

"Adieu, darling."

The Morning

I shall never forget the land of the sun; let's make, for the beloved phantom, a poem like those the camel-drivers sing on the road to Lagouath.[60]

When I was rich, I deflected the river and I led it, through a thousand conduits, into the arid plain where the sun burned the merchants.

The plain became a garden, but when, poor, I went past the merchants sitting in the shade, they shouted: "Look at the madman!"

"Madmen tear up trees, but they don't irrigate them," my soul murmured in my ear, and I became a camel-driver.

When I saw the road encumbered by cadavers I said the leaders of the caravans: "Let's find a virgin route bordered by clear springs." They left me to search on my own, and when I came back with a dry mouth, they shouted: "Look at the madman!"

"Madmen get lost on beaten paths, but they don't trace new ones," my soul murmured in my ear," and I fell in love with the sultan's daughter.

The sultan's daughter is more beautiful than the moon. I shall make a poem for her as profound as the night.

---

[60] A version of this section appeared as "Le Poème du Fou" in the *Revue des lettres et des arts* in 1867 and a revised version was subsequently included in *Les Amoureuses* as "Meyrin."

When my poem is similar to a rose-bush I shall perfume my mouth and I shall sit down in front of the one that I love on an embroidered carpet. To my right and my left I shall light cassolettes, and I shall declaim my verses slowly, marking the measure.

The sultan's daughter is whiter than jasmine, a smile sings at the corners of her lips.

My poem is like a honeycomb, and I am sitting on freshly-cut flowers.

I shall sing softly, swaying my head. If the sultan's daughter does not give me her hand to kiss when I have sung a thousand verses, if she does not give me her lips to kiss when I have sung ten thousand verses, I shall say: "I'm mad!" and I won't love her any more.

Light of my eyes, put a cushion under your elbow, light your nargileh, take your little feet out of your green slippers and listen to the poem I've made for you, while gazing at the moon.

Listen to my poem; you are the sultan's daughter, but it is the son of amour.

Houri with a woman's heart, put a cushion under your elbow in order to be able to sleep, if the weight of your eyelashes in causing your eyelids to fall.

Listen:

Further away than Gizeh, further than Memphis, further than Thebes, going up the Nile, I lay down one evening in a round valley, which resembled an amethyst cup half full of sand.

I had been going upriver all day, and saying to myself all day: "Why does the Nile, when it floods, not pass over the grass on that plain?

Half of my soul, the feet swell quickly when one asks "Why?" at every step.

Sing, warbler, without ever asking yourself why you sing, and your days will flow like a stream in a channel of faience.

I lay down and I saw, on the crest of the mountain the color of amethyst, great crouching sphinxes.

Sister of blonde corn, let my verses caress your soul with a wing-tip as they fly away.

Close your azure eyes, and my verses, flapping their wings, will sway your soul as the evening wind sways fields of barley.

While I was gazing at the sphinxes, the simoom drank my water-skins.

The Nile is nearby; but the crowd drinks from the Nile. As I only like new cups. I lay down on the sand and, as the vultures soared above my head, I said to them in beautiful verses:

When, in order to eat my eyes, you settle, wings dangling, upon my still-warm forehead, you will see in my eyes the portrait of my beloved; her sweet face is engraved in streaks of fire in my pupil.

Since I have contemplated that star fallen from the sky, I am like a man blinded by the sun, who sees in the darkness that star at which he has gazed...

I have only sung a hundred verses, and you have given me your hand to kiss! You have, therefore, divined that my heart is a cool oasis in which the flower of amour blooms brilliantly? You have divined that my heart is a profound sea on which the boat of our amour will never run aground?

You have given me your fingers, more transparent than cloudless amber, you have given me your nails more brilliant than a drop of blood on a golden stirrup, you have given me your wrist, more delicate than an ivory flute, and I have only made a hundred verses! Sweet incense of my soul, my verses will be ardent coals, and your heart will be changed into an embalmed cloud!

Oh, my poem, do not progress any longer like a hare, which takes ten steps and looks round; run like the white camel that traverses the desert without stopping.

Listen, beloved:
Lying on the plain, I gazed at a cloud that floated in front of the moon.

That cloud descended, and when it touched the earth, three almahs emerged from it. The thinnest had a cup, the most beautiful had a flute, the palest was naked to the hips.

The thinnest said to me: "Drink, and you will never be thirsty."

I replied: "My love is a fresh spring from which I drink long draughts."

The vultures looked at me sideways.

The palest of the amahs said to me then: "Come into my arms and you will see the heavens.

I replied: "My love is a garden in which the tree with golden fruits grows."

The vultures stretched out their bald necks.

Then the most beautiful of the almahs played the flute, the sphinxes crouching on the summit of the mountain got up, and I saw two palm trees, and under the palm trees, a woman who resembled you.

Messaouda, what I have seen tonight has made me an infidel; I believe, now, what the old men taught under the cedars of Lebanon.

Those old men said that the life of the soul is a stairway that resembles a crescent, the middle of which is in darkness and the two points in the light. They say that at every death the soul, when it is young, descends one step, and that it climbs one when it is old.

If what those old men say is true, we have lived before, and I shall rediscover on your lips the perfume that intoxicated me in the valley of the Nile...

I have rediscovered the sweet perfume on your lips. What the old men say is true,

Listen, Messaouda, to the story of our last amour:

The sphinxes descended from the mountain bathed in the waters of the Nile. I forgot that men called me mad and I said: "My heart can see the one for whom it is waiting..."

Alight, nightingale on that pomegranate bush whose bloody eyes are gazing at the sister of my soul. Clutch in your little feet a branch of the smooth bark, draw back your pretty gray head into the feathers of your neck and sing your most beautiful song of love; you alone can repeat what I have heard, in my dream, under the palm trees of the Nile, Yes, you alone can repeat what the virgin with the perfumed lips has sighed in my ear.

Listen Messaouda, to the song of the nightingale.

....
....
....
....
....

No, my Messaouda, no, I shall not tell you, briefly, the end of our story. It is necessary nowadays, if one wants to be called a poet, to say very little in many words.

Once, a poet was similar to a palm tree, which heads straight toward the sky; now he is similar to a vine, which, in order to rise up two cubits, climbs along walls.

When I sang for you, my verses flowed like the waters of the Nile; my verses were composed of images and not of words, of perfumes and not of letters. Today, I sing for the crowds; I want your name to be written, in letters of azure, on the doors of the Kaaba. Sleep, if the weight of your eyelashes causes your eyelids to fall; I shall speak to the crowd.

When the sphinxes had sung the nuptial song, the virgin that resembled you brought me to a palace where men of stone were dreaming, their hands on their knees.

I know the route that leads to the palace of amour, daughter of the sultan, would you care to follow me as you have followed me before? When I go past, the crowd cried: "Look at the madman!" But what do you care about the cries of the crowd?

Yes, I'm a madman! I've sown my ideas in the furrows of others. Yes, I'm a madman, I've emptied my head in order that the sun might shine there, in order that the wind of the desert might extend its wings there.

Let the crowd speak; the spirit of God resides in empty heads.

The crowd is malevolent... Hide yourself, white aspho-del, under the leaves of the laurel; when the madman has fin-ished his poem, the cavalier will jingle his spurs, and instead of laughing, the crowd will tremble.

Balm of the tree with golden fruits, hide yourself like a dewdrop in a calyx; tomorrow you will shine like a pearl on the hilt of my flyssa, and the heads that do not bow down will roll in the dust.

You do not want to hide like the lover who is waiting; you want, like a proud wife, to stand upright on the threshold? Come with me to the residence of the kadi.

Come, you shall be the shadow of my body, and I shall put your heart in my empty head.

Your heart will find in my empty head a garden in which streams twitter, a sandy path bordered by clear springs.

Come to the residence of the kadi, blonde sister of the roses; he will read the two verses and you will attach, with my name, the pleats of your veil, and your veil will be retained by a solid pin.

"Look at the madman! Look at the madman!"

They are crying: "Look at the madman!" and they have nominated a blind kadi!

When I conducted to that man the star fallen from the sky, when I said to him: "She wants to be my wife," he replied: "You are alone, and you have nothing in your hand but a handful of sand."

Come, my Messaouda, into the round valley where the waters of the Nile no longer enable grass to grow since the flame of our amour has changed the sand into rubies.

Come into the palace where we have loved one another before, when the old plane tree was only a seed.

Come, the great sphinxes are waiting for us on the steps of the terraces.

The Evening

My dear monsieur, I've spoken about you to my sister, and she doesn't know you. She has even been quite astonished by your visits.

Her husband, who is a skeptic, has claimed that I was conversing with my image, which I saw in a mirror. Not liking argument, I made no reply.

But that is not what I wanted to talk to you about. Since this morning, I have been in love.

Don't protest; I'm not in love with a woman...I'll wager that you're going to laugh. I'm in love... You'd certainly laugh if I told you, without preamble, with whom I'm in love, and I'd be annoyed. I'll tell you the story from the beginning.

This morning, when I quit this frightful château, where the weather-vanes were grating, I took a sunken path and I arrived on edge of a pond—an amour of a pond, very transparent, very blue.

As it was a trifle cold, I made some verses—rhyming always warms me—and as I didn't know what to make verses abut, I made one about the pond. This is it:

> Between a clump of pines and great woods of oaks,
> Sleeps a little pond, calm...

It was impossible for me to find a rhyme for "oaks";[61] I'm not a poet; but I am a botanist; I picked a furze flower and opened its calyx,

---

[61] In the original, the word here translated as "oaks" is *chênes*, but it is just as easy to find rhymes for *chênes* in French as it is to find rhymes for *oaks* in English.

230

We scholars are habituated always to look into the depths of things, so we often break something and find nothing inside.

I opened the corolla and I found a drop of dew there. In that dew-drop the sky was reflected, and the little pond, and the great woods.

I thought about many things on seeing everything that a drop of dew can reflect, and I said to myself: "Perhaps it's easier to confine the sky in a dew-drop than to hang a dew-drop on the sky."

You don't understand me? I have however, said something beautiful. I've said: perhaps it's easier to animate a dream than to enable a woman to live in the middle of a dream; I've said; perhaps it's easier to make a soul germinate than to acclimate one already grown in a country that isn't its own.

After having turned that idea over and over in my brain I made a camel-driver's song, which I won't sing you, because I've forgotten it, and I met a young woman.

I chatted with her and I saw that she had no soul.

Let's understand one another: I saw that she didn't have the soul of a woman, which doesn't prevent her from having a soul like trees that grow and dogs that love.

I thanked the Creator; I had found the drop of dew into which I could put the sky.

My dear monsieur, this is what I intend to do: I intend to put a woman's soul into that charming creature and love her until death. Help me to make a beautiful woman's soul...

"Uncle!

"I beg your pardon; my niece is knocking, I'm going to open the door. Darling, this is the monsieur... Why, he's gone!

"You know uncle, Mère Tiennette says that that monsieur is the devil."

"Ah!"

"That's why I knocked on your door, because Mère Tiennette says that the devil runs away from little children. I don't want you to talk to the devil; he'd make you a sorcerer."

"I wasn't talking to the devil. Adieu, *chérie!*"

"You know, uncle, I also want to tell you that Louise is very upset."

"Which Louise?"

"My Aunt Louise, the one who knows tales. You met her yesterdays and you didn't want to recognize her."

"I didn't see her."

"Tomorrow, it's necessary to embrace her. Adieu, Uncle."

"Adieu, darling."

The Morning

"You've never seen me?"

"I've seen you in the snow that falls immaculate. I've seen you in the wave that has never touched the shore and I've seen you in my most beautiful dreams.

"You resemble the daughter of the bards who told me the legend of Merlin under the dolmens of Carnac; you resemble the daughter of the druids who talked to me on the hills of Champagne.

"But you have no soul, flower of the woods."

"I have a heart!"

"I know, and I'll give you a soul, a soul with great wings. For you, I'll ask the muse of Armorica for mercy. I want you to be the gracious symbol of the inspired race that didn't believe in death."

"You saw me yesterday for the first time?"

"Yes, my veronica, I saw you yesterdays for the first time. I saw you when I was dreaming of a soft nest for my amour."

"Your niece bid you adieu yesterday?"

"My niece is still a little bird; unfortunately, tomorrow she'll be a woman. You're weeping?

"*And Solomon, the poet king, who only liked flowers in sheaves and pearls in necklaces, has been spelling the same word for three thousand years without wearying.*"

"Who taught you that, my violet?"

"A man I loved when I was only a child, a man I would love again, if he wished…a man that I loved when he called me little Louise."

"I really was mad, then."

233

POEMS IN PROSE

Jephthah's Daughter

There is no God but God!

All of you who are going, along the roads, seeking the flower of poetry, stop! The flower of poetry does not grow on the roads, the flower of poetry is a flower of paradise. Open the book in which the word of Allah is flamboyant, and you will find the flower you seek, the rose without thorns that hides dewdrops and golden scarabs between its leaves.

If you read the sacred book with your eyes, you will find wisdom; but if you read it with your heart, you will scent the perfume of its rose, you will see Heaven in the dewdrops and you will hear the music that the golden scarabs make with their emerald wings.[62]

When I look with my eyes at the book of Allah I read: *The daughter of Jephthah wept on the mountain.* But if I approach the rose to my nostrils, if I touch the golden scarab with my heart, I see the mountain of cedars; I see the gray waters of the Dead Sea at sunset; in the depths of the valley, in the oleanders, I see Jephthah's brown tents. I see the virgins of Gilead weeping, their heads in their hands, and the Levites

---

[62] Although the Quran only references the story of Jephthah as narrated in *Judges* 12 very briefly, it offers a slightly different slant on the insistence of his daughter on her father keeping his vow, permitting an alternative explanation of the relevance of the story to the practice of human sacrifice.

heaping up the stones of the altar that the blood of Ephrata will redden.[63]

Ephrata is sobbing, holding out her arms: "I shall never hear a word of love!"

Mohammed, make your flute say what the reeds of the salt lake say before a storm; Ephrata sobs, wringing her arms: "I shall not see the sunset again; I shall never hear a word of love; like a date-palm that has grown alone in a crevice in a rock in the sea of sand, I shall never hear the word that make the beloved palms in the round oasis sing."

The virgins of Gilead sigh: "Alas, alas, she will not hear the word that makes the crowns of date-palms sing when the embalmed flowers tilt their golden urns. Her mother has named her the fertile valley, but the laborer will never come. Weep, weep, daughters of Gilead!"

Ephrata sobs, wringing her arms: "I shall not see the sunset again!"

Gazelles, listen, this song has been made for your sisters. Listen, gazelles, to what Jephthah's horsemen are saying in the plain:

"They are coming from the mountains like a torrent; blood is fuming under their hasty footfalls…in the valley they are all dead.

"Throw, daughters of Gilead, throws flowers to the horsemen!"

Listen to Ephrata, gentle gazelles, she will not say what you say as you braid your hair. She says: "I have never thrown

---

[63] Ephrata is a place name, derived from the name of the river Euphrates but often applied symbolically to Bethlehem; Jephthah's daughter is not named in *Judges* and L'Estoille's employment of the name appears to be idiosyncratic; other authors who give her a more detailed identity her usually name her Selia or Adah.

my necklace…like the shackled mare whose stallion is in the desert, I shiver as soon as the wind blows from the orient.

A woman needs love as grass needs water. Ephrata sobs: "My heart is a wave, a hill of sand, an inflamed cloud; it shivers as soon as the wind blows from the orient."

Mohammed, make your flute say what the cymbals say when the Aga mounts his horse: a chief is about to speak. Play softly in order not to wake Ephrata, who sighs: "I am the wife, the husband is waiting for me; sing, my sisters" Let the couch be perfumed! Let the tent-flap be lifted!"

Play, Mohammed, the chief is speaking.

"Star of the Orient, show me the route, my heart is thirsty for love…"

The chief with the long hair sees Ephrata asleep, and amour, like dew, lifts up the flower of poetry in his heart. Listen to him: "Sylph with the tender lips, sylph of the nights of summer, you who open the lilies and wither the orange-blossom. Carry the soul of the horseman to that asphodel."

Do you hear tender gazelles? Ephrata sighs on awakening:

Crested with striped plumes, beautiful bird of the sun, you who see so far, do you see a horseman on the plain? Do you see my betrothed on the plain?"

The horseman advances and says: "I am the breath that will inflate the vermilion apple in the roseate calyx."

The virgin responds: "I was waiting for you as grass waits for the rain."

She is beautiful, Jephthah's daughter, as beautiful as the morning, as beautiful as the middle of the day, and the horseman cries: "Sing, beautiful blue birds! Sing, great woods of oaks! Sing, mossy cedars! Sing, gilded palms! Your friend is no longer alone, your brother is beloved.

"Come, I have a chariot of maple-wood lined with bear- and leopard-skins near a wood; I have white bulls, I have red

236

cows and gray colts with astonished eyes. Come, I teach you how the stars flower, as brilliant as furrows in the sky. Come, I will teach you how a man can rise without ever dying, I will love you as the sparrows love in their nest."

Ephrata weeps as she replies: "I am the promised victim of the god of armies. Go away, go away! I am Jephthah's daughter."

Make your flute vibrate, Mohammed; the voice of the chief is loud. Make your flute vibrate; you can still hear the chief say, pressing the lily of Gilead to his bosom: "My horse is stronger than a wild bull, gentler than a heifer, lighter than a hind, and my arm can bend an ash-wood spear. Come, come, I love you!"

Then the one who ought not to have a husband sighs in the arms of the horseman: "He has said the word that the south wind brings to the tall palms; I am a wife; sing, my sisters."

Sing, gazelles, a wedding song. Ephrata is shivering in the horseman's arms.

"We have put under white linen loves the color of honey and two grains, three grains of incense. If you are hungry, come, come! Come and find the loaves the color of honey!

We have put under white linen the open pomegranate and two grains, three grains of incense. If you are thirsty, come, come! Come and find the open pomegranate."

Gazelles, fall silent; the Levites are coming up from the valley, they are singing: "The Eternal his taken in his hand the sword of Israel; before him our enemies have fled like the grouse before the eagle, his breath has swept them away like wisps of straw, and his gaze has consumed their squadrons more tightly packed than grape-pips, than seeds of maize."

Pity the man who only reads the book of Allah with his eyes; his heart will dry up instead of becoming as verdant as the lily of spring. The man who only reads with his eyes will burn like the straw,

237

The Song of Arthur

Be silent, Messire, and you will hear a glorious song.

I

One day, Merlin said to Arthur: "If you were only a man you would have the right to repose, but you are a king, Arthur, the son of a mysterious cloud. You can repose when you have found a bard capable of writing in immortal verse the story of your life. It's necessary that, in dolor, your sons can sing your glory; it's necessary that, in the intoxication of triumph, they can sing your virtue."

"Where can I find that bard?"

"I don't know. True bards are rare, and they hide, preferring to speak to the ear of the woods than to the ear of princes. Instead of following the chariots of chiefs, like empty reeds that think they can sing because they snore, true bards only follow the roe-deer that gazes at them, the sparrow that listens to them, and the woman who flees them.

"I shall have it announced in the lands where Gaelic is spoken that there will be a poetic combat at Kerleon, and that Arthur will give a golden shield to the victor. The prize being fine, all the bards will come, and I shall say to the most skilful: 'Write my story; you shall have a piece of red gold for each of your verses.'"

"True bards do not sing for a golden shield, they do not exchange their verses for pieces of red gold; true bards sing because they love the sound of their voices. Let the heralds say simply: 'King Arthur wishes to bequeath to the future the history of the past; men savant in the art of poetry, be in Kerleon on the day of June's full moon.

"Why choose the day of June's full moon? The venison is only good in September."

"I would like to witness the combat, and I must quit you on the night of Saint John; I have sworn to the friend who is waiting for me under the hawthorn bush. Your life has been beautiful, King Arthur, you will find a bard; when the Almighty forges a great sword, he stretches the strings of a sonorous harp."

"I shall do as you desire."

Arthur was the son of a virgin and a cloud. The earth trembled when he mounted a horse, and the queen's hair was so beautiful that singers compared it to flowers of gorse. He was as savant as a forest, as mild as a meadow and as strong as a torrent.

II

On the day of June's full moon, a hundred bards and a thousand knights are sitting at Arthur's table in the palace of Kerleon.

The table is well served.

The king, on a seat of green rushes, a carpet the color of dawn beneath his feet, a cushion of red cloth beneath his elbow, has set Queen Guinevere to his right and Merlin to his left. Messire Keu, the seneschal, is supervising the cooks. Beduyer, the cup-bearer, is sampling the hydromel and Gauvain, the herald,[64] is calling the guests by name when the

---

[64] The names Keu, Beduyer and Gauvain (of characters generally known in English as Kay, Bedivere and Gawain) are linked to these functions in a passage in Léon Gautier's *Les épopées françaises* (1865) translated from *Le Roman de Brut*, describing a banquet, but the names of Caerléon and Mordred are rendered in their more familiar form therein. The chapter in Gautier includes an elaborate commentary on Hersart de Villemarqué's interpretations of the romances cited, which probably assisted Duclaux to make up his own variant.

king designates them with his hand. Modred, the Scotsman with the yellow eyes, is opposite Guinevere.

The feast is gay. The warrior, as vigorous as a bear, is laughing heartily and empties his ivory horn; the blonde Guinevere has white teeth; the sword-bearers have no worries, the harp-players no anxieties.

Only Merlin is not laughing; he is gazing at the Scot and muttering into his white beard: "The wild boar has not killed all the vipers." Merlin can see the future; like Arthur, he is the son of an aerial spirit and a Breton virgin. He understands the language of gazes and he mutters into his white beard: "That viper will bite the woman with the golden tresses."

When hunger is appeased, the pages place before each guest a cup of honeyed wine, and King Arthur says: "Men savant in the art of poetry, it is necessary that the future knows how I have vanquished the enemies of the Gaels, and only beautiful verses are immortal; so tune your harps and sing the best that you have, in order that I might choose my historian."

The oldest tunes his harp and sings the praises of Guinevere's blonde hair. He sits down again. Guinevere gives him a gold ring, and Arthur thanks him.

The second bard sings the praises of Guinevere's blue eyes, the third of Guinevere's white teeth, the fourth, fifth, the sixth, and all of them until the last, sing the praises of one of Guinevere's beauties.

The queen is as beautiful as a flowering eglantine, as an apple-tree charged with apples; but she is a woman, and when the last harp falls silent, her eyes are shining.

The sword-bearers are asleep.

"These are empty reeds," Merlin murmurs in the king's ear.

"They're gallant," Arthur replies. Then addressing Modred: "Sing as well, nephew; you're not a Gael, but you have my blood in your veins."

Modred smiles. He sings: "The one I love is so beautiful that I dare not sing her praises. The most beautiful verses tarnish the lips of the beloved, and the silver strings of a tortoise-shell harp can never sigh a kiss."

A stranger appears on the threshold—there are no locks of the doors of Arthur's palace. Modred looks at the queen and sits down.

"Be welcome, stranger," says Arthur.

The stranger comes in. A heavy sword hangs along his right thigh; a wolf follows him, holding a maple-wood harp in its white teeth.

"King of the Bretons," he says. "I am a Gaelic bard."

"We do not know him," whisper the bards.

"Be welcome once again," replies Arthur. "What is your homeland?"

"Gaul. You are the last of the Gaelic kings, Arthur, son of the mysterious being; I am the last of the bards."

"He is the last of the bards!" howl the empty reeds.

"Be silent, arrangers if words!" cries Merlin

"He is the last of the Gaulish bards," says Modred, smiling.

"You don't understand the language I speak, son of darkness; shut up!" replies the Gaul.

The Scotsman leaps over the table, sword in hand. The Gaul has taken the harp from the mouth of the wolf; he covers himself with it like a shield, and Modred's sword breaks on contact with it. That sword had cleaved many shields, however.

"Friends, don't stain my queen's robe," says Arthur. "Tomorrow the day will be long, and if you wish, you can settle your quarrel at sunrise. Sit down, Modred. Eat, Gaul; drink from my cup, and then you can sing."

Modred goes out, pale with anger. The Gaul takes the golden horn, pours a few drops of wine on to the table, and says: "You are the blood of the earth where the oaks grow; always flow red for the Gaels! Flow for them like a river! Give them the strength that renders good and the gaiety that renders brave."

He empties the horn in a single draught, and then he touches the strings of his harp. The sounds that fly from it resemble the sound of the wind in the leaves of the birch, the murmur of a stream between leaves of cress. He sings: "Blonde daughter of oaks. Gaul with the vermilion lips, virgin to whom I have given my soul, enable my harp to say what your great woods say."

The bards mark the measure with their hands in order not to let a fault escape, but the sword-bearers are asleep and Guinevere is pricking the fir-wood table with the point of her knife. The Gaul shakes his long hair and draws such a powerful chord from the harp that the warriors shiver as if the trumpet had sounded.

"Sword-bearers, I am not singing for the ear, I am singing for the heart; wake up!"

The voice of the bard is louder than the voice of a king. He sings: "The sun rises over the bloody plain, the dying shiver, the wounded horses whinny and die. The Gaulish army is vanquished, and the last defenders of Alise have not drunk since the battle.[65]

"I see the day of tears!

"The chief with the broad forehead gazes at the bloody plain ad sighs—the chief who has never been afraid—'They were young, they were handsome... the forest no longer has great trees!'

"I see the day of tears!

"The chief with the broad forehead gazes at the bloody plain; his foot collides with a cadaver. He leans over, kisses the blue lips, and he says—the courageous chief—'You have

---

[65] The town of Alise-Sainte-Reine was regarded by many nineteenth century scholars as the site of the last stand of Vercingetorix in his resistance against the Roman invaders led by Julius Caesar, which ended when the besieged Gauls were forced by thirst to surrender. A statue of Vercingetorix was erected in the town by order of Napoléon III to symbolize the strength of Gaul.

left a joyous swallow on the hill; she is waiting for you and you are dead... They were so brave! They were so strong! They have been vanquished... It is my fault!'

"I see the day of tears!

"Then the wounded, who have not drunk since the battle, raise themselves up on their hands and cry: 'You are the king of war! Vercingetorix, may your name be blessed!'

"I see the day of tears!

"The courageous wild boar is weeping like a child; then the druidess of the waves places her hand on the shoulder of the king of swords. She says: 'Make a fine funeral for Gaul, which is about to die; let her find her druids, her bards and her soldiers again on the plains of the heavens. Children, gather the chariots, the saddles. The javelins, the arrows and the lances; make a heap of them and set fire to it; Gaul will have a beautiful funeral, and the wind of Heaven will not be strong enough to disperse our ashes.

"I have seen the day of tears!

"Then Vercingetorix said: 'It is necessary that Gaul should not die.' He mounts his horse and emerges from Alise. He emerges from Alise—the courageous boar—he puts his feet in shackles himself and he says to the victor: 'Leave my people free and I will be your slave.'

"I have seen the day of tears! I have seen the boar in an iron cage and my heart is filled with hatred. I have seen the king of swords shackled like a slave. And the thirst for vengeance had cleaved my lips.

"I have seen the day of tears; I want to see the day of triumph. Gaels, Gaels, do not let your swords rust under the kisses of women."

"He is a true bard," Merlin murmured in the king's ear.

"Friend," says Arthur, your voice reminds me of the clash of swords and the rattle of breastplates."

Guinevere is pricking the fir-wood table with her golden knife, and she smiles disdainfully. Guinevere is as beautiful as the mountain lake where the swan makes its nest; she is as beautiful as the solitary valley where the heather is white; but Guinevere is a woman.

"How do you like that song?" Arthur asks her.

"I only like love songs."

"Queen, I also know love songs," says the Gaul, and he sings: "The virgin walks alongside the stream, in the green forest; her long hair floats loose over her linen robe, her lips smile at the butterflies. Her fingers caress the fern-leaves. A goldfinch follows her, and as soon as she stops it perches on her shoulder...

"The tree of those who sing is the birch. The branches of the birch sigh on winter nights: *Do not trust the stranger*.

"The goldfinch says in the virgin's ear: *I have a palace in the forest bluer than a spring evening, more luminous than a summer evening, more gilded than a beautiful autumn evening, more brilliant than a beautiful winter evening*. The virgin replies to the goldfinch: *Little bird of the woods, you're lying...*

"The tree of those who think is the hawthorn. The branches of the hawthorn sing on winter nights: *Do not trust the stranger*.

"The sun is hot, the virgin follows the stream into the somber forest; she stops under an oak and lies down on the moss. The goldfinch perches on a green branch and he chirps, while flapping its wing: *Close your eyes the color of the sky...*

"The tree of those who seek is the hazel. The branches of the hazel sigh on winter nights: *Do not trust the stranger*.

The virgin wakes up in a crystal grotto and the goldfinch sings over her lips: *Morgane, our son will be the king of Bretons, Arthur of the heavy hands...*[66]

---

[66] The character of Morgane—whose name is spelled in more than half a dozen different ways—featured in numerous Medieval romances, in which her relationship to King Arthur is vague and various, although a consensus of sorts was eventually forged by Chrétien de Troyes, who represented her as Arthur's sister. That notion was carried over into Malory's

'The tree of those who fight is the ash. *Guinevere, do not trust the stranger.*'"

Guinevere blushes.

Arthur murmurs in Merlin's ear: "I thought that you alone knew that." Then, filling the heavy cup: "Gaul, you are my bard, would you like to be my brother?"

"I would like that, King Arthur."

The two Gaels each open a vein, letting three drops of blood fall into the wine, and they drink one after the other.

"Arthur," says Guinevere, "the torches are burning the fingers of the pages; it's time to retire."

The warriors wanted to finish the feast with a great combat, but Arthur cannot refuse Guinevere anything, and he retires with her to the chamber with a sanded floor. The knights lay down on the benches, the Gaul headed toward the oakwood, and the diviner sat down on the threshold.

III

The two ladies-in-waiting, Enid and Teyaf of the golden bosom,[67] comb the queen's hair and uncover the great bed with crimson curtains.

She is very beautiful, Queen Guinevere, in her fine linen tunic; but Arthur is a soldier and his mouth cannot say what his heart says...

Arthur is asleep like a sword in its scabbard; the queen gets up and leans on the window that overlooks the meadow where the mares have been hobbled. She thinks about the flat-

---

Morte d'Arthur, which established her usual English appellation as Morgan le Fay, and which calls her mother Igraine. The attribution of her name to Arthur's mother is idiosyncratic.

[67] The name Tayef appears odd as well as idiosyncratic; Enid is frequently cited as one of Guinevere's ladies-in-waiting, sometimes coupled with other names, but none resembling this one.

teries of the bards, she thinks about Modred, and she says to herself: "Around me, no one speaks of anything but combats fought for beauties, but I have no knight."

A voice replies to her: "If you wished, Guinevere, I would be your knight."

She has been intoxicated by the flatteries of the bards; she makes a semblance of not having heard. "Beautiful Guinevere," says the voice, "I am Modred, your nephew, come down into the meadow; only the sound of the Oliphant can wake the sleeping Arthur."

"What do you want?"

"To sing you a love song, to repeat what Arthur says to beautiful demoiselles in the enchanted castles whose walls he has overturned."

"The dew is falling and I have red satin slippers."

"The dew will not wet your slippers."

Modred bestrides his black horse and takes the queen, leaning out of the window, in his arms.

"Let me go!" says Guinevere. Modred raises the bridle, clenches his knees, and the horse leaps over the hedge of the meadow.

IV

Arthur has two birds for friends: a blackbird who whistles so sweetly that the flowers tell him their secrets, and an owl whose sight is so piercing that it sees the soul of rocks. The blackbird was on a hawthorn, the owl on a birch, when Modred abducted Guinevere. They cry so loudly that Merlin awakes.

Merlin understands the language of the birds and he sighs: The queen has fled with Modred! Woe, woe! My noble friend will be alone in the danger, the last star will bear me away tonight!"

He runs to the royal chamber, lifts the leather curtain and tugs Arthur's arm.

"Guinevere," says Arthur, half-asleep, "my heart will henceforth be a court of amour, and I shall no longer quit you."

"Arthur, wake up!"

"Where is Guinevere?"

"You are not a man like other men; you must be strong before dolor as before death. "Queen Guinevere will no longer sleep by your side."

"My sword!"

And he runs out of the room.

"I can see the future, but I cannot change the future," sighs Merlin. Having said that, he takes the form of a swallow and flies away in the direction of the land of Bretagne.

Arthur runs into the courtyard, his sword naked. He summons the porter, Gleouloued of the broad hand.[68]

"Why have you let the queen depart?"

"Father, I was sleeping behind the door."

Then the blackbird speaks on the hawthorn: "Modred's horse has leapt over the hedge of the meadow, it carried Queen Guinevere away."

The warrior, as vigorous as a bear, sits down on the ground and began to weep, and Gleouloued, stupefied, sees the Gaulish bard beside him. The Gaul says to Arthur: "Why are you weeping, King of the Gaels?"

"I'm mourning the love that has flown away and the honor that is dead."

"Nothing can kill honor that has not failed, and no one knows when love flies away. Pick up your sword, I shall fight beside you.

"Companions, saddle your horses!"

The knights wake up; the watchman lights the beacon fire on the hill, the herald strikes the shield with sonorous studs with blows of his ax.

"Where is Merlin?" Arthur asks.

---

[68] *Gleouloued à la large main* is Arthur's porter in Edgar Quinet's *Merlin l'enchanteur*.

No one had seen him depart, neither the light sleeper Gleouloued, nor Goudueï with the cat's eyes. Then the owl speaks on the birch: "Merlin has returned to the Armorican forest."

"Yes, I remember," says Arthur. "He had to quit me to-night; I shall be alone in dolor. Companions, saddle your horses! Men of my family, avenge my honor!"

V

At the head of the army march Arthur and the Gaulish bard, Behind them come Messire Keu the seneschal. Beduyer the cup-bearer and Gauvain the herald. They are three good warriors.

Behind those three famous warriors march three warriors no less celebrated: Landlé, whom swords dare not touch, he is so handsome; Morvean, at whom no one dares look, he is so ugly; and Gleouloued, whom no one can knock down, he is so strong. The other knights are all as similar as the ears of a field of barley.

When the army had set forth, the women had uttered sobs; but the Gaulish bard had said to them in a harsh voice: "Women ought not to weep when men go to battle."

Arthur is mounted on a horse the color of foam, whose rounded rump is protected by a large shield. The bard is mounted on a horse the color of fog, which stopped in front of him ready saddled. The heart of the King of the Bretons is beating beneath a silver breastplate; his blond hair escapes from a silver helmet. The bard had scarlet braces and a wolf-skin for a cloak. A gold necklace resonated over his bare breast, a golden bracelet squeezes the top of his right arm, gold powder falls from his blond moustache. The maple-wood harp is hanging from his saddle-bow.

Arthur has the air of a king. but the bard also has the air of a king.

VI

The horses being weary because of the heat, the bard sings: "My beloved has for a palace the azure-tinted cloud, the cornflower of the golden harvests ripened by the sun in summer evenings, under the fiery sky.

"If death summons you what will you reply to death?"

The knights strike their shields three times with their lances and cry, in unison: "We will say to death, gaily: 'Yesterday, we were already waiting for you gaily; today we will follow you gaily!'"

"The eyes that I love have the color of wild myrtle; they are milder than a May wind, more profound than a frozen pond and purer than a golden shield.

"If death summons you, what will you reply to death?"

The horses have begun to trot. The knights cry in unison: "W will say to death gaily: 'Yesterday, we were already waiting for you gaily; today we will follow you gaily!'"

"My beloved has for a palace the azure-tinted fog, the tent lined with gold that the night deploys on summer evenings over the embalmed meadows.

"If death summons you, what will you reply to death?"

The last ranks can no longer hear the voice of the bard, but they cry with the others: "We will say to death, gaily: 'Yesterday, we were already waiting for you gaily; today we will follow you gaily!'"

"The breasts that I love have the perfume of a vermilion apple; they are whiter than fresh milk, sifter than the silvery swan and sounder than a golden shield!

"If death summons you, what will you reply to death?"

The horses, clenched by knees, bound; sparks spring from shields. The knights cry in unison: "We will say to death, gaily: 'Yesterday, we were already waiting for you gaily; today we will follow you gaily!'"

"My beloved has for a palace the azure-tinted gulfs, jewel-cases of golden pearls that the moon rounds out on summer evenings under the nacreous waves.

"If death summons you..."
"Halt! Here is the enemy!"

VIII

Arthur's army has stopped, six bowshots from Modred's army. The Gaels sit down around large fires; then, as night arrives, they go to sleep with their heads helmeted.

The moon rises, a darker cloud emerges from the fog and heads toward the mound on which Arthur is talking about Guinevere to the Gaulish bard. Gradually, the cloud takes on the form of a man. Arthur, attentive, distinguishes a muscular torso, a broad brow over which thick curls of chestnut-colored hair fall, large bright eyes and a blonde moustache.

"Vercingetorix!" cries the bard.

The phantom is as handsome as a wild bull and his gaze is mild. He says to the bard: "Friend, we are going to rejoin one another, not to quit one another again. Then, addressing Arthur: "My son, I am content with you."

"If you are the living cloud who loved the Breton virgin, if you are the goldfinch whose kiss engendered me, give victory to your son, mysterious director of battles.

"I am the King of War. I engendered you with a Breton virgin under an oak with profound root and sinewy branches, and you have the sword of the Breton. I am the man of the past, you will be the man of the future."

A crimson band lights up on the horizon; the cloud pales and disappears, Modred's army moves off. Arthur sounds the horn and the Bretons mount up.

The earth trembles under the feet of the horses.

VIII

The Gaulish bard is on a green mount in the middle of the plain between the two armies; his horse had flown more rapidly than a sea-eagle.

250

The bard is on the green mound, a virgin beside him on a white stallion. She is crowned with violets, the virgin of battles; she has large tender eyes, the virgin with the heavy sword; perched on her white horse, she is reminiscent of a drop of milk on a marble breast, a Valkyrie with red hands.

She sings, the daughter of the sun, and her voice is as sweet to the ears of warriors as the crepitation of beer in a new cup. She says: "Rocks, silver your crests! Gorse, sway your golden butterflies on your green branches! Swords are about to open the doors of the palace of the brave.

"The table is served! The horns are full! Swords are about to open to the gates of Heaven to the souls of men!"

The Valkyrie extends her hand, and in the first rank, horses fall, their heads broken.

IX

The old men, the women and the children are gathered in the inclined plain of Kerleon. They are gazing northwards.

They have gazed until sunset, they have gazed until moonrise; now they are sobbing: "Arthur is dead!"

The old men tear their beards, the women press their nurslings to their breasts, and the children say: "Why have our handsome knights not come back?"

The old men tear their beards and sob: "Our army is dead, and there is no bard worthy to sing its funeral song.

Then a voice resounds in the oak-wood—a voice as loud as the voice of thunder, a voice as full as the voice of the torrent. That voice sings: "A child, he was already a man. A child, he was already valiant in combat. A child, he plunged the sword into the anvil. He has fallen at Camlan."

"He did not quit the battlefield while the blood flowed; he scythed through breastplates as a reaper scythes through stubble; he was sage in counsel. He has fallen at Camlan.

"His warriors are dead; but they died brave men. At midday their lances traced a bloody path on the ground; at midday

251

they had chipped their great swords. They have fallen at Camlan.

"They died brave men. At midday their shields resound-ed like thunder; at midday their great swords cut through leather and iron. They have fallen at Camlan.

"The armies are in battle on two hills; between them runs a stream bordered with willows. Who will be the first to cross the stream?

"It was Arthur. First, he launches forward, crying: 'A heart for an eye! A head for an arm!' His silver breastplate was as resplendent as the morning frost.

"Arthur launches forward first; shields tremble under the point of his lance; under shields in pieces the soil roe up. His impact is more terrible than that of the wild boar; he runs like a herd of wild oxen, like blazing heather.

"When there is mention of the battle of Camlan, peoples will weep.

"Behind Arthur, as tightly-packed as the seeds of an ear of corn, as prickly as a hedgehog, the chiefs with golden neck-laces advance. Their swords are wings.

"Modred's Scots resemble waves driven by the tempest. They wind in sinuous waves along the green hill. They flow in somber waves all the way to the stream bordered with wil-lows. But Arthur's army is a rock, and the somber wave breaks in red foam.

"When there is mention of the battle of Camlan, peoples will weep.

"The waves roll along the green hill…they roll until evening; but every wave is shorter than its sister, and by each wave the rock is eroded.

"It is a fine battle, a battle of men.

"The sun sets; there is no longer anyone on horseback but Arthur and Modred; all the others are dead! They died for a woman, the valiant warriors!

"Then Modred says: 'Let us lower our lances,' but Ar-thur cries: 'Guinevere! Guinevere!' and the lances splinter into smithereens. They draw their swords, as trenchant as the north

252

wind, as heavy as hail, and they whirl them around their heads.

"It is a fine combat.

"Armor crackles under blows like iron in the anvil; blood pearls on hands; breath makes a fog, and the horses rend one another's breasts.

"It is a fine combat.

"The two horses battle, and the warrior as vigorous as a bear clutches the Scotsman in his arms. The two breastplates are cleft. Modred opens his mouth and falls, but Arthur also falls, his breast split.

"Do not search for Arthur's body in the valley of Camlan; do not search for his sword in the valley of Camlan; it is with his body in the round isle of the blue Ocean..."

X

Arthur falls on the bloody grass and his eyes close.

When he opens them again the moon is shining. He raises himself up on his elbow, sees nothing around him but cadavers and crows, and lets his head fall back on to the grass. He thinks about Queen Guinevere.

A skylark is singing. "Why is that skylark singing," he says to himself. "Are skylarks like women, then?" But the skylark is singing softly, and he perceives a woman who is coming forward, looking at every cadaver. Arthur's eyes are troubled; he can scarcely see in the midst of the crows. She approaches slowly, but when she is near the stream bordered by willows Arthur murmurs: "Guinevere!"

"Arthur! My master!"

"Guinevere, I loved you."

"As soon as he had seated me on the rump of his horse, I wanted to flee..."

"My knights are dead because of you... I forgive you, and up there I shall ask them to forgive you too. They all loved you, and me.... I still love you."

"Arthur, Modred's lips have not touched my cheek."

"Don't tell me that if you're lying..."

"Arthur, Arthur!" Having said that, her beautiful blonde hair inclines slowly, and her eyes the color of cornflowers close, and then open pale.

A glow illuminates the west.

Arthur tries to sustain the head with the golden lashes, which slides over his shoulder, but the hand that cleaved anvils when it was still the hand of a child can no longer lift a lock of hair. Guinevere smiles, but every time her eyes the color of cornflowers close, they open again even paler... An embalmed breath caresses the king's lips; the soul of the white eglantine flies away; Guinevere is dead.

"I must die standing up," says Arthur, and he gets to his feet.

XI

In the western Ocean there is an isle as green as an emerald, an isle that floats on the blue waves. Fays have taken the unconscious Arthur there.

Arthur is lying next to a spring bordered by sage; Guinevere is sustaining his head and Morgane is washing his wounds. The water is closing the gaping wounds.

Gaels, Arthur is still on the round isle, but while the fays were carrying him away his clenched hand opened and his sword fell into the sea.

Arthur's sword is still in the waves, but on tempestuous days, one commences to see its tip shining, and the forests have told me that the King of the Gaels will be reborn.

Rachel and Lia

In the name of the clement and merciful God!

I

The caravan is in the plain.

THE ANGEL OF THE SAND
The stars are shining!
On their blonde radiance,
Like a pink flamingo
Of the saline pool
Wings open...

ELPHA[69]
Hey, watchmen, are you asleep?

THE WATCHMAN OF THE NORTH
The plain is silent.

THE WATCHMAN OF THE WEST
The desert wind is blowing.

THE WATCHMAN OF THE SOUTH
The camels are getting up.

---

[69] Although the name Elpha does appear in some versions of the Old Testament it is not in connection with the story of Rachel and Leah (rendered as Lia by Duclaux) recounted in *Genesis* 29, which offers no basis for the story recounted here.

THE WATCHMAN OF THE EAST
The Orient is reddening.

THE ANGEL OF THE PALM TREES
Sleep, ashen wood-pigeons,
Sleep, white doves;
I have chased away the owl.

ELPHA
Children of the night, you who reap in the darkness, do not approach; our sabers are heavy and our lances are long.

The voice of the camel-driver traverses the echoless air like an arrow.

II

A slender crescent trembles between the stars.

THE BEGGAR
I can't sleep. As soon as I go to sleep I see Isaac's men; as soon as I go to sleep I hear the cry uttered by Sullalinn.[70] Sullalinn, the sun is about to rise, the warm sun whose rays dress with flames your bodiless soul.

The old man walks in order to loosen his numb legs.

---

[70] This name does not seem to appear anywhere else, but it might be worth noting that a character named Sullallin features in the poems of Ossian, faked by James Macpherson, where she is the wife of Cathmor, a name that L'Estoille appropriated as that of a bard in another of his fakeloristic drams, "Gyptis" (in *Les Amoureuses*, translated in the third volume of the present set), providing evidence of a sort that L'Estoille was familiar with Macpherson's work, which as greatly admired by many writers of the French Romantic Movement.

III

Can you hear, in the distance, singing in the plain? By night, when you approach a douar, sing loudly and make your stirrups ring.

THE VOICE
I have put in my heart the Euphrates with the green waters. My heart is too vast, nothing can fill it!

THE WATCHMAN OF THE WEST
Elpha! A voice is singing in the plain.

ELPHA
Horseman, if your intentions are good, peace be with you

THE HORSEMAN
I am Jacob, son of Isaac.

Jacob, the son of the patriarch, and Elpha, the son of the maidservant, have clung to the same teat; they have slept in the same cradle, and they love one another as the thumb and the forefinger love one another.

IV

The two men talk about their childhood.

THE BEGGAR
Can you hear them, Sullalinn? Can you see the son of Isaac? The day of vengeance is near. Tomorrow, you will recover, in the Tigris, your pink body, which the waves have paled, and you will wait for me in the living forests where the flowers never fade. You will not wait for long; my soul is stifling in this crushed breast, in this unsteady head.

The two young men talk about their amours.

ELPHA

I only love the plain, where the wind effaces the traces of my footsteps. Erect a tent, Jacob; for myself, I want to live under the blue vault. You will be the root of the tree whose branches buckle under its fruits, and I will be the last bud of the blasted tree. My father was a king; I too want to be a king, a king of the empty desert whose roads are known to me alone. I am not of your tents, sons of tents; I was born in the land of birds, the land where the trees hide your mute sky, the land where the earth speaks.

JACOB

Today is man's, tomorrow is God.

The last star is extinguished.

V

The men have their foreheads in the sand; Elpha is kneeling on his white camel.

ELPHA

O you whose sight is straight, you who knows the roads, show us the route! Drive plague and fear away from us. Give water to the wells and grass to the soil; give the laden camels roads without stones; give the great stallions loving mares; give men peace.

THE CAMEL-DRIVERS

You are the mighty!

The beggar is leaning on his staff.

JACOB

Who is that beggar?

ELPHA

A madman. When the sun is flamboyant he speaks alone, then stops and lends an ear to listen as if someone were replying to him. I let him drink from our water-skins.

JACOB

The Spirit of God dwells in empty heads.

ELPHA

Children, are you ready?

THE CAMEL-DRIVERS

We're ready.

Sing, if you want your camels to march.

ELPHA

Beautiful lily, why, sadly
Do you close your calyx?
Beautiful lily, why do you close
Your snowy calyx?

A CAMEL-DRIVER

Camel-driver, I have seen pass
Your dark-eyed gazelle;
Her haïck was open
I have seen her round throat
And I am jealous!
And I am jealous!

THE CAMEL-DRIVERS

Trot, trot, brown camels!
This evening you shall have barley and dates.

The caravan extends over the sand like a snake in search of water.

THE BEGGAR

A long time ago my people died. It is a long time since I was a king.

THE CAMEL-DRIVERS

Trot, trot, brown camels!

The voice of men is faint. Only their sobs make a sound above the clouds. You can no longer hear the camel-drivers, but you can still hear the beggar sighing.

VI

The caravan is now no more than a line, the beggar no more than a dot.

THE ANGEL OF THE SUN

When I awake,
The great lion, Roars amorously.
Under my golden lips
The palm-tress twist
And the aloes
Fume on the plain
Like incense-burners.

THE BEGGAR

Sullalin! Sullalin!

THE ANGEL OF THE SAND

When the sun is flamboyant,
I have transparent lakes
In the midst of the clouds.

The caravan has disappeared behind rocks of salt.

Fortunate are those who understand the words of the book.

VIII

In front of the caravan three scouts are marching.

THE SCOUTS

They are more numerous than the leaves of the cedar.
And their pontiff has a golden breastplate.

When you flush out a partridge, what do you say, camel-driver/

I say: "The well is nearby."

They are mounting horses with curly manes.
They are filling carts with long bronze poles...

When you see an ostrich running, what do you say, camel-driver?

I say: "The spring is far away."

They are emerging from the reeds like white flies.
And before them flies a great winged lion...

When the earth smells of musk, what do you say, camel-driver?

I say: The tents are nearby."

The camels are trotting, their necks extended. The beggar is walking slowly.

THE BEGGAR

If I kill the son of Isaac, the soul of Sullalinn will go to recover, in the river, his pale body, and I shall no longer see it in the sun's rays. Sullalinn, I do not want you to quit me. If the sun no longer weaves you a cloak of radiance, the sun will be nothing for me but a globe of darkness. If the dew no longer gives you a necklace of pearls, the dew will be nothing for me than muddy water. If the morning air no longer lifts you up in its blue arms, the morning air will be nothing for me but a noxious fog.

THE ANGEL OF THE SAND
The road of the desert is the road of Allah;
Each must seek it, but my wings efface
The tracks of camels in the golden sand.
Prayer and faith guide caravans.

THE BEGGAR
I can no longer march alone. When I see Sullalinn following, on the sand, the turning sun, I follow Sullalinn without paying any heed to the road.

Elpha's camel flies like a bird, Jacob's horse bounds like a panther.

THE SCOUTS
Here are the tents! We have traversed the land of thirst; here is the clear stream! We have traversed the land of fear; here are the smiling virgins! Blessed be Jehovah!

Women have always loved the camel-drivers; they clap their hands.

God is great
When he wishes, he can make the gazelle
and the lion drink from the same spring.

IX

The camels are unloaded.

THE YOUNG WOMEN
Braid your hair, daughters of the desert.
Let your striped belts float in the wind;
Our young men have returned.

*The mares paw the ground, and the meager stallions prance
and whinny.*

RACHEL
*They are stronger than the old cedars
Of the mountain with white crowns;
They are prouder than the antelope,
And their eyes are as profound
As serene nights.*

ELPHA
The asphodel bud has blossomed and its perfume is intoxicating.

THE YOUNG WOMEN
*If we had wings,
Like the partridge...*

ELPHA
I believe that amour grows slowly in the human heart.

*The camels are unloaded and the bouquet of roses sheds its
petals in the wind of amour.*

X

Listen, a man is talking to another.

JACOB
I have watched your flocks as the quail watches over her
chicks, and when I do not see Rachel my days are full of darkness.

LABAN

You have a right to the promised salary. Take Rachel, and may happiness enter your tent this evening in the haïck of the one you have chosen.

JACOB

When the tender jasmine enlaces the solitary date-palm, my tent will be an embalmed oasis.

The jasmine gives flowers but the olive-tree gives oil, Why does Jacob prefer the jasmine to the olive-tree?

LIA

How quickly the sun moves today!

Laban tells the shepherds to gather the flocks, for the flocks must witness their master's wedding.

Fortunate are those who understand the word of Allah!

XI

Watch the almahs turning; in admiring the creature, one renders homage to the creator. The shepherds and the camel-drivers have sat down at the wedding feast.

THE IMPROVISER

The flocks are in the plain
Where the perfumed grass grows;
The joyful lambs are bounding,
And the great stallions
Are resting their fine heads
On the shiny rumps
Of silvery foals,
But the pastor is pale;
He is thinking of the blond cluster

That is ripening on the olive-trees...
Turn, almahs,
As the star
Turns on it burning axis!

Women, who believe they have the right to weep, listen to the brown-haired Lia. She is behind the tents.

LIA
A drop of water in the dust is ugly, but if a ray of light travers-es it, it shines like a ruby.

Rachel reddens the palms of her hands with henna. Jacob gaz-es at the sun.

LIA
The sun is about to hide and the dust will drink me.

The almahs turn.

LIA
Jacob, I would have been for you the dog that watches while its master sleeps.

Jacob does not hear what Lia says; he is gazing at the sun. Who is that man who is walking so slowly? There is no empty place.

LIA
Dry up, my eyes; on a wedding day, the tears of a maidservant bring misfortune to the husband.

Why are the almahs no longer dancing?

LABAN
The lips of the poet have dried up. Elpha, your voice is soft; sing to make those women turn.

ELPHA

I only sing in the desert.

JACOB

Brother, are you sad?

ELPHA

I am happy; your heart is half of mine. Your bride is beautiful, Jacob, but mine is even more beautiful. Men of the tents, fill your cups and drink to the bride of the camel-driver. Almahs, let your veils fall!

Turn, turn as the star
Turns on its burning axle...
When the wind of the desert rises
When the reddened sand
Buries the palm-trees,
When the lightning flashes,
When men tremble,
Out there out there,
A pale virgin appears...
It is the camel-driver's bride!
Turn, Almahs!

Her arms are as white as ivory,
Her eyes are as soft as the night,
And her lips are so fresh
That after having kissed them
One no longer returns to one's tent...
Out there, out there,
Where the sky touches the plain,
I shall seek the pale virgin,
I shall seek my bride.

Elpha draws away. The men look at one another, astonished, and Jacob says, in his soul: "His father was a king; I shall give him half my people." Lia is weeping behind the tents; the beggar stops nearby.

THE BEGGAR

I can no longer march alone. When I see Sullalinn following, on the sand, the turning sun, I follow Sullalinn without paying any heed to the road. Why is that woman weeping? Only amour makes young women weep. Her eyes are golden dots like Sullalinn's eyes. When I was a king, I dried up tears. I am no longer a king, but I know the secrets of flowers; they have given me the key that opens the blue door.

LIA

The sun is about to hide and the dust will drink me.

THE BEGGAR

I cannot let eyes that resemble Sullalinn's weep. Are you in pain, young woman?

LIA

Stranger, in the tents of Laban no one will ask you where you come from, nor where you are going.

THE BEGGAR

Keep your secret and take this gourd; if you empty it, sleep will come, sweet sleep full of beautiful dreams. Your eyes resemble eyes that I never saw weeping.

The beggar disappears into the shadow of the palm-trees.

LIA

Only a king can give a golden gourd—a king, or an envoy of God.

Lia goes back into the tent. Elpha saddles his white camel, the one that is never thirsty.

ELPHA

Get up, my runner, we're going to the salty pond; my bride is waiting for me. My marriage bed will be worthy of a king, it will have the color of the sky.

The great camel gets up and departs, swaying its head like a swimming swan.

XII

The almahs fall, palpitating, on the striped carpet. The sun sets.

THE YOUNG WOMEN

We have a gazelle, a gazelle with bright eyes.

THE SHEPHERDS

We have a tawny lion with a spoiled heart.

THE YOUNG WOMEN

We have a cup full of milk and honey.

THE SHEPHERDS

Rachel, Rachel! The star of amour is rising.

LABAN

I am giving you to Jacob in order that he will have sons whose tents cover the plain, in order that his name will not die. Jacob, always be good to your maidservant, and your maidservant will obey you.

JACOB

Let your eyes be, for me, what the dew is for the plain.

The blush of the bride belongs to the husband, and men must not see the virgin lift the curtain of the tent.

God does what he will!
It is God who extended the white daylight
and rendered it luminous; it is him who
folded the night and blackened it as if he
had burned it.

XIII

Jacob is gazing at the stars, which are riding. Lia is perfuming Rachel's hair. The beggar is hiding in the shadow of the palm-trees.

THE BEGGAR

The God of the murderer is a powerful God, he has twisted the reed like a creeper, he has inclined his superb head toward the ground; but amour is stronger than the God. The God of the murderer is a powerful God, he has filled with darkness the brow that illuminates peoples; but the star of amour has remained brilliant in the night.

The fires are extinguished, the tents are folded up. Lia is braiding Rachel's hair.

XIV

The partridge always returns to the spring; the lover always returns to the beloved tent.

ELPHA

Why has the sand not swallowed me? Why has the sun not caused my head to burst?

THE BEGGAR

Stand up, twisted body; obey the soul of the king.

THE YOUNG WOMEN
Rachel, Rachel! The star of amour is rising.

ELPHA
She shall not enter that tent.

JACOB
Lord, the future is in your hand.

THE BEGGAR
I can no longer pounce like a tiger; I shall crawl like a snake.

THE YOUNG WOMEN
In a sky without storms the star will shine.

ELPHA
How beautiful she must be with her hair braided and her eyes darkened! How white her hands must appear with their rails red! I adore them, hose dainty hands; I have so often held them in mine when she was small and she said: "Elpha, my good Elpha. Sing me one of the songs that make the camels trot..." I must kill her!"

THE YOUNG WOMEN
Rachel, Rachel! The star of amour is rising.

ELPHA
It' must be done! It must be done!

THE BEGGAR
It must be done!

ELPHA
Does that voice come from within or without?

THE BEGGAR
It comes from within and without.

ELPHA

Go away madman!

THE BEGGAR

You love her, then?

ELPHA

Get away, or...

THE BEGGAR

Saddle your camel and return to Jacob's Tent.

ELPHA

And then?

THE BEGGAR

The desert is vast and Rachel loves you. Go saddle your cam-el. The madman is not mad.

Lia hides Rachel under the white veil; the blush of the bride belongs to the husband.

XV

You shall take an eye for an eye and a tooth for a tooth, but you shall not arm a foreign hand in your quarrel, or you shall be cursed, and the missile that you believe that you are launching against your enemy with return to your own heart.

THE BEGGAR

He will not have killed Rachel; but when he returns she will be in her tent, He will hear the sound of a kiss and he will kill Jacob. I shall hear the saber grate. The day of vengeance has come.

The fires are extinct. The sand muffles the sound of footsteps.

XVI

Lia has emptied the golden gourd; she takes Rachel to Jacob.

RACHEL
Let me look at the stars for a moment longer. I am still as free
as them, but tomorrow…you're trembling?

*The camel-driver throws his thick burnoose over Rachel. He
carries her away, and Lia enters Jacob's tent. The beggar
writhes on the sand like a snake with a broken back. The angel
of silence opens his velvet wings over the tents.*

As an apple-tree is among forest trees, so is
my beloved in the hands of men. I have
reposed in the shadow of the man I have
desired so much and his brow in soft to my
lips.

XVII

Lia is running, her hair loose.

LIA
I was only a drop of water in the dust; the sun gazed at me and
I shone like a ruby.

THE ANGEL OF THE DESERT
The dew is moistening my wings.

THE ANGEL OF THE NIGHT
Stars, draw the folds of your veils over your tired eyes.

LIA
Where am I? I'm afraid… Rachel! Rachel!

THE ANGEL OF THE NIGHT
Stars, draw the folds of your veils over your tired eyes; the red
hair of the impatient sun is rising.

LIA
I don't know! I don't know!

THE ANGEL OF DREAMS
Errant spirits, return to your somber grottos until dusk; the
angel with crimson wings has placed his golden heel on the
threshold of the Orient.

LIA
What have I done?

The sun rises. Horsemen are riding over the plain.

XVIII

*Elpha has been gazing into Rachel's eyes instead of gazing at
the motionless star, and his camel has described a circle.*

RACHEL
Why has Lia abandoned me? Jacob! Jacob!

ELPHA
Don't call for Jacob.

RACHEL
I hate you! Let me go!

ELPHA
No.

RACHEL
Elpha! My good Elpha!

273

ELPHA

No…no, you hate me.

RACHEL

I'm afraid!

ELPHA

She's afraid...

RACHEL

Don't touch me.

Blood springs from Elpha's breast. A diver sees the bottom of the sea, but which of you can say: "I have seen the bottom of a woman's heart?" Blood springs from Elpha's breast. Rachel tears her veil.

RACHEL

I don't want you to die!

ELPHA

Her arms as are white as ivory
Her eyes are as soft as the night,
And her lips are s fresh,
That after they have lowered,
One no longer returns to one's tent...

RACHEL

I will go wherever you wish.

ELPHA

Out there, out there,
Where the sky touches the plain,
I shall seek the pale virgin...

Elpha is dead. Which of you can say: "I have seen the bottom of a woman's heart?"

May God enable you to die in holy war!

XIX

The book in which the word of Allah sleeps is a cluster of
thunderbolts; do not look at it to closely, you will be dazzled.
Rachel was the mother of Joseph. Laban died in old age and
Jacob had twelve sons.

Like Attar the perfumer I have burned my
soul in order to illuminate believers, and
my brain is as smoky as the niche in which
a lamp is placed.

Symphony

ROSE-DES-EAUX

I

As a child he lived in a castle in a gorge in the Cévennes. He was as wild as a tercel, and the grandfather called him Luern,[71] which means "wolf" in the old language of the mountain.

In the castle, at the back of a flower-garden, between two yellow marble vases full of apples and pomegranates, a granite woman leaned over a basin. That woman, it was said, was a statue.

Luern spent long hours watching the serious head of the statue tremble in the water of the basin.

For long hours, lying in the grass, he sang vague poems accompanied by the crickets.

The grandfather listened to the vague poems, and then he took the child by the hand and led him into the sunlit vine-yards where the cicadas sang in the twisted peach-trees, and into the shady meadows where shy walnut-trees dipped their roots in transparent springs.

He said to him: "Do not crush snails underfoot, do not pull the wings off cockchafers, do not throw stones at the toad crawling between the vine-stocks; the Creator has given souls to the ugliest creatures."

---

[71] Luern was the name of a legendary king of the Arvernes, who allegedly ruled then in the second century A.D.

They went slowly, the child as joyful as a butterfly, and the old man as pensive as the crenellated towers that watch swallows soaring in the gulf. They went slowly, and the grandfather said: "March straight, and don't be afraid of anything."

By night, the stone woman descended from her pedestal and leaned over Luern's bed. She carried his soul away to strange lands, full of flowers and sunlight.

II

It is the night of the summer solstice. A bright fire is burning on the Plateau de la Madeleine and the mountain folk are dancing and singing: "Saint John, Saint John! Come and dance, girls! Girls and boys, dance a round!"

At midnight, the fire is extinct and a great voice is heard over the heath; that voice says: "The blasted oak will be green again."

The next day, the foresters found in the ashes, which were still warm, a little girl with hair the color of gold. They took her to the castle, and as she was perfectly beautiful, the grandfather gave her the name of Alona.[72]

III

The years passed. The grandfather taught Luern what a man ought to know. He told him about Oberon and Titania, Morgane and Merlin, Arthur's knights and Charlemagne's peers.

He said to him: "The Gaels were the bravest and finest of men. They knew that the earth is only an arena in which the

---

[72] In the greatly expanded and substantially different version of this narrative contained in the 1880 *La Chanson de l'alouette*, the girl mysteriously recovered from the ashes is named Alauna, that being the name of a Celtic river goddess.

soul learns to be brave, a school in which it learns to be free, and in which, from time to time, death looms up like a ladder before the fatigued soul, which climbs it, reposes and is reborn."

Alona accompanied them in their long walks.

Every night the stone woman leans over Luern's bed and carries his soul away to strange lands full of flowers and sunlight.

The years pass and Alona's eyes have acquired the color of periwinkles. Listen to Luern telling her what he had dreamed.

The statue took my soul into the middle of silent forests interrupted by marshes and heaths, traversed by a great river.

Herds of red deer passed under the oaks; aurochs bathed their black manes in the marshes and eagles soared over the heaths. Only a few wicker boats moored under the willows, a few blue-tinted clouds rising from the woods and a few mild and guttural strophes rolled by the breeze over the florid heath indicated that humans were there.

My soul went forward, and in a wood it saw a pond in which water-lilies grew. The whitest opened and a fay emerged. She said to me: "When I cut the mistletoe with evergreen branches with a golden sickle, you were a chief and we loved one another. Now I'm a fay; would you like to reign with me over the ponds in the woods?

"Enlaced like the bindweed hanging from the maples, we shall glide by night over the silvery meadows, we shall drink the dew from the lips of periwinkles, and in the water-lilies we shall sleep by day, rocked by the blue waves.

"The stars are shining; come on to the heath where the dead await the poet who seeks and the fat who remembers. I am Rose-des-Eaux, the undine with the soft lips.

The fog dressed the oaks with satin mantles, the stars decorated the ponds with necklaces of carbuncles, glow-worms dotted the grass and roe deer, necks extended, trampled the moss with their tawny feet. I followed the fay.

We walked in sunken paths, hand in hand; we traversed forests, hand in hand.

Rose-des-Eaux stopped. Forms emerged from an oak-wood. Some had wolf-skins on their shoulders, others blazoned robes, others burnished breastplates; the last had a gray hood. Among those shades I saw women as beautiful as poems.

Rose-des-Eaux said to me: "They are the souls of those who died for France. They are coming to our wedding, to the wedding of the poet who seeks and the fay who remembers."

Oberon appeared, cup in hand, and he sang: "Drink from the emerald cup; your lips are pure. Inebriation never empties it, disgust never breaks it. The Master has no put ashes in Oberon's cup."

I drank. Then a cloud emerged from the cup, which was still full: as cloud of velvety wings, luminous scarves, loose hair, pink legs and bare shoulders. The cloud had a conical form; it was spinning on its point, and with every rotation a couple fell from the swarm like an overripe grape from a red cluster.

The cloud spun, and with every rotation a couple fell from the swarm—fays of the woods with their green scarves, fays of the heath crowned with gorse, fays of the springs, roses in hand, fays of the rivers with glaucous eyes, fays of the waves with sift eyes, and fays of battles with open wings. Then follets with bodies of flame, sprites with inflated cheeks, elves with silver feet, sylphs with lips tinted with flower-pollen, gnomes with large heads, chilly dwarves in mouse-skin cloaks, kobolds and korrigans—with every rotation a couple fell from the swarm like an overripe grape from a red cluster.

I grew wings and Rose-des-Eaux said to me: "Look, the stars are going out."

Oberon blew his horn and the entire crowd followed us. The follets, the gnomes, the korrigans and the dwarves rode behind us on goats with gilded horns, and ahead of us the valkyries, perched on their horses as white as foam, whipped the nacreous morning mist with their bloody wings.

The heaths disappeared, the forests were effaced. We were now flying more rapidly and rising ever higher. The fay said to me: "We are going to where I shall rediscover my golden sickle plunged in the trunk of the eternal oak. We are going to the radiant star where blood never flows, where science and amour reign; we're going to the star of the Gaels, the green isle of the Ocean of the heavens.

We slid between the worlds, which went by, leaving a wake of stars behind them. We flew so rapidly that the radiance of dawns could not keep up with us, and we shone in the midst of those flames like dewdrops on the leaves of brambles.

The worlds sang: "The God of the Gaels is the God of the suns!"

Rose-des-Eaux furled her wings. We were in a garden as large as a kingdom; but the garden resembled a flower-garden and the statue was smiling there above a basin, under linden trees

I woke up. A voice murmured:

"Rose-des-Eaux is the one you have loved since the beginning".

"It is time for you to be a man," said the grandfather. "Go and look at death."

The ship left a luminous wake behind it and Luern sighed as he gazed at the declining coast:

"If I were a star I would love you, sea of blue smiles; but I'm only a fire follet and I love the round basin bordered by purslane and mint. I'm only a fire follet; your great waves would extinguish me.

The ship left a luminous wake behind it, and Luern sighed as he gazed at the peaks of the Balearics.:

"I'm going where the green jasmine opens its snowy stars to the evening wind. If I were a nightingale, I'd be happy; but I'm only a tercel and I weep for my fir-trees."

The ship left a luminous wake behind it, and Luern sighed as he gazed at the rising coast:

Here is the coast where the women resemble bronze statues leaning over the rims of wells. Daughters of the desert, you will not make me forget Rose-des-Eaux."

Since Luern's departure, Alona has been sad. She spends her days in the woods, on the edges of ponds where water-lilies flourish, in the sunken paths where bindweed hangs from the maples.

She does not know what she is seeking, but she searches and she waits

Luern is a spahi at Tlemcen, where the olive groves are dense, where the Moorish women are beautiful, and he is amorous. He loves the Gaulish fay, the undine with the fresh lips.

At Tlemcen, where the olive groves are dense, where the Moorish women are beautiful, he has not forgotten Rose-des-Eaux.

It is a mild autumn evening; sunlight is reddening the hornbeam hedge, the leaves are falling, one by one, from the crowns of the lindens. And the last roses, sensitive to the chill, are turning westwards.

Alona, sitting on the laws where the crickets are no longer singing, is gazing at the dull sky, at gray clouds shredded by the wind. She has put her hands together because large tears are falling from her somber eyes.

She says to herself: "Since his departure, the violets no longer have any perfume, the wings of the butterflies have no more splendor, and I weep without knowing why." She looks at the statue. "I hate you! You have shown him a fay."

The granite lips murmur: *A great army is camped on the sand at the foot of a rock beaten by the waves. O the rock, a man with bright eyes is clasping a blonde virgin in his arms...*

"Luern has bright eyes!"

It is a mild autumn evening; the leaves are falling, one by one, from the crowns of the lindens.

The grandfather is dead. His grave has been dug in the little cemetery, in the middle of the vineyards.

In the oasis, under the palm trees, next to the stream, Luern has a house of marble and faience; but he is sad.

The women of the ksour come, after the sun has set to listen to the players of flutes and derboukas under the pomegranate trees, he avoids their laughing groups. Wrapped in his burnoose, a cigarette in his lips, he walks with slow steps and the gazelles of the desert whisper: "Look at the kebir who only loves his horse, the kebir with gray eyes."

When the sun is hot, Luern reads the Bible, the Koran and the fantastic poems of Arabia, while indefatigable horsemen pass by without saying where they have come from or where they are going.

By night he watches the stars shine.

He is sad because he does not find Rose-des-Eaux in the poems or in the stars.

She is pretty, with wide-open eyes and tousled hair!

"She does not have the eyes of our women; she has the eyes of the women painted on Egyptian sarcophagi, eyes that have the air of having seen the commencement."

"Look at that one, a little further away; she is as wild as a swallow, and tomorrow, she will be fifteen years old."

She goes upstream; if a warbler chirps, she stops and listens; if a sunbeam glides between the branches, she stops and looks.

"With her floating hair, her trailing robe and her bare arms, she resembles women who bear the temples of Elora[73] on their heads."

"She is as wild as a swallow, and tomorrow, she will be fifteen years old."

She says to the stream: "Stream with the clear voice, my soul is as old as the rocks that shine in your bed; would you like to know who I loved when the earth smiled, young and florid, at her luminous spouse? Listen:

There was a temple, a palace and a hut on the bank of the Ganges. The temple was so high that its summit disappeared in the rays of sunlight, the palace was so large that one could not count its windows, and the hut was so small that a magnolia hid it completely. In the temple a god was dreaming, in the palace a queen was smiling, and in the hut a potter was working, making clay pitchers to draw water.

One morning, without knowing why—it was spring—the potter was weeping, His tears fell so abundantly that they stained the white clay, so he left the unfinished pitcher on the

---

[73] This enigmatic reference is the first of several to "Elora," by which the author is presumably referring to the ancient temple caves of Ellora and their carved monuments, incorporated into his pseudohistory of reincarnation along with the banks of the Ganges.

turntable and went to the temple whose summit disappeared in the rays of sunlight.

"You're weeping because you do not love," said the god.

The potter returned to his little yard, and as a flower was blooming on the magnolia, he sighed: "Only a flower can love a potter." Then he returned to the pitcher he had begun, but as he was still weeping his tears diluted the clay and it became so soft, so very soft that it took on the form of a magnolia flower between his fingers.

He had only ever made pitchers for drawing water.

That night the potter dreamed that a woman was hidden in the clay flower. He woke up and ran to look at it, but he only saw a dewdrop.

"Dewdrop," he said, "Why are you not the woman I saw in my dream?"

He took a handful of earth, but tears began to flow and the clay became so soft, so very soft, that it took on the form of a woman between his fingers. He placed the clay flower on the head of the statue.

He had only ever made pitchers for drawing water.

That night, the potter dreamed that the queen was hidden in the clay flower. He woke up and ran to look at it, but only saw a sunbeam.

"Sunbeam," he said, "Why are you not the queen that I saw last night?"

The sunbeam was extinguished, and the potter went to sit outside the palace gate. A loud noise shook the vaults of the temple; the Brahmins cried: "The god of Love has taken the form of a sunbeam."

The potter did not hear the cries of the Brahmins; the queen came out on a white elephant. He lifted the cup and said: "Queen, I'm only a potter, but I made this cup while thinking of you."

The queen took the cup, and a sunbeam emerged from it.

284

The potter drew away, but instead of returning to his hut he went to the blacksmith to obtain a chisel and he went into the mountains. The queen had said something to him that no one had heard.

He walked for weeks, and when he found a rock as hard as iron he chiseled temples of Elora. At the entrance he put two panthers with human heads; on their pedestals, clematis branches were enlaced with oak branches...

Clear stream, talkative stream, my soul has been a queen on the banks of the Ganges and the soul of Luern had drawn from the void all the great gods of India. Clear stream, talkative stream, when Luern returns he will dig grottoes for me more profound than those of Elora.

Luern has read the Bible and the Koran in order to find a remedy for his sadness; but as he has drunk with avid lips, he has only found thirst at the bottom of the divine cup. Now he no longer reads; he dreams.

Woe betide the man who dreams under the Saharan sun; the sun pierces his skull and engraves lugubrious images on his brain.

Luern has dreamed while traversing the plain and he has seen Bible verses, like birds with wings of fire, perching in the trees of the old castle, carrying the granite woman away in their beaks, and singing, with Rose-des-Eaux, a savage hymn to the woods and the rocks.

Alona, sitting on the grass where the crickets are waking up, while watching the red mantle of the statue tremble in the somber water of the basin, says: "When Luern returns, we will love one another as we loved one another under the fig-trees of India."

The blackbirds whistle in the hornbeam hedge: "Rose-des-Eaux now has hair the color of gold."

Luern, in the middle of the plain, says to the passing breeze: "On the edge of an azure-tinted pond, between rocks and flowers, I would like to have a hut with a thatched roof, a hut with a mossy roof."

The breeze replies: "When the falcon wants to find a gazelle, it searches in the grass, not in the sun."

Luern is galloping over the plain; he turns round and he says: "Adieu, emerald of the sparkling diadem that the Creator has placed on the unwrinkled brow of the black virgin with velvety eyes.

"Adieu, oasis where the wood-pigeons inflate their ashen necks when the tender wind casts in loose tresses the opals of roses and the rubies of pomegranates.

"Adieu. I am going, like the grouse that the vulture has hunted, to drink at the cool spring; I am going beneath the fir-trees of the snowy Cévennes."

The mountain folk are singing in the depths of the valleys: "Saint John! Saint John! To the fires of Saint John bring bundles of furze and box, to chase away the demon."

The fires are extinct and the granite statue is marching over the heather. Then a great voice cries in the darkness: Why, blonde lioness, have you put a heavy golden collar around your neck? Whether it is gold or leather, a collar is always heavy."

The granite lips reply: "My golden collar is the collar of a chief, the collar of a soldier; I shall give it to the Gael who will draw Arthur's sword from the waves."

The great voice cries in the darkness: "Why O blonde fay are you hiding under that mantle of linen and faded silk? Why do you not pass proud and naked before the nations, in your resplendent beauty?"

The granite lips reply: "Poets speak Latin, master masons speak Greek; they have carved me this heavy mantle."

The mountain folk are singing in the depths of the valleys: "Saint John! Saint John! To the fires of Saint John bring bundles of furze and box, to chase away the demon."

The great voice cries in the darkness: "The blasted oak will be green again."

The granite statue is back on her pedestal; tears are falling from her eyes, and she sighs: "My bard has not returned! Is he asleep too in the shade of palm trees? Has he forgotten the druidess? O you who created me to watch over Gaul, bring back the one who will not speak Latin or Greek."

IV

Greetings, my beautiful village with faltering houses; I have come to sleep under your peach-trees, to wander over your heather, to refresh my hands in your stream. I am sad, friend, I have come to ask your sun for my gaiety of old.

Brambles have grown over the grandfather's grave. Their leaves murmur in his ears what he already understood when alive, and the dew that drips from their flowers glides like tears over the heart that loved them.

"Grandfather, I have marched straight, and the brambles have lacerated me. I have looked down from on high and I love a phantom. Tell me the secret that renders happiness."

Greetings, old castle! Greetings, dense hornbeam hedge; I still have the heart of a child.

Luern says to Alona: "Your eyes shine like a sunbeam; your somber eyes are more profound than the Saharan lakes,"

The blackbirds whistle as they stir the leaves reddened by the autumn.

Alona replied: "I as cold in this old castle; I was about to leave in order to join you. You would have erected a tent for me next to your own, and we would have talked, under the cloudless sky, about the statue and the grandfather."

The blackbirds whistle as they stir the leaves reddened by the autumn.

Luern sighs: "Child, never love a phantom!" He goes away; Alona lowers her head.

The blackbirds whistle in the ivy.

Alona is running along the mountain path. Luern cannot see Alona. She is running along the mountain path; but she only caches up with Luern at the foot of the Pic d'Ange.

The Pic d'Ange is a rock as high as a church. Goats have never climbed to its summit, shepherds have never collected the coral berries of the beautiful service-tress that grown in one of its fissures.

Luern gazes at the rock and he says: "One evening in September I engraved my name in the smooth bark of the beautiful service-tree. One evening in September I was dreaming up there , and I saw the plain like a yellow carpet, and the great fir-trees like a field of wheat. Beautiful service-tree, I am, like you, alone on a vertiginous rock, alone in a crevice to which blue butterflies never rise. My mistress is within me and her kisses make me weep."

Luern hears a sigh in the dense shadow cast by the rock. He turns round and he sees a white form. The white form flees into the meadow. It flies over the grass and disappears behind a juniper bush at the corner of a thicket.

The blackbirds whistle as they stir the leaves reddened by the autumn.

Luern is on the edge of the basin. Alona is shredding anemones. The same moonbeam caresses then, and the statue's tears fall slowly into the granite shell.

"Beautiful statue," says Luern, "you don't walk at night? You're not a woman, then?"

Alona is shredding anemones.

"My dream was only a dream" Alona, never love a phantom."

"I love a poet."

The night is clear; Luern looks at the child with the golden hair

"I've loved him since the day when the earth, young and florid, smiled at the Creator."

Alona puts her hand on the shoulder of the statue, and sings:

A long time ago, a very long time ago, an oak said to a clematis: "Embalmed clematis, my heart beats beneath my bark when your tender arms hug my knotty trunk. Climb, clematis, into the branches of the oak."

Along time ago, a very long time ago, the clematis replied to the oak: "Over the silvery sand the azure-tinted wave twitters; over the limpid spring the buttercups shine and dew spangles the emerald grass where the glaucous irises open their large blue eyes."

The oak said: "Climb, clematis, my head overlooks the forest.

The clematis replied: "If I climb, I will no longer hear the spring twitter, I will no longer see the blue irises."

A long time ago, a very long time ago, the oak said to the clematis: "Climb and you will see the sky, where the sun sows changing flowers over the crimson of the evening; climb and you will hear the stars singing."

A long time ago, a very long time ago, the clematis replied to the oak: "I can see the sky, I can see the sea. The sea is greener than the grass, the sky is bluer than the iris, and the quivering of your leaves is more harmonious than the twitter of the stream."

The oak said: "Hug me, I will give you strength.

The clematis replied: "Sustain me, I will give you my perfume."

The blackbirds were whistling in the ivy.

The lamps are extinct, and Luern is dreaming in the square bed where he slept as a child.

The curtain opens, a warn hand touches his forehead. He takes the hand and, pressing it to his lips, he says: "I've been expecting you for many nights, sweet friend of my childhood; why have you not come for such a long time?"

The warm hand shivers.

"You're shivering like a woman?"

Luern tries to get up, but the warm had presses on his forehead and a voice murmurs in his ear: "I'm not the statue; I'm Rose-des-Eaux. Sleep, child, and I'll carry your soul away to the land where we loved one another when I was a woman."

The arm hand rests of Luern's brow and the soft voice murmurs:

Near the palace where the sun forges its golden arrows there are great plains dotted with water-lilies and irises, the leaves of which are silvered every night by the kisses of the sea. In those plains the horses of the Gaels grazed when Boun taught strings to speak.

Boun was born under an oak tree and he understood what the stars were saying. Boun was a warrior, and when the bulls were asleep with their legs folded, he sang t the daughter of chiefs what the trees said. The young woman did not understand yet, but she smiled, showing her teeth, and her teeth were so small that Boun sang in order to see them shine,

In spring, Boun no longer sang to his friend while the bulls slept.

He spent long hours sitting on the edge of the sea, with the waves licking his feet, and his bright eyes gazing westwards. He listened to what the blue waves were saying to the green waves; he understood the two voices, but he was sad. He was sad because the young woman did not bush under his gaze.

He was so sad that he made the strings of his harp weep, one evening when the wind cast hawthorn blossom into the sea.

As soon as the waves heard his lament, they too began to weep, and the young woman got down from the heavy cart. Then the harp rented sweetly and Boun sang: I have for my bride a chariot drawn buy twelve white bulls with ivory horns and a heart that fear has never entered; would you like to be my bride?"

The young woman replied: "I have for my fiancé a heart that love has never entered..."

She fled, and Boun, making the strings of his harp vibrate, sang: "Mountains, flatten beneath the feet of my horse! Rivers, solidify beneath the feet of my horse! Forests, open beneath the feet of my horse! I want the earth for my bride!"

While Boun was speaking to the earth, men had cut lances of ash-wood; they came to form a circle around him.

That circle was so wide that a skylark which tried to traverse it fell with rigid wings. Boun placed it on the wood of his lance.

So the circle was wide; but the voice of the chief as so powerful that the warriors trembled when he sang raising his ax: "March, sons of the sun, march westwards! March, children of the oaks! Our swords are thirsty, strike, strike! Strike the blue swords on the shields!"

Then the skylark sang: "Chief with the strong hand, instead of crushing the skylark you have placed it on the wood of your lance; the skylark will be the bird of the Gaels. Where your sons camp I shall sing over their chariots, where your

291

sons sow I shall sing over their furrows, and I shall teach your daughters to love their hearth as I love my nest."

The skylark rose into the sky, and when it seemed no larger than a bee, it sang: "The earth belongs to the Gaels!"

The men had hardened their ash-wood lances; the young woman had put on a bridal crown; the druids had planted a stone as tall as an oak; the druidesses has collected the sacred herb; Boun lifted his ax and cried: "Let's go!"

The young men armed with arrows marched ahead, then came the bards, then the horsemen, then the heavy carts, then the foot-soldiers. The bards sang the round of swords, the horsemen struck their blank shields, the women uttered shrill cries, the stout bulls bellowed, and the foot-soldiers, applying their bark shields to their lips, howled like wolves.

The bride was sitting on the rump of the gray stallion, with her arms around the neck of Boun, the long-haired chef. The skylark indicated the route.

Child, you have the soul of Boun,[74] look before you and you will see what you seek.

Luern applied the warm hand to his lips. The warm hand withdrew abruptly, the heavy curtains fell back, and he remained alone on the wide serge bed.

---

[74] The invented character named Boun does not appear in the variant version of the narrative contained in *La Chanson de l'alouette*, where reference is made instead to the similarly-invented Ar-Braz, also featured in *Vercingétorix*. Braz is a Breton word meaning "Great." In 1868 the author could not have been aware of the existence of the would-be Breton bard who signed his poetic and folkoristic work Anatole Le Braz (Anatole Lebraz, 1859-1926), although Le Braz probably read L'Estoille's work.

The nightingale is singing in the lilacs, a silver thread designs in the sky the jagged profile of the western mountains. Alona sighs: "Why did I flee?"

The quail wakes up in the clover, a golden thread designs in the sky the rounded curves of the eastern mountains. Alona, smiling, say to the last star: "We shall go to the land of the sun, we shall have a white house in an orange grove."

The nightingale is singing in the lilacs, a silver thread designs in the sky the jagged profile of the western mountains. Luern, his heart overflowing with love, says to the last star: "I am no longer alone; a soul is floating above me."

The quail wakes up in the clover, a golden thread designs in the sky the rounded curves of the eastern mountains. Luern sighs: "I love a phantom! I shall have neither a companion nor sons."

Alona has fled into the meadow where the walnut-trees dip their roots into transparent springs; she says: "When his soul soars with extended wings, he loves me. Dream, my poet."

Luern is going upstream; he is thinking about Rose-des-Eaux; he is thinking about Alona, and his soul is torn. Luern is one of those who only want to have one amour. He gazes at the mountain, he gazes at the plain, and he says: "Adieu, beautiful land where the grass is green, sweet land where the sky is blue!"

Luern is in the bedroom. Alona is sighing behind the door: "I would like to be loved as a woman."

Luern is pacing back and forth; he says: "I would like to kill my head or kill my heart."

Alona comes in. "Go away," says the man who has dreamed under the Saharan sun. Go away, pale phantom! I love a woman."

"I'm not Rose-des-Eaux, I'm Alona."

"What do you want?"

"To be your friend...your sister."

Luern gazes at the child with the golden hair; her lips are pale, her eyes are bright. He gazes at the child with the golden hair and says in a harsh voice: "The violet is not the friend of the fir-tree; the dove is not the sister of the tercel."

Alona totters and Luern sobs: "The fir-tree loves the sweet perfume of the violet, but its trunk is too hard to bend as far as the grass. That is why it sighs so sadly. The tercel would like to caress the feathers of the dove, but it has sharp claws, its caress is a wound, and when it sees blood, it becomes cruel...cowardly...mad."

Luern has dreamed under the Saharan sun; his hands tremble and his eyes shine.

Alona is leaning on the table; her unbound hair hides her entirely; she says:

"Near to the river with the bed of clay, near to the warm river that bloodies the reeds, in a dense thicket of lilacs and lianas, a tawny panther is licking its white underbelly.

A frisson arches her back, a vague glimmer lights up in her eyes, she gets up, and, her paws extended, her muzzle in the grass, she mewls. A hoarse roar rolls over the red waves, a shadow passes, two flashes gleam; the panther stands up and, mad with amour, lacerates the flanks of her beloved."

Luern is pale, Alona is leaning on the table, her hair hides her entirely; she says:

"When the moon silvered the sand, we ran in circles in the desert; when the sun made the rocks fume, we slept under the lilacs, and when the buffaloes went to the Euphrates, we felled the strongest and we drank, in long draughts, from its open throat."

Alona leaps up and her lips touch Luern's lips...

Luern caresses the golden hair, and Alona, her breast heaving, says: "The granite woman has taken my soul into the land full of flowers and sunlight, where it took your soul as a child. She has lifted before me the veil of the past.

"I have seen the sea with flamboyant waves, which beat the rock on which we loved one another as immobile crystals. I have seen the forest where you were an oak, where I was a clematis. I have seen the jungles where we were two panthers. I have seen the caverns of Elora that you hollowed out for me. We are the two halves of an eternal soul..."

A sun the color of ruby is shining over the green star, and the Gaels have gathered on a beach bathed by the Ocean of living waves.

They are there, those who have fought bravely, those who have loved, those who have searched. They are there with their bodies, as handsome as dawns, as strong as tempests, as light as mists, and clear as springs. The warrior caresses his horse, the bard makes the strings of his harp vibrate, the priest sings the true name of the Creator, and the couples, like white gulls, pass over the blue sky.

An old man is on a grassy mound. His beard is gray, but his eyes are flamboyant and his figure is upright, That old man is a acorn that the Creator has sown; that old man is the oak whose roots cover the earth; that old man has son the face of the Almighty. Seated at his feet are a priest and a warrior; between them there is an empty place.

The patriarch gazes at the heath, he gazes at the Ocean, he lends an ear and he says: "Why do I not hear the bard's harp resonating? A man ought only to leave the circle where no one any longer dies in order to teach or to love. When one loves a woman, one sings; when one loves a people, one sings."

"Then a voice more vibrant than the voice of the skylark rises from the earth; that voice says: "Bards must search like men, and weep like men, before speaking the secrets of the heavens."

The crescent of the moon, as slender as a sickle, turns its points toward the Orient. Tears are no longer falling from the eyes of the statue into the granite seashells.

The leaves are motionless, a nightjar flies soundlessly, a silent owl puts its head out of its hole and a guard-dog, lying in front of its niche, wags its tail gently. The statue descends from its pedestal.

The violets open their large eyes in the grass; the narcissi in order to see better, stand up on their stems; a rose in love with a glow-worm calls to her sleeping sisters and the bells of the hyacinths say to the stars of the jasmine: "Look at the statue walking along the path alongside the hornbeam hedge; the old hornbeams are saluting her and the snakes in the ditch are making bracelets of topazes and sapphires for her.

Luern, his head on Alona's heart, says: "My lovely sparrow, when shall we build our nest?"

The statue stops in front of them. A diadem of ears of corn retains the heavy tresses of her ashen hair; a belt of vine-branches tightens her green robe sown with golden reeds, and a star shines on her forehead. She puts Alona's hand into Luern's hand, smiles and disappears.

The blackbirds are whistling in the ivy: "Gaul has taken up her fay's robe, the bright robe of the past."

The trees, the rocks and the flowers are singing a sublime symphony, and a great voice cries in the darkness: "Guardian of my race, you are beautiful in your fay's robe. Soul of Gaul, render to my son the maple-wood harp, and the blasted oak

will be green again, and the sword of Arthur will be flamboyant in the sunlight."

The voice sweeter than he voice of the skylark responds:
"Bards must weep like me before telling the earth the secrets
of the heavens; but I have already stretched he strings of the
maple-wood harp."

The voice sweeter than the voice of the skylark rises all
the way to the green star, and the patriarch says to the priest:
"You will render the golden sickle to Gaul," and he said to the
warrior: "You will render Arthur's sword to Gaul."

The granite statue is no longer on her pedestal; she is
broken at the bottom of the basin.

ALONA

I

They were listening to the nightingale singing. "Let's talk about the past," said Alona, "The great and poetic past. The potter chiseled the rocks of Elora for his queen. I want my love to light a torch in your hand that will illuminate the world.

"We shall have the green forest for a nuptial bed. The most skillful sculptor cannot make a leaf of a tree, and the sound of the most beautiful poem does not rise as high in the heavens as the sound of a kiss."

Luern gazes at the debris of the statue in the round basin. He says: "When a soul animated those granite eyes I read long poems therein; now the eyes are extinct and my brain is only a troubled mirror that reflects palely the images that Alona evokes. Sweet child of my childhood, if it is true that I hollowed out the grottoes of Elora, dissipate the darkness that hides my heart from the one I love."

A voice spoke in Luern's soul,

The moon trembles in the sky like a swan's feather on a woodland pond; Luern presses Alona's hands between his own and he says:

The Gaels marched for one winter and two summers before arriving at the sea that has only one shore; then, the land being Boun's, he wanted to give it to his bride, and the chiefs were summoned to his wedding feast.

When the cups were empty, the crowd cried: "Let the bride always be queen!"

Boun looked at his bride. He looked at her once, and then he smiled; he looked at her a second time, and then went pale. "It's necessary that you know, swallow," he whispered to her, "that your friend is the strongest." He drew his sword, the guests drew theirs, and he felled them as a woodcutter fells elders.

The guests were Boun's men, but the chief wanted to be sure that no one could take his bride from him, that no one could make his swallow weep.

When the sword was wiped clean, the crowd cried: "Boun, it requires so little, you know, to make a swallow weep: a passing cloud, a flash of lightning, a whistling wind.

Boun looked at his bride. He looked at her once, and then he smiled; he looked at her a send time, and then went pale. "It's necessary that you know, swallow," he whispered to her, "that you will never feel the weight of the tempest." He saddled his gray horse. Clouds were running in the sky, lightning was flashing, an icy wind was whistling; he made his bride sit down on the mane of the horse. He rode northwards, and then southwards; he rode to his right, and then to his left, and when the horse fell dead, not one drop of rain had touched his bride's forehead, not one a breath of wind had undone her hear, and not one flash of lightning had dazzled her.

Boun loved his gray stallion, but he wanted to be sure that its breast was broad enough and his arm strong enough to prevent the rain from wetting his bride, and o prevent the wind from carrying his swallow away.

The cups were full and the crowd cried: "Boun has vanquished the tempest, but will not death vanquish him? When death touches Boun, who will console his swallow?"

Boun looked at his bride. He looked at her once, and then he smiled; he looked at her a send time, and then went pale. "It's necessary that they know, swallow," he whispered to her, "that death does not touch the soul of the Gaels. It's necessary that they know what you know."

Blood sprang from the chief's breast, and he said to the crowd: "Sons of the sun, death does not touch the soul of the Gaels. When their bodies are used up, their souls quit them and go to grow to ennoble other bodies that are stronger and more beautiful. On the day when death summons you, have no hear and no regrets."

The bride placed her crown of eglantines on his red breast.

The moon is trembling in the sky like a swan's feather on a woodland pond; Alona stands up, shivering, and she says: "I can hear the great army weeping. I can hear the bards singing the death song. I can hear the noise that the stones make as they are piled upon the chief's body; but a thick cloud is before my eyes."

Luern presses Alona's hands between his own and he says: "The soul of the land where the oaks grow has spoken through your lips."

"This cloud is crushing me. The druidess is dead, I am no longer anything but a woman."

Luern sighs. "We loved one another in the plains of the sky, when the days of earth were only hours, when a cry rose toward us; the skylark was struggling in the claws of an eagle. You said to me: 'This people is your people, we shall not be happy as long as they are not free. Stop your chariot of clouds.'

"Then a voice spoke in the bottomless blue. That voice said: 'If you stop your chariot in the middle of the road you will have all the blood shed on your hands, and all the tears shed in your heart.'

"I stopped my soldier's chariot, my king's chariot, and our souls were incarnated in the bodies of two children. My name was Kenrik, and I was a bard; your name was Moina, and you were a druidess."[75]

"If you have been a bard, sing."

"I'm weary; let me sleep at your feet."

II

Luern looks at his sister, and he makes this poem for his beloved:

1.

The Arvernes are seated at the table of Vercingetorix; Kenrik the bard stands up...

KENRIK

O you who have only sung death songs for a long time, wake up, sleeping harp! And you, father of Gaels, you who are sleeping out there where the sun rises, part the veil of the past before me!

Under a sky always blue, strewn with stars by night, like a limpid like in a florid valley, our ancestors lived. But one day, the storm wind swelled the profound waves, the lake broke its dikes; the children of the dawn marched toward the night.

They marched for a long time, without ever looking backward, without turning aside for anything.

Time, where is your source? Between what banks have you flowed? I only see a pale glimmer n your waves, paler

---

[75] The name of Kenrik—who features as the bard of Vercingetorix in the subsequent drama—appears to have been improvised by L'Estoille, but the name Moina can be found in Macpherson's Ossian fakelore as well as the similar improvisations of Frank Sayers.

than that of the moon when the idle fog lets its gray mantle trail.

Sleeping harp, wake, that your chords might enlighten me.

In you, great chief of the hundred heads, last branch of the tree in the shade of which so many brave men have lived, listen to what your fathers did. Son of Celtill with the neck as white as snow untrodden by any foot, the arm as strong as a twenty-year-old ask, and the heart as large as the valley where the Allier warms in the sun, son of Celtill, listen to what your fathers did.

When the horsemen with the white shields shone over Gaul like foam on the crest of a wave, they broke at the feet of the Arverne mountains. Their tumultuous flood beat our black rocks, but the rock did not tremble, and the invincible Kimris recoiled before the Arvernes.

The hawk wants to live alone, it wants to have a large sector of sky without division. One of your fathers, seeing the crows circling, flew away. A crowd followed him.

On the edge of the blue sea, in the rounded gulf into which the rapid river flows, he encountered a foreign woman. She was weeping; her cheeks had the color of honey, her lips had its perfume. You who come from afar," she said, "and who are going far, protect one who has quit for Gaul the land of the crimson."

Your father drew his sword and said to the enemies of the Phocean foreigner: "Woe betide anyone who touches her!" His sword was so heavy that they all fled; it as so long that when he went, none dared return. He had crossed the mountains of ice.

One day, long, long after, Rome wanted to brave the Gauls. The Gauls crushed the soldiers of Rome in their bare arms.

Sons of conquerors, you are as strong as your forefathers; like them, you will crush the bronze breastplates. Vercingetorix, the cock has crowed, lift your ax and lets us depart...

While he sang, Kenrik gazed at Moina, the druidess with the golden hair.

2.

Kenrik has sung the victory, but the gaze of the druidess has drunk his heart, as the gaze of the sun drinks the water of ponds in summer. He sings his sadness...

I have read on the leaves of the oak verses older than the bark of the oak; I have read on the leaves of the birch verses more brilliant than the bark of the birch; I have read on the leaves of the hawthorn a history of amour.

That history is also written on the necks of swans, on the hooves for horses and on the blades of swords, because that history is as old as the word, Listen:

One day when the sun was shining on the hill where the bees go to seek their honey, a woman as beautiful as a battle was sitting on a rock. She was as beautiful as the foamy wave, as a storm-cloud, as snow stained with blood.

She sang: "Be silent, nightingale; my forehead shines like daylight! Be silent, skylark; my eyes are as profound as the night! Be silent, winds; my voice vibrates like brass! Stop, torrents, my fingers are as strong as bronze."

In order to listen to her, the nightingale no longer sang on the willow; the skylark no longer sang on its nest; the wind no longer sang in the branches of the larch; the torrent no longer sang under the cress.

A hawk soared, crying. The virgin, as beautiful as the flame that burns the ripe crops, said to the hawk: "Be silent." The wild bird flew higher, and cried more loudly.

Then she sang what the forests say when the lightning furrows them, what the meadows say when the furious bull rips them with thrusts of its horn, and what the cliffs say when the wave slaps them.

The hawk soared, crying. Young men approached. The virgin with the white teeth smiled, and the sonorous harp sighed like the heather when the storm wind glides tenderly through the fading flowers.

A man emerged from the path of the tombs, He gazed at the sun and the grass, the stream and the forest, the glacier and the plain; then he drew his sword and cut out his heart.
He cut out his heart, put it in his hand and said: "Proud bird of the clouds, hawk with the powerful wings, take my heart and carry it into the rays of the sun."
The hawk rose so high that the palpitating heart caught fire in the sun's rays. It burned slowly, and the ashes fell slowly on the sonorous harp....

Kenrik sings his sadness. He has given his heart to the blonde druidess, but the bagpipe is calling the clan of Vercingetorix to arms, and he descends from the mountain.

3.

Kenrik is weeping on the edge of the Ocean. Caesar has had Vercingetorix killed...

THE WAVES
The sand is soft.

KENRIK
Weep, heather of Arvernia! Weep, gorse of Bretagne! The heart of Gaul is no longer beating, Vercingetorix is dead.

THE ROCKS
Waves, we are thirsty! Come, come!

KENRIK
A king must not sit down alone at the feast on high. Adieu, heather of the Dore mountains where the bees buzz! Adieu, heaths beloved by the proscribed bards!

THE WAVES
The sand is soft, soft, soft!

THE HARP
Waves, close your emerald lips; I am going to sing. Awake,, echoes of the rocks; I am going to sing. A bard, I want to sing.

THE WAVES
We are the harp of the Unknown; our voice covers the voice of humans.

THE HARP
Bard?

KENRIK
Be silent!

THE HARP
Her eyes are darker than the cherries of the wood, her hair has the color of autumn ferns. Her arms are as pink as

the foam of the stream, and her bosom resembles a nacreous cloud crimsoned by the fires of the evening....

THE ROCKS
The waves are motionless. Why?

THE HARP
Her feet are as light as those of the roe deer, her lips are...

KENRIK
Wind, break these strings! Torrent, carry this wood away! Fire of the heavens, strike the bard!

THE ROCKS
When the harp vibrates, our sleeping souls awake again, the sun enters into our frozen brows, the warm wind inflates our granite veins. Sing, bard's harp!

THE HARP
Breaths that comes from the heath where the gorse flourishes; breaths that caress the branches of old oaks; embalmed breaths, make my strings vibrate...

KENRIK
Be silent! The skylark does not sing in a cage.

THE HARP
The skylark is not in a cage. The skylark of the Gauls cannot be put in a cage. Skylark, touch my strings with the tip of the wing that is believed to be broken and the conqueror will tremble in his bloody toga. Since the bard wishes to be silent, sing alone, strings of bronze! Sing alone, strings of gold!

THE WAVES
Sisters who come from the open sea, glide soundlessly.

THE GOLDEN STRINGS

The Gaels have bright eyes and broad chests. The Gaels are the sons of the sun. Their women have arms so soft and lips so fresh that the clouds are jealous of the sons of the sun.

KENRIK

My dolor is like a great plain, my soul is fatigued in wanting to traverse it.

THE CROWS

Kenrik is summoning us. Why is Kenrik sad?

THE GOLDEN STRINGS

Vercingetorix is dead.

THE CROWS

Is that true?

THE BRONZE STRINGS

It is true.

KENRIK

Adieu, crows with great wings, my soul is about to quit its body. You still have the dew of the woods on your wings; accompany my soul to the milieu of the clouds.

THE CROWS

A boat is coming over the sea.

KENRIK

There are no more men to heap up turf on my tomb; waves, carry my body into a cavern that the rays of the setting sun enter.

THE CROWS

A woman is in the boat.

THE WAVES
Druidess, do not set foot in our foam; we will push the boat on to the sand.

KENRIK
Sun, take my soul in your fiery arms!

THE ROCKS
Druidess, tell the bard to sing; as soon as he sings, our sleeping souls will awake again, the sun will enter our frozen brows, and the warm wind will inflate our stony veins.

MOINA
Kenrik!

KENRIK
The crows are about to bear away my soul.

MOINA
I love you...

The druidess says to the bard: "Let us leave out bodies on the earth; we will find others in the plans of the heavens. Come, soul of Boun, our people will be free."

4.

Two clouds passed by, chased by the western wind; one was gray, the other white; the druidess spoke to them:

"Gray cloud," she said, "you shall be the horse of the bard of tempests. White cloud, you shall be the horse of the virgin of battles, the Valkyrie with bloody wings."

The two clouds changed into stallions and the last rays of the setting sun made one body of the two souls.

Do you remember, Alona? My body resembled that of a bard and my harp had the winds for strings. Yours resembled that of a virgin, but two wings quivered on your naked shoulders.

The stallions carried us over the Rhine with green waves, the Danube with pale waves, and the great river with red waves; they carried us over an icy region in which nations were wandering.

Then you said to me: "Sing, to those peoples who only see the Sun for a moment, when his horses launch themselves fuming from the palace of the night, sing the splendors of the sunset Sing, to those people who only have rugged prairies, the intoxicating perfumes of the sunset. Sing, to these people who only have iron, the golden palaces of the sunset."

I sang, and all those peoples gathered their flocks together and, simultaneously, they marched westwards. Then you said to me: "Return to the land of oaks and prevent the sons from forgetting the language of their fathers."

Do you remember our adieux, Alona...?

The Valkyrie is in the plain bordered by four rivers; her horse snorts, her great wings are open.

She hears a muted sound, and she sees black stripes on the yellow plain, which fan out like the feathers of a peacock's tail.

When the sun set the chiefs marching at the head of the peoples had crossed the river; they stopped in front of the Valkyrie.

They formed, of their own accord, a crescent so large that a galloping horse could not have gone from one point to the other in a day. Behind them, the peoples fanned out like the feathers of a peacock's tail.

Each chief looked at the chief next to him. They spoke to one another, but they did not understand one another. Then the Valkyrie spoke:

"Kings, sit down," she said to them, "and eat together. I am the virgin of battles; I will guide you toward the west, where the sun is flamboyant, where the meadows are perfumed, and where the palaces are made of gold."

The warriors uttered a cry of joy, brandishing their weapons; then they sat down next to one another. It was a fine feast.

The next day they all marched westwards, and they only stopped in the middle of the Forum.

"Our souls are the two halves of one eternal soul," said Alona; "nothing has been able to separate them in the past, nothing will separate them in the future. And yet I sense, between the two of us, something that prevents our souls from dissolving in a kiss. When we were wandering over the sea of the commencement, we were united in the same crystal; when we were floating in the sap of a clematis and an oak, we recognized one another; when, souls devoid of will, we animated the bodies of two panthers, we were united; but since we have had human bodies, we have been pursuing one another without being able to attain one another. Why? Oh, tell me why, if you know, tell me why I am not a woman like other women."

"We loved one another in my chariot of clouds."

"I'm not a woman, I'm a Valkyrie. I'm thirsty…always thirsty…"

She utters a sigh and flees. Luern sighs:

"She is still Moina, but I am no longer Kenrik. She is still the druidess, but I am no longer anything; my sword folds like a wisp of straw, and the song of a cricket covers my voice. Where is the stone ax that opened the forests of the west to the Gaels? Where is the maple harp that made Caesar tremble?

310

Where is my chariot of mist? Where is my horse of cloud? I have been a soldier, I have been a poet, but I am no longer anything. What have I done, for my soul to crawl on the ground above which it has soared?"

Where the Almighty created life, he said to the souls, all equal, that were shivering under his gaze: "You shall forget what you know; but you will learn it again in conflict, and for recompense, you shall have an eternal individuality." He spoke, and the flames were no more than pale sparks that his breath dispersed in the immensity.

When those sparks animated human bodies they gradually grouped together, the brightest going with the brightest. Then the Almighty said: "Humans ought to love one another. They are the buds of the same root; they ought to love one another as the leaves of the same tree love one another; but the tree has branches, some of which look downwards and the others upwards; let us give each one a direction and a will."

He spoke, and the souls of nations stood up radiantly before him. In their various languages there was nothing in common but the name of the Creator.

He showed himself to each one under one of his faces and he said: "Go, watch over the human races, sustain them in their struggles; when you understand one another, the promised hour will sound and the victory will be won."

The soul of the Gaels shone, in the midst of those souls, as the evening star shines in the midst of the stars.

"Saint John! Saint John! To the fire of Saint John bring bundles of furze and box to drive away the demon!"

The fire is extinct on the Plateau de la Madeleine, and the song of the mountain folk is lost in the depths of the valleys

Then a great voice resounds in the darkness. That voice says: "You are beautiful beneath your crown of vine-branches and gladioli, blonde guardian of my race. The sword of my sons will emerge brilliant from the scabbard; the harp of the Gaels will sing; you have donned your fay's robe, your bright robe of the past."

The great voice that speaks in the darkness is the voice of the patriarch who has seen the face of the Almighty; it comes from the green isle of the ocean of the heavens.

The luminous being crowned with gladioli and vine-branches, who marches, without buckling them, over the crowns of the furze, is the soul to whom the Creator has taught the language of the Gaels. She responds: "When the Master wanted the wind the fecundates the palm trees to come to gild the leaves of the oak, I imprisoned the Gaulish sylphs under the menhirs; I imprisoned the Gaulish fays in the path of the dolmens, and I hid myself in the forehead of a granite statue.

The wind is no longer blowing from the east, it is blowing from the west; awake, blonde fays! Sylphs with luminous wings, awake!"

The fire of Saint John is extinct on the Plateau de la Madeleine, and a cloud is swirling over the heather, a cloud of velvety wings, luminous scarves, pink legs and naked shoulders. That cloud has the form of a cone, it is spinning on its point, and at every rotation a couple falls from the swarm like an overripe grape from a vermilion cluster.

The fays sing as they circle on the silvery grass:

When the moon rises,
We dance in the meadows
* Variegated!*
When the dawn lifts
Her sapphire robe,
* The zephyr*
Cradles us on its wings,
* Sparks,*
In the covered paths
* Of the green woods.*

The sylphs sing as they flutter over the silvery grass:

Flower, violets,
Grass of the paths!
Open your cassolettes,
Branches of eglantines!

Then a great voice resounds in the darkness. That voice says: "Where is the first-born of my sons? Where is the long-haired chief? Why, if he wants to remain mute, has he quit his place between the prayer and the sword? Why, if he does not want to guide the Gaels over the rising route, is he tearing with the brambles of the ground the foam-colored feet of the daughter of the dawn?"

The soul of Gaul replies: "Men can only hear human voices Boun is a man now; when he has wet, he will tell the earth the secrets of the heavens."

The fires of Saint John are extinct on the Plateau de la Madeleine, the song of the mountain folk is lost in the depths of the valleys, and Alona sighs as she combs her hair: "I'm not a woman, I'm a Valkyrie! I'm thirsty, always thirsty!"

III

Luern is sitting on the grass; Alona, standing up, is gazing at the sky.

A SOFT VOICE
The sky is blue, the buds of the oak are opening.

THE STREAM
I am in love, pebbles, with a glaucous iris; sing, blue pebbles! sing, pink pebbles! and my beloved will turn her large azure eyes with the fine golden lashes toward you.

LUERN

I'm weary, my beloved; I would like to stop for a moment. My head is heavy, my knees are trembling; let me sleep at your feet. When they clench under my lips, these feet the color of foam, my heart leaps like a kid, my head sings like a bird and my soul opens its wings.

ALONA

If I were the mist floating over the poplars, the sun would drink me.

LUERN

I'm weary, my beloved; let me reread on my knees, my eyes in yours, the endless poem, the poem of our amour. You're smiling? Smile, beloved; your smile is as sweet as the kiss of the wave, and your lips sweeter...

ALONA

In the desert without flowers, in the desert without water, the sphinx smiles. Its head overlooks the plain, and it smiles because the great eagles cannot climb as high as his brow, because the great lions break their claws on its bare breast. The sphinx smiles because it is stronger than the desert wind, because it knows more things than the waves of the Nile know.

Bring me, wings tied, the wind that lifts the sand; tell me what the stars write on the leaves of the lotus.

LUERN

I'm weary, my beloved.

ALONA

The Sphinx smiles when the great eagles fall on the sand, wings open; it smiles because it is never weary.

The Sphinx smiles when the great lions drag themselves, roaring, on their bloody feet; it smiles because it has never shuddered, whether under a threat or under a kiss.

LUERN
Do you remember the night when we listened to the nightingale under the willows?

Luern is alone.

A SOFT VOICE
The grass is green, the sky is blue. The buds of the oaks are opening.

LUERN
I loved her as the wood-pigeon loves his dove, as the wolf loves his she-wolf, as the mist loves the meadows.

Luern is weeping; the crowd comes.

THE CROWD
Amour is a flower that opens in the evening and fades in the morning.

LUERN
Amour is a flame that the wind does not extinguish. Amour is a spring that the sun does not dry up.

THE CROWD
Avenge yourself.

LUERN
I love her.

THE CROWD
Forget.

LUERN
I am one of those who do not forget anything.

THE CROWD

Die.

LUERN

If I died, who would love her as I love her?

Proud symbol of eternal lover, of the strong and pure love that the Gaels dream, wild hawk, will you take my soul and burn it in the rays of the sun?

THE HAWK

Give it to me...

Luern is weeping; the crowd passes by.

THE CROWD

Who is that weeping madman with the bloody breast?

LUERN

Paw the ground no longer with your impatient hoof, El Biod, my beautiful horse, we are going to return to where the plain is wide and the sand is fine. We shall follow the tawny greyhounds into the clump of lentisks, we shall follow the falcons over the white hill where the gazelles are sleeping, we shall see the oleanders again, and the great palm trees, and we shall hear again what the bullets say when the blue burnooses float in the desert wind.

A YOUNG WOMAN

Let's not draw nearer; his breast is bloody it would stain our white dresses.

LUERN

I am no longer in love.

THE OLD MAN

You're a coward or a fool.

LUERN

Well, I shall have a mistress, a mistress so beautiful that everyone will be jealous. Statue with the soft smile, angel with the starry brow, you shall be my mistress...

Luern is saddling his horse; Alona advances with slow steps.

ALONA

The warm wind is numbing me...I can no longer think..., My knees are buckling. I'd like to lean on an arm.

LUERN

Shake your silvery mane, El Biod! We're going where the bullets are whistling,

ALONA

Luern?

LUERN

My hand can still lift Boun's ax; I want to die like a man, in the sunlight. Adieu; I'll prepare out nuptial bed in the green isle.

ALONA

He never loved me.

LUERN

Let flowers grow where the ashes of my heart fall...

Alona is drawing away; Luern, his foot in the stirrup, is weeping as he gazes at her.

LUERN

Where to go? Out there? I already have too much blood on my hands. I'm weary.

A SOFT VOICE

The grass is green, the sky is blue" Spring is sowing white daisies on my bosom. The grass is green, the sky is blue; apples trees are snowing on my brow,

Snow, apple-tree branches; snow, hawthorn branches, snow, snow on my hair.

THE CRICKET

Cri-cri. Cri-cri, the leaves are growing!

THE SOFT VOICE

The grass is green, the sky is blue, the sun has crumbled its golden rays on my lashes and the sylph of spring has burned the sweet incense of forests on my lips.

Snow, apple-tree branches; snow hawthorn branches; snow on my blonde hair; an inspired bard will sing my youth, will sing my beauty.

The grass is green, the sky s blue! Sing, sing, poet! I am the virgin with azure eyes, the virgin with fresh lips; I am the queen of the sunset.

LUERN

You are the voice that spoke in my soul in my childhood dreams.

THE SOFT VOICE

You're weeping? Your breast is bleeding? Come; my lips will dry your tears and my hand will close your open wound.

Come, I have a fresh garland of gladioli and periwinkles; we shall go into the reeds, under the willows, under the aspens, to listen to what the wave says to the caressant branches.

Come into the shadow of the rock, between the blasted oak and the flowering hawthorn; I shall sing you the beautiful verses of the past. I have put on my fay's robe again.

THE CROWD
Who is that madman who is talking to the trees and the rocks?

Alona hears the voice and she stops.

THE SOFT VOICE
Sleep, and if, when you awake, your wound is not closed, nothing will flow from it but red blood, pure blood. Gaels ought to die with a smile on the lips.

LUERN
The children of men need a clear gaze when it is necessary for them to fight bravely.

A VOICE FROM ABOVE
The bud on the oak is opening.

LUERN
The grass is as green, the sky as blue, as the evening when the two of us listened, under the willows, to the song of the nightingale. That evening, the air was full of perfumes and vague sounds—the sounds of great kisses and the perfumes of new saps; she gazed at me, and I mistook her eyes for two stars.

THE SOFT VOICE
Women are flowers, and the angel of spring gives a drop of dew to their hearts in the morning, as to the calices of the irises. So long as the sun has not drunk the tear fallen from the sky, the iris only loves the azure and the woman only loves the dream, but when the sunset reddens, the thirsty iris opens its lips and the weary woman seeks a broad heart and strong arms in order to repose.

ALONA
Luern, do you remember our long kisses in the crimson of the sunset, when the wind drove its chariot of clouds over the plains of the sky?

LUERN
Woe betide those who sing; they are forgotten! Woe betide those whose heart is broad; they are slain.

THE SOFT VOICE
Be silent, my bard; you are talking like the crowd.

LUERN
My heart has burned in the claws of the hawk; the wind will roll me like a dry leaf.

Skylark, when you alighted on the wood of my lance, you said to me: "I shall teach your daughters to love their nest as I love my nest." Skylark, you still sing over our furrows, but our women no longer love.

THE SKYLARK
When you sat your bride on the rump of your horse you said to her: I will give you the earth," and when the earth was hers, your first kiss gave her the sky; Luern, what have you given Alona?

Gaels, on the day when you want it, your women will love their hearth as I love my nest, but let them dream; their soul is a great as yours,

Instead of lying at their feet sighing: "I'm weary!" say to them: "Swallows, open your wings; we are hawks, and we want to overtake you above the clouds."

LUERN
Alona?

ALONA
Come and build our nest.

THE SOFT VOICE

Snow, apple-tree branches; snow, hawthorn branches; snow on the two fiancés who will sing my youth, who will sing my beauty.

THE VOICE OF THE FOREST

Perfume, violets, the grass of the pathways; here come the bard and the druidess.

The breeze, as mild as a gaze, enlarges the leaves and casts the catkins of the hazel-trees into the lips of the torrent the. In the first fir-trees, under a mossy rick fringed with white lichens, starred with anemones, on the thick and slender grass, like two finches in a nest, the amorous couple is chirping.

"Enlaced, like the bindweed that is hanging from the maples, we are gliding by night over the silvery meadows, we are drinking the dew from the lips of the periwinkles.

"When your velvety wings caress the gorse, the glow-worms dot the grass and the roe deer, necks extended, tread the moss with their tawny feet."

"We are going hand in hand along sunken paths, and the campanulas ring joyously, and the honeysuckle opens its cassolettes, and the nightingales in the eglantine-bushes salute Rose-des-Eaux, the blonde fay.

"We are flying over the forests, had in hand, and the birches say to the oaks: "Wake up, wake up! Here comes the sylph with green wings, the sylph that sows the mistletoe."

"We are two rays of light, two breaths of wind."

A luminous form advances toward the amorous couple. "The granite statue!" says Luern.

"I am the soul of Gaul," replies the luminous form, smiling. "You are my bard, Alona is my druidess. The days of proof are over...

The soul of Gaul spoke for a long time, but only Luern and Alona heard her words.

IV

The boat descends the river. Lying on a leopard-skin, they huddle together, one against the other, like two wood-pigeons in a nest, and they do not speak, having too much to say.

The boat descends the river, the moon rises over the palm grove.

"Do you love me?" says the young man with the bright eyes to the lips of his companion.

The boat glides soundlessly, and a stork traversing the Nile hears what the vermilion lips reply. The word that she hears is so soft that she glides in order to listen, but the vermilion lips only say one word, and she goes to perch on the head of a sphinx whose feet are licked by the waves.

The child with the golden hair folds her arms beneath her head and sings, while gazing at the silvery stork:

The warbler loves for a day or two on the rose-bush, but the stork loves forever on the azure-tinted tower. The warbler sings, the stork thinks; the stork is the bird of Allah!

"Close your eyes, your large soft eyes, and the houris will bring you the oranges of paradise."

"The stork is the bird of Allah," replies the sphinx, whose feet are licked by the waves.

The child with the golden hair sings while gazing into the bright eyes of her friend:

"The warbler loves a butterfly on the rose-bush; the stork loves a horseman on the azure-tinted tower. The warbler sings, the stork thinks; the stork is the bird of Allah!"

The boat glides soundlessly and the sphinx sings: "Close your eyes, your large soft eyes, and the houris will bring you the oranges of paradise."

The moon is shining over the ruins; the river widens, the sphinxes sing:

"Amour is immortal!" sighs the child with the golden hair to the lips of her friend.

All the sphinxes sign in unison, turning toward the Nile their long eyes devoid of gazes. They all sing in unison, and then the one whose feet are licked by the waves sings alone:

"I am the imperishable image of amour such as God has made it; I am the immobile sphinx with the broad brow and the lowered eyes.

"I have the smile of the virgin and the rump of a lion; milk swells my teats, my claws are ready to kill. I am the imperishable image of amour such as God has made it.

"The beauty of my lips attracts, the milk of my teats intoxicates; but after the kiss is given, my claws rend the heart into pieces, and the wind sows the crumbs as soon as I have fecundated them.

"Nothing dies in nature, but in order to revive it is necessary to die. Death is the fecund earth in which the divine seed swells, and like a reaper when the corn is ripe, lust passes."

"Death does not touch the soul of the Gaels," replies the child with the golden hair.

The river widens, the boat glides soundlessly, and the young man lifts the blue veil.

The boat glides soundlessly…is it a kiss or is it a caress of the breeze in the foliage of the plane trees that wakes the sleeping swan?

A lion roars in the reeds. The current pushes the boat toward it and it passes its paws over its wrinkled muzzle; but the child with the golden hair says to it: "Great lion, why are you extending your claws? We understand what your emerald eyes are dreaming. Come to lie at our feet, and I will tell you what you ask the rocks when the sun is hot."

The lion leaps into the boat and the plane-trees sing; "We have a living soul beneath our bark, a soul that thinks, a soul that knows. Every spring, our hearts grow with our leaves. Love! Love!"

The plane-trees sing; "Every spring, our hearts grow with our leaves. Love! Love!"

The lion roars: "Love! Love!"

The sun rises; the morning wind rolls columns of sand over the plain, and the child sighs, folding her arms beneath her golden hair: "Night, you were the most beautiful of nights!"

The morning wind rolls columns of sand over the plain; the lion licks the child's feet; the young man takes the tiller and says:

"Swallow, where do you want to go? I know beautiful temples and old forests. The temples I know have marble columns with fluted shafts, but the forests I know are full of birds and flowers. Swallow, where do you want to go?"

"To the land of the sun."

"Like an amorous swan, Algiers extends its wings over the sleeping gulf where the moon bathes."

"Let's go further."

"Like a wounded lion. Balbeck sleeps in the desert, and like a white reed, Bagdad the poet perfumes the Orient."

"But near the waves where the stars sow sparks as they twist their hair, in Saba, the ardent city illuminated by the fires of the sunset, in Saba, the eternal city where men no longer go..."

The boat has disappeared and the reeds of the Nile sing to the blue lotuses: "They are going to Saba, the city where one loves."

TO THE ONE I LOVE
Do not forget what the Gallic bards said:
Three things diminish continuously: obscurity, error and death.

A. de L.
Sunday 12 May 1867.

VERCINGETORIX

PART ONE

THE HARP

Celtill was the chief of the Arvernes.[76]

He was strong, he was rich, he was generous, his bed was empty; he went among the Belges in search of a companion.

The Belges gave a beautiful young woman to the man whose beard was gray.

The Belges placed the gentle hand of Ida in the hand hardened by the friction of a bridle; but Ida's blue eyes wept.

They wept on the evening of the betrothal; they wept in the morning, when the willows of the Escaut disappeared in the dust raised by the Arverne stallion; they wept even more the next day and the day after.

---

[76] Celtillus is cited a chief of the Arverni in Julius Caesar's *Gallic Wars*, which provides the basis for the present story, although the character of Ida and the account of the birth of Vercingetorix given here—and expanded in *La Chanson de l'alouette*—is L'Estoille's own invention,

Then a butterfly alighted on Ida's pale lips...

Since the butterfly settled on her lips Ida no longer weeps, and she goes every evening to listen to a voice under the larches of Sancy. For nine months she has climbed the path bordered by holly every evening.

One evening, she did not come down again. She was dead on the moss, and Celtill had a son.

The chief found the child beautiful; he named him Vercingetorix and he confided him to Divitiac, the savant druid.[77]

Celtill was strong, he was rich, he was generous, he wanted to be king; but instead of a crimson mantle, the Gauls gave him a mantle of flames.

Then the person who was known as the son of the traitor was no longer anything but the chief of the clan of the Monts Dore, and he grew up solitary in the grotto of the savant druid.

I

THE VOICE OF THE BATTLEFIELD
Kill! Kill!

THE HARP
Arioviste is fleeing. The sun is setting. Caesar is alone in his tent. Listen.

---

[77] Divitiacus of the Aedui is the only druid who is mentioned by name in the *Gallic Wars*. There he is said to have travelled to Rome following a battle in which Gaulish forces, including the Arvernes were massacred by Germanic forces led by the king of the Suebi, Ariovistus, There he met Cicero, on whose authority Caesar names him as a druid, His request for Roman aid led to the next phase of the Roman invasion of Gaul, when Caesar went to confront and defeat Ariovistus' forces. His association with the education of Vercingetorix is an invention of L'Estoille's.

327

CAESAR
Do they know now why they are dead? No, they don't know, even now.

A beautiful night! Humans, for nature, are less than the leaves on the trees; when the leaves fall, the sky veils itself.

A WOUNDED GERMAN
The crows have red wings, where the Suebi have passed! I see the table of the feast, I see... The daises are red where our horses have browsed...

CAESAR
At the head of our laws, if it had been written: "Death is only a door that opens on a better life," the earth would belong to Rome.

THE SILVER STRINGS
Chariots drawn by weary oxen are approaching. Two horsemen precede them, do you know them?

CAESAR
Where is Arioviste?

IMPERADORIX
Here are his chariots; but he has been able to traverse the Rhine on a boat run aground in the branches of a willow.

CAESAR
He has no more to fear.

If you had caught him I would have been glad, because at twenty years you would already have had a celebrated name.

This young chief is your brother?

IMPERADORIX
We each opened a vein over the cup and we drank from it; since that day Vercingetorix has been my brother.

CAESAR

I had been told that the son of Celtill was a bard. I see today that he is also a man. Your father has been unjustly condemned, Vercingetorix.

VERCINGETORIX

The past is past.

CAESAR

The past is irreparable, but you ought not to suffer any longer from an injustice. I shall mention you to the chiefs.

VERCINGETORIX

Vercingetorix is proud of the amity of Caesar.

IMPERADORIX

Permit us to go and unbridle our horses.

THE HARP

Listen.

IMPERADORIX

Vercingetorix, your men are mingled with mine; tomorrow we'll separate them, it's necessary that each one has his glory.

THE SILVER STRINGS
They're jealous and avid to command.

THE BRONZE STRINGS
Woe, woe! The bald man knows.

CAESAR

I shall be the counselor of all those who want to rise, and I will aid all those who want to fell heads that are too high.

THE GOLDEN STRINGS
The moon is rising, white. A breeze agitates the poplars of the Rhine. That breeze passes warmly over the battlefield, and the open veins allow a last drop of blood to flow.

THE HARP
Moina the druidess is leaning over the cadavers. Listen.

MOINA
Ah, here's a Roman! There's only one carcass of a jay for a hundred cadavers of vultures.

THE BRONZE STRINGS
In spite of his helmet and its crest, how small that Roman is!

THE HARP
An ant is feeble, but an ant-hill is powerful. Ar-Braz! Ar-Braz! Emerge from the tomb; the hour of danger is sounding.

MOINA
They speak the same language, they worship the same God, the land is empty out there, but they fight like two bulls, and the she-wolf watches then with famished eyes.

THE GOLDEN STRINGS
Ar-Braz! Ar-Braz! Where are you?

MOINA
Fortunate are those who fall in their force, like green fir trees under the North wind.

Open your wings gladly, souls of Gauls; in the fog, out there, your horses of cloud are pawing the ground. Impatient, they are chewing their bits. Can you hear them whinnying? Depart; they are as light as an eagle, as strong as a torrent;

their rumps are like a meadow silvered by spring; their manes are like the plain, gilded by autumn.

Open your wings gladly, souls of Teutons; in the moonlight, the Valkyries are descending on their white mares. They are calling you. Depart; their lips have the perfume of withering violets, their arms are like the wave that sways the reeds.

Fortunate are those who fall in their force!

Depart, souls of Gauls; in the green star the warrior rediscovers his horse, the bard rediscovers his harp, and couples soar in the blue sky like swallows.

Depart, souls of Teutons; in the bright palace where shields resonate, the hydromel is fuming, the wild boar fuming on the bronze platter, and the daughters of the dawn are undoing their long hair.

THE SILVER STRINGS
The wounded are dead.

THE HARP
Caesar is writing in his tent. Look.

CAESAR
Is it the wind of my fortune that has pushed that boat into the branches of a willow?

III

THE SILVER STRINGS
Where are we?

THE HARP
At the foot of the Sancy.

THE SILVER STRINGS
The horses are bridled, the young chief quits his clan.

THE HARP

Caesar summons his friend Vercingetorix, and the young chief quits his clan in order to join him. He departs joyfully; next to Caesar there is a young woman from Narbonne. Caesar's ward is as beautiful as a sunset; Praxinoe, the daughter of the ally of Marius, is as beautiful as an evening in September.[78]

THE GOLDEN STRINGS

While the horses are bridled, Vercingetorix is dreaming on the heath. Listen.

VERCINGETORIX

On the flowering heather, she would be like a hind listening; under the silvery fir trees, she would be like a roe deer waiting. Flower under her footsteps, violets. Blush under her hand, raspberries of the woods. Torrent, you shall not wet her feet; where she was born, the water is warm. Mountain breath, you shall not touch her cheek; where she was born the breeze is mild.

THE GOLDEN STRINGS

There, behind that menhir, Moina the druidess.

MOINA

Ar-Braz! Ar-Braz! Where are you?

VERCINGETORIX

I wasn't everyone to love her, everyone to envy her. I want her to be the golden bough of the growing oak.

---

[78] L'Estoille presumably adopted this name from the idylls of Theocritus, where it is attributed to a maid. He did not retain it in *La Chanson de l'alouette*, where a markedly different character is substituted for Praxinoe.

MOINA

Where are you going, Vercingetorix?

VERCINGETORIX

To rejoin Caesar.

MOINA

You're going to make your horse prance before his? You're going to measure your sword with his?

VERCINGETORIX

I'm going to command the Gauls, who will learn the art of war in his company.

MOINA

Why are you showing the wolf the path to the cowshed? Why are you showing the crow the path to the walnut tree? The wolf will bite the legs of the great stallions and will bite the necks of the foals. The crow will carry away the ripe nuts, and its chicks will eat them.

VERCINGETORIX

Druidess, Caesar is a friend of Gaul; he wants her to be free and strong. He wants a florid garden outside his tent. He wants to give the matron crowned with towers a sister crowned with vervain.

MOINA

I have seen tears on the clover! I have seen blood in the spring! I have seen signs of death under the leaves of the apple tree!

VERCINGETORIX

Women will weep, blood will redden the guard of the sword, the men of the past will tear their cheeks; but the mistletoe will grow green on the vigorous trunk. Gaul is only a shoot of the oak; it's necessary that it be a tree. Let she who has rounded the pearl of the west give me wisdom, and you will be able to plunge your sickle into healthy bark, and the wild boar will be able to gather his piglets in the shadows.

MOINA

Ar-Braz! Ar-Braz! Where are you?

VERCINGETORIX

Bless me, Druidess, I am going to forge the sword of Ar-Braz.

IV

THE SILVER STRINGS

Caesar has a court, like a king

THE HARP

He has a court finer than a king's, since Arioviste has come to sit down at his table.

THE SILVER STRINGS

At the table of the man who only drinks water the wines are passing in full cups.

THE HARP

At the table of the man who never loved, three amours grew around Praxinoe. The Gaulish woman to whom Marius has taught Latin. The bald man wants the smile of the Narbonnaise to separate the three men forever, who would crush him if they were united.

THE GOLDEN STRINGS

At the bottom of the steps. Moina is gazing at the flamboyant windows. Listen.

MOINA

The druids no longer have faith, men in longer have marrow. Ar-Braz! Ar-Braz! Where are you?

THE SILVER STRINGS
The chiefs, the elders and the druids look into the bottom of their cups without seeing.

THE HARP
Caesar looks at the German, the Eduen and the Arverne, all three in love with the almond branch, whose flowers have been perfumed by the Ionian wind.

MOINA

Women no longer have courage. Ar-Braz! Ar-Braz! Where are you?

THE SILVER STRINGS
The Arverne and the Eduen quarrel. Imperadorix falls.

THE HARP
Caesar smiles; he sees Arioviste giving his ring to Praxinoe.

MOINA

Ar-Braz! Ar-Braz! Where are you? Drunken Gaul is letting her two arms dangle, and those who pass kiss her pale hands, and those who desire to rivet golden chains to her weakened wrists.

THE SILVER STRINGS
Caesar descends the steps with Arioviste.

THE HARP
He is taking his leave of him. Moina bars his way. Listen.

CAESAR

When going to his plow the laborer sees the skylark; it's a fortunate presage.

MOINA

What field are you laboring?

CAESAR

The field of a friend; I am buying horses from Arioviste for Vercingetorix's horsemen.

MOINA

And why are you buying horses for my sons? You have aided us, we shall repay you; go away if you don't want your breastplate to rust under a dolmen tomorrow.

CAESAR

My soldiers are passing over the Alps again, taking nothing but wounds from Gaulish land.

MOINA

There is still Roman gold at the bottom of our lakes; it will be repaid. And what do you want? Rome? Blood is repaid with blood; we shall retake Rome and give her to you. But depart this morning if you do not want tonight to redden the granite table.

THE SILVER STRINGS

Did you hear, Caesar? Why don't you strike her? You're afraid.

THE HARP

He's smiling. Beware of men who smile under an insult. He's summoning a soldier. Listen.

CAESAR

Follow that woman and kill her without anyone seeing you. When you've killed her, find me and bring me the hand-guard of your sword. Go.

They wanted to cut down the oak and their ax has broken; I shall only tear away the mistletoe, and the oak will fall, eaten away by the worm that erodes the others. Beautiful land of the west, I shall rip out your heart, but I won't gash your cheek.

THE SILVER STRINGS
Where is he going?

THE HARP
To rejoin Praxinoe.

THE GOLDEN STRINGS
The druidess is hidden by the shadow of a lilac... The legionnaire goes past... Piercing eyes are required to follow a skylark in the furrow.

THE BRONZE STRINGS
Vercingetorix has carried the wounded Eduen to his tent; he returns; the druidess wishes to speak to him, the legionnaire will hear, and... Why, Vercingetorix...?

MOINA
Where are you going, Vercingetorix?

VERCINGETORIX
To take my leave of Caesar.

MOINA
On the edge of the blue lake that the dust does not tarnish, I shall recite to you as before the beautiful verses of the past; then you will mount your horse and...

VERCINGETORIX

Yes, you will recite to me the beautiful verses of the past; I'm only a bard, and a bard of the past.

MOINA

He isn't only a bard! Ar-Braz! Ar-Braz! Where are you? Your bride must have a fresh crown, and my crown is withering. Come, I'm waiting for you, as the snowdrop awaits the sun

V

THE HARP

The slaves have carried away the sleeping guests, they have washed the marble pavement, they have put Corinthian cups, fruit and flowers on the table. Caesar is alone with Praxinoe, lying on a lemon-wood bed encrusted with tin.

PRAXINOE

You said to me: "Be loved by them and you shall have that of which you dream." They have fought because of me; give me that of which I dream.

CAESAR

You have a beautiful ring on your finger. Is it a betrothal ring?

PRAXINOE

If I wish. It's Arioviste's ring.

CAESAR

Listen—I trust you, no one else can give you what I'm offering you—I want to go to Rome, and I'm afraid that the Gauls might forget me; it's necessary that I leave them a master who is my…friend, and that master will be Vercingetorix.

PRAXINOE

A child.

CAESAR

Yes, that child, and you shall be his wife. If he forgets me…you understand?

PRAXINOE

Yes, I'll warn you.

CAESAR

Here he is; he's armed. It's necessary that he doesn't leave.

THE GOLDEN STRINGS

The daughter of the south gets up. Her copper-colored tresses are flamboyant. Smiling, she advances toward the Arverne, her little teeth shining, her beautiful bare arms rounding out, and without speaking, she places on her head a helmet with bronze wings.

THE SILVER STRINGS

Why?

THE HARP

Listen.

PRAXINOE

Do I resemble the virgins who carry the souls of the brave away from battlefields?

VERCINGETORIX

The Valkyries are pale violets; you are a cluster of privet.

PRAXINOE

At the first combat you'll take me on the rump of your horse; your horsemen will say that you resemble the god of war when your heavy sword is raised again, bloodily.

THE SILVER STRINGS

He won't go.

THE BRONZE STRINGS

Be careful, son of the wind.

THE GOLDEN STRINGS

Praxinoe is lying on the lemon-wood bed, and drunkenness with an opal mantle emerged, laughing from an amphora of Campanian earthenware. She emerges cheerfully from the brown amphora, the goddess with the caressant arms; her tresses stream like golden waves over her throat, which descends to her yielding breasts.

THE BRONZE STRINGS

The legionnaire stops on the threshold...he puts his hand to the guard of his sword. Eternal shame to the man who strikes in the dark! Your pedestal will crumble, fox who has stolen the skin of a lion!

CAESAR

If your horsemen resemble this soldier, you'll have good horsemen; they'll obey without thinking.

THE HARP

Vercingetorix doesn't hear Caesar; he is gazing into his heart.

THE BRONZE STRINGS

The bald man is whispering in Praxinoe's ear. Listen.

CAESAR

He's just cut the branch with which you were weaving your royal crown.

PRAXINOE

Vercingetorix, your horsemen say that you're also a bard, and I've never heard Gaulish songs...

VERCINGETORIX

Our songs are like the fog; they only show the forests, they only caress the heather.

PRAXINOE

And why should I not be a branch of heather?

THE GOLDEN STRINGS

Listen; Vercingetorix is singing to the daughter of the south the poem of Ar-Braz, the one for whom the Gauls are waiting.

THE SILVER STRINGS

I've heard mention of that chief, who led the Gaels from the land of Asia. His body is under a dolmen in Morbihan, and his soul will be reborn in order to give the world to the Gauls.

THE GOLDEN STRINGS

His bride was called Fleur d'Épine.[79]

THE HARP

Caesar's brow is furrowed. His whispers to a slave. Her breast quivering, Praxinoe listens.

---

[79] The name Fleur-d'Épine [Mayflower, in English] had previously been used as that of a symbolic female character in one of Comte Antoine Hamilton's satirical fantasies.

VERCINGETORIX

The men had hardened their lances, Fleur d'Épine had put on a bridal crown, the druids had lifted a stone, the druidesses had torn up grass. Ar-Braz cried: "Let's go!"

THE SILVER STRINGS
Two Almahs and a flute-player!

THE GOLDEN STRINGS
The flute sighs, slowly, the Almah's turn. The goddess of the vines kisses Vercingetorix on the forehead. Caesar smiles. The flute sighs, and slowly, slowly, the Almahs twirl. Caesar gets up and leaves. The flute sighs, and Praxinoe's arms fall back on the lemon-wood bed.

THE BRONZE STRINGS
Look, oh look! Under the lilacs, the druidess is dying.

THE GOLDEN STRINGS
Fays are cutting flowers on the edge of the stream. Listen.

MOINA

Where am I? A luminous land is floating before my eyes... Oh, the handsome warriors with azure breastplates. They're smiling at me... I'm cold.

THE FAYS

With cress and iris we are weaving a shroud for the pale druidess.

MOINA

What will those say who are guiding the Gaulish conquerors through the world? He has struck me with his sword.

THE FAYS

With clover and mistletoe, with sage and vervain, we are weaving a shroud—for whom? For whom?

MOINA

Ar-Braz! Ar-Braz! Where are you? The eagle is soaring and the skylark... I'm thirsty...! Thirsty!

THE FAYS

With cress and iris we have woven a shroud for the pale druidess; but for whom are we weaving this embalmed shroud that is floating like a dream?

MOINA

They no longer know why the branches turn green, why the flowers wither, why... Ar-Braz! Ar-Braz! He is born! His eyes are soft, his forehead is broad, his back is like an ash tree. Vibrate, silver strings; under his heel the she-wolf will howl... Blood...! Blood...! Gaulish blood...! Death is the fecund earth in which the future germinates; vibrate, silver strings, the enchained will be reborn. Alight on his spear, skylark of the Gauls, tell him...

THE FAYS

Sleep in your cool shroud of green cress, sleep in your soft shroud of blue irises; with your hair the goldfinch will make her nest, with your lips the bee will make her honey, with your eyes the stream will make pebbles, those pretty pebbles that glisten. But why have we woven you this embalmed shroud, which is floating like a dream?

THE SOUL

You will no longer marry the flowers, you will no longer fill the basins of springs, you will no longer light fires on the marshes, you will no longer erect stones for two thousand years; sleep in the bright shroud that is floating like a dream.

THE GOLDEN STRINGS

The goddess of the vines leans over the lemon-wood bed, smiling. The blonde friend of the bards flexes her broad back, and her tresses fall all the way to her feet, parting like the strings of a harp. She vibrates the ivory harp softly, and the hawk sings like a nightingale, and with wild torrent snakes like a stream, caressing the flowers of memory one by one.

The daughter of the south leans over the Arverne. The chief's eyes have the color of woodland springs, springs on which emerald beetles spin...

THE HARP

The warbler was thirsty.

VERCINGETORIX

In the sunlight of amour the apple ripens! In the sunlight of amour, the sword is steeped!

PRAXINOE

Oh, my beloved, finish the poem of the one who is to come.

VERCINGETORIX

While his blood flowed, he said: "Death will give me a larger heart, a redder blood.

The crowd cried: "That's good!"

When the blood was no longer flowing, the crowd brought three rocks. Under those three rocks they laid the chief; then, to his right, they laid the gray stallion. As there was still room, Fleur d'Épine was laid to the chief's left.

Then the Gaels saw a chariot in the clouds, and in that chariot a man with eyes the color of the sea next to a woman crowned with violets and vervain.

How will Ar-Braz be called, when his eyes have the hue of his waves? How will Fleur d'Épine be called when she has exchanged her bridal crown for the crown of a druidess?

PRAXINOE

I have seen the eyes that have the hue of the waves. What ought a druidess to know?

VERCINGETORIX

What men knew yesterday, and what they will know to-morrow. Your kiss has burned my veins!

PRAXINOE

I don't know anything. Will you still remember me when you love the other?

VERCINGETORIX

I am one of those who only love once.

PRAXINOE

Your eyes have the color of the waves; you are Ar-Braz, the one who was to come.

VERCINGETORIX

No, my swallow, I'm not Ar-Braz; Ar-Braz could stifle a horse by tightening his knees, he could heard the voice of the leaves; he could read the book of nights. No, I'm not Ar-Braz; but if you love me, I might perhaps be his bard.

PRAXINOE

Will he still remember me when he loves the druidess?
Caesar said to me: "I want to be the king of Gaul, but it's necessary that I hide behind someone, and Vercingetorix is the only one tall enough."

VERCINGETORIX

He said that?

PRAXINOE

I was to be Caesar's spy.
I love you now, and...

VERCINGETORIX

I don't know whether you love me or the man who wanted to be king. Perhaps you can't know yourself, today. Adieu; if you love me, tomorrow you will rejoin me.

THE BRONZE STRINGS
He's a man; he's gone.

THE SILVER STRINGS
Praxinoe isn't weeping; she's as green as grass. What will she say to Caesar, who is coming in?

CAESAR

I promised you a royal fiancé, you have one; Arioviste is waiting for you.

Ah, you're singing in the sky, skylark! I'll change your furrow into a marsh. Can you hear the German river that is breaking its dikes?

VI

THE GOLDEN STRINGS
Why are you weeping under the willows, Praxinoe?

THE SILVER STRINGS
Look at that woman crowned with vervain.

THE GOLDEN STRINGS
That isn't a woman; the willows are greeting her. Listen.

THE INDIVIDUAL CROWNED WITH VERVAIN

On Arioviste's couch a ring is shining whose imprint is an order; why are you weeping?

PRAXINOE

Do you know a gulf were the water swirls?

THE INDIVIDUAL CROWNED WITH VERVAIN

You'd be cold on a bed of sand; the fish would eat your eyes, and your beloved would no longer recognize you when the wave cast you up on the grass.

PRAXINOE

My beloved no longer loves me.

Can you see the fire that is alight? Before it oxen are being slaughtered; when the oxen are roasted, Arioviste will summon me, and when he is sated...he's the king,

THE INDIVIDUAL CROWNED WITH VERVAIN

You are the fiancée of Ar-Braz, the long-haired chief. Take my sickle; the sheaf will be red, but the bread will be white.

THE GOLDEN STRINGS

There is no longer only one light bathing Praxinoe.

PRAXINOE

The closed book has opened, and my eyes are dazzled.

ARIOVISTE

Why, instead of combing your hair have you fled? I ought to break your head with the blow of an ax. Roman, throw away that sickle.

THE GOLDEN STRINGS

The moon is trembling in the sky like a swan-feather on a woodland pond.

PRAXINOE

King, why do you say to the druidess that she is Roman? Do you no longer recognize your sister? Have you forgotten, then, that my father played in the same meadow as yours, and drank from the same spring? Listen to the one you call Roman.

THE GOLDEN STRINGS
The moon is setting, but the golden sickle is gleaming like he celestial crescent.

Praxinoe spoke for a long time. She spoke until morning, and the men of the North listened. They thought they were traversing prairies devoid of hills; they thought that they could hear the pale waves of the sea lamenting. The druidess knows all their names; she has seen all their combats.

The druidess spoke until morning, and when the rising sun caused the gleam of the sickle to pale, the men of the North bent their knees, and the old king kissed the hem of her robe.

VII

THE SILVER STRINGS
The men of the clans are descending by all the paths; why? On the stony heath, Vercingetorix is marching head bowed; why?

THE HARP
He is thinking about the Narbonnaise.

THE VOICE OF THE HEATH
The grass is green, the sky is blue; snow, branches of the apple tree; snow, branches of the hawthorn.

VERCINGETORIX
When I took the foals to pasture I was happy. I slept in the sun like a gray lizard, and the heath spoke to me.

THE VOICE OF THE HEATH
Come into the shade of the apple tree, come into the shade of the birch. I will teach you the song of the cricket, and

348

when your hair is white, the triads will fall from your lips as the flowers fall from the hawthorn in the month of May.

VERCINGETORIX

The road before me leads to an unknown country; behind me darkness is thickening over a glorious past. I shall be the last man of a crumbling past; I shall be the last bard of those heroes who will no longer be reborn.

THE HARP

The clan has gathered.

VERCINGETORIX

Children, listen to me and then respond as free men ought to respond.

THE CLAN

Speak.

VERCINGETORIX

There are men in the isles of the west who know the secret; I am quitting you in order to go and learn from them the divine laws that make people happy and strong.

THE CLAN

If those laws are divine they are written in your heart, and you have no need to quit us in order to read them. Stay in your clan; you can always have your granary full, wine in your cellar and meat in your larder. Marry a beautiful young woman; mount fine horses; render justice; from time to time, to amuse the young, go into the plan to burn a village...

VERCINGETORIX

The past is being effaced, and the poems of the Gaels are not yet made. When I come back, I will tell you what I have learned, and your sons will repeat it to their sons.

THE CLAN
Who will defend us?

VERCINGETORIX
Sheep need shepherds to defend them; chamois have no need of them.

THE CLAN
Our blood is red; instead of reviving the heroes of the past, be a hero yourself.

VERCINGETORIX
Keep your blood for Ar-Braz. Await the promised hour.

THE SILVER STRINGS
Who is that man who is stopping, out of breath?

THE HARP
He's a senator from Gergovia.

THE SENATOR
The Belges are menacing the Eduens; Caesar is going to march against them, and he requests your alliance. Knowing the amity that links Vercingetorix to Caesar. we have promised him our help and yours.

VERCINGETORIX
I was the friend of Caesar when I thought he was the friend of Gaul.

THE SENATOR
Gaul! Gaul! You speak of Gaul as Celtill spoke of it. Do you want to be with us or against us?

VERCINGETORIX
I shall be with the Belges.

THE SENATOR

Then we shall have no need to march for long in order to encounter the enemy.

THE CLAN

They have forgotten the day when the mountain men entered Gergovia! You want to attack us? Out paths are too steep for your rickety legs, chestnut-merchants. Let us descend to nail to their doors these owls that dare to show themselves to hawks.

VERCINGETORIX

Stay here; I'm leaving, because it's necessary.

KENRIK

I shall leave too. I shall take my white bagpipe, and no piper in Gaul will sound more loudly than the piper of the Arvernes.

THE CLAN

We are too many here to stop the merchants down below; let the old men stay and the young ones set forth. Do you want that, Father?

VERCINGETORIX

Yes.

THE CLAN

It is decided. The wild boar of the Arvernes will not go forth without his young. Let's go drink to your return, Vercingetorix, and may the earth be warm for those who don't come back.

PART TWO

I

THE SILVER STRINGS
In the Roman army the Centurions are inspecting the spear-heads and the straps of the shields; is the Belgian army still asleep?

THE HARP
It won't take long to bridle the horses, and before the Belgian army, Vercingetorix's horsemen are on watch.

VERCINGETORIX
Caesar, Caesar, I would have been your man if you had wanted it. If you had wanted it, the Gauls would have aided you to conquer the world, and they would only have shared the glory with you.

It isn't the Roman army that my horses will charge first, it's the Eduen army, the army of Imperadorix, my brother's army... What if the will of the master is not on my side! What if I am only a madman dreaming of the impossible! O you to whom the Creator has confided Gaul, speak to my soul! When Imperadorix mingled his blood with mine, a fragment of your chariot fell into the cup; you blessed our amity; and now we are enemies, and perhaps it's because I'm here and he is out there.

THE GOLDEN STRINGS
Here comes the daylight; the skylark is singing.

THE SKYLARK
Where the Gaels camp, I sing on their chariots; where the Gaels sow, I sing over their furrows. Listen, Gaels, listen to the skylark.

To those who labor I say: Be cheerful; all grain sown rises. To those who bind the sheaves I say: Be cheerful, amour is a full ear of corn. Listen, Gaels, listen to the skylark.

To the man whom the East wind brought I say today: I am the bird of Ar-Braz, who will be reborn when Gaul awakes...

THE HARP
The trumpets sound, the bagpipes bellow, the harps vibrate. Like the flame in the heather, the Belgian army rises to its feet. Vercingetorix mounts his horse,

VERCINGETORIX
Bird of Ar-Braz, you have perched on the wood of my spear; you will always fly toward the Gauls.

Children, tighten your knees!

THE BRONZE STRINGS
That is not a fuming torrent on the lain; it is the clan of Vercingetorix.

THE BELGIAN ARMY
Sing of the blue blade that loves the flesh! Sing of the blue sword!

O sword! O great chief of the battlefield! O sword! O great chief...

THE GOLDEN STRINGS
On the hill the bards are tuning their harps. Two Valkyries are weaving crowns of violets.

II

THE SILVER STRINGS
Like a wave on a granite rock, the Belgian army breaks over the legion. The rock totters...

THE HARP
The rock has tottered; but the wave is no longer anything but foam, which the wind sweeps away,

THE SILVER STRINGS
What is that tight-knit squadron, whose horses are stumbling at every step?

THE BRONZE STRINGS
Can't you see the chief with the glaucous eyes? Can't you see the silver wings of the skylark gleaming? They're the horsemen of Vercingetorix. The horses are stumbling because their breasts are bloody, because each of them is carrying a wounded man on its rump. Even those who strike from a distance, the Spaniards and Numidians, dare not pursue them.

III

THE HARP
Their chins in their hands, they are crouching around smoky fires. Large tears stripe their cheeks.

A BARD
Brambles will grow in the hearth, the fox will hollow out its hole beneath the threshold. The owl will nest on the beam: Du Lug is dead![80]

---

[80] "Du Lug" is presumably a reference to the Celtic god Lug, or Lugh, mentioned in numerous inscriptions found throughout western Europe and particularly associated by Julius Cae-

The horse will no longer have oats, the ox will no longer have hay, the bloodhound will no longer have bones: Du Lug is dead!

The beer will no longer flow, the bacon will no longer smoke, the honey will no longer spill: Du Lug is dead!

The shield will no longer gleam, the young woman will no longer laugh, the harp will no longer sing: Du Lug is dead!

VERCINGETORIX

Chiefs, why are you weeping? I have traversed all of the plain, and I have seen as many Romans there as Gauls.

A BARD

Nettles will grow in the hearth, the toad will make its hole under the threshold, bats will nest in the roof: Du Lug is dead.

VERCINGETORIX

Bard, why do you say that he is dead? Are we dead? It's not with tears, it's with blood that out tombs will be washed; we won't be mourned, we'll be avenged, in order that we can say, when we arrive up above: Our friends are brave. Do the birches have no more bark, because all those wounds are bleeding? Bandage them, and mount up!

THE HARP

They have all risen to their feet; they have picked up their dented shields; tomorrow's sun will see naked swords again.

---

sar (who regarded him as an equivalent of the Roman god Mercury) with Gaul.

THE SILVER STRINGS
The Belges have not retreated; to the last man they are dead, and the Sambre has carried away their cadavers. But why have three legions conquered all the land from the Seine to the Loire?

THE HARP
Because the bald man's tongue is like the serpent's tongue, because Gaul is not a tree but a stump, and to every scion he has whispered. He had spoken, and then he had crossed the Alps, believing that the winter wind will not be strong enough to bar away his words.

V

THE GOLDEN STRINGS
With the buds hearts open.

THE HARP
Vercingetorix knows it, and as soon as the snowdrop stars the mountain he descends into the plain. He marches straight ahead—the Romans are everywhere—and every evening his horsemen have heads on their saddle-bows. Where he passes, the young women crowd the thresholds and the young men buckle their sword-belts in order that the young women will not say: We would like to be of the clan of Vercingetorix.

THE BRONZE STRINGS
The anxious chiefs consult one another. The centurions and the tribunes threaten them; but every night, in every village, a band forms, and the Roman sentinels are removed and the Roman merchants are killed.

THE GOLDEN STRINGS
Red hands are not washed in one night.

THE HARP
Vercingetorix knows it, and he marches on, leaving be-hind him desert places full of men, who would be murderers if they unbuckled their sword-belts. Couriers are on horseback, the legions are concentrated, Caesar is informed. He writes to the chiefs: Your heads will fall if these cutters of the roads are not nailed to trees by the roadside. *He writes that, but in that vague glimmer he divines a conflagration.*

THE SILVER STRINGS
In the evenings there is talk of Ar-Braz, the one who will return.

THE HARP
Under a dolmen that the sea only uncovers at the equi-noxes the bones of Ar-Braz are whitening between the bones of his horse and the bones of his fiancée, and every spring a crowd gathers to hear the breath growling under the dolmen when the soul of the chief comes to visit his bones. But for twenty-four years the soul with the broad wings has not been heard to pass, and the crowd says: Ar-Braz is born. That is why there is talk of Ar-Braz in the evenings, and the young women are beginning to say: The Arverne's eyes have the col-or of water.

VI

THE SILVER STRINGS
Blood is flowing from the Rhine to the Pyrenees, and from the Ocean to the Alps.

THE HARP
It has been flowing for a long time, and will flow for a long time yet. The bald man's tongue is like a serpent's tongue, it whispers to every scion, and the entire stump will fall under the ax.

THE GOLDEN STRINGS
Let us close our eyes.

VII

THE HARP
Vercingetorix is lying on the white cliff. The Bretons have also been vanquished by Caesar.

VERCINGETORIX
My legs are like those of an old man; my heart no longer has the strength to fill my veins. Why has my blood not flowed to the last drop?

KENRIK
The sky is black today; it will be blue tomorrow.

VERCINGETORIX
If I were dead, perhaps I would command fine armies in a victorious Gaul...kill me, Kenrik.

KENRIK
When you command, I shall obey.

VERCINGETORIX
I have done what I could. They said that I was Ar-Braz, but my hand can no longer pull a sword from its scabbard. Promised liberator, I would have liked to sing your advent and die beside you; if you are not yet born, may I be reborn with you!

KENRIK
Father, let's return to the Monts Dore.

VERCINGETORIX

The wolves have licked their wounds, the crows have eaten their eyes, the snow has blanched their bones, and they were like elks.

KENRIK

Today they are like hawks above the clouds. The boat is waiting for us, let's return to the Monts Dore.

VERCINGETORIX

I would return alone! No.

KENRIK

We will say to them: Ham died dragging two Roman soldiers into the Aisne; at Vannes, Luern had his arm cut off on the side of a galley; in the isle of Bretagne Alain stopped a cohort and the bards are singing his name at feasts.

VERCINGETORIX

Ws departed a thousand strong, and we would return two!

KENRIK

The children have grown. Those who followed us on the day of departure with wooden swords will come to meet us with bronze swords; we will have enough to make a fine squadron, and the earth will tremble again under the iron shoes of our horses.

VERCINGETORIX

My skylark is now a coin with the effigy of Caesar.

KENRIK

The Druids have seen Fleur d'Épine; Ar-Braz is born.

VERCINGETORIX

I am not retreating; I am falling; my veins are empty.

THE GOLDEN STRINGS

He gazes at the sea, which the setting sun is setting ablaze, and the circling gulls.

THE HARP

The breeze is blowing from the land, it has passed over the hayricks, over the flowering hawthorn, over the pines whose resin is beginning to pearl; the breast of the Arverne swells, his pale cheeks are colored.

VERCINGETORIX

I have more blood! Let's go, Kenrik; it's necessary to struggle until death.

KENRIK

When you hear the skylark, the skylark of the Arvernes, you can sow, and the crow will not come to eat our seeds; instead of feathers in its wings, our skylark has spikes, spikes that burn.

VIII

THE SILVER STRINGS

The leather sail rises up the fir-wood mast; the boat plunges its prow into the foam.

KENRIK

Instead of feathers, on its neck, our skylark has swords, swords that bite. When you hear the skylark, the skylark of the Arvernes, you can draw the wine: the wolf will not come to leap on to the table.

VERCINGETORIX

I have done what I could, but one is weak when one is not loved. Amour is the torch of the soul; if it is extinguished, all is darkness; one loses one's way and can no longer deflect others from the precipice.

THE GOLDEN STRINGS
The moon passes over the sky like a tear over blue eyes. An undine puts her hand on the side of the boat. Her long hair shines, and pearls fall from her breast as from an open jewel-case.

THE UNDINE
I have for the man I love a sapphire palace, a bright palace with florid walls, a palace where time has no wrinkles, where the cup has no lees. Bard of the heavy sword, come repose your head on my bosom; it will rock you as the wave rocks the swan in the depth of the woods. Come, I will take you into sonorous grottoes where the harp of the waves vibrates. Come, I will take you to the isle without winters, which floats like a dream where the Ocean touches the heavens.

VERCINGETORIX
The woman I love has no more than a roofless cabin and her lacerated breast bleeds. The woman I love I do not desire, and I shall die content and proud if my eyes, as they close, see a smile on her lips.

THE GOLDEN STRINGS
If you only listen with your ears, you will not understand. Listen with your heart, and the released divinity will part the veil.

IX

THE SILVER STRINGS
Why, like a woman, is Praxinoe weeping on the bank of the Rhine?

It is not the druidess, it is the woman of old who is weeping. Listen, and you will understand.

PRAXINOE

Where the azure wave caresses the shiny trunks of the green laurels, the flowers have an intoxicating perfume and the fruits are the color of gold...

In the plains dotted with irises the horses of the Gaels passed when Ar-Braz was chief. Ar-Braz was a chief; but when the bulls slept he sang to Fleur d'Épine what the trees say and what the stars write on summer nights...

Where the grapes ripen the wind is a kiss of the good goddess, a kiss that reddens the lips. Here the fog hides the sun... Here one does not live, one dreams...

Life is eternal; today only lasts an hour, but tomorrow will not end. After the sad dream the soul sleeps momentarily, and then awakes, reposed...

Like a swallow I should like to build a nest in the marble frieze of a temple in the depths of a gulf. Like a dove, I should like to build a nest in a cypress...

Lightning demolishes marble friezes, the wind breaks cypresses; I shall build my nest in the immobile azure, where the stars are rounded out like pearls in the sea. Ar-Braz, stop your chariot of clouds; my impatient soul is beating its wings...I am coming to rejoin you...

You died alone, my beloved! You are dead; I no longer hear your harp, I so longer see your sword gleaming. He died under the carriage-pole, the proud charger, because I did not want to harness beside him the aurochs with the muddy flanks. You are dead, my handsome stag, and only a foreign forest has sung your last combat.

THE HARP

Vercingetorix has tightened over his blue tunic the green belt of a bard; he goes through the fields, enters into the circle of the watchers and slips into the tent of those in the pay of Caesar.

The poet is always heeded when he talks about the liberty of slaves and the glory of the vanquished, and if he talks in a low voice, everyone hears him. Gaul has heard him; silently, swords are being forged, and young women are saying: The eyes of the bard have the color of water.

Only one has not sharpened his blade.

THE BRONZE STRINGS

The bard no longer sits down under the beams of cabins; his brow furrowed, he is marching Northwards. The forests have said to him: Ar-Braz is born; but he had not found him on the soil of Gaul, and he is marching with a furrowed brow because he would not have wished Ar-Braz to be a Suebe.

The waves of the Rhine are beating the fetlocks of his horse.

VERCINGETORIX

Gaulish river, do you recognize me? Don't drag down my horse; I am the man who sings in order that impure gods do not bathe in your waters.

PRAXINOE

It's him! He is gleaming like a hill after a storm.

He isn't dead! Sing, birch leaves; holly leaves, sing. Apple tree with the florid crown, let your apples fall; wild boar, summon your young; he isn't dead! Caesar, the skylark has not fallen from the sky, and you have not changed his furrow into a marsh! Caesar, if the German river breaks your dikes, it is you that it will drown. Sing, birch leaves; holly leaves sing!

I am here, my roebuck.

VERCINGETORIX

Soul of Gaul, speak on my lips, put the hand of the Suebi in the hand of the Gauls. You did not wish to have the savior born in our vanquished clans; you wanted to make the fruit grow on a virgin branch; put honey on my lips for the wild bear. The Gaels need a heavy sword; the German sword will vanquish; but after the victory, animate the strings of my harp,

363

in order that I can teach the victor the sweet language of the Gauls.

X

THE HARP
The Germans are crowding around the foreign bard.

VERCINGETORIX
Night furls its wings, and the daughter of the waves tells the beads of her necklace, laughing—the Dawn smiles when her heel does not wipe away tears or blood from the thirsty grass. That is not thunder rumbling; it is steel ringing under the hammer; it is a sword that is being forged out there in the west!

The Dawn went to sleep und two similar ash trees, the leafy branches of which enlaced in the azure; the Master leaned over on his throne of clouds, and one of the ash trees was the first of men... That is not lightning flashing; it s a sword flamboyant beneath the chisel, it is a word engraved on the blade out there is the west!

One of the ash trees was the first f men, the other was the first of women, and the first couple of the Purs[81] was created, on the breach, in the sunlight, while the Dawn slept... That is not thunder growling; it is the word speaking on the steel, it is a cry that is flying, out there in the west.

We are a leafy tree; that is why the buds dry up when the bark is torn away, that is why there bark dries up when the buds are torn away... That is not lightning flashing; it is the word that is lighting a fire, out there is the west, the fire that summons the brave!

---

[81] Many of the original readers of the present work would have construed "Purs" as "Pure Ones," because the French *pur* is the equivalent of the English *pure*, but in fact the term is probably a transcription of the syllable attributed to a rune that only resembles a P, and whose probable meaning is "giant."

Sons of Teuth, will you light your gaiety at the fire of the Gauls?

ARIOVISTE
The druidess is asleep under the horns of my bulls, and my bulls lower their heads when Roman clarions sound. The earth is our domain; when we want fresh grass, we march and others recoil. I am the chief of the Purs; I will defend your land because it is mine.

XI

THE HARP
The hundred tribes of the Suebi had harnessed their chariots; at the voice of the druidess, they stopped.

VERCINGETORIX
Why are you stopping them? They are not foreigners.

PRAXINOE
Listen

THE VOICE OF THE GAULISH LAND
Under the feet of my druidess the hyacinths are blue. Her gaze flowers the apple trees, her breath ripens the grapes. My druidess is the middle of a summer day; the German soul is as pale as the dawn of a snowy morning.

VERCINGETORIX
Our wounds are adjacent!

PRAXINOE
An ear of wild corn is not an ear of domestic wheat. My sons have broad foreheads, my daughters have soft voices, the Gauls are not Germans.

VERCINGETORIX
Ar-Braz! Ar-Braz, where are you?

PRAXINOE
The sheaf will be red, but the bread will be white.

XII

THE BRONZE STRINGS
In the forest of the Carnutes[82] *the Spirit speaks under the oaks.*

BARDS
O you who have no name, you whose throne is immobile above the errant stars, enlarge our hearts and harden our arms! Cause the lightning of the somber night to spring forth; let the lightning re-temper the Gaulish sword!

THE SILVER STRINGS
Praxinoe appears under the dolmen.

BARDS
The soul of Fleur d'Épine, the fiancée with the white arms!

DRUIDS
The golden sickle has emerged from the waves, the starry belt has fallen from the sky.

CHIEFS
When the soul of Ar-Braz has a body, the sword of Gaul will shine like lightning.

---

[82] The Carnutes were a Gaulish tribe whose territory extended between the rivers now known as the Seine and the Loire. The term was also used as a place name, for an area centered on the site of the modern town of Chartres.

PRAXINOE

The moon trembled in the sky like a swan-feather on a woodland pond, and Koridwoen has spoken to me. She said: The clans are like a flock without a shepherd, the she-wolf will eat them; the she-wolf will eat them one by one if they do not give themselves a chief whose head is high enough to count them all.

CHIEFS

In a wheat-field the ear that surpasses all the others is an empty ear. Who will enable us to know the man greater than us?

DRUIDS

Does the soul of Ar-Braz have a body?

PRAXINOE

He had conducted his chariot in the plans of the sky, the one who knows what men do not know. Who is the man whose heart has been large enough for all your angers? Who is the man who said to you yesterday: Sharpen your swords? Who is the man who is saying to you today: Swords cut, draw them!

THE CROWD

Vercingetorix!

PRAXINOE

Who is the man who has said aloud what you dare not say to your wives when they are dreaming in your arms?

THE CROWD

Sing of the blue blade, which loves the flesh! Sing of the blue blade!

DIVITIAC

The old men no longer have sons, the children no longer have fathers; war is a bad thing.

BARDS

The sword is the plowshare that traces the furrow of the future. It is the sword that cuts the brambles of the path. It is the sword that trims the vine whose wine will give strength and gaiety, amour and wisdom.

THE CROWD

How it shines, the sword of Ar-Braz!

PRAXINOE

Then a butterfly alighted on the pale lips of Ida, Ar-Braz had descended from his chariot of clouds... What name will Ar-Braz have when his eyes have the hue of the waves?

THE CROWD

Vercingetorix!

BARDS

Vulture, sharpen your beak; wolves, sharpen your teeth! The sword will pass over men like the scythe over the furrows.

PRAXINOE

Get up, reapers! The sheaf will be red, but the bread will be white.

DRUIDS

Vercingetorix is the one who had to come.

THE CROWD

O sword! O great chief of the battlefield! O sword! O great chief!

PRAXINOE

You will march where he says, you will stop when he says.

THE CROWD

That's sworn!

PRAXINOE

Let the sons of the perjurers pale before a shield! Let their daughters sell themselves!

THE CROWD

King of war, draw the sword.

VERCINGETORIX

I shall not return it to the scabbard as long as there is a foreigner in Gaul, and the day when I wipe it I shall break it in front of you.

PART THREE

I

THE SILVER STRINGS
The clouds are passing over the peaks, the wind is growling in the gorges, and the water of the torrent is black; a horseman presses his weary horse. Where is that horseman going, who is looking behind him?

THE HARP
He is going to tell Caesar the names of those who have sung the round of the sword.

THE VOICE OF THE GLACIER
Imperadorix, do not go any further!

THE VOICE OF THE FIR TREES
Imperadorix, do not go any further!

THE VOICE OF THE GRASS
Imperadorix, do not go any further!

THE BRONZE STRINGS
He has not heard, but his horse has heard; it rears u and Imperadorix falls into the brambles.
The brambles stretch out like snakes; like snakes they enlace the chief of the Eduens.

THE VOICE OF THE BRAMBLES
You shall go no further.

IMPERADORIX
One might think that these brambles were binding me.

THE GOLDEN STRINGS
A great voice is speaking from the summits. Listen.

THE GREAT VOICE

Let the traitor pass; he always does what he wants to prevent.

THE HARP

The sun is resplendent on the glacier, the breeze is singing in the fir trees, the rocks of the bed of the torrent are iridescent, the brambles relax their arms. Imperadorix gets up.

He has not heard anything.

II

THE HARP

Can you see the Gaulish army going up the Loire? At every town, every village and every cabin it increases. Can you see Vercingetorix in the midst of the chiefs covered in scintillating armor? Like the Gauls of the past he wears neither a helmet not a breastplate.

The army extends. At every step a file is added to the squadrons, a cart is added to the baggage train, a flock is added to the flocks. It is not an army, it is a people on the march. On a white mare, Praxinoe is galloping, torch in hand; she is setting fire to villages, cabins, crops and forests. Before Caesar can be informed, the Roman army will have died of hunger on a bed of ashes.

THE SILVER STRINGS
Praxinoe is stopping. Why?

THE HARP

Listen.

A SHEPHERD ON A HILL
Yesterday, at sunset, Caesar crossed the Allier.

PRAXINOE
Vercingetorix, do you hear? There was a traitor in the sacred clearing.

VERCINGETORIX
We shall be victorious; our cause is just.

THE GOLDEN STRINGS
On that white mare, it is not a woman who is passing with scattered hair, it is the indomitable soul of old Gaul, the soul as profound and somber as a forest.

III

THE HARP
Night is falling, the army stops. The faces are anxious.
Caesar has crossed the Allier; the Bituriges and the Arvernes think of their children, who are between them and the enemy. They think while leaning against the granite blocks of a long serpent of raised stones.

A VOICE
Let us pray to Teutates![83]

THE ARMY
Let us pray to Teutates!

THE HARP
Vercingetorix passes his hand over his brow.

---

[83] Teutates , or Toutatis, earlier cited in the present text as Teuth, is one of three Celtic gods mentioned by the Roman poet Lucan.

THE GOLDEN STRINGS
Like a seagull in its nest of foam, the druidess is sleeping in the silvery mane of the mare with the red hooves. She wakes up...

PRAXINOE
Let us pray to Teutates!

THE BRONZE STRINGS
She leaps on to the heather. She raises her ax. The mare falls, its throat cut. The army kneels...

THE ARMY
What does the heart say?

THE BRONZE STRINGS
The druidess extracts the heart, but the heart does not quiver.

THE ARMY
Let us pray to Teutates!

VERCINGETORIX
Why does the one who created life like the odor of blood?

PRAXINOE
The past...

VERCINGETORIX
The past is the night, the future is the dawn. If it is necessary again that a man fall under its knife, I shall be that man.

PRAXINOE
Don't say that! When the voice speaks, it's necessary to obey.

VERCINGETORIX

If he voice speaks, you will obey; I am a man like the man you have killed.

THE ARMY

Let us pray to Teutates!

PRAXINOE

Do you hear?

BARDS

Let us pray to Teutates!

DRUIDS

Let us pray to Teutates!

THE HARP

The prisoners are trembling. Vercingetorix climbs on to the altar of turf.

VERCINGETORIX

One does not offer a trembling victim to Teutates but a free man who offers himself freely. Druidess, search for the secret of the future in my heart.

THE BRONZE STRINGS

He lies down on the altar, his arms in a cross. The harps quiver... The knife escapes from Praxinoe's hand.

VERCINGETORIX

Strike; my heart will tell you whether blood pleases the Creator.

THE CROWD

The knife has slipped from the hands of the druidess; the god does not want you.

THE HARP
Vercingetorix gets to his feet. He picks up the knife.

VERCINGETORIX
A knife can fall from a woman's hand; if the god no longer wants blood he will break the knife on my breast.

THE SILVER STRINGS
Blood springs forth.

THE BRONZE STRINGS
It is not the chief's blood that springs forth. The daughter of Keridwen had stood up, and the jade hilt is gleaming between her shoulders.

PRAXINOE
Let blood no longer flow over the altar!

THE GOLDEN STRINGS
It is not a druidess who has died, it is the faith of the past.

IV

THE HARP
Vercingetorix is thinking, his hands crossed over the pommel of his heavy sword.

THE GOLDEN STRINGS
In the stars of the Gaels, in the green isle of the ocean of the skies, the druidesses of the past are singing under the flowering apple trees. Listen.

THE DRUIDESSES OF THE PAST
Before the sun the moon pales; let us sing, the daylight is rising.

THE SOUL THAT HAS JUST FLOWN AWAY

The circle of the past has closed, the time of Gaul is finished; the song of the skylark of the west will no longer be heard. O Master, when the races slept in your bosom like the fruit in the bud, you said to me: Soul of the Gaels, you are the daughter of my heart; you shall always carry in your hand the torch of verity, and when the earth, like a rose, embalms the heavens, the earth will belong to your sons.

The time of Gaul is finished; how will my sons call the divine skylark tomorrow?

THE VOICE OF THE CREATOR

They will call her Liberty!

V

THE HARP

The Gauls have delivered numerous battles. They have sometimes been victorious, sometimes vanquished.

THE GOLDEN STRINGS

Why, since their cause is just?

THE BRONZE STRINGS

Death is the fecund soil in which the future germinates.

THE GOLDEN STRINGS

The Romans are fleeing before Gergovia like smoke under the autumnal wind. In the breath of the Gaulish horses, the legions writhe... They are throwing away their eagles!

Oh, the beautiful dew! How green the grass will be tomorrow! The sun is setting, the sky is black. Stars, why are you not opening your eyes? Today you shall see rocks of coral!

Look at the father! That is not a sword that he is holding in his hand, it is an iron wheel. The wheel is heavy; look at the rut. How beautiful he is! Under his knees the stallion cries.

He stops, the white stallion. He swings his enormous head slowly. He trembles. He falls. He is dead.

VERCINGETORIX
You were a brave horse; I shall mount none but you up above. Sound the retreat, Kenrik; our horses are weary. They have abandoned their machines, they have thrown away their ensigns; they are defeated. Today they are fleeing, tomorrow they will die.

VI

THE HARP
The Roman army is floating like a galley whose oars are broken. It is groaning under the impact of waves with blond crests, leaving crushed cohorts in its wake, The flooded Allier stops it for three days.

CAESAR
What if what their druids taught were true! What if the nations had one soul, an indomitable soul, an eternal soul that laughs at conquerors…!

THE SILVER STRINGS
An exhausted centurion without weapons approaches.

CENTURION
Salut, Caesar! Labienus has not dared to give me a letter; he has sent me to request reinforcements

CAESAR
Reinforcements?

CENTURION
We were on the banks of the Seine, facing the isle of the Parisis when news of the affair of Gergovia arrived in the Northern regions. It flew with lightning rapidity; we knew by

sundown what had happened when it rose. Then the Gauls all rose up, and now Labienus is blockaded between the Seine and the Parisis. They have burned the bridges, and when I left, the army of the Belges had been announced.

CAESAR
You'll depart again tonight. Go! Go to Labienus! I dare not even wait for him. He has defeated me—me, the invincible! I believed myself to be above amour, above amity, above hated; I had never been defeated... I would give half of what I want to take him alive.

A SENTRY
The Gaulish cavalry!

VII

THE HARP
The last joists of the bridges are burning, Vercingetorix is talking to the chiefs. Listen.

VERCINGETORIX
It's necessary to follow him night and day and only to charge his rearguard. We'll cross the Allier tomorrow when they lift camp.

THE ENSIGN-BEARER
Father, shall we set up your tent here?

VERCINGETORIX
No, the valley is too green; I'll camp on the sand with the horsemen. If I set up my tent here, there would no longer be a single leaf or blade of grass tomorrow. War doesn't only kill men.

KENRIK

The plow has crushed the flowers of the heath, but the harvest will be fine.

VERCINGETORIX

While the ears don't fume over the area, the laborer trembles. I'd like to be on the eve of the harvest.

KENRIK

At the whinny of the Gaulish horse the she-wolf is fleeing without daring to look back; tomorrow she will fall, breathless, and the stallion with the silver mane will crush her under his hooves.

VERCINGETORIX

Who wants to take a message to Arioviste?

KENRIK

When a bleeding bloodhound holds a stag by the throat, the dog that had hidden in the bushes arrives with its fur bristling; it bites the dead beast, and is given its share of the spoils because it is believed that it has aided the courageous bloodhound. You have no need of Arioviste.

VERCINGETORIX

The more numerous we are, the less bloody the struggle will be.

A CHIEF

Fortunate are those who fall in their force like green fir trees under the North wind.

VERCINGETORIX

If he isn't with us he'll be with Caesar.

A CHIEF
Then we'll have no need to mount our horses twice. The hunt will be fine; we'll bring back a she-wolf and a bear.

VERCINGETORIX
The German forests have sheltered proscribed druids.

A DRUID
The German is still only an ear of wild corn; don't mingle him with the wheat.

VERCINGETORIX
You have wanted what I dared not want; you're braver than I am. We shall be victorious, children.

KENRIK
Instead of feathers, the wings of our skylark have spikes, spikes that burn!

VIII

THE HARP
In the middle of the battle Arioviste has joined the vanquished Caesar and the Gauls have retreated as far as Alise. Many have remained on the battlefield. There are many of them, as many Romans as Gauls, and as many Germans as Gauls.

The earth is no longer drinking blood, the streams are no longer running. The crows, sated by six years of carnage, are waiting before settling for the cheeks to turn green; the fat wolves have licked the living wounds and are lying down, their muzzles on their paws.

The victors have followed the vanquished; no fires are seen on the heights, nor marauders in the valleys; no harps are heard lamenting, nor trumpets sounding the retreat. Silence is everywhere; the wounds were mortal and in the soil labored by horseshoes the crickets have been crushed.

THE SILVER STRINGS
A wounded man is stirring. Is it a Gaul or a German?

THE HARP
It's a Gaul.

THE BRONZE STRINGS
Why is the Valkyrie not taking his soul? Virgin with caressant arms, a brave man is summoning you.

THE VALKYRIE
I don't take away the souls of traitors. Let the earth take it.

THE GOLDEN STRINGS
The wind is carrying away the virgins like thistledown.

IMPERADORIX
Gaulish soil, take me entirely; let my soul, accursed shadow, not go to howl on the reefs of the shoreless sea. Make of my soul a nettle on the roadside, which all feet trample' but may it be reborn one day in order to wash away its stain.

THE EARTH
I don't want your bones.

IMPERADORIX
Vercingetorix! Vercingetorix!

THE SILVER STRINGS
In the black sky a circle brightens; in the middle floats a blonde form in a starry robe. She touches the ground and leans over the dying man. It is Praxinoe; but her breast is broader, her forehead higher and her eyes prouder. Listen.

381

THE BLONDE FORM
He will have pardoned you. Come!

IX

THE SILVER STRINGS
What is the ensign-bearer Luern looking at?

THE HARP
He is looking into the ditch at those who were expelled from Alise because they ate but could not fight.
The wounded are moaning. Listen.

A WOUNDED MAN
Water!

LUERN
It is necessary to have ourselves killed today; tomorrow we shall be too thirsty.

THE SILVER STRINGS
A scorpion launches a dart. Luern totters.

THE BRONZE STRINGS
He's dead; but he has drawn the dart from his wound and hurled it at the enemy. Fortunate are those who fall in their force, like green fir trees under the North wind.

AN OLD MAN
It's thus that the men of old died.

VERCINGETORIX
They were young, they were strong, and I have got them all killed! The forest no longer has tall trees.

A WOUNDED MAN
Oh, the beautiful grapes!

KENRIK
Sing of the blue sword that loves the flesh! Sing of the blue sword!

THE CROWD
O sword, O great chief of battle. O sword, O great chief!

VERCINGETORIX
My beautiful army is dead! Luern, you have left a joyful swallow on the hill where the bees are buzzing; she is waiting for you, and you are dead.

KENRIK
Let the rainbow glisten at your point, master of battles

VERCINGETORIX
They were so brave, ad thy have been vanquished... It's my fault! Throw your blood in my face,

A WOUNDED MAN
Vercingetorix, may your name be blessed!

THE CROWD
We have sworn to die with you, we swore it of our own free will; may your name be blessed!

A DRUID
Let us give Gaul a beautiful funeral. Let us all kill ourselves.

THE CROWD
Yes.

VERCINGETORIX
Children, in an hour you will have water; in an hour you will be free.

THE CROWD

But...

VERCINGETORIX

You have sworn to obey until death; obey!
Climb on to the rampart, and let no one follow me.

X

THE HARP

Gaul is dead!

THE GOLDEN STRINGS

Listen to the skylark.

THE SKYLARK

The man is mad who weaves a cage for the bird loved by the sun, for the skylark of the Gauls!

The man is mad who believed that the sound of the trumpet can cover its song!

The man is mad who thinks that the skylark is dead because he can no longer hear it.

When the skylark no longer sings over the furrow it is listening in the blue sky for the voice of the Almighty; and as soon as a harp quivers, it descends with new words that make masters pale and armies tremble.

The man is mad who thinks the skylark is dead because he can no longer hear it. When a harp quivers, the skylark will say to the bard the word that will make the master pale and make armies tremble.

XI

THE SILVER STRINGS

That old man's hair is as white as snow. Children are playing at his feet. Who is that madman?

THE HARP

He is only six years older and you don't recognize him? That's Kenrik.

KENRIK

I was honored in the days when I was a bard; I was honored by all men. As soon as I entered into the residence of the chiefs, the crowd uttered cries of joy; as soon as my harp sang, red gold fell from the trees. Now... Sleep, my child, sleep... O daughter of the king, you are as beautiful as the morning dew. The rising sun is delighted when it looks at you; do you not know that? Sleep... Sleep, children; here are cherries.

A SMALL BOY

Tell us a story, Grandfather.

KENRIK

About Vercingetorix.

A LITTLE GIRL

He kissed me, before departing for the war; Maman told me so.

THE OLD MAN

Far, far away, in the direction of the rising sun, there are mountains as there are here, and in those mountains a town surrounded by walls. It was larger than Gergovia, and it was called Alise. Six years ago this autumn, we were there with Vercingetorix. It was hot that year, and we had nothing left to drink.

KENRIK

We had nothing left to drink.

THE OLD MAN

You see, children, if you are here to eat cherries, it is to Vercingetorix that you owe it. He gave his life in exchange for yours; don't forget that, and the day when you can kill a Roman, kill him. Where was I?

A SMALL BOY

And we had nothing left to drink

THE OLD MAN

So we were going to die. Then Vercingetorix put on his silver helmet and he went on his own to find Caesar. We were on the walls and we...

KENRIK

Caesar was sitting down when the father arrived n his white horse; he was sitting down, and he didn't get up. How stiff his legs were! I've given you cherries; say, children: How stiff his legs were!

THE CHILDREN

How stiff his legs were!

KENRIK

He didn't get up, and the father circled around him three times. On the first circuit he threw away his golden shield; on the second he threw away his silver helmet, and on the third, he threw away his blue sword. Caesar pushed it with his foot. May his foot rot! Say it, children: May his foot rot!

THE CHILDREN

May his foot rot!

KENRIK

Caesar smiled, and he said to his executioners: Bind his hands. And the executioners bound the king of war, and they struck him, and his blood flowed. The executioners wept, but Caesar did not blush. May his eyes go blind!

THE CHILDREN
May his eyes go blind!

KENRIK
Caesar did not blush, and he said to the hero: "Why have you come?"

"I have come to exchange my life for the life of my people.

"Your life is mine."

"My body, yes; my life, no. If you let those who are in Alise leave, and if you swear never to go to the abode of the Arvernes, I will swear to live until the day when you want to attach me to your chariot in the streets of Rome.

The bald man's eyes gleamed with joy... Listen! Can't you hear anything? Can't you hear wheels grinding on paving stones? I can see a crowd. There are as many heads in it as there are needles on a fir tree. Here come horsemen; they're Romans. May they be cursed! May all those who speak their language be cursed!

O my soul, you who are no more than a little bird, fly away. Fly, my soul, all the way to the hawthorn bush, all the way to the flowering furze; listen to the cricket singing, and no longer listen to what they say out there... Can't you see him bound with chains? Can't you see that merchant throwing mud at him? The chariot stops, and he's untied.

A LITTLE GIRL
Who are you talking about, Kenrik?

KENRIK
About whom should one talk? I'm taking about the man who prevented your hair from being cut off... A man is next to him, a sword in his hand... The man raises the sword, the fa-

ther smiles... A king ought not to sit down without his bard at the feast on high...

THE BRONZE STRINGS

The Roman crows have eaten the eyes the color of the sea, but they have not eaten the soul with the mighty wings. Ar-Braz will be reborn.

The Roman has thrown his crimson mantle over the luminous name, but he has not extinguished the torch of the past. Ar-Braz will be reborn.

Ar-Braz will be reborn, and the day will be as bright as the night was dark.

FANTASY FROM BLACK COAT PRESS

( ) Marie Catherine d'Aulnoy. Tales of the Fays 1
( ) Marie Catherine d'Aulnoy. Tales of the Fays 2
( ) Honoré de Balzac. The Last Fay
( ) Mme Barbot de Villeneuve. The Naiads Beauty and the Beast
( ) Cyprien Bérard. The Vampire Lord Ruthwen
( ) S. Henry Berthoud. The Angel Asrael
( ) Aloysius Bertrand. Gaspard de la Nuit
( ) Charlotte-Rose Caumont de La Force. The Land of Delights
( ) Comte de Caylus. The Impossible Enchantment
( ) Félicien Champsaur. Pharaoh's Wife
( ) Comtesse D.L. The Tyranny of the Fays Abolished
( ) Alexandre Dumas (w/Paul Lacroix). The Man who Married a Mermaid
( ) Marie-Antoinette Fagnan. The Enchanter's Mirror
( ) Paul Féval. Anne of the Isles
( ) Charles de Fieux, Chevalier de Mouhy. Lamekis
( ) Judith Gautier: Isoline and the Serpent-Flower
( ) Jules Janin. The Magnetized Corpse
( ) Gustave Kahn. The Tale of Gold and Silence
( ) Paul Lacroix. Danse Macabre
( ) Louis-Guillaume de La Follie. The Unpretentious Philosopher
( ) Etienne-Léon de Lamothe-Langon. The Virgin Vampire
( ) Etienne-Léon de Lamothe-Langon. The Mysterious Hermit of the Tomb
( ) Maurice Level. The Gates of Hell
( ) Marie-Jeanne L'Héritier de Villandon. The Robe of Sincerity
( ) André Lichtenberger. The Centaurs
( ) André Lichtenberger. The Children of the Crab
( ) Monsieur de Listonai. The Philosophical Voyager

( ) Jean-Marc & Randy Lofficier. The French Fantasy Treasury (Vol. 1) (anthology)

( ) Jean-Marc & Randy Lofficier. The French Fantasy Treasury (Vol. 2) (anthology)

( ) Jean-Marc & Randy Lofficier. The French Fantasy Treasury (Vol. 3) (anthology)

( ) Charles Lomon & P.-B. Gheusi. The Last Days of Atlantis

( ) Marie-Madeleine de Lubert. Princess Camion

( ) Charles Malato. Lost!

( ) Maurice Magre. The Marvelous Story of Claire d'Amour

( ) Maurice Magre. The Call of the Beast

( ) Maurice Magre. Priscilla of Alexandria

( ) Maurice Magre. The Angel of Lust

( ) Maurice Magre. The Mystery of the Tiger

( ) Maurice Magre. The Poison of Goa

( ) Maurice Magre. Lucifer

( ) Maurice Magre. The Blood of Toulouse

( ) Maurice Magre. The Albigensian Treasure

( ) Maurice Magre. Jean de Fodoas

( ) Maurice Magre. Melusine

( ) Maurice Magre. The Brothers of the Virgin Gold

( ) Catulle Mendes. The Little Fays in the Air

( ) Louis-Sébastien Mercier. The Iron Man

( ) Joseph Méry. The Tower of Destiny

( ) Hippolyte Mettais. Paris Before the Deluge

( ) Henriette-Julie de Murat. The Palace of Vengeance

( ) Marie Nizet. Captain Vampire

( ) Charles Nodier. Trilby The Crumb Fairy

( ) Pierre-Alexis Ponson du Terrail. The Vampire and the Devil's Son

( ) Pierre-Alexis Ponson du Terrail. The Immortal Woman

( ) Pierre-Alexis Ponson du Terrail. The Police Agent

( ) Edgar Quinet. Ahasuerus

( ) Edgar Quinet. The Enchanter Merlin

( ) Restif de la Bretonne. Discovery of the Austral Continent

( ) Restif de la Bretonne. Posthumous Correspondence (Vol. 1)

( ) Restif de la Bretonne. Posthumous Correspondence (Vol. 2)

( ) Restif de la Bretonne. Posthumous Correspondence (Vol. 3)

( ) Restif de la Bretonne. Posthumous Correspondence (all 3 volumes)

( ) Restif de la Bretonne. The Story of the Great Prince Oribeau (The Fay Ouroucoucou 1)

( ) Restif de la Bretonne. The Four Beauties and the Four Beasts (The Fay Ouroucoucou 2)

( ) Marie-Anne de Roumier-Robert. The Voyages of Lord Seaton to the Seven Planets

( ) Louis-Claude de Saint-Martin. The Crocodile

( ) Nicolas Segur. The Human Paradise

( ) Nicolas Segur. Penelope's Secret

( ) Pierre de Sélènes. An Unknown World

( ) Brian Stableford. The Queen of the Fays (anthology)

( ) Brian Stableford. Funestine (anthology)

( ) Brian Stableford. The Origin of the Fays (anthology)

( ) Brian Stableford. Tales of Enchantment and Disenchantment (anthology + non-fiction)

( ) Charles-François Tiphaigne de La Roche. Amilec

( ) Simon Tyssot de Patot. The Strange Voyages of Jacques Massé and Pierre de Mésange

( ) Louis Ulbach. Prince Bonifacio

( ) Willy. Astral Amour